A handful of spells

A handful of spells

a novel

by Kimberley A. Shaw

Savvy Press

2014

Dedicated

to the memory of
Mr. Richard Bettcher
of the Camden-Rockport High School
who showed by example
how to be a proud hard-of-hearie in an audist
world.

Contents

Chapter 1 - Mainstream USA

Caitlin slid her breakfast dishes into the dishpan as carefully as she knew how. Plate bumped against mug; could anyone outside the kitchen hear that? She looked towards the living room where her mom sat keying an article into the family computer. Good. She then tiptoed towards the "studio" on the other side of the kitchen, where her dad stood staring into the depths of a Steinway, with tuning wrench in hand. Now's the time. She shouldered her bookbag and slowly opened the side door to the driveway where her bicycle stood, leaning against the house. She closed the door carefully so that it wouldn't bang against the doorframe and reached down to unlock her bike.

But a shadow fell before her. Cait looked up to see her mother scowling at her. "Caitlin Leo, you're not taking that to school. Your balance is too shaky for all that traffic."

"But Mom, my balance is totally normal during daylight."

Her mother frowned and pointed toward the street. "Bus stop. Now."

The bus driver looked just as grumpy as Cait felt as she boarded the yellow schoolbus and picked a seat behind Megan and Brynna, who weren't as snobby as Erin and her clique. At least this gave her time to read. Cait pulled out a novel, tucked a chestnut ringlet of hair out of the way, and settled in as the babble of Megan and Brynna's conversation continued..

"... had to wait two days ... got a new cat ..." said Brynna.

1

Instantly alert, Cait thought of her own beloved family cat, Nini. She turned up the volume on her hearing aids and leaned forward. "Who got a new cat?" she asked.

Conversation stopped as Megan and Brynna turned to stare at her. "Cat?" asked Megan.

"Cast, retard," said Brynna, "my big sister had to get a new cassst." And they broke out into giggles as Cait buried herself into her novel. Another try at being normal gone bellyup. Would this ever change? thought Cait. As far back as Cait could remember, she'd been on the edges of conversations she couldn't quite catch. Books were so much better, with everything right there on the page before her, with nothing to go missing or turn into blurry mumbles. She hunkered down more, wishing she weren't bigger than everyone else besides. All because "lack of social skills" put her in kindergarten at age six instead of age five.

Cait thumped her fist against her seat in exasperation as the words "cast, retard" echoed in her brain. Why did this bus have to have such a loud engine? How could the other kids understand each other above that noise? In the aisle, a handful of grit fanned out with her fist-thump. Cait noticed the motion, and thumped the seat again. A couple of pebbles shot forward, but the rest now stayed still. Not mad enough any more, she guessed.

This was the other thing that made her different. Making things move without touching them was fun, but she had to be in a really bad mood for it to work at all. Or a fantastically great mood. Cait buried herself in her book and tried to ignore Megan and Brynna's ongoing chatter.

In homeroom, Mr. Carlin smiled as he handed her the school's FM receiver, a boxy cellphone-sized device that carried the teacher's voice through a "neckloop" headset to Cait's hearing aids. "All charged up so you won't run out

2

of sound during math class," he said, while attaching the transmitter's microphone to his lapel.

Social science and language arts classes went by uneventfully. Then during writing practice, Mr. Carlin announced, "Work on your two-page essay outlines quietly. I'll be back in five minutes." As he went out the door, Cait could still hear his shoes going squeak, squeak, squeak down the hall. Oh no, he forgot to turn off the FM, thought Cait. What if he's on his way to the restroom? As if he read her mind, there was a "click", and the sound through her hearing aids went off. Cait turned to her outline with relief.

But her pen was out of ink. As she reached into her bookbag for another one, the FM receiver slid off her lap and swung for a moment from the neckloop. Cait grabbed it and tried to stuff it into her undersized dress pocket.

"Robot!" called out one voice to a chorus of giggles. Cait looked around to see Mike Mullin snickering at her.

In the next instant, he stopped, and Cait turned to see that Mr. Carlin was back at his desk. And that she could barely understand what he was saying about their essay deadlines. Should she interrupt to tell him to turn the FM on again and risk having the whole class stare at her? A new idea lit up within her. What if she could shift the transmitter's switch to "on" the way she made the gravel in the bus move? Even if she weren't mad, could she make it work anyway? Cait visualized the transmitter while her index finger imitated the motion of moving the switch. Just one quarter-inch this way, I really need it over here ... uh oh, was Mr. Carlin saying her name?

"Ms. Leo ... all right?" Mr. Carlin looked right at her.

3

"Um, no. Sorry, but the transmitter's not on," said Cait. Out the corner of her eye, she could see Mike smirking.

"You're right, apologies," said Mr. Carlin. "Let me know next time that happens, alright? Now let me repeat those deadlines."

Cait was all too glad to collect the FM transmitter at the end of class and escape to lunch. Maybe the afternoon math and science classes with Mr. B. would go better than this. She knew that art class would be fine. Nothing ever went wrong in Ms. Finner's art class.

During recess, Cait sat sketching the trees that ringed the playground. She struggled with one in particular; it was full of brilliant pink blooms. How could anyone show that with only a lead pencil? She began doodling leaves in the margins, imagining them colored in bright oranges mixed with reds and yellows. Just like they were a year and a half ago. That was the very first time she made something move without touching it. Zoom, she remembered how she would pick up a hand, and the leaves followed. Zoom, there they went again. What a great afternoon that was.

That was after the best school assembly Caitlin could remember. Most school assemblies involved some sort of "listening up," whether it was the rock band with incomprehensible lyrics and silent bass that everyone else loved, or the fast-talking un-microphoned poetry-slam champions.

This assembly featured a magician who didn't talk at all, but with every expression on his face, every sweep of his satin cape or tip of his sequined hat, let you know exactly where to look, and what was going on. Afterwards, everyone ran around the playground imitating the tricks they'd just seen, Caitlin included. She smiled at the memory. All those beautiful leaves around them made it even better.

And when she swept her hands down towards the ground to stir up a bit of breeze, how would she know those leaves would follow her hands instead? And so she moved off behind the old broken swingset to figure out what was going on. Cait remembered looking around to see if the magician were nearby, pulling a few more tricks before he left school property, but there were only the usual students, plus Ms. Healy, the recess monitor.

Nervous yet thrilled, Cait swept her hand once more at a set of bright leaves. And there they went, again following her hand, making her bubbly mood even bubblier. And again. Whatever this was, it was great.

Caitlin winced as she recalled the shout that destroyed this mood.

"HEY there! You deaf or something?" And there she was, surrounded by Erin's whole clique, with Lisa asking her, "We can't do that, how come you can?" Cait stalled as much as she could, and told them something about wires and thread. But she could tell they didn't believe her, and the whole school called her "weirdo witchy Cait" ever since.

"Brrrrrrrnggg." The end-of-recess bell brought Cait out of her recollections, and she closed her sketchbook with a bang. That was one noise she never had trouble hearing, unlike the basso mumble of Mr. B., who taught both math and science. His voice was always blurry, even with the help of the school's FM set.

By the time she arrived home, Caitlin was in a truly foul mood. Math class had been abysmal. Thank you, Mr. Carlin, for putting such a great word on their vocabulary list. Abysmal. She'd answered three questions wrong

5

during one math class. And Mr.B. accused her of not listening hard enough. Again.

And to top it all, somebody Vaselined her locker door. Gross.

She flumped down on the front steps of her house. Time to fling some rocks around.

Flick. Finger met thumb, and flew out with the force of Caitlin's exasperation. A piece of gravel jumped an inch off the nice smooth walkway which led from house to street, and lay wobbling atop a neighboring stone.

Bet this mood's bad enough to get two stones to jump. Abysmal.

Flick. Three tiny pebbles flipped over in unison.

Nini watched cautiously from under a nearby bush, her long gray fur blending in with the shadows, except for a white blaze that went from forehead to chest. A couple of feathers lay nearby from when she'd taken a swipe at a nearby sparrow. She sat with eyes fixed on Caitlin, however, not even budging when a bright green beetle flew past her nose.

Cait hated to spook Nini like this, but how much worse could a day get? Let's see if I'm mad enough to get this big rock to move. Middle school next year had better not be like this.

Flick. An oblong stone flopped over on its side, rather than jumping up at Cait's finger-flick. Too heavy, thought Cait. A thrill went through her. I really like doing this. Wish I didn't have to keep it secret.

Cait rearranged the skirt of her jean jumper to shelter her bare feet from surnburn as she looked about for a new rock. She couldn't wait for the school year to be over. And then there'd be family reunion, and maybe her great-aunt May would tell her some new ghost stories.

She tried one more flick, but nothing happened. The energy was gone.

"People should be more like cats," Caitlin told Nini. "You think my rock trick is totally normal, and you don't care what I can or can't hear."

Nini gazed back at Caitlin, then turned her attention to a passing bug.

Feeling better, Cait pulled out her math homework and began on problem sets. By the time she was halfway through her English essay, the sun was low in the sky, and Cait decided to take a break.

She pulled out her sketchbook, and began to draw the giant sugar maple in front of her. She loved this yard. Next to the sugar maple, which lit up in three shades of red-gold every fall, were a pair of tall oaks, which her dad said were over two hundred years old. The two-story wooden house behind her used to belong to a farm, and had a pointed gable over the front porch.

Best of all was the triple-paned bay window in the front of the house, perfect for showing off the Christmas tree her dad put up every year, the acrylic menorah her mom set in the middle window every Chanukah, and everybody's carved pumpkins at Hallowe'en. And the middle window was where Cait sat watching for the headlights of arriving cars before Thanksgiving dinner and Passover seder, the one other Jewish holiday her mom observed.

A motion in the sky caught Caitlin's attention. Hawks throve in the area, drawn by huge old oaks like the ones before her, and she loved to watch these birds spiraling in the air. But this bird looked on a mission, flying straight across the sky rather than watching for dinner in lazy circles.

"... Cait, don't forget ... get the mail" came a voice from behind her. She turned to see the curvy silhouette of her mom against the screen door, hand on hip holding a sheaf of manuscript pages, unruly dark hair barely restrained by a single barrette. At least when her parents' voices went muddy on her, it was way easier to figure out what they were saying than her teachers, or those kids on the bus.

"Yes, Mom, I'll go get it," she answered heading for the mailbox at the end of the walkway.

Caitlin looked up again. The bird was closer now, and it was heading right for her. But whatever it was carrying didn't look like prey. Weird. And didn't this bird realize there's a cat right here?

She stood and watched as the brown-spotted hawk landed on the mailbox, a rolled-up piece of paper in its claw. It stared and bobbed its head at her. It's pigeons that are supposed to bring letters, not hawks, Cait thought, remembering what Mr. Carlin taught them about Napoleon and pigeon post.

"Somebody's playing a prank," she told the bird, as it stared and then clicked its beak in an annoyed fashion. It didn't seem nervous about Nini's presence at all. Caitlin glanced briefly at the tuxedo cat. Nini made no signs of preparing to pounce on the hawk, but sat oddly still, sniffing the air.

"Am I supposed to take this?" Caitlin carefully reached for the paper. She expected the hawk to spook and take off, but it just bobbed its head, ruffled its feathers, and began preening as she read the writing on the outside of the scroll. There was her name in black ink, with the thick-to-thin line of a dip pen, like the crow quill used in her art class. This thing should be in a museum, she thought as she carefully untied the cord that held the paper rolled up.

"The Witches' Academy of Salem is pleased to invite Caitlin Leo to join its incoming class of firstyears." An odd feeling began to grow inside her. A witch academy? Yeah, right. "We believe that all people of magical ability need and deserve a full education in how to use their talents. This school, located in the historic coastal town of Salem, Massachusetts, has provided New England witches with an outstanding education for over three hundred years." And at the end of the letter, "We await your immediate reply." The hawk clicked its beak and bobbed its head as if saying: "So write already."

Would the hawk sit there all night if Cait didn't write back? Would Nini get tired of whatever was holding her back and go after this bird the way she got the neighbor's bumbling bulldog off the front lawn the other day?

"Cait, the mail."

"OK, Mom!"

Caitlin stuffed the scroll in her pocket and reached into the mailbox to pull out a handful of letter-size envelopes and a rolled-up magazine. The hawk continued to sit and stare, beak still working, click click click. This must be a hoax, she thought as she went into the house and handed her mom the mail.

Who would set up something like this? There was the time someone scribbled "weirdo witchy Cait" all over her locker in ugly orange paint. Another time, some wit had parked a black-covered math book with "Spells" written on it at Cait's study-hall desk. But this letter-carrying bird wasn't her classmates' style. Not unless one of them got help from a genius high-schooler or something. Well, she wasn't going to let them mess with her head.

Cait plopped down on the front step, tore a sheet of blank paper from her sketchbook, and wrote, "Dear

9

Witches' Academy: I only read stories. I don't go and live in them." She handed the letter to the hawk, but it only bobbed its head at her. Right, gotta roll it up so the bird can carry it, Cait reminded herself. This time, the hawk grasped the paper in its talons and flew off with it, while Nini stretched and strolled over to sit next to Cait. They both watched the bird disappear against the clear May sky. Who trained this hawk? wondered Cait. And why didn't Nini try to pounce on it?

Chapter 2 - The Gift

The letter-carrying hawk was still on Cait's mind the following day. She sat in the living room after school, working on a picture of the bird sitting on their mailbox while her mom keyed an essay for "the bigheaded do-gooders at Audubon" onto the family computer. Watching TV was never allowed while her mom was writing, which made it easier for Caitlin to concentrate on choosing exactly which shade of cream was right for the brown-spotted front of the bird. A slam of the keyboard tray pulled Cait's attention away from her drawing.

"Son of a sea biscuit, I can't believe the ink's out already," snapped Miriam Leo, her voice ringing out clearly in the quiet room. She glared at the printer, then softened her expression as she turned to Caitlin. "Care to ride with me into town? Need any more art supplies?" She waved towards Caitlin's sketchpad.

"Bookstore, Mom. Please?"

"Let's go. I'll drop you off on the way to Staples." Miriam peered at Cait's ears. "Are your hearing aids in? Good girl. Don't roll your eyes like that. It took us a whole year to pay for these new aids, and you know that they help. And once those new earmolds come in they shouldn't hurt any more, either. "

The town's bookstore was Caitlin's haven. The books were always interesting, and sometimes the other customers were interesting, too. And it was an easy place to have conversations, besides: quiet, with carpeted floors and background music kept low. Nothing at all like her classmates' favorite arcade, where sound bounced off bare floors and walls and voices all sounded like "waah wah, blabbity bla" no matter what they were saying or who was saying it. Trying to hang out at the arcade only got Cait laughed at, so she gave up on it long ago.

As she scanned the bestseller rack, Caitlin became aware of a very familiar scent nearby, that of "English Rose" perfume. She looked around to see a diminutive and thickwaisted woman with a straw hat and white ponytail in the greeting-card section.

"Aunt May! How come you're here already? Family reunion isn't until next weekend." Cait threw her arms around the elderly woman, who hurriedly stuffed a card back on its rack.

"Wanted to surprise you, for what that's worth," said May, as she pushed her hat back into place. "Unexpected events brought me into town early. Have you received any unusual letters lately, by the way? Delivered by bird, perhaps?" Aunt May's bright blue eyes peered directly into Cait's.

"How did you know?" was all Cait could say.

"Your black mood, my dear, we have your black-mad mood to thank." May chuckled as she said this. Cait frowned. What was going on? "Let's have some tea, shall we? Cures all ills," May continued as she took Cait's elbow and steered her toward the bookstore's tiny café. They were the only customers.

Over steaming cups of Constant Comment and chocolate-covered butter cookies, May went on. "Now mind you, I don't condone having a temper. Can be dangerous, you know. And so, when I saw the mood you were in the other day, I decided to turn around and come back once you'd simmered down. But when I saw what you were doing with those stones, oh, my dear, you have no idea!" Aunt May beamed at her as Cait stared at her great-aunt in bewilderment.

"No idea, what?" she asked, toying with a half-eaten cookie.

"The Gift!" Aunt May's voice dropped as she said this, and she looked over to where the waitress was busy stacking glasses. Gift? Was that what Aunt May said? What gift? Cait tapped the table for attention and pointed at her hearing aids.

May turned back to face Cait. "Don't worry, have I ever forgotten about your ears? As I was saying, you're just like my cousin Joyce. But we thought we were the only ones. Your father got none of it at all, nor did his brother, nor did any other cousins. And just last week, I've met the loveliest fellow who told me there's a whole school just for people like us. And all this time I had no idea. If only Joyce were still around." May shook her head slowly as she sipped her tea.

"You never knew? But nobody ever told me anything about you and Aunt Joyce," Cait retorted, pushing her chair from the table. "And I still don't know what you're talking about."

May put her hand on Cait's. "We couldn't exactly run around telling people, after all. People who talk about seeing ghosts and hearing weather reports from plants tend to get sent to the funny farm. So, it was easier to talk about The Gift and we knew what was meant. But now that we know about you, well ..." she raised both hands in a there-you-go gesture and beamed once more. "It was almost too much to ask for. It was pretty lonely after Joyce died, thinking I was the only one. Ah, Joyce, if only you were still around! If only you could have known about that Salem Council and its school." Aunt May shook her head and gazed at her tea. "Now that's one ghost I wish would drop in and visit more often, unlike that idiotic Civil-War

13

poltergeist who likes to rattle my best china plates." She pushed away her teacup, straightened her hat, and looked at Cait. "Well, I've got some more arrangements to make now that you're in the picture. You did answer that letter, didn't you?"

So it wasn't a prank. The cookies sat like a rock in her stomach as Cait stared at the floor and nodded slowly. "I told them no," she mumbled.

May sighed. "Oh Cait, Cait." she answered. "But how could you have known?"

Cait poked at the half-eaten cookie before her. A real-live witchy weird school and she blew it. How could she ever stand regular public school now, knowing that there was this whole other place where she ought to be instead? A long silent moment dragged by as Aunt May stared at her tea, and cookie crumbles piled up on Cait's plate.

The silence was broken by a knock at the doorway. The bookstore owner poked his bald head in to tell them that Cait's mom was parked outside and honking for her to get out of the bookstore already.

Aunt May waved Cait ahead. "I have things to do, but will see you soon. And next time you see a bird-delivered letter, for heaven's sake, tell them 'yes'!"

As Cait got into the car, her mom's eyebrows arose in surprise. "I don't think I've ever seen you not buy a book before."

Cait shrugged as she tamped down her nerves. "New Peach Fuzz didn't come in yet." She was dying to ask all about her aunts and their talents, but should she? What should she tell her? Or not? "Does Aunt May sometimes say really strange things?" Cait finally asked. "Besides her ghost stories, of course."

Miriam held her hand on the ignition key, but didn't yet turn it. "She is a bit of a free spirit sometimes. You

14

should ask your father that one." Then she started the motor, and Cait was left to her thoughts, giving a thin smile whenever her mom cast a concerned glance her way.

Once they got home, Cait's mom rushed inside to put the ink into the printer, "deadline" being the only word Cait could catch of what she was saying as she left the car. Cait got out slowly, scanning the sky in case there was indeed another letter-carrying hawk.

But as she walked to the front door, something bumped her foot instead, making her stop abruptly to recover her balance. It didn't take much to throw off Cait's balance, which was just as bad as her ears. She looked down to see a squirrel flicking its tail at her as it stared up. Yes, it carried a letter.

Caitlin bent down and took the tightly rolled-up scroll. Not exactly bird-carried. Then again, this letter had the same old-fashioned ink as the other one, and the same cord tying it up, and a text which now read: "The Witches' Academy of Salem, which is very much a real school, is pleased to invite Caitlin Leo ..."

A real school, where flying leaves and jumping rocks were normal. Somewhere she could actually fit in. And she would be far away from the kids who thought she was an idiot since kindergarten. A school that even Aunt May knew about. She hadn't blown her chance to go there after all! How could middle school be anything but wonderful there?

Caitlin ran up to her bedroom and retrieved a sheet of the grown-up fancy stationery Aunt May gave her last August for her birthday, and wrote: "To the Witches' Academy of Salem, I accept, Caitlin Leo, May 2007." She rolled it up, wishing her knot didn't look so sloppy as she retied the cord. Caitlin slipped back outside, handed the note to the squirrel, and wondered what would happen next.

Up in her bedroom, while she slogged her way through history timelines and long division, she couldn't help but wonder what a whole school full of magical people would be like. Bubbling cauldrons full of eye of newt and toe of frog. Eww, she hoped not. Crystal balls and fortune telling, stuff that's in the stars; maybe it would be like astronomy. She liked the six weeks of astronomy her class was taught when the school won an experimental grant last year. And broomstick-riding instead of general gym. With her balance? Yeah right, she'd flunk that class for sure.

But first, she'd have to get through what was left of fifth grade.

On her bus ride home the next week, Cait sat immersed in one of her favorite Sammy Keyes books. As she giggled at a scene where Sammy and her friends decided to show up at a fancy party as rowdy pirates, a loud "Ha, ha, hardy haw", interrupted her. Cait looked up to see Mike and Jack staring at her, their friends sniggering in the background.

"So, you gonna answer Mikey's question?" said Jack.

"What question?"

"See?" Jack turned to his buddies in the front of the bus. "Told ya she goes off somewhere else when she's buried in one of these," and he grabbed the book.

"HEY!" But Caitlin wasn't fast enough. The book flew from hand to hand, followed by laughing. Cait's face flushed as she stood up, speechless with anger. If only everybody would just stop, she thought. Her fist clenched at this last word. She felt a pop as if something had burst, and then the bus dipped on the right-hand front side.

16

The bus driver was visibly annoyed as he pulled over. "We've got a flat tire, everyone. Stay put while I fix it, don't go making any trouble." He glared at the busload of students as he stepped out of the now very quiet bus.

Jack was ready to start making cracks again, but Mikey glared at him and hissed, "Don't get her more mad. Remember how that blackboard cracked all the way across when Mr. B. yelled at her for not listening?" His voice carried clearly in the quiet bus. Across the aisle, Erin and her friends smirked and shot "told ya" looks at Jack and Mikey.

As Cait eyed the crescent shapes her fingernails left on the palm of her hand when she made that fist, Caitlin got a roiled-up feeling in the pit of her stomach. She'd just stopped a whole schoolbus because she got mad. This was getting dangerous. What else would she end up doing without meaning to?

After a quick look out the window, she headed to the front of the bus. "I'm close enough to walk home from here," she told the driver after snatching her book from a girl in the front row.

He paused from wrestling a stubborn lug nut, looked down the street and nodded. "You're only half a block from your stop. Go ahead." Then he growled at the bus doorway, "Rest of you stay put!"

As she started down the sidewalk, so did the buzz of voices on the bus. "Blablabla   find her flying saucer. Blabla beam her up blabla --- haha!"

Witches' Academy of Salem. She liked the way it sounded. Please let me fit in there, Caitlin prayed as the rhythm of her footsteps carried her home.

Caitlin rounded the corner to her street, where the only sound was that of her feet going crunch, crunch, crunch on the gravel on the edges of her neighbors' lawn.

As she neared her house, she saw a squirrel awaiting her at the front steps, but it carried no letter. What now?

Cait blinked; there seemed to be a kind of shimmer as she looked at the squirrel. Then suddenly it wasn't there anymore, but a tall thin man in a gray wool suit with a short fuzz of salt-and-pepper hair stood there instead.

He stepped forward to shake Cait's hand.

"I am Tom Seekins, Admissions Officer for the Witches' and Wizards' Academies of Salem. You must be Caitlin Leo. Pleased to meet you." His voice was clear and easy to understand. "I hope to have a word with you before your parents arrive home, when I'll explain your new school to them. Do you still believe it to be just a story?" he asked, but there was a smile in his eyes.

Caitlin dared to ask the only question that happened to be in her brain at the moment, still trying to grasp what she'd seen. "Does the suit match your fur, or is it the other way around?"

He broke into a real smile as he answered. "I can wear anything at all, and prefer robes to suits myself, but this happens to be less conspicuous if the glamour wears off while I'm in squirrel mode."

Cait wanted to know what a glamour was, but first things first. "Will I get in trouble for making the bus tire go flat?" she blurted out. "I didn't mean to, but the other kids were teasing me again, and I got mad. All I did was make a fist and it went pop."

"No doubt at all that you've got magic." He shook his head a little. "This school will be exactly the place where you'll learn to rein in that kind of energy and make it do what you want it to do. Something I guarantee that everyone will be happier with, you included." Then, as her mom's car pulled up, he asked, "Shall I introduce myself to the rest of your family now? We have a lot of ground to cover."

Chapter 3 – Good-bye Public School

Miriam Leo sat erect on the edge of her wing chair as she poured coffee all around, even to Cait. Her notebook now lay nearby with two pens next to it, and Caitlin could tell from the crinkle between her eyebrows that her mom was thinking up lots of things to ask. Caitlin's dad radiated bemusement as he leaned back in the other wing chair, thin and nimble fingers playing with a hex wrench from his piano-tuning kit. Aunt May was there as well, beaming with self-satisfaction from the computer chair. Mr. Seekins had the sofa all to himself, and silver-edged cups and saucers from the holiday china sat in front of everyone. Cait fidgeted with excitement from her ottoman, while Nini watched from under the coffee table.

Once everyone was served, the official interview began.

"Why does she need to go off to some special school?" asked Miriam, gazing directly at Mr. Seekins.

"Many parents want to know that right away," he answered. "Untrained magic can be a ticking time bomb. Unexpected and dangerous things can happen when magical abilities and adolescent emotions get mixed up, as you may well imagine, and a little training leads to much less danger in that department." Caitlin breathed a silent thanks that he didn't tell her parents about the flat bus tire.

"But she'll be hours away from home," Miriam pointed out.

"But they'll be people like me!" Cait blurted out. "My regular school thinks I'm weird and nobody talks to me there." Aunt May nodded in understanding.

Miriam turned to Cait with a peculiar expression she'd never seen before. "But what about that girl you used to be friends with, Susan?"

"Moved away in fourth grade," said Cait.

Miriam's frown lines deepened and Donald's hex wrench stopped its gyrations. "What about Erin? Lisa?"

"Won't even look at me since I spooked them with some flying leaves." Cait leaned forward to stroke Nini's fur as the cat purred in reply. Miriam's frown lines were now a full-out scowl, but Donald nodded slowly.

"A new school could be exactly what she needs," he said as the hex wrench spun again in his fingers. Miriam held his gaze for a very long time before turning back to Mr. Seekins for her next question.

"How on earth will she earn a living?"

"There are many ways. Academy graduates rarely find themselves unemployed. Magical arts are very useful in the healing arts and law enforcement, and many skilled weatherworkers become meteorologists."

The crease between Miriam's eyebrows was smaller now, but still there.

"We've never heard about this place. How long has it been around?"

"Three hundred and two years," proclaimed Mr. Seekins. "You can rest your mind that it won't go anywhere anytime soon."

"Disability access?"

"Mom! That's what these are for," Cait blurted out as she flipped the red hearing aids out from behind her ears. She wasn't about to risk being too different for this school.

Mr. Seekins was ready with his answer. "Provided as needed, upon request. Levitation spells, talking books, whatever is needed. Sometimes tutoring instead of regular classes." There was a tense pause as Cait put her hearing aids back and Miriam tapped her pen against the notes she'd just made. Please, no special tutors, prayed Cait. Nobody at school made friends with Special-Ed kids.

21

Then Miriam looked up once more at Mr. Seekins. "How are we going to afford tuition?"

Caitlin restrained herself from cheering. Money talk meant that her mom would say "yes". From across the room, Aunt May winked and gave her a thumbs-up sign. And her dad? She could see the hex wrench spinning around in his fingers. He grinned and winked at her, too.

Mr. Seekins smiled as he took another sip of coffee. "The entire cost of this school is covered by the magical community; students' families are responsible only for books and apparel. We really do want to make sure that all New Englanders with 'The Gift', as Ms. Wildner puts it, get their education." He nodded towards Aunt May. "Of course, if we know that a family does have the means to pay their own way, then we encourage them to make an extra contribution to the school fund. We're lucky to have many generous families. And if even the cost of books is an obstacle, then the Sorcerers' Aid Society will be glad to help."

Donald Leo finally pulled in his long legs, sat forward, and asked, "Won't she fall behind in her reading and math while studying all this magic?"

"Not at all," replied Mr. Seekins quickly. "There's plenty of math in Astronologia, and multilingual literacy is required for Spellwork."

A grin grew across Donald's face. "Miri, I think this is the right thing to do. If my Aunt Joyce were still around, I think she would've been very pleased to know about this school. Many thanks to Aunt May." There was pride in his eyes as well as bemusement, as he raised his coffee cup to May, who saluted him back with hers.

Mr. Seekins nodded as he reached for another cookie. "Magic very often runs in families, and it's extremely rare that a child of ability would be the only one in their

22

extended family. Possible, but rare. Many of our students have parents who've also graduated from Witches' Academy and Wizards' Institute. Please keep in touch with our extension office about your new fall classes, Ms. Wildner." Mr. Seekins now addressed Aunt May. "It sounds like they'll have much to offer you."

At last, even Caitlin's mom ran out of questions. Mr. Seekins drank the rest of his coffee with a flourish, setting the silver-rimmed cup down on its saucer with a precise "tik". As everyone stood up to see him off, Mr. Seekins' gaze fell upon the computer, scanner, printer, and small photocopy machine that took up one corner of the living room. Miriam Leo called it her "writing headquarters", but Caitlin grabbed the family computer every chance she got, so she could spend hours playing games, roam the Internet, and read the latest chapters of W.I.T.C.H. fanfic.

"By the way, there's no need to bring any electronics to the Academy. You won't need them there, and there'll be nowhere to plug them in on campus," Mr. Seekins said. He paused at the front door to wave at everyone just before turning the knob and vanishing into a twist of wind that ruffled Cait's hair.

"Now that's the kind of stuff I can't wait to learn," said Aunt May, as she watched maple leaves flutter with Mr. Seekins' disappearance.

Cait's mind reeled with this new information. How could there be no electronics? Everyone needed computers. Did that mean cell phones too? TV? And what did he mean about "nowhere to plug them in"?

During the next few days' family reunion, Cait's aunts, uncles, and cousins came and went from the Leos' farmhouse, on their way to hike, picnic at open-air concerts, or go antiquing. And Cait spent hours with Aunt

May as they both speculated on what their new classes would be like.

Summer flew by and dragged its feet, all at the same time. Sometimes Caitlin couldn't wait – no more Mike and Jack tormenting her, no more being called "weirdo witchy Cait". And then sometimes a chill gripped the pit of her stomach. What if her ears messed things up and she got stuck with a tutor? Or she couldn't catch up with kids who already knew all about magical things?

The acceptance packet from Salem showed up two weeks after the meeting with Mr. Seekins, delivered by eagle this time. It was a rather large stack, what with the student handbook (one copy for her, the other for her parents), the list of required textbooks and other supplies to be bought upon arrival in Salem, and the letter with the details of exactly how to get there. ("Please be at Long Wharf in Boston at ½ hour before the high tide on Sept. 9. You must be prompt, as the school schooner Schoodic will not wait for latecomers – even upper-level witches cannot turn tides. Soothe-Sea remedy will be freely available to all those who need it. Upperclass students only may elect to arrive at the Academy via commuter rail from Boston.")

"Yay, we get to go to Boston," Caitlin said, squealing with delight. "Can we go eat in Quincy Market the way we did last summer?"

Miriam frowned as she pushed in her keyboard tray, turned off her radio so they could easily talk, and took the letter from Caitlin. "Depends on when high tide is, hon. We may have to leave the house at dawn just to get to the boat on time."

Caitlin then handed her the "Parents' Handbook to the Witches' Academy of Salem" and watched her mom nod as she skimmed it. "Good. Self-contained campus with dorms, classroom building, and dining hall all adjacent.

24

I'd forgotten to ask about that. Rare luxury for an in-town school. Off-campus travel, athletic and social events all contingent on maintenance of reasonable grades, good. Accommodation of disabilities provided by the infirmary as needed." Miriam looked up from her book at Caitlin. "Promise that you will ask for accommodations right away, that's what they're for, OK?"

Caitlin sighed. "Yes, Mom." What did "accommodations" in the magical world mean? Would she still have to drag around some strange device nobody else had? Or – hope leapt within her – what if magic could fix her ears, so she really didn't have to "be good, listen up, fit in" any more? What if that were their "accommodation"?

"I'm going to read mine upstairs, Mom," Caitlin said, and Miriam waved at her to go ahead while she turned back to her latest manuscript and music poured once more from the radio. Flute and violin – two of the instruments Caitlin could hear best.

Caitlin flopped down on her bed to read. Four paws landed on her back; she could feel Nini purring as she kneaded Cait's shoulder blades, then settled herself down. Witch Academy – witches had cats, didn't they? Was she supposed to bring Nini along? On the other hand, Nini was really her mom's cat; she'd raised Nini from kittenhood just before Cait was born. She flipped to the back of the book to look up "animals", but found no index there.

"How am I supposed to find things here? Like if I'm supposed to take Nini with me?" Caitlin spoke aloud, ready to toss down the book. Something bright caught her eye. Was the edge of that page glowing? Cait turned to the glowing page to read: "Students may bring a small familiar of their choosing with them during their time at Witches' Academy in both the Hedge and Above-Hedge divisions.

Bring only one familiar, no canids please." But there was no further explanation. How were people supposed to know what a familiar was? Or if you had to ask, did that mean they weren't? Caitlin bit her lip as she reached back to pat Nini. She wondered if Nini would even get along with the other animals. She'd never had to share our house with other pets. Plus, she's a hunter. What if she decided to eat somebody else's familiar?

Cait decided to look up something else about this place. Could she get another page to glow?

"How old is Witches' Academy?" she asked the book, remembering that Mr. Seekins said that it was very old. A different page had a glowing edge now. Cait turned to it and read:

"The Witches' Academy was founded in the year 1705 by the Greater Boston Council of Witches, which to this day monitors magical and nonmagical interactions. It was founded as a direct result of the unfortunate events of 1692 and 1693, which are known to the world as the Salem Witch Trials. Its mission is to ensure that all magical residents of New England receive an education appropriate to their talents." Caitlin remembered learning about that in history class. Wouldn't her teachers freak to find out there were real witches in Salem, both then and now? She skimmed over the next few paragraphs until "wealthy families" caught her eye. Would she need to put up with upper-class snobs? Those "generous" families Mr. Seekins had mentioned? She hoped that she wouldn't be the only one whose family had to ask for Sorcerers'-Aid help.

Then there was the problem of how much stuff she could bring. Caitlin looked across the room to her bookcase full of novels, manga, and art books. The desk next to it overflowed with sketchpads, ink, watercolors, and a set of charcoal sticks she loved using but were too fragile to carry around. If she brought all her favorite books, there'd be no room for clothes in her suitcase, let alone art supplies. What was it she'd read about luggage?

"Luggage," she said to the handbook, and there it was, "One suitcase or trunk, plus a book satchel and if bringing a familiar, a carrying case."

This was going to take a while. Nini jumped down and watched Caitlin haul her suitcase out of the closet and put clothes into it: her favorite jeans, dress, t-shirts, and the sweater from Mrs. Graham down the street who'd taught her to knit. That's enough clothes, Caitlin thought. I guess the robes on our shopping list are the school uniforms. I hope they're comfortable and not totally ugly. And that they have real pockets. And I want books. Caitlin stared at the bookcase for ten minutes before giving up and moving on to her desk. This was easier. She put two new sketchbooks into the suitcase, one giant one for big drawings, and a little one to fit into her pocket for when she got a good drawing idea away from her desk. One box of watercolors, even though the colors in the tubes were prettier. Lots of pencils, one of them charcoal. And erasers.

A little brass menorah she'd had since she was five twinkled from the top of her bookcase. Would she still be in school during Chanukah? When did the holiday fall this year anyways? She put the tree-shaped menorah in alongside the watercolors just in case and wondered if there'd be Jewish kids at this new school. Even half-and-half ones like her.

Caitlin stood back and looked at the suitcase. Still room in it. Good. She decided to leave it where it was. During the rest of the summer, things came and went: gotta pack that red shirt, I'll miss it. What was I thinking?

I've outgrown that red shirt. The three volumes of Swan I've not yet read. No room for them, better read them now. And maybe I can copy a couple of the best pas-de-deux pictures out of them to put up on my wall in the dorm. Whatever the dorm rooms are like.

The rest of the time during that long summer, she wrote long letters to Aunt May, who had already begun classes in spellwork and mindcasting with a tutor in her tiny New Hampshire town.

On her birthday, she finally got to open the box Aunt May left in the living room during reunion; it contained a dozen little amber glass jars with typewritten labels and dried herbs inside: "For memory help (exams?) take a spoonful steeped in ½ cup of water ½ hour before studying." "For cramps, take one pinch in a spoonful of honey once an hour until pain gone." "To see spirits, chew one twig under a full moon outside." Weird, but useful, although she was in no hurry to find out what "cramps" were like. Better make suitcase room for that box.

Her favorite birthday gift was the old-fashioned leather bookbag which Uncle Rudi the historian had sent all the way from Germany, where he was researching his latest book. Ever since a childhood misunderstanding of his name, Caitlin got to call him "Uncle Rude."

Then there were the books from Mom and Dad. Each of the books was hidden in a different spot in and around the house and its front yard, with a hint written on it as to where to find the next book. Then, as usual on her birthday, Mom, Dad, and Mrs. Graham sang "Happy birthday," and they all ate strawberry shortcake on the front porch. As she finished her shortcake, a thrill went through Cait. She had never bothered trying to have a birthday party since her friend Susan moved away, especially since hardly anyone was in town during the summer. On the other hand, what if she made some real friends at this Salem school? Maybe when she turned thirteen next year, she would be sitting here having a party with people besides just her family. Cait smiled as she put her empty shortcake bowl on the porch floor for Nini to lick out, and watched fireflies zoom around their front yard.

Chapter 4 - The Schoodic

And then Sunday, September 9th finally arrived, and the Leo family stood on Boston's Long Wharf near a sign that said "WAS charter", surrounded by hundreds of other girls and their assorted family members, all in various stages of excitement and nervousness. Only a few of them appeared to have animal carriers with them, to Cait's great relief. She was afraid all the other students would have familiars already.

One nearby girl stormed and shouted as parents tried to reclaim the cellphone she clutched.

A chill grew in Caitlin's stomach as she watched. The boat ride itself didn't worry her. Because of inner-ear "vestibular damage", she never got motion sick, no matter how many whitecaps surrounded a boat, or how fast the summer-fair Tilt-a-Whirl went. Same thing that made her bicycle tip over after sunset.

But being surrounded all the time by all these people she didn't know – what was that going to be like? She had never been away from her parents for more than one week of summer camp, and now she was going to be living hours away from them. And further away from Aunt May as well. Caitlin stood between her parents, holding their hands. She now squeezed their hands more tightly as she looked up at her dad on her right, her mom on the left.

"You're going to be all right, babe, I know you can do it," her mom said as she smiled, but her hand was gripping Caitlin's much harder than usual, and her dad's eyes were getting red.

"Write to me!" burst out Caitlin. "I want to know when the front-yard maple changes color, and if Nini catches any moles, and if that diva with the Steinway gets the role she's auditioning for. Write to me -- the handbook says

30

how. Don't forget!" Caitlin wished for the hundredth time that computers and cellphones were allowed at Witches' Academy.

At that moment, a bit of motion in the distance caught her eye. A sail the color of sunset was coming around the granite corner of what used to be a warehouse and was now overpriced apartments, and then another sail, and another ...

"A real four-masted schooner," breathed her father, who had grown up on the coast. "But no motor noise at all. How do they maneuver like that with so little wind today?"

And now people were hugging and good-byeing and making their way to the end of the dock.

A stocky, bright-eyed woman in a burgundy "Schoodic" sweatshirt and jeans jumped from the boat onto the dock with an armload of heavy rope, which she wound around a dock mooring with quick and practiced motions. Hands on hips, the woman addressed the crowd, bawling out, "Firstyears ... left! Upper classes ... red sign ... right! Firstyears ..." She scurried among the crowd, directing girls toward two gates where signs now appeared. "... see your families ... Halfterm ... tide won't wait."

Caitlin hadn't thought someone with such a solid frame would scurry about so fast. She looked so much like a chipmunk zooming across the lawn, that Caitlin stifled a giggle, wondering if she were like Mr. Seekins. Maybe she really was a chipmunk sometimes.

Cait's parents pulled her into an enormous bearhug; it was time. She picked up her suitcase and headed for the green sign. "Love ya, Mom, Dad. See you in October!"

Ahead of her in line, a slender girl who was almost Cait's height seemed to be talking to something in the palm of one hand while pulling her suitcase with the other. Her hair fascinated Caitlin. It hung string-straight and looked dark, but showed random flashes of copper in the sun. When she looked up, Caitlin caught her eye and asked, "Are you a firstyear?" while watching for her answer.

"Yeah, are you? My toad here really hates being cooped up so I'm trying to talk him into putting up with this cage." The toad's amber eyes gazed out through the bamboo slats of a cage barely larger than himself. The girl's voice carried easily in the outdoor space despite everyone else's chatter. So much better than being indoors, where sound bounced around and got all mixed up.

"He's cute," Caitlin said.

"Thanks. Nobody outside the magical world ever says that. His name's Nick." The girl paused and frowned; her eyes were green with a bit of brown. "How come you're leaning your head like that? Do you have a bad ear?"

Caitlin stepped back self-consciously and cranked up her hearing-aid volume. It was that obvious? "Neither ear is exactly normal, but this one's better," she said, pointing to her left ear.

Penny's expression cleared as she continued talking, keeping eye contact with Caitlin. "I'm Penny. Can't shake hands right now, though."

Caitlin's eyes flicked to Penny's hair.

"Yeah, my parents have no imagination," replied Penny. "Your name is?"

"Caitlin."

"Your name goes with your hair, too. Looks just like the hairdos they put on the Irish dancers."

"Ugh, I hate those poodle wigs," groaned Caitlin. "These corkscrews are a pain, always getting snarled. I'd swap in a minute."

"I bet there's a charm for that. We're supposed to learn all sorts of shapeshifting stuff. My mom's been telling me all about the classes and Salem and everything. And Nicky told me this morning that all day's going to be beautiful. He makes the cutest burbling sound when weather's going to be good. Of course, that was before I had to coop him up in this cage."

Nini doesn't do anything like that, thought Cait with dismay. She must not be a familiar.

"Next!" boomed a voice from under under the green banner, which had changed its lettering to now read, "Welcome new WAS students!" The voice belonged to a tall long-nosed woman in crisp black academic robes with voluminous sleeves and a silver-and-blue hood. Her neatly-cut chin-length hair was clear white, threaded through with hairs of true, metallic silver, which gleamed in the sun. Penny turned away from Cait to give her attention to Silver Hair.

"Name, please," she said. Despite the chattering crowd around them, Silver Hair enunciated her words with a crispness that carried more clearly than Caitlin expected. She sounds like my speech therapist, she thought.

"Penny Dingle, daughter of Sophia White and Phil Dingle."

"Welcome to Witches' Academy. Your mother ..." Here, Silver Hair's voice dropped, then rose again: "...1986 I believe ... hope you will as well. Next!" And Penny's name magically checked itself off on a list sitting on a nearby stand.

Caitlin stepped up. "I'm Caitlin Leo, daughter of Miriam and Donald. No magic-school graduates in my family." She watched Silver Hair closely for her answer, noticing that the witch's eyes were the same shade of gray as that on the wings of the seagulls perched on posts nearby.

"Welcome aboard, and welcome to the magical world. You are in good company." Silver Hair returned Cait's steady gaze as she answered in that speech-therapist voice. "There are plenty of other students who also come from non-magical families. I'm sure you'll find each other. Next!" And Caitlin's name checked itself off. Wait a minute. What about Aunt May? But Silver Hair was already busy with the next student in line.

As they proceeded aboard, Caitlin felt a little giddy as she realized that everybody on this ship was a witch. And if there were so many people running around with magic, why did everybody back home think she was so strange just for moving a few leaves around? Where did all these people hide the rest of the time? She eyed the burgundy-shirted women who supervised boarding, adjusted sails, and stowed boxes and baggage, hoping somebody would pull out a wand and perform a spell or two. She was disappointed that only Silver Hair wore fancy robes. And there was not one pointy hat in sight.

Penny was talking to the toad in her hand again. Caitlin could see that his eyes were blinking very fast, and that his throat was rapidly pouching out, then in, out-in, out-in. "The ocean scares Nicky," explained Penny, when she saw the direction of Caitlin's gaze.

"When do we get to see spells and stuff?"

"Not yet. Not where Plods can see, unless there's a really, really good reason. My mom gave me fourteen lectures about Plain Sight all the way from home to here, and I told her I know, I've known since I was six years old. It was a loooong ride from Connecticut. Maybe we'll see something once we're out of harbor."

"Let's stay on deck. I want to wave goodbye to my folks."

They passed a tall broad-shouldered blonde witch with the palest skin Caitlin had ever seen, who was loudly announcing, "No running on board, no flying, no hexing. We arrive in Salem in fifty minutes. Please keep all familiars safely confined until we arrive at the school." For a moment, Cait was glad to not have Nini along with her. How many familiars would she try to eat? Especially once they got to the school and weren't confined to carriers any more?

Then she spotted one familiar that wasn't in a carrier.

A crow sat on one of the deck railings with its feathers fluffed and beak open, while staring up at a scowling girl in a blindingly white dress who replied, "... not a fledging ... get your own food! ... never asked you to hang around me ..." She waved angrily upwards and stalked off as the bird sat for a moment longer, then flew off.

Nearby, a petite witch with very short hair, a rounded nose, and eyes so dark they were nearly black, quietly and inconspicuously floated pieces of luggage into the ship's hold, murmuring a charm over each one. She held a wand of pale wood, slender and unadorned.

"Penny, magic!" Caitlin said, elbowing her new friend while she stared.

Dark Eyes smiled at them and tilted her head at their suitcases. "Yours, too." With a murmured word, and a small motion of her wand, Caitlin's suitcase, then Penny's, floated through the square hatch in the deck and into the hold.

As they took their place at the railing with the other students, the morning light put a pale-gold glow on the Boston skyline, and Caitlin could barely make out her parents among all the other people gathered at the end of

35

Long Wharf. She wondered if her dad was jealous. He'd grown up hearing stories of all the four- and five-masted schooners that used to haul cargo up and down the coast, and she wished that he could be aboard, too.

"Penny, where's your family?" asked Caitlin, catching Penny's eye and leaning in for her answer.

"Back there, to the right," Penny began in a flat tone, then put her voice up a notch as Cait leaned in more. She pointed towards the wharf, then looked back at Caitlin. "Do you see the bratty kid trying to climb the flagpole? That's my brother Stu." Then she paused. "Heeey. I'm about to get a whole semester without babysitting the twerp. Maybe even all year." A grin broke out on her face.

The last student was finally aboard, the ship untied from the dock, luggage stowed, and Chipmunk, Loud Voice, and Dark Eyes now stood at the helm. To anybody outside the boat, they appeared to be consulting the chart.

Penny elbowed Cait, her eyes bright. "Oh, they're about to do a teamwork spell. Those are the most powerful ones."

The trio raised their wands in unison, began a low chant Caitlin couldn't catch, and a soft wind came up, filled the sails, and sent the boat on its way. Threading its way among the harbor islands, the Schoodic soon left Boston behind. Caitlin leaned against the deck railing and gawked at the open sea which stretched out endlessly on their right as the ship turned north toward Salem. For a "powerful" spell, that one was rather boring, but the ocean really was beautiful, with sun flashing off its blueness in bright sparkles. Many students drifted below deck, while others, especially firstyears, gazed around them.

"Violet, look, isn't the ocean so amazing? ... stare at it all day ... gorgeous!" said a plump girl on Caitlin's right who hopped from foot to foot as she looked out at the water, loud voice carrying clearly among the general chatter.

Cait agreed with her. How could those other kids not want to sit and stare at this all day? The ocean really was gorgeous. "Did you grow up inland?" Cait asked her. The girl turned huge pale-blue eyes on Caitlin as the breeze ruffled blonde curls around her lightly-freckled face. "I'm from Fitchburg" – Caitlin lost a few words here – "... hardly ever get to the ocean" – she swept her hand toward the water – "but we do ... Fitchburg Flitters, and Witches' Academy has got ... good at flying ... our team ... won't have a broomball team ... owe me five Quillers ... got to have a team ... watch broomball?" She finally paused her torrent of words and continued more slowly. "Oh, I'm Meg ... my friend Violet ... grew up together." A skinny girl with rippling black hair waved at Caitlin and Penny, her many bracelets flashing in the sun.

Caitlin tried to make sense of the bits of Meg's speech. "Um, broomball, is that what you said? What's broomball?"

"Get out! Everyone knows broomball."

Caitlin racked her memory. "That's this game they play on ice, right? Up north?"

Meg stared at her in disbelief, then burst out in hoots of laughter.

"Take it easy on her. Not everyone grew up in a magical family," Penny said. She caught Caitlin's elbow. "C'mon, let's go below. I hear they sell snacks on board."

Cait began to worry as she followed Penny. Was the whole school going to be like this? The other kids all knowing things that she didn't?

As they arrived below deck, the sound of two hundred babbling voices swamped Caitlin's ears. She couldn't even tell that Penny was talking to her until Penny turned

37

around to look at Cait with a frown on her face. Then her mouth began to move: something about stairs?

Caitlin held up one finger and looked about for a quieter corner. Almost all of this deck consisted of one large, open room, filled with comfortable chairs and a few sofas. Little round tables scooted around, stopping wherever it looked like somebody needed a place to put a full glass or a loaded plate of goodies, and a tall box marked "Soothe-Seas" was zipping around presenting itself to anybody who was looking at all pale or wobbly.

Although a good amount of light filtered in through the portholes and the prisms set in the deck above, softly glowing globes hovered overhead, filling in wherever the daylight didn't quite reach.

But there wasn't a quiet corner in sight, nor any smaller room to retreat to. Caitlin sighed. With all this magic, how come they didn't have some spell making it easy to hear in crowded rooms? She bellowed to Penny, "Can't hear you! What'd you say?"

"Food, over there." Penny gestured to a counter beyond the stairs with her free hand. In her other hand, Nick looked much calmer now that they were out of sight of the ocean.

They went over to the counter, and the background noise dropped down a bit. Caitlin hoped there'd be some chocolate, peppermint patties maybe, or a cream soda. She scanned the racks of clear-wrapped cookies, little white boxes and bags marked "Peppermill", and neat lines of bottles labeled "Single-fizz cider". Even the bowls of dark ridgey nuts and peachey-colored apples weren't as she expected. Behind the counter were more bottles labeled "Double-fizz cider" and a flashing red sign that announced, "POSITIVELY NO SALES OF DOUBLE-FIZZ TO ANYONE GRADUATING AFTER 2008. We know who's not a senior. And aging glamours don't fool us." Caitlin guessed that a "glamour" must be some sort of spell.

At last, Caitlin spotted something familiar. "I know that red box with the bricks on it!" But she nearly dropped it as soon as she'd picked it up; the "beans" were jumping around inside. She could feel the candies hit the sides of the box. The "Boston Baked Beans" she knew never did that.

Penny grinned and pointed to the box, which actually read Salem Baked Beans. "These things are great. Mom always gets them for us at the summer Solstice broomraces back home."

The price tag was marked "60 cents" – no, wait, it said something else now. "2 Blatt"? Then it became blurry. No, it was the ink. It was moving, breaking apart and moving like little worms and shaping itself again to read, "60 cents". Caitlin looked at the other boxes and bottles and bundles on the counter. All of them had the same kind of label which wove back and forth between the two prices. Watching those tags made her dizzy. Great. More things she didn't know about.

"You pick. What's good here?" she asked Penny. "Then tell me what's up with these weird price tags."

"Oh, I'll treat you. Gotta introduce you properly to witchy goodies. Make up for stupid people who laugh at Plod-raised witches. No offense to your parents." Penny added quickly. She took a bag from the cashier, sat it on the counter, and began to fill it one-handed with snacks while Nick blinked his amber eyes from her other hand.

"Plod? What's that?" asked Cait.

Penny reddened as she paused, a box of Salem Baked Beans in her hand. "It's not a very nice word, but that's what we call nonmagical people. Mom prefers to use the term 'nonmagicals', but she has to be extra polite 'cuz she works in retail. Same with teachers." She continued to peruse the snacks before her.

Caitlin took Nick so that Penny would have both hands free, and went to find a pair of empty chairs as she thought over what Penny had said. Plod. To plod. She mulled this over as she took a seat and returned Nick's amber gaze. Well, it was true that lots of grownups plod around not really noticing what's going on around them. Especially that bus driver back home. And half her public-school teachers. She wondered what the teachers at Witches' Academy would be like.

"Taa-daah!" Five minutes later, Penny presented two bags of snacks with a flourish as a table zoomed underneath to catch them. Penny kept eye contact with Cait as she sat down, reclaimed her toad, and leaned forward towards Caitlin. "Can you hear me OK?"

Caitlin blinked in surprise. Wow, only my family remembers to ask me that, she thought, impressed with her new friend. "You're OK right now," she answered, catching a bean which flew out from the carefully-opened box Penny held out to her.

"The magical world has its own currency," Penny began. "Smallest is the Blatt, something like a quarter. Ten Blatt equals one Quiller. Ten Quiller makes an Orso, and ten Orsos equals an Adel. Goes all the way back to colonial days."

"An Adel's gotta be a pretty big amount of money."

"It is. Not too many people carry them around. Mom told me about mage banks where we can swap in our dollars, and we'll probably do that right away when we get to Salem. And she lectured me and lectured me to never change money outside of a mage bank. You could get stuck with pixie Orsos, which look real, but turn into a

40

handful of leaves at just about the time you want to spend them."

"So, how come the magical world has its own money, anyways?"

"Because it's too easy to fake Plod money. Anybody Hedge level and up can do it. So there's supposed to be all this spellwork built into proper Mage Geld" – Penny looked down her nose with a haughty air as she said these words, while pretending to count out money, sending Cait into giggles. She went on. "So that when you know what to look for, you can tell a pixie Orso from a real one. My mom's got a secret part of her shop for magical folk, and there's this great spell on the cashbox there, so when someone tries to pay her in fake Orsos or Quillers, they fly right back at the customer."

"What happens then?"

"Usually people get mad and stomp out, but one woman spent a whole half hour trying to talk Mom into accepting the fake coin anyways. Summer people can be really weird sometimes, and magicals can be even worse. But without them Mom wouldn't have any business, so we have to be nice to them." Penny bit off a tiny bit of peach-colored apple and dropped it into the cage for Nicky.

"Yeah? How weird?"

"Let's see. There was this wizard who wanted to ship a ton of seaweed to Arizona so he could create this mini ocean there, complete with lobsters. Mom tried to tell him that wasn't possible, but he went and bought all the stuff anyway even though it was way expensive. We ate really well that week." Penny paused and sighed. "It was great. Scallops and stuff we usually can't afford. Then another time there was this Plod who thought that sea beans were wonderful, wanted a half pound of them sent to her hotel every night for her supper for two whole weeks. So I got to run the sea beans to the hotel and watch all the people there. And when I'm done school, I'm going to go stay in fancy hotels in different places with people talking all kinds of languages. And Nicky here will tell me all about when it's safe to broomride and when I'd better stay put."

"How does Nicky tell you that?" Cait felt a quivering in her chest. Maybe now she'd find out the difference between a pet and a familiar.

Penny frowned and looked at the toad. "Hard to explain. I get kind of an image in my head. No, not really an image. More of a feeling of what the weather will do, and I know it's him." She shrugged. "Oh, and here's another weird story. This one very pale lady was in the shop once buying some roses. And while I was getting the paper to wrap them in, Mom asked if she were engaged or something, and the lady went as red as her roses, said 'Loreleis don't get engaged', and walked right out without the flowers. Even though she'd paid for them already. So when I grow up, I'm going to go to Germany because that's where Loreleis are from. They live all by themselves on these riverside cliffs and hardly ever come to the States."

"Sounds like a great trip, but I want to know more about all these animals. How did Nicky become your familiar? Do other people's familiars tell them things?"

Before Penny could reply, a breeze through the room made Cait look up. With a start, she realized that people were picking up bookbags and familiars and making their way to the stairs.

"Top deck, everyone, we're nearly in dock." Silver Hair swept through the room with long strides that made the hem of her voluminous robes billow out behind her as the silver tassel on her hood swung from side to side. "Hello you in the corner, you need to wake up, we're here.

42

Firstyears to the front starboard gate, everyone else to the back starboard gate."

As Penny and Caitlin made their way abovedeck, they saw a small island crowned with an assortment of maples and oaks, a sandy beach at its foot. A grassy lawn and green-painted mansion stood beyond the beach; rough boulders divided beach and lawn. Picnic blankets in all colors were already arranged on the sand, and a flotilla of canoes, kayaks, and rowboats waited nearby. The older students were already filing down a long ramp to a dock which wound its way among a set of red stone ledges as Loud Voice handed them something that looked like tickets. The words "... Seven Gables ... four o'clock ..." drifted over on the breeze.

Caitlin hoped there'd be plenty of food left for the firstyears. She and Penny made their way to the bow of the ship, where Silver Hair calmly surveyed the proceedings.

"I do believe everyone's here now," she said. "Welcome firstyears. I am Mirtha Greatwood, Associate Director of Witches' Academy of Salem. We will very shortly be joining the other students at lunch, and then afterwards we will take you on a tour of Salem and show you where everything is. Right now, we have this beach to ourselves, so you can relax at the moment. Enjoy yourselves, and be back at the dock in one hour."

With that, Caitlin, Penny, and the rest of the firstyears trooped off the schooner.

At the end of the dock, Chipmunk and Dark Eyes handed out flat white boxes.

"Anything which should not be in your lunch?" Chipmunk asked Caitlin, as Dark Eyes gave Penny her box.

43

"I eat just about everything," said Caitlin. "It would be nice if there was no Swiss cheese, though."

Chipmunk smiled, concentrated for a moment, and passed her wand over the box she held. She handed it to Caitlin, eyes twinkling. "Have a good lunch."

Caitlin and Penny settled onto a green and purple blanket and picked up their lunchboxes. Caitlin noticed that other students kept glancing their way. What was going on?

She decided to ignore them and concentrate on her lunch. She carefully opened up the box, which seemed to be the same kind of thin cardboard doughnuts and fudge came in. Inside it lay a sandwich, an apple, some grapes, and a cookie. As Caitlin smoothed out the folds in the cardboard to flatten it, it began to ripple. Then she felt china, not cardboard under her fingers. A real plate lay in her hands instead of the box.

As her jaw dropped, a nearby student remarked, "Eating off cardboard would be pretty boring, huh?"

Halfway through her sandwich, Caitlin realized that there was something missing. No sounds of clattering china obliterated the conversation, which was usually the worst part of a shared meal like this.

She looked around. The older students must be finished eating by now. Where were the plates going? At the next blanket over, one girl put down her empty plate with a sigh. Then it began to shrink, crumpling in on itself, and became ... a leaf? A light breeze picked it up, and sent it skimming over the sand. The same thing was happening all over the beach as upperclass girls finished eating and made their way over to the boats. In groups of threes and fours, they rowed and paddled out from the beach, heading away from the ship, and disappearing around the other side of the island.

44

"Boy, do I want to take a stack of those dishes home with me. I hate washing dishes," mused Caitlin. "I wonder if we'll learn how to make leaves turn into dishes and back?"

"I bet we will," said Penny.

"Actually, you have to be a pretty advanced student for the spell to last for any useful amount of time," volunteered the nearby older student who had talked to them before. "So better not serve up hot soup on your first try. Ouch!"

"How soon do we get to learn that kind of spell?" asked Penny.

"Not until your second semester. You'll have to learn to run a glamour before you can do any transformations, but the Spellwork teacher's great."

"How many teachers are there? Are any of them mean?" asked Cait.

"And do we get to broomride right away?" asked Penny.

The older student was happy to answer all their questions, but before Penny and Caitlin could ask half of what they wanted to know, they could see Associate Director Greatwood waving them back to the dock.

It was now time to go to Salem itself.

Chapter 5 – Quillers and Orsos

Once all the firstyears were assembled, Greatwood said, "Follow me," and led them along a path that materialized among the rocks that divided beach from mansion, then continued alongside the grassy lawn to a narrow road. A bright yellow trolleybus with filigreed decorations around the windows awaited them there; their luggage was already piled atop the bus in a matching rack.

"All aboard, please. There are numerous things to be accomplished before you arrive at the school," said Greatwood in her speech-therapist tones as the last of the firstyears took their seats. "First and most importantly of all the things which you must remember is that whenever we are not on school property, we must Hide in Plain Sight. Very important skill. " Greatwood punctuated these last three words with downward jabs of her right hand, making her voluminous sleeve flutter like a giant wing. "Some schools have the luxury of having entire castles at their disposal, in remote locations, surrounded by undeveloped acreage. We do not. And the Council of Witches gets very upset with us if they have to go about doing rumor control every time a student gets careless or carried away. Showing off in front of the tourists who come to see the "witch city" is very tempting. Don't do it. Don't even consider doing it." A steely edge crept into her perfectly-enunciated voice as her piercing gaze reached to the back of the bus. Is there some kind of punishment for students who tease the tourists? Cait wondered, as the engine started and the bus pulled away from the green mansion.

It soon became clear that they weren't really on an island after all, as the road became a causeway with water on both sides. Then the causeway ended and they reached the mainland, but the road still hugged the water on the left. Greatwood still stood at the head of the bus, facing the students. They'd never allow somebody to stand there like that on a regular bus, thought Caitlin. How come she's not totally losing her balance?

"Allow me ... bit of history about the ... Salem, the oldest witchcraft school in the US," began Greatwood. Kssh, kssh, kssh, the sound of the bus tires on pavement and the whoosh of passing traffic obliterated half of Greatwood's words.

Penny nudged Caitlin, crossed her eyes, and mouthed "BO-RING."

Greatwood continued, "Witches' Academy ... 1705 ... same one ... today. I am sure ... unfortunate events of 1692 ... Witch Trials ... not one of those poor souls ... for all the Council knew ..."

Caitlin gave up trying to make sense of the bits and pieces she could hear, and figured that Greatwood was probably telling them the same information that she'd already read in her student handbook. She gazed out her window on the left side of the bus, watching blocks of close-packed wooden houses go by. From time to time, a gap between houses showed a flash of ocean beyond.

The ebb and flow of Greatwood's lecture stopped, and students yawned and shifted in their seats. Caitlin looked up to see Greatwood glance out the window and nod to the driver, who slowed the bus and pulled over. Greatwood's voice now rang out clearly. "Attention to your right, everyone."

There, they could see only a plain wooden building painted pale-blue, with a sign reading "The Peppermill". How come everyone's looking at this? Cait wondered.

47

Now that the bus was no longer in motion, Greatwood's voice once again stood out clearly. "This building, besides being a place to buy excellent fudge -- do not use up all your book money there – is important for you to remember. Why? Because that place exactly opposite" – she pointed at the left side of the bus, and forty-two heads swiveled to look – "is the House of Seven Gables, and if you are downtown in Salem and need to get to the school quickly, that is where you can do so. There is a secret staircase, and once all of you are equipped with wands, you'll learn how it works. Always done out of the sight of nonmagical people, naturally. Now, painful administrative tasks are demanding my attention, and so I must leave you here. Until we meet at the school, you will be in the capable hands of Lucia Corwin, our Spellwork teacher."

Chipmunk -- that is, Ms. Corwin -- stood up as Greatwood stepped out of the bus and set off with her long strides in the direction of an ancient-looking wooden house, large and brown, with a very peaked roof. Cait frowned as she watched Greatwood. Was she wearing that oversized trenchcoat before? What happened to her fancy academic robe with the big sleeves and silver hood?

As the driver started the bus, Ms. Corwin asked loudly, "How many of you ... mage money ... wands and books?" About three-fourths of the students put up their hands.

"Wizards' Bank is near ... need to visit ... get your wands, robes, and books. ... other magical shops .... later how to find them ..."

Penny put up her hand. "You said wizard's bank, not witch. Where do the boys learn magic?"

Everybody perked up to listen; some of the girls began fussing with their hair and clothes. Nobody was gabbing now. Two rows ahead of Caitlin, the blonde who had laughed at her on the Schoodic leaned forward attentively. Ms. Corwin suppressed a smile, then shot a look of warning as she kept talking with raised voice. "There is a school for wizards ... Boys' Wizarding Institute of Salem ... nonmagical people think it's a D.S.S. asylum. School founders saw fit ... boys and girls separately, when the first local boys ... soon after our school was established. So, no sneaking back and forth ... will be found out." Groans broke out around the bus as she continued. "... have plenty of chances to see the boys ... such as Halfterm. ... attention around you, please. Marketplace is coming up on the right, and the Old Town Hall ... get off there."

They passed a couple of blocks of assorted cafés and shops. As Cait scanned the storefronts, a bookstore with a pentagram on its sign made her heart jump. Was that their bookstore? But the bus kept on without slowing. A square plaza opened up on their right, surrounded by old-looking two- and three-story brick buildings. One more building of the same brick, with tall multipaned windows, stood in solitary splendor in the exact center of the plaza.

As soon as the bus stopped, Ms. Corwin jumped up and whirled about to face the students, once again reminding Caitlin of a chipmunk. "Here we are. After me," she announced, and the students all trooped off the bus and followed her to the plaza. Instead of leading them to the town hall, however, Corwin bustled off to the left, towards a tiny street of nondescript rowhouses. There was no traffic here, and the quiet felt wonderful after all the bus noise. Corwin nodded as she stopped in front of a house with a windowless brown-painted front door. A black-capped chickadee watched them from a ledge above the door, and cheeped loudly as they approached. Corwin

49

looked up, smiled at it, then turned to face the students. "Here we are. We go right inside this house, and will be on our way to getting our Mage Geld."

From somewhere in her sweatshirt sleeve, Corwin produced a scuffed-up dark-colored wand with an elaborately carved handle. She tapped it on the wooden door, which swung open to reveal a very ordinary-looking hallway with oatmeal-colored walls, and three doors of fake-oak veneer on the right. She waved them briskly into the house. "The sooner we're all in here, the sooner you get to see the shops." Once everyone was inside, the door swung shut, and Corwin strode to the center door of the oatmeal hallway. For a long moment, she stood with one hand pressed flat against the center of the door, while everyone stood about her in silent confusion. The door vanished without warning, to reveal a narrow brick staircase which led down below street level. A set of the same glowing globes that had illuminated the ship hovered at the top of the doorway. As they went down the steps, the globes accompanied them, floating a little bit ahead of them to light their way. When the stairs ended in a bright marble lobby, the glow-globes floated back up the stairs to await the next customers.

A very tall, old-fashioned wooden desk stood at the end of the lobby. Looks a couple of centuries old, thought Caitlin. Then it occurred to her that it probably was really that old. When was it they founded this school? 1705?

A spare and sharp-eyed wizard in full black robes and a matching tall hat sat on a high stool behind the desk. He looked older than old. He made Caitlin's grandmother look young. As they approached, he said, "Another new class of witches for our town, Ms. Corwin? So good to see the youngsters."

Caitlin couldn't imagine how many incoming classes he must have welcomed to Salem, but decided not to even try to do the math.

"I expect that some of you are in need of Mage Geld," he continued. "If you would, please form a line to my right." He swept his wand in that direction, and a window with an old-fashioned grille in front appeared in the wall behind him. A wizard with green eyes, the beginnings of a beard, and a wide-brimmed pointed hat hastily stepped in place behind it.

"Who needs to make withdrawals?" asked the ancient wizard. About six hands went up. Another sweep of the wand, and another doorway appeared, with a pointy-nosed skinny blonde witch with a matching wide-brimmed hat stepping into place there. Behind her appeared a large brick cylinder, with row upon row of small doors in it. As the first girl stepped up and gave her name and information, the cylinder revolved around about halfway, sank two levels, and a door opened itself in front of her, right at shoulder level, so that she could easily reach in and take out what she needed.

Caitlin tore her gaze away from the spinning column so that she could remember how many Orsos she was supposed to change her dollars into, besides the two Adel that were allowed for book-buying, courtesy of the Sorcerers' Aid Society. They had given her a certificate to cash at the bank, but she hated the thought of handing in that piece of parchment with its fancy calligraphy in purple ink and gold ornamentation. She hoped there would be enough left over for something else once she had bought all the things on her list. Better leave a few dollars in her pocket as well, so that she could find out about that fudge.

Cait opened up the parchment to admire it one more time. As she did so, a small motion across the way caught her attention, and she looked up to see the white-dressed girl from the Schoodic sneer at her. The crow still accompanied her, tugging at her shoelaces. She gestured towards Cait's parchment and said something to the girl next to her, who stepped out of the line slightly and craned her neck to look at the parchment, then smirked back at her friend. She was just as well-dressed, right down to a crisply-pressed plaid dress with matching ballet flats, and her dark hair rippled onto her shoulders in perfect waves. For a fleeting moment, Cait imagined Nini catching Crow Girl's familiar for dinner.

Cait tucked away the parchment and turned to Penny. "How much do you have to buy?"

"Not a lot," Penny answered. "I already have my robes. My mom's good with sewing, and she made sure I wouldn't have to buy any. And I've inherited my grandmother's wand. She wanted me to have it. It's lucky that it works well with me, but I'd rather have my grandmother back. It's only been a month."

As Penny's eyes teared up, Caitlin returned her gaze to the brick column to give Penny some privacy, but gave her a hand-squeeze in sympathy.

"Sorry to hear that," Caitlin said. Penny nodded.

The line seemed to take forever. A few students had already brought Mage Geld with them from home, and they chatted in the marble lobby while everyone else waited. Finally, Caitlin stepped away from the counter with the two Adel for the bookstore, one Adel for the robemaker, and assorted Orsos and Quillers. The pale-gold Orsos and silver Quillers looked disappointingly like regular coins, except that she had never seen a porcupine on a coin before. Moving those coins aside in the palm of her hand, something crystalline winked at Caitlin in the dim light of the bank lobby. A bright-gold rim surrounded a center of pure crystal, and in the center of that, a carved eagle soared. Penny grinned at Caitlin's wide-eyed expression of wonder as the coin reflected bits of light around them.

"To the bookstore," called out Ms. Corwin, raising her wand, and causing a glow-globe to float over to a low doorway in the lefthand corner of the lobby. The ancient clerk smiled, consulted something on his desk, and said, "Best of luck to all of you, and welcome to Salem."

They all followed Ms. Corwin's lively step to the doorway and into a tunnel. It was narrow, mostly stone, and there were no longer marble slabs underfoot, but packed earth. A faintly damp smell reminded Cait of the unfinished cellar in her own house. Overhead, an especially bright glowglobe hovered over Corwin, and as Caitlin's balance began to go unsteady in the darkness, another glowglobe floated over to accompany her. After a short walk, the tunnel opened into sort of underground room, or was it really a street? There were shopfronts here and there among walls that were sometimes earth and sometimes brick, and glowglobes zoomed around everywhere overhead. It felt like a street, but there were no vehicles around, unless Cait counted a pair of teenage boys in tall hats trying out brooms in one far corner. "Plain Sight" was clearly not needed here. Witches and wizards of all ages strolled about in robes and hats of all shapes and colors. The firstyears' regular clothes now looked totally out of place. Remembering Greatwood's robe-to-trenchcoat change, Cait glanced at Corwin, but the roundfaced teacher still wore her own Plain Sight jeans and "Schoodic" sweatshirt.

A loud squeal ahead caught Caitlin's attention. "Ooh, hey look – boys! Over there! ... cute!" It came from the pudgy girl who'd laughed at Caitlin for not knowing what broomball was. Meg. Boy-crazy twit, thought Caitlin, as the girl's friend toyed with her bracelets and both of them began to strut. The two teenagers paused from trying out their brooms to eye them in return.

Near the end of the underground street, Ms. Corwin stopped and whirled about to face the students. Caitlin suspected an announcement was about to follow, and maneuvered closer to the teacher so as to hear her better among the general chatter. "Here's the bookstore where all of the Witches' Academy textbooks will be stocked throughout your time at the school. Go to the counter at the back and tell them your name. They've set aside a set of the required firstyear texts for each of you, and they'll tell you how to get to the robemaker and the wandmaker. Have fun browsing the other shops, but be sure to meet me right back here at four o'clock."

With that, she gestured at a sundial that hung above the center of the street. A sundial underground? What sense did that make? Nevertheless, Caitlin could plainly see on it the usual pattern of light and shade that would be on an outdoor sundial on a clear day, with the shadow pointing exactly at II.

As she walked into the bookstore, Caitlin was pleased, in the midst of all this strange newness, to note how comfortingly familiar it felt, very much like her favorite second-hand bookstore back home. The volumes lining the walls of this shop were of all shapes, sizes, and colors. Most of them were new, but some of them appeared truly ancient. The smell was right, too: paper, leather, a slight bit of mustiness from the older books. She wanted to begin browsing immediately, although she didn't understand a lot of the titles. Then there were the books written in letters she didn't even recognize. Cait squinted at a book whose spine was completely covered with curls and squiggles, and wondered if Uncle Rude would know what kind of alphabet it was. And there was another shelf of books over there, all with flowing lines that looked like dropped ribbons. And that whole section of books looked like Hebrew. Did this mean they would get to learn other languages at this school? Back home, she had so badly wanted to learn how to read those German newspapers Uncle Rude wrapped gifts in, understand those prayers she'd recited at Passover and Chanukah, read the Spanish and French magazines that had their own corner in the bookstore back home. And her teachers had always said the same thing. Wait until high school, you can learn then. What would her new textbooks be like? Are any of them written in these other alphabets?

As she hurried past the stacks and shelves of books towards the textbook counter, a soft, rustling, breathy sound met her ears. It had a speechlike rhythm, but didn't seem to be coming from any of the chattering customers around her. Were the books themselves whispering? She leaned towards a table which held an elegantly-bound red leather volume, and the flustery whisper grew a little louder. Holding the book up to her better ear, the sound sorted itself out into words.

"Four hundred and thirty-one ways to flummox whoever is sending bad charms against you, no permanent harm to the spellcaster, only one Adel and three Orso, and you can take me home to make your life easier." Caitlin hastily – but oh, so carefully -- put the book back on its table. She had never in her whole life handled such an expensive volume. Since when did stores put two-hundred-dollar books out on tables for people to handle? she wondered. What kind of security do they have here? No way she wanted to find out what witches or wizards did to perceived shoplifters.

Again, she headed to the back counter, ignoring everything else along the way. The line wasn't as long as she'd feared, but she was surprised to see a couple of boys among the Witches' Academy students waiting to buy books. A short boy with freckles all the way up his broad neck turned and saw Caitlin. "Did you just get in on the Schoodic today?" he asked, voice clear in the quiet shop.

As she nodded, he continued, "I saw it come in with the out-of-town BWIS students yesterday. I'm local, so I get to live at home. But I should have bought books before there were any lines."

Then a clerk yelled "Next!" and he turned his attention back to the book counter.

A bored-looking wizard fetched her stack of books, tied up with a red cord, and Caitlin handed over the one Adel, two Orso due with a sense of relief, glad that they didn't cost the full two Adel that had been allotted to her by Sorcerers' Aid.

As she tugged one of the books out of the stack to have a better look at it, a tingle went up her arm and a clear voice called out "Book unpaid! Book un-" as the red-faced clerk tapped the cord around the books. The voice stopped abruptly, and the cord turned green.

"So sorry about that. They're truly all yours now," he said.

Caitlin picked up her books, moved away from the counter, and hoped there were no more hidden hexes to be found. Would she be better off browsing the nonmagical bookstores for fun? With caution, she slid the smallest book towards her. It was a solidly-bound black hardcover titled Elementary Spellwork. About an inch thick, it sat comfortably in her hand and seemed about the right size to slip into a pocket. She flipped through it quickly. There, she knew those letters – they were Hebrew. This was going to be great. No "waiting for high school" for other languages at this Academy. The Astronologia book, in contrast, was big and bulky, its deep-blue cover ornamented with silver spangles which rearranged themselves into new patterns every time her gaze drifted away from the design. There was a book on Alchemy, nearly the size and shape of the Spellcraft book, only with a deep-green cover. And the text inside was full of all kinds of symbols and shapes that weren't quite like letters, but what were they? I'll find out soon enough, she figured. She turned to the next book, Greenwitchery for Greenhorn Witches. It was on the large side, had no odd symbols in it, and was printed on very lightweight paper, with the smell of a sunlit meadow coming from its pages. Zoomorphia for Beginners, on the other hand, didn't smell anywhere near as pleasant: somewhere between unwashed dog and low tide. Cait wondered what Nini would make of that one, and hoped she wouldn't miss the cat too badly during her time at Salem. At the bottom of the stack was Mindcasting: Knowing the Vibes Around You, which was plainly bound, in an elegant shade of burgundy.

As she stuffed the last book into her bulging bookbag, Penny showed up with an overloaded shopping bag.

"Oof, I can't wait 'till we learn to put flying charms on things so my muscles don't have to lug stuff like this," she puffed, as she took her place in the textbook line. "Be glad your parents don't send you off to school with their magical-book shopping list. I know I'm going to be stuck in some hideous line at the Broomcourier while you're picking out your new robes. Don't forget to get at least one heavy lined wool robe, by the way. Mom warned me that the classroom building is really cold in the winter."

"Sounds like our house. It's sooo drafty all winter long. But what's Broomcourier?"

"Oh yeah, I forget you're new to all this. Well, sending magical books through US Post doesn't work too well. The talking ones set off security and it gets kind of complicated. So, if you need to get magical things shipped to people, Broomcourier will do it. They're down the hall that way," Penny turned around and pointed to her left, "and two doors over."

Once Penny had her textbooks, the two girls headed out the door, and Penny showed Caitlin where the robemaker's shop was.

"I'll find you at the wandmaker's. They're right next door," she called out as she lugged her load of books to Broomcourier's, Nick perched majestically atop the smaller bag with her texts.

The robemaker's proved a quicker errand than Caitlin expected. As soon as she stepped into the tiny shop at the end of its own earthy cul-de-sac, a birdlike elderly witch with a blue-beribboned hat looked up from a book of robe patterns to throw a piercing glance at Caitlin. Before the door had even closed behind her, a sample robe was in Caitlin's hands. As she pulled the garment on, Caitlin was delighted to note that it fell at exactly the right length to walk around in without being tripped over, had lots of pockets all over it, even on the sleeves and at the hem, and when she waved her arms around, had plenty of room in both arms and chest. Now this was the way she liked to dress. Comfy, with lots of pockets. Did the magical world have fashions? She hoped not. At the robemaker's quick

58

gesture, Caitlin handed the robe back with reluctance, receiving two paper-wrapped bundles in return. One was much bulkier and heavier than the other, and Caitlin guessed that it held her winter woolen robes and cloak.

"No pointed hat?" asked Cait with disappointment, as the dressmaker plopped a round cap onto her head.

"If you study, it will be," was the cryptic reply. "Time to choose your dress robe." Blue Ribbon walked over to a wall filled with bits of fabric in all shades and textures. She pointed to the center of the wall. "These are the standard fabrics for the Academy," she said with a sweep of her hand, as two rows of shining fabrics fluttered in response. Her voice was clear in the quiet shop. "The robe itself must be black, but lining and trim can be whatever you like." She then pointed out two more rows of flimsier fabric below it, whose colors looked muted in comparison. "Those are the budget fabrics, two quillers less per yard." Then she gestured upward to where bright jewel-hued fabrics began to wave. "For two quillers extra per yard, there is silk." Up near the ceiling, one row of brilliant colors was still stationary. "And for five quillers above the standard rate, I have available real dryad-woven silk bespelled from the worm." This last row now fluttered in response. Cait couldn't help reaching up towards a brilliant cobalt swatch, which responded by unreeling itself down to where she could feel that that the fabric was every bit as sumptuous as the brilliant color looked. Cait wondered what "dryad-woven" meant. Then she realized that it was one of the most expensive fabrics in the shop and let go of the swatch, which returned to its spot near the ceiling. Blue Ribbon's gaze was sharp as she awaited Cait's response.

"I like this shade," said Cait. She pointed to a purple silk in the row below, admiring the soft shine of the fabric

59

as it billowed out towards her, the swatch becoming a full bolt-width of fabric as it went. Even though Cait could only afford standard fabric for the dress robe itself, there were just enough quillers to buy real silk for its purple lining, and gold piping for the edges. "And the hemline is self-adjusting, in case you aren't quite finished growing," said Blue Ribbon, while a Cait-sized manikin wearing purple, black and gold swatches vanished through a doorway in the back of her shop.

Now, to buy her wand. As Cait left the dressmaker's, and headed towards the brightly-lit wandshop next door, she was startled to see one student standing still among the bustle of the corridor. The boy-crazy blonde, Meg. But instead of ogling the lanky youth exiting the shop with broom in hand, she stared at a display of brooms with brightly-polished handles. "Two whole Adel," Cait heard her say, with a huge sigh. Realizing Cait was looking at her, she pointed at the middle broom. "That's what pros get to ride. Luckeeee." Meg sighed again and stared at the display once more.

The familiar smell of sawdust and cedar filled her nose as soon as Cait opened the door to the wandshop and walked in. A large table in the center of the shop held nearly a hundred wands, all made of plain wood. Students gathered about it, supervised by a redheaded, bearded wizard.

It felt so much like her dad's workshop that Cait just stood there for a few minutes. She remembered the flash of her Dad's whittling knife as he shaved down a pale piece of wood which needed to fit into one specific groove in the depths of a piano he'd repaired last year. Whittle, whittle, shave, shave, pale curls of wood falling to the floor. Then a pause as he fitted the piece to its destination, shook his head, and shaved it down some more. "What if you cut it too much and it breaks?" she had asked. He caught her gaze briefly before holding it again to the gap beyond the piano strings. "That's why I go slow, keep checking. And make sure it's the right shape when I start."

A pang of worry prodded at Cait's mind. Would she miss him while being at Salem? And Mom? Pushing the thought aside, Caitlin jostled her way closer to the tableful of wands.

A thrill ran up her spine as she went. This sure wasn't school as usual any more. Wands were for fairy tales. No, wands were on the shopping list for this new school. Her new school. Weird witchy everyone. But how did one go about choosing a wand? One sturdy-looking wand was elaborately carved at the handle like Corwin's and looked too long to fit inside a bookbag. A pale one about the size of a drum-player's stick had barely a dent or two where fingers should go, and no carving at all. One tiny white wand (holly?) was as thin as the band-director's baton at Caitlin's old school, and only as long as a ballpoint pen, while two long dark knobby wands at the edge of the table looked more like walking sticks than anything else.

There were also more kinds of wood than she'd ever seen before. They ranged from the palest of blond pine, to the deeper-toned rosewood, and an unbelievably dark ebony. Like piano keys. Don't get homesick, Caitlin told herself.

Her wand ended up being American chestnut, which looked like oak. It wasn't the prettiest or fanciest one there, but it sat in her hand so comfortably she didn't even want to pick up any of the others. While the wandmaker described what a rare tree it had come from, Cait wished that she didn't have to wait to show it off to her family. A bout of homesickness washed over her. What

61

had that teacher on the boat said? "You'll see them at halfterm." A whole month from now.

There was just enough time to buy a snack at a nearby stand – mooncakes and single-fizz cider – and then the sundial stood at four o'clock, with all of the firstyears under it. With a flash of panic, Cait realized that her shopping list hadn't included pens, pencils, or paper. How was she going to take notes? Her sketchpad didn't have enough pages for a semester of classes. Were they going to go to other shops after these underground ones?

"Good work, firstyears, no latecomers at all," said Ms. Corwin, as she confirmed that all forty-two of them were there. "Now, follow me up these stairs, and when we go out the door, board the bus right away." She led the way up a wooden flight of stairs at the very end of the underground street. As before, glow-globes hovered overhead.

At the top of the stairs, Corwin held her wand against what looked like a plain wall for a few moments, waiting for something.

Then, a wooden door appeared. "Together everybody, now." She ushered them through the door and a small foyer. A shop on the left caught Cait's eye as the students hurried along. The twiggy brooms propped up outside its doors looked cheap and undersized compared to the ones downstairs. She remembered Greatwood's words: don't tease the tourists who come to see the "witch city." As the students piled onto the bus, Caitlin saw Ms. Corwin exchange nods with a middle-aged woman who leaned against the shop's doorway.

Caitlin looked back at the shop from the bus: "Crowhame," read the sign on the front of a narrow wooden house. Was that shopkeeper also a witch? Was she Hiding in Plain Sight with her touristy shop?

62

Ms. Corwin stepped into the front of the bus, scanned the seats full of students, and announced, "Please remember this shop. That is the easiest way to get to the bookstore, bank, and Broomcourier from our school. Just direct your wand at the exact center of the wall opposite the front door. If there aren't any nonmagicals nearby, voilà, your door will show up. Go down the stairs, and there are your shops. Now, let's go to the school."

Chapter 6 – Sisterly Bonds

The bus left Salem's bustling downtown and drove through a tree-lined neighborhood full of old-looking wood and brick houses. After passing a huge yellow house that said "Museum", several wooden houses turned sideways to the street and a brick mansion marked "Town Library", the bus stopped.

"We're here," announced Ms. Corwin. A collective groan went up as everyone looked out the window.

"A Catholic school? No way I'm going back to one of those."

"It can't be. Maybe it's got a disguising spell on it."

"My parents'll croak. I'm Jewish."

Ms. Corwin stood still for a moment, listening to the babble as a smile tugged at the corner of her mouth. She raised her hands for attention. Then she said, "Actually, our school is on the other side of the street."

Everyone turned to look out the other side of the bus, but there wasn't much to see, only two ordinary wooden houses. A pair of red-brick pillars stood between them, each of them topped with a flat stone slab. A path between them led to a yard behind the house on the right.

Ms. Corwin gave no answer to the confused chatter around her, but simply motioned for them all to follow her off the bus. Once they were gathered around the brick pillars which stood at almost her shoulder height, Corwin again signaled for silence as Cait worked her way up front. Then Corwin announced, "Here we finally are, at the end of today's travels. I give you the Witches' Academy of Salem!" And with that, she touched her wand to the center of the stone atop the left-hand pillar and pronounced a strange-sounding word. Pitoch? B'tohach? Peto'ach? Cait hoped that this school wouldn't expect students to learn their spells by ear.

A broad and grassy path appeared to the left of the pillar, and an ancient-looking wooden house with diamond-paned windows stood at its end. Beyond it, they could see bits and pieces of other buildings. One of them appeared to be topped with a giant glass globe. Wow, Cait thought. If they can hide a whole school like this, what else can they do?

"Onward," cried Ms. Corwin, and they all followed her to the front door of the old house where Greatwood stood awaiting them, again attired in her big-sleeved black robe with the blue and silver hood. Only a few students were whispering; most were still gazing about drop-jawed at the school's sudden appearance. Greatwood's voice rang out clearly from her podium of the house's front stoop as if she were in a grand auditorium.

"Welcome to Witches' Academy of Salem, firstyears," she boomed out. The surrounding chatter stopped. "You are about to enter ... first witches formally studied magic in North America ... proud to add your numbers to the illustrious ranks of magicworkers ... unbroken chain from 1705 up until the present day." Greatwood paused, beaming proudly at the firstyears. She swept her hand before the crowd, making her sleeve flap like a flag as she continued to speak. "Doubtless there are those among you ... highest ranks of magicworking ... remembered with pride among the sisterhood of the Witches' Academy of Salem."

At this point, Corwin cleared her throat loudly, caught Greenwood's eye, and glanced off in the direction of the other buildings. The Associate Director frowned, pushed at her sleeves, nodded, and continued. "It has been a long day ... doubtless quite tired ... chance to settle into your dorm, put away your Plain-Sight clothes, rest up, and be ready for the term-begin banquet … your ordinary robes. I look forward to seeing all of you then. Welcome." And her giant sleeve fluttered in the direction of the hallway behind her, which went through the whole of the house, and opened onto the rest of the school.

A large two-story building stood before them as they exited the house. Its yellow-brick second story was full of tall multipaned windows with rounded tops, and its first story was bisected by a granite archway. The tall windows reminded Cait of the Town Hall near Wizards' Bank. The archway led to a courtyard covered with a plush plump-leaved little groundcover. A sandy path around its the edges was bordered by slender trees full of apples, pears, plums, and tiny yellow fruits that Cait didn't recognize. To the right and to the left, beyond the trees, stretched a pair of white-painted wooden two-story buildings; the glass globe stood atop the nearest one on the left. A solid-looking stone building stood at the courtyard's far side, with a seamless sheer-glass front contrasting with all the other antique-looking buildings. It had a greenhouse on its roof.

The sound of a voice caught Cait's attention as she absorbed the details of her new school. "… right, everyone," It was Corwin talking, and Cait moved closer to catch what she was saying. "Partridge Hall was named for Willa Partridge … had the idea to found our school … stubborn enough to get the other Council members to agree." Corwin's voice rose as a few students began to fidget. "Attention, please. If any of you need to send a message to your families, please note that the school aviary is on the roof of this dorm … plenty of birds to go around, and a crow or a dove is just as good at delivering a note as hawks or eagles. The library," Corwin turned around briefly to point out the building to the group, then turned back, making Cait miss half her sentence. "... straight ahead ... classrooms tomorrow morning. We have just walked under the Commons." Corwin nodded in the direction of the yellow-brick building. "That is where the term-begin banquet will take place. You will hear a bell when it's time to gather. When it rings, make for the staircase over there." Corwin gestured toward a double staircase which curved up to the level of the tall windows on the second floor of the Commons. Cait glanced at it quickly, and turned her attention back to the teacher. "Go on in and settle into your rooms. I'll see you at the banquet." And she strode off back towards the wooden diamond-paned house beyond the granite archway, leaving the firstyears at the dorm door.

How were they supposed to find their rooms? Caitlin looked at Penny, who shrugged her shoulders. But since the door already stood ajar, all the students entered as a group. There was a bright sitting room with pine paneling, comfy seats, a fireplace, and on each side of it, hallways stretching to the right and to the left, both containing staircases which led to the second floor.

A tawny dog napping in front of the fireplace raised her head to look at the students as they entered. Then she went up to the nearest firstyear, who clutched her cat-carrier more tightly, although neither cat nor dog seemed perturbed by the other's presence. How come all these animals are so good? wondered Cait, recalling the hissing, spitting, puffed-up fury that Nini became whenever she was near a dog. The tawny dog sniffed the girl's palm, looked up slightly, and did a retriever-dog point toward the left-hand hallway.

"Guess I'm second-floor then," said the girl, walking off.

One student at a time, and sometimes two by two, as with Meg and Bracelet Girl, the process repeated itself, until Caitlin and Penny were both pointed to the first floor, right-hand hallway. As they started down the hall, a medium-height girl with magenta fur trim on her robe strode the other way towards them, checking the trim as she went. She found a trailing thread, paused, bit it off, then continued her imperious stride. Cait had seen that perfectly rippling hair before. On the bus? At Wizards' Bank?

Penny flagged her down. "Excuse us, but how do we find which rooms are ours?"

The girl's bright blue eyes narrowed and the corner of her mouth rose in a sneer, as Cait recognized Crow Girl's friend. "Read the door, of course," she said with a toss of her hair, then she paused and added, "You're the one who needed Sorcerers' Aid money," staring right at Cait. "No wonder you don't know these things." She then rushed off towards two other fur-trimmed girls who were giggling and gossiping in one corner of the sitting room. Cait recognized one of them as Crow Girl, but the bird itself was nowhere in sight.

Cait fumed while Penny peered down the hallway. From behind some of the closed doors came the sound of muffled chatter.

"Hope she's not our neighbor," said Caitlin.

"Never mind her," said Penny. "Some people have more money than brains. We've got some hidden writing to find. My mom told me about it. We'll probably be the only ones who can see it, because we're the only ones who need to see it. Look for a light." Penny turned away from Cait to walk down the hallway. As Penny mumbled something, Cait spotted a pale glow on one door to the right. Once they stood before the door, it formed the words "Caitlin Leo" and "Penny Dingle."

"Good, we don't have to worry that we'll hate our roommates," said Penny. "My mom had terrible roommate stories." She pushed the door open to reveal matched desks, wardrobes, and beds, all of plain pine, lined up along each side of the room. Under a wide multipaned window at the far end of the room was a pair of small tables. Penny parked Nick on the lefthand small table, then began to unpack her book bag onto the nearby desk.

"Hey, I could snore, or sleepwalk, or be a closet thief. We might still hate each other," said Caitlin, only half-joking. She'd never had to share a room before. What if they didn't get along after all?

"Nah – I'd know it if you were someone like that purple-trim girl," Penny said, jerking her head at the hallway and grimacing. "I'm good at sussing out people. Have to be, when I'm helping out Mom. Poor Nicky needs some water, so I'm gonna go find some."

"All I want to do is sleep," said Caitlin. "My brain will burst if I try to learn one more thing today." She pulled out her hearing aids and plopped them on the other little table, then curled up on the nearby bed only to spring up again. "Hey, my bag's here. How'd they know where to bring it?"

"Cait, we're in a magic school, remember? Go have your nap. Oh, is it OK if I call you Cait?"

"Mmmf, sure."

And Cait wasn't aware of anything else until she felt Penny shaking her awake, and then she heard the muted tones of a bell ringing from somewhere outside.

"C'mon, we have to get robed and get to dinner. Wake up."

69

"Okay," she muttered as she looped her hearing aids back behind her ears.

"Hey, red's a great color by the way," said Penny. "Beige hearing aids are so ugly."

"Um, they're my mom's idea, thought they'd be cheery," said Cait. "Besides, even when they're this great color, people still don't notice them. Or they notice them for two seconds and then forget, and go right back to mumbling. You're great at not mumbling, by the way. Wish more people were like you."

"Thanks," said Penny, turning abruptly to open her wardrobe and swiping at one eye.

As Cait opened the thinner of the wrapped bundles the robemaker had handed her, she groaned. "This robe has wrinkles all over."

"Nah, you're okay, it looks more like fold lines than wrinkles," said Penny, stowing her bookbag on the floor of her wardrobe. Then she addressed the darkness within, leaving the door ajar. "Don't eat any spiders Nicky, remember that. But go after all the moths and flies you want." Cait could just see the glow of the toad's eyes as she pulled on her robe and followed Penny out of the room.

The gathering firstyears walked across the courtyard to where a large group of girls waited atop the Commons' double staircase. Mirtha Greatwood stood with them, wearing a tall hat shot through with silver and a silver-trimmed black silk robe with sleeves that reached all the way to the floor. Cait maneuvered to the front of the group not only to hear Greatwood better, but to also admire that shimmering robe.

"Now that our firstyears are safely here," announced Greatwood in her clear, crisp voice, "shall we find out who your Little Sisters are? Firstyears, you'll have many wonderful and assorted things to learn during these inaugural days of your magical studies, and your new Big Sisters will be there to help you along." She waved at the secondyears. "Wands out, please! And remember that it is the wand-impression doing the choosing, not your eye-impression." Some of the secondyears pouted and scowled at that. "So, eyes closed, and no cheating; I will be watching. One at a time, alphabetically. Ruthann Appelbaum, please begin."

A slight girl stepped forward hesitantly, swallowed hard, and faced the group. She closed her eyes, drew her wand, and swept it in a slow arc before her, from left to right, until a freckled girl startled, a look in her eyes something like recognition.

"Abigail Zunz, I believe? A to Z last names, who could have predicted? You two can proceed into the Commons. Your table's right up front near the faculty table. Next, Lori Aspen."

Four names later, tiredness set in as the voice went on. Cait dropped her concentration, letting the names blur into incomprehension, being aware only of their unbroken rhythm as pairs of girls were matched. A dark, swooping motion in the courtyard caught her attention, and she watched it out the corner of her eye. Was there a bird out there? Or two? But the flight motion wasn't quite birdlike, it was too erratic. Then Cait felt a light tap right in the center of her chest as if somebody were playing tag, but nobody had touched her. She looked up to meet the gaze of a pair of green eyes belonging to a tall girl with skin the color of cinnamon, and brought her attention back to Greatwood.

"Caitlin Leo. Please proceed to the Commons, and enjoy the banquet. Next, Sheila Travers."

71

Frustration built up with Cait. She didn't even know what this girl's name was, but decided to not interrupt the Little-Sister ritual to find out. This is my big chance to fit in, she reminded herself. Weird witchy everyone. I'll find out her name once we're inside.

Green Eyes waved at Cait to follow her, then pushed open the tall door and marched into a noisy, brightly-lit room. Its pale blue walls ran up to a high cathedral ceiling crossed by exposed roof beams of dark wood, and golden late-afternoon light gleamed through its tall windows. Stone fireplaces as tall as people stood at each end of the room, one to the right and one to the left, and broad gray stones with flashing bits of mica paved the floor. Round tables filled almost all of the space, and one long table stood against the back wall. Cait could see all the grownups gathering around it. The room was also filled with hundreds of chattering voices. How could Cait begin to understand anybody in all this noise? Green Eyes glanced back once as she walked into the room, and Cait could see that she was saying something, but what? So much for finding out her name.

The hovering lanterns which lit the room gave Cait an idea. They matched the changing leaves outside, and she recognized the flaming orange-red of maple, the bright yellow of birch, the dull brown of oak. Instead of keeping up with Green Eyes and pretending to understand her chatter, Cait decided to stop walking and continue her absorption in the lamps. Fit in, she thought. I've got to fit in. I'll pretend I was distracted by these lamps and that's why I don't know what Green Eyes was saying.

Cait watched the girl arrive at a half-filled table, reach for a chair, and look around wildly as if Cait had pulled a vanishing spell. Typical hearie, Cait thought to herself.

Green Eyes hadn't even noticed that I'd stopped following her.

Cait continued admiring the lanterns until she felt a tug at her elbow from Green Eyes, who kept on talking as she escorted Cait to a half-filled group of tables near where the grown-ups stood. Only when she turned to face Cait, could anything understandable filter through all the noise. "... seats saved ... four times ... favorite subject ... " They were now at their table, where four girls already chattered away loudly. As Cait sat, she turned her chair to face Green Eyes, hoping to catch more of the monologue, and switched her hearing aids to "directional" mode. "Strict and always ... every week she gives --" Green Eyes turned to point at a green-robed witch who was holding a lively conversation with Dark Eyes, and the rest of her sentence was lost. Turning back to Cait, she continued, "Gotta remember the door-charm! And here's ... get to classroom up ... turn up on ... third floor, not till bell ... Oh, Shannah!" Green Eyes shouted over Cait's head. "Over here! How ya been?" Green Eyes shot a look of apology at Cait, who waved her to go ahead and talk with Shannah. Just as bad as the public-school cafeteria back home, thought Cait. Even with fancy hearing aids. Penny better show up soon.

A flutter of colorful fabric drew Cait's eye back to the group of teachers Green Eyes had pointed out. None of her teachers at home dressed like that. These teachers wore silk and velvet robes in rich, bright colors that made Cait think of the tubes of watercolors she'd left behind. There was ultramarine and cobalt blue, viridian green, and carmine red. Cait recognized Ms. Corwin in black-on-black robes with velvet and satin playing off each other, while black feathers ornamented her small cap. In contrast, another teacher wore robes of flame orange with red and

73

yellow, topped by an orange and gold turban. In the very center of their long table sat a tiny, elderly witch who appeared quite firmly in charge of the whole thing, although she hardly seemed to be doing anything at all but casting the occasional word this way, or the occasional glance that way. Her robes were the most elaborate of all, black and red, embroidered in gold, with matching feathers in her tall, pointed hat.

The complexions of the teachers varied as much as their regalia, making Cait realize how white-bread boring her home town was. She recognized the bright-haired blonde from the Schoodic, whose pale skin glowed in the lamplight; the woman in orange looked quite dark in contrast to her. Then again, an ebony-skinned and very rotund witch with an elaborately-feathered hat at one end of the table made everyone else look light. Greatwood appeared to be introducing Feather Hat to the rest of the faculty. An image burst into Cait's brain of all that bulk atop a tiny broomstick, making her giggle.

She felt a tap on her shoulder. Penny had arrived with her Big Sister, and their table was now full. Cait pulled out her pocket sketchbook to make a quick drawing of Feather Hat atop a broom, and was rewarded by a loud snort of laughter from Penny. Penny then added a drawing of Greatwood drowning in a pair of gigantic sleeves, followed by Cait's drawing of Corwin as chipmunk. As she drew the last whisker on the chipmunk, a tap at her mind made Cait drop her pencil in surprise as Penny looked up at exactly the same moment. It felt almost like the tag-you're-it tap at the Little Sister ritual. Around them, everyone else had stopped talking and now watched the faculty table. Cait flipped her sketchbook to a clean page and left it on the table before her, hoping none of the teachers had seen the sketches.

Greatwood stood next to the tiny woman in charge, her silver-shot hat flashing in the lantern-light, and then loudly announced, "Welcome, students of Witches' Academy. And welcome to the new school year. Do I hear the outgoing seniors of the class of 2008?"

An enormous cheer went up from a group of three tables in the back, where students were dressed nearly as impressively as the teachers, complete with wide-brimmed, pointed hats.

"2009?" Another deafening cheer.

"2010?" More cheers, and likewise for "2011?"

"Our nearly-Hedge-certified thirdyears?" The table next to Caitlin and her classmates erupted in cheers and clapping.

"The returning secondyears?" Around her, Big Sisters cheered and clapped.

"Finally – firstyears please rise – I present to you our newest students. Please welcome our firstyears to the Witches' Academy of Salem." Everybody was cheering for them now. When would they ever get to eat? Caitlin wondered.

But there wasn't long to wait. Greatwood sat down, and dishes of all kinds floated their way through a small door to the left of the faculty table. An enormous platter with a whole roasted pig led the way, followed by a flock of roasted chickens on their own individual platters, all parading in a grand sweep around the Commons. The pig headed to the faculty table, while the chickens flew over to all the student tables. A platter hovered near Cait, but as she reached up for a drumstick, she paused as she had a better look at the roast. It was too long to be a chicken, and wasn't shaped quite the same, and since when are chickens that dark? But it smelled delicious, and as she reached up again, a drumstick neatly unhinged itself from

75

the roast and floated down to her plate. Beside her, Penny elbowed Cait, rubbed her hands together, and mimed calling the pig roast over to their table.

Cait forgot all about the pig roast however, once the fish course swam in. A pair of whole roasted salmon floated around the room on silver platters, followed by schools of smaller fish on their own platters, mackerel, sole, and trout. Side dishes of squash, potatoes, new corn, and all kinds of cooked greens followed. One very bright green dish looked familiar, but it took Cait a moment to figure out that it looked just like seaweed. Who ate seaweed? she wondered. How many kinds of people went to magical school?

Once the eating slowed down, individual plates of salad came out for each diner, and the empty plates and platters took themselves off toward a small and inconspicuous door to the right of the faculty table.

During the entire meal, brown jugs of fizzy cider hovered at each table, plus some green ones at the faculty table, as well as what looked like wine bottles. When a flock of green jugs headed towards the three senior tables, Cait craned her neck to read their labels, which said "double-fizz" in bold black ink. As the green jugs arrived at the senior tables, a cheer went up. At the faculty table, Green Robes held up a glass in salute to the seniors.

Cait picked up her own glass to see what would happen; a brown jug with "single-fizz" written on it appeared, filled her glass, and zoomed off again. Penny had noticed the jugs of double-fizz as well, raising her own glass whenever a green jug was nearby, but none of them so much as paused on its way to the seniors. Cait continued to watch with fascination as the empty jugs and bottles flew off through the little door to the right of the faculty table and newly-filled ones flew back into the room from the other little door.

Conversation now hummed all around Caitlin. Penny was now busy asking questions of her own Big Sister, but broke off from time to time to grab the sketchbook and scribble a note to Cait. "Did you know only about half the students here stay in school beyond Hedge level?" "The BWIS coach is supposed to be awesomely cute." "Wow, broomriding's a whole class here. Witch driver ed!"

Green Eyes, on the other hand, spent most of her time gabbing with the secondyears. Every so often she'd turn to Cait as if she'd forgotten something, but Cait would just shrug and let her go back to her friends. Too much noise, way too much work to understand people, even if she did have a ton of questions to ask. Annoyance prickled at her. Why did it have to be so hard to have a regular conversation, even here? Why didn't it occur to anyone to use magic to make noisy rooms easier for talking? Were there no hard-of-hearing witches?

Cait looked around around the room; everyone was in groups of four, six, eight as they chatted away with all the energy of a brand-new school year. How could they possibly all understand each other? she puzzled.

But new excitement filled Cait as she watched lanterns floating overhead and all those people in their real-live pointy witchy hats. Weird, witchy everyone. So unlike her poor aunts who had only each other for so long. After having to hide her rock trick for all this time, it was especially fun to watch those zooming jugs, bottles and platters, all those hovering lanterns. I may be half deaf, Cait thought, but it's great not being weird any more. Wonder what we'll learn in class tomorrow?

A raucous hoot and set of giggles erupted from the back of the room. Turning around, Cait tried to figure out which of those three senior tables had made all the noise. Boy, were some of them grown-up looking. And it wasn't just their big hats either, which were so much more grand than the firstyears' nondescript caps. That tall blonde with the broad cheekbones, she could be a model, Cait thought. And that bouncy girl talking with her hands would fit right in at the faculty table. She looks a lot like Green Robes, actually. Cait remembered one boy at her old school whose parents were both teachers, and wondered if anyone here had a teacher for a parent. With surprise, Cait noticed that the robes everybody wore gave away very few details about the figures underneath. Looking around the rest of the room, she tried to guess which of her classmates had developed already, but there was no telling. Sweet. She'd hated being the curviest girl in fifth grade.

Once salads were finished, the tiny, ancient witch in the red, black, and gold robes rose from her place, and the entire room fell silent. Despite this, Caitlin could make out very little of her low-voiced speech, except that her first name was Penthesilia, and that she had been director of Witches' Academy for longer than Caitlin's parents had been alive. But the words of the speech didn't seem to matter. With or without words, there was a heavy aura of power about her which commanded instant respect.

Finally, a flock of elaborately-iced cakes came out, accompanied by silver coffee and tea pots pouring themselves as people wished. At last, diners began to drift out of the Commons and down the double staircase to the courtyard and off to their respective dorms, apartments, and houses. As soon as Caitlin, Penny, and their new Big Sisters were outside, Green Eyes' speech became clear. "See that huge globe on top of that dorm? That's where everyone wants to live their senior year, but there's only

78

eight rooms on that top floor. So there's a lottery among the top Astronologia students to decide who'll get a room." At the foot of the stairs, Cait stopped, stepped aside from the other students exiting the hall, and motioned for Green Eyes' attention.

"What's your name, by the way?" Cait asked her. "There was all the noise in the Commons, and I never got it. And don't all those flying dishes ever crash into each other?"

Green Eyes grinned. "I'm Luatha. And yeah, a soup tureen and this big old wine bottle crashed into each other during last year's term-end banquet. Poor Ms. Broadleaf looked like she was about to cry. She's the Greenwitchery teacher, and she's in charge of the wine, which only the faculty and muckamuck guests get to drink. And Ms. Greatwood looked like she was about to throttle someone. But four of the upperclass students stepped right up to clean up – probably sent it by wand to the nearest front-yard tree – and you should've seen Ms. Corwin crack up. She stopped real fast when Greatwood gave her this dirty look." Luatha began walking towards Partridge Hall, as the other three girls followed. Fireflies were now out, and filled the courtyard with their tiny lights.

"What kind of name's Luatha?" asked Cait. "I've never heard it before. My name's boring."

"From my great- great- great-grandmother, best herbalist in three Councils of Witches." Luatha straightened her hat with a flourish. "Sorry Plod names are so boring. Upperclassers get to change theirs if they want."

"I hope classes don't begin too early in the morning. I could sleep for a week," said Penny with a yawn. As the group proceeded, Cait hurried to keep Luatha on the side of her good ear, and her face within eyeshot.

"If you're lucky, you'll be scheduled for evening classes tomorrow. Half the firstyears have evening classes on Wednesday and Thursday, everybody else on Monday and Tuesday. You'll get your schedule tomorrow morning. Not too early, don't worry."

"What if I oversleep?" worried Cait. "I kind of sleep through things."

"She's right," added Penny. "She tried to sleep right through the banquet bell, but I wouldn't let her."

"Oh, they'll get you up on time, don't worry," said Luatha, as they neared their dorm door.

A shout interrupted their conversation. "Aw, the cute little chicks are toddling home!" teased a passing upperclass student.

"Oh chill, you Woolie," replied Luatha. "Lucky girl," she told Cait and Penny. "She got one of the Astronologia-dome rooms. She's been bragging about it all day. Oh, there's Melisande – gotta catch up with her. See you tomorrow." And she took off to join a chattering group sitting among the courtyard fireflies.

Caitlin watched Luatha go with resentment. Wasn't her Big Sister supposed to stick around now that Cait was somewhere where she could finally understand what everyone was saying?

At the dorm door, Corwin awaited the firstyears as they trickled back from the Commons. Caitlin raised her hand automatically at the door, then caught herself. No knob? No handle?

Corwin explained, "Your wand will open it."

"Um, er, shoot, it's in my room," stammered Cait as a flush of frustration travelled up her face. How was she supposed to know that going to dinner required a wand? She'd just lost her first chance to learn real magic.

Penny proudly held her wand at the ready. "What do we do now?"

But first Corwin addressed Cait. "Always keep your wand on you. And never leave it out unattended. That's why we have these pockets." She pointed at a very narrow pocket on the front of Cait's robe. Then she stepped back to address both of them.

"What did the Schoodic look like in dock today?"

Penny and Cait shrugged, completely confused.

"The password's Schoodic. Just hold the image of the ship in your mind, then send it through your wand to the door," and she waved at Penny to try it.

"Couldn't you just say the word Schoodic?"asked Cait.

"You could, and yes, it's easier to use the word than the image, but somebody might overhear it who shouldn't. Not so safe." And she gestured again at Penny, who was concentrating very intensely; her wand trembled as she raised it. There was a moment of concentration, and the door shook a little.

"Trying too hard," said Corwin. "Just see it."

This time, the door shook and then opened. "Good night," Cait and Penny called to Corwin, "Thank you."

Once in the lobby, Penny did a little dance. "I did it! We're really at a witch school. We're really witches!" And even Cait's annoyance at forgetting her wand melted away when Penny grabbed her arm and they do-si-do'ed all the way down their hallway.

Chapter 7 – Weird Witchy Everyone

Cait had been enjoying a lovely dream about Nini being at Salem; there even seemed to be a weight on her bed as if the cat really were there. She felt the warmth of sun on her face, and a light brush of something soft against her nose. But it didn't feel quite like fur, it was more like ... feathers? Cait opened her eyes to look into those of a huge black bird. Cait stared in disbelief. This bird was as long as her forearm, and weighed as much as Nini. Lots bigger than the crows back home. Seeing that she was awake, it gave a throaty "krrrk", dropped a scroll in front of her, and looked hopefully at the little table near Cait's bed, which had a small drawer she'd overlooked before.

Penny was already up, studying her copy of the class schedule as Nick blinked his amber eyes from a corner of her desk. She laughed at Cait's expression. "Look what they send you for trying to sleep through the dinner bell! Not everyone in the magical world has ravens. There's birdseed in that stand. They get a treat in return for bringing messages," she said.

Cait pulled open the drawer, hoping that this bird really was just a raven, and not a transformed person. "Here you go, and thank you," she said, and watched the bird leave by way of a hinged pane in one corner of their window. As the bird left, Nick leaped from desk to bed to a terrarium under the window which Cait was sure hadn't been there before.

She unrolled the scroll. Words wrote themselves in black ink as if by an invisible hand, each line disappearing as she looked down to the next line.

"Monday, September 10th.

Firstyear schedule, group A.

Breakfast 7-7:50.

Greenwitchery 8-9:50.

Spellwork 10-11:50.

Lunch 12-12:50.

Alchemy 1-2:50.

Swimming at 3:30, meet at the gate under the Commons.

Dinner at 7:00 pm. No tardiness tolerated."

Upon reaching the end of the list, Cait glanced back at the beginning of the scroll, only to see the words begin writing themselves again: "Monday, September 10 ..."

Caitlin looked up. "Swimming? That's not magic."

Penny lifted her chin as she answered. "I bet it's a weatherworking prerequisite. Maybe the courtyard's really a pool."

Cait turned back to her schedule. Looked pretty full. What would her new teachers be like? Would they mumble through their noses like her old math teacher did, or whisper like Ms. Hope in third grade? Then she remembered that Corwin was a teacher. She liked Corwin. If the teachers here were all like that, then it would be all right. Not that it looked like there was any spare time to get to the infirmary to check out accommodations for hard-of-hearies.

Outside, a bell struck the hour. Seven times its deep tones floated through the air at the edges of Cait's hearing, lingering for moments after the clapper finished striking. Cait looked out in time to see two eagles drop the pull-cord from a bell which hung in a cupola in the center of the Commons' peaked roof. "They're gorgeous," she sighed. Then her nerves jangled. Time to find out if magic school was better than public school. Better grab extra hearing-aid batteries just in case.

They scrambled for robes and books – Cait's robe in a heap on the floor, Penny's neatly hung back up in its wardrobe – ran down the hallway, and pushed open the front door.

Cait wheeled about as the door swung shut. "I'm gonna do that spell."

"We'll be late, we have to eat and get to class," Penny protested.

Cait saw the ship clearly in her head, held it there, pointed her wand, and sent the image through it. An electric buzz flowed through her arm, through the wand, and to the door. She could feel the latch as it popped. Bingo, the door opened.

"Yay! I did it too!"

Penny just rolled her eyes and walked briskly toward the Commons.

Once they were stuffed with tea, bread, eggs, cheese, smoked fish, and bacon -- Cait was disappointed that the dishes stayed put on their buffet this time -- the bell rang again, and the roomful of students cleared out and set off toward the library building.

To Cait's relief, everyone's Big Sisters showed up at the library door to help navigate the crowds and to point firstyears towards their proper classrooms. By the time they'd trudged up all the stairs to the greenhouse, only about twenty-five students remained, "group A" from the schedule, apparently. Cait groaned as she recognized the two girls who had laughed at her Sorcerers' Aid parchment, still wearing their robes with magenta and yellow fur trim. A girl with a green-trimmed robe stood with them as well. There were five new faces in the group as well, and she wondered if they were local like the freckled boy in the bookstore. As everyone caught their breath from all the stair-climbing, the babble of their chatter stopped abruptly. It was then that Cait heard several things popping, and the unmistakable sound of cursing.

"Go ahead and take your seats, you're in the right place," said an exasperated voice. A short freckled witch with frizzy hair and a deep-green workrobe smudged with soil stuck her head out of a doorway at the far end of the greenhouse. Cait recognized her as Green Robes from the banquet, who continued talking. "And for Flora's sake, will somebody grab that mop by the front door and send it over to me?" Cait sighed with relief. So far, this teacher was easy to understand. Maybe she wouldn't have to worry about "accommodations" after all.

While students settled on the stools provided among the tables full of small clay pots, Cait making sure to claim a seat near the front, Green Robes took the mop and disappeared for a few minutes behind the door, then returned, more composed but still a bit frazzled.

"Welcome to beginning Greenwitchery, I am Rosa Broadleaf. Had some overeager plants in the other room, nothing to worry about. Do you all have your books? Good. Please open them to page 5, 'One hundred most useful magical plants,' while I show you the plants themselves. I'll expect you to know the first twenty-five plants on this list for tomorrow." She glared as they all groaned. "Plant knowledge is the heart and soul of witchcraft, do not forget that. Wandwork is flashy, flying is fun, but herbs are essential. Why? Well, working spells takes energy, and you could tire yourself out creating a spell to cure a stomachache, and then need a nap besides. Or you could just throw an enhancement spell on a sprig of peppermint and let it do the work instead. But it's no good unless you know the difference between peppermint, spearmint, and the rather dangerous rue. So, onward. Firstly, Artemisia!"

Cait relaxed in her seat as she listened. This teacher gets an "A" for diction, she decided. Not too much of what she said seemed to be going muddy. Then Cait wondered how many of those one hundred plants were in the little jars Aunt May had sent her, and wished she didn't have to wait until next summer's family reunion to ask her all about them in person. Good thing the school aviary was right at the firstyears' dorm. Cait was going to be writing lots of letters to Aunt May. Also, good thing Nini wasn't here. She'd think the aviary was hunting heaven and that would be a disaster.

From the table of small plants before her, Ms Broadleaf took a silvery, lacy-leafed plant. Tapping it with her wand, twenty-five silvery Artemisias appeared, one before each of the students. "Observe the pale green foliage, silver beneath, and with deeply dentellated leaves, and its light scent." She put it down, tapped the pot again, and the Artemisias disappeared from their tables. With another wand-tap, the reddish-leafed "Beebalm" also appeared before them, as Broadleaf described its properties. So went the rest of the two hours.

Entering the spellwork classroom on the second floor, Cait was glad to see Ms. Corwin at the front of the room with its ordinary-looking rows of desks. Eagerly, she laid her wand on the smooth desktop, choosing a front-row seat out of habit.

This room looked far more interesting that her old classrooms back home. Posters with all kinds of letters hung on the plastered walls; Cait recognized the squared-off script on the poster behind Corwin's right shoulder. It was labeled in English: "Hebrew characters, printed form." How many languages they were going to know by the time they graduated? Cabinets stood about the edges of the room, containing books, blocks, plants, teacups, paper of all colors, branches, shells, feathers, and stones. On a shelf all its own a whole tea set stood, complete with tray.

"Ooooh, we're back in kindergarten, look at the alphabet charts," said Crow Girl to Magenta Trim, as she smoothed the yellow fluff that decorated the edges of her own sleeves. "I knew how to read those letters when I was five." But the chart she pointed at was nothing like Cait had ever seen before, consisting of bunches of lines that seemed like a giant card-game scorecard, some parallel, some crossed, some diagonal. Two more charts showed the ribbony script and the curls and squiggles Cait remembered seeing in the magical bookstore. What did everyone else make of all these charts? She watched the other students for their reactions.

Penny walked past the charts slowly, scanning each one. Meg chewed her fingernails as she plopped down at a nearby desk, barely glancing at the walls. One nearby girl had her textbook open and was looking back and forth from page to wall.

"Good morning, everyone," said Ms. Corwin. She gazed around the classroom, making sure she had everyone's attention. "I see that some of you are more than ready to pull out wands and begin work. Good. We'll have plenty of hands-on practice here. But spellwork is not just simply a matter of making the right sound, waving a wand, and poof, there's your result. But we all know that from our own Partridge-Hall front door. Don't we, Claire?" She looked pointedly at Magenta Trim, who squirmed and tried to hide her embarrassment. Cait gave Corwin a mental thumbs-up and assigned her an "A". This teacher definitely knew how to talk so people could understand her. Extra points for looking around and getting people's

87

attention first. Or maybe there was a spell on the classrooms to make it easy to hear? So why didn't they use it on the Schoodic or in the Commons?

Corwin continued her lecture. "There are many, many magical languages which the wizarding world employs. Over in areas of the former Roman Empire, such as in England, Latinate forms are preferred. Venny sky foos," and the teapot on the shelf flew over to Corwin's desk. Cait wondered what those strange words looked like written down, and if they were anything like what she thought she heard.

"And the Grecian tradition has its own loyal following. Erkho...." A rapid-fire series of syllables was lost to Cait; a china sugar bowl joined the teapot.

"But here in America, Aramaic forms are standard, and not only because of Puritan influence, even though we are very much rooted in the British tradition here at Witches' Academy. Boh-ee kos!" This spell was said more slowly and clearly than the other two had been, and a teacup with a mismatched saucer flew over. Corwin poured herself a cup and put in two lumps of sugar. "When the European witch persecutions began, much magical knowledge was preserved by certain families of renegade Jewish magicworkers, who already had a few centuries' experience in how to thrive underground and out of the sight of unfriendly governments and disapproving rabbis. As soon as they were able, some of these families, mine included, fled over the Atlantic to North America in the aftermath of the Inquisition, and were able to mentor many later refugees." She took a drink. "Feh, cold." A wand-wave, a word Caitlin couldn't at all catch. Steam now rose from the cup. "Of course, when those refugees from Europe arrived here, there already was an established magical community -- many communities, as a matter of fact – among the native tribes of this continent. America contains hundreds of Indian tribes with many, many languages, and varied magical traditions of their own. The spell you just heard was from one of the woodland languages, a few hours north of here. Not too far from where one of you grew up, as a matter of fact."

A thump came from the direction of the Magenta Trio, as Cait turned in time to see a red-faced Claire pick up her dropped spellbook.

Corwin ignored the disruption. "There is a wonderful wizardry school in Arizona for those who wish to study Native American magic in depth."

She paused for a moment and stirred her tea. "There is also a school in New Orleans which features its own strong magical tradition." Corwin pronounced another unrecognizable phrase whose syllables all blurred together, and a scone perched on the edge of her saucer. A wave of worry roiled about in Cait's stomach as she tried to figure out what Corwin had said. That was two phrases in a row she couldn't get. Was this how their spells were going to be taught? What if she flunked this class?

Corwin's voice continued. "This year's visiting teacher, Ms. Auclair, comes from that tradition. You'll be meeting her soon, in your Mindcasting class." A girl with bright beads woven into her many braids looked up attentively at that, while Corwin took a bite of scone.

"Not to worry. I will teach you only Aramaic-based spells, although acquaintance with these other alphabets" – Corwin waved her scone in the direction of the posters – "will follow in the second and third years of your coursework. And in your above-Hedge years you'll be learning the languages themselves, as well as their scripts." Cait felt torn between the thrill of learning all these languages, and the worry about being able to hear enough of them to learn them in the first place. Corwin took another bite of scone, then put it back on her saucer. "More importantly, the most well-written spells are absolutely useless without the proper intent to give them meaning and force. Without intention, you have no more magic than a common stage illusionist." She put down her teacup, and regarded the tea things in front of her. "Enough lecture. Let's play! Gamarnu, nelech!" With a tap of her wand, the tea things returned to their cabinet shelf.

A girl with short spiky hair and a defiant look waved her hand furiously; Corwin nodded at her. "What about Asian magic? China? Korea?" she asked loudly.

""My oversight, apologies," answered Corwin. "Yin is correct. In the United States, we also have Dragon Academy in San Francisco, which teaches pan-Asian magical techniques. And now, wands out, books away, choose a few little and light objects to practice on. Preferably something unlike your neighbor's things." Once everybody had chosen their objects and were again at their desks, Corwin said, "We will now practice sending the objects back to where we got them, one object at a time, please. The phrase is" – she slowed down, enunciating clearly – "'Lech na.' And remember, intention."

The room filled with the sound of twenty voices, some hesitant, some imperious, some having a terrible time producing the "ch" sound in the middle of lech. Caitlin's neighbor, a wispy and shy girl was saying "Lek na, lek na" to a persistently immobile scrap of paper. Caitlin, fortunately, knew that sound already, because Uncle Rude had drilled her years ago in how to properly say "Weihnacht" when he showed her pictures of tabletop Christmas trees from Germany.

Sink or swim time. Did she indeed hear this spell right? Cait pointed her wand at the blue robin's eggshell on her desk, visualized it flying back to the top shelf of the middle cabinet, and pronounced, "Lech na."

She felt a shimmering wave of energy travel down her arm and through the wand to the shell, which traveled the same arc she had visualized, back to the shelf. At the same time, a fluttering "fffftt" resounded from both hearing aids. She let out the breath she didn't realize she'd been holding.

"Brava! What a beautiful first try," crowed Corwin, appearing at Cait's elbow. "Does your family speak Hebrew? Yiddish? German?"

"A bit of German, and enough Hebrew for blessings," said Cait, glowing. She hoped that the spells would all be this easy to understand.

There was a faint voice from Cait's left side, and she turned to face the sound. "Can you help me?" asked the shy girl wistfully. "How on earth do you say that sound?"

"This is how my uncle explained it to me," began Cait. "Your tongue's in the same place as when you say the 'k' sound, but you brush it against the back of your mouth, 'kh', instead of striking it like this, 'k' ..." By the end of the class, they were both reliably zipping their chosen objects from their desks back to various shelves.

"For tomorrow, everyone, begin learning the Alef-Bet on page 18, same letters as these ones," announced Corwin loudly. She pointed to the Hebrew chart behind her as the bell rang for the next class.

As Cait got up to go, she nearly bumped into Claire, who had just put her practice object back on the shelf by hand, and now stood by Corwin's desk. "But why can't we just use the Latin words like the old families do over in

England?" she fumed at the teacher. "These Mideastern languages have too many weird noises."

Corwin's left eyebrow shot up as she regarded the petulant student. "You might do well to stop by the library on the way to lunch, and look up the good and very old name of Abulafia. Bring me a one-page essay tomorrow on what you find."

Penny snorted as she elbowed Cait and headed out the door. "That girl sounds just like the tourists back home who think every ice-cream shop should have fifty flavors."

"Yeah, and only their personal favorites, please," added Cait with a giggle. How'd she get so lucky? All this time hanging out with Penny, and she'd not even had to say "what?" once. How long would this last?

Over lunch, Penny swapped notes with the girl who couldn't say "kh", shared plant advice with a townie, and had four other girls clustered around her by the time their sandwiches were gone. Cait watched and worried as incomprehensible babble swirled around her. The Commons was much noisier than it had been at breakfast, and Cait had to work hard at understanding anything at all of the surrounding conversations. Would Penny be in some sort of clique with these other girls by October, leaving Cait out?

But when the eagles coasted past the Commons windows to ring the bell for classtime, Penny stood at Cait's side, bookbag on shoulder. "Grab one of those cookies on your way out," she said, pointing to a nearby plate. "Peanut butter. They're really awesome."

Everybody arrived at the Alchemy classroom on time, where curtains were drawn and lamps lit. The dark-eyed and graceful teacher wore a set of flowing burnt-umber robes, nothing at all like the simple workrobes of Corwin and Broadleaf. Cait had hoped there'd be cauldrons, crystals, and lots of wandwork. But these desks were bare, save for rolls of paper, pots of ink, piles of quills, and one penknife each. Once everybody settled in, the teacher spoke in a soft, slow, but clear voice. "You may remember me from the Schoodic. I am Graciela Melendez, and will be teaching you the first rudiments of the ancient art of alchemy, without which all of our other branches of magic and indeed this school, would not be in this world. Wands away, please." This was directed at Cait and a few others who were putting wands on desks in hopeful readiness. "When we are ready, we will use our wands, later in the semester. But to properly do magic, we must first learn the essence of things as they are." Melendez' voice began to drop as she went on. "I will not make you create your own ink today, nor paper. But you will ... very good reasons ... fraudulent Disappearing ink, for example, have ... to be secure." Cait leaned forward as Melendez' voice dropped, watching the teacher closely in an attempt to catch as much as possible of her low-voiced speech. Did they forget to put a listening spell on this room? Or were Broadleaf and Corwin unusually easy to understand?

"Or there is the embarrassment .... wrong person ... ink-making will be another day, potable, Disappearing, toxic, therapeutic ... papermaking. Milkweed silk for flying ... clay in the pulp ... plates you enjoyed using at yesterday's lunch."

Yesterday? It felt like a week ago to Cait.

"Today, we shall cut our own quills." Melendez' voice rose to where it was more audible as she waved a quill in emphasis. "You all need to know how to do this. Only when your fingers know how to cut a quill without conscious thought, will you then be ready .... Papermaking ... later, as will simple Transmutations." And the two hours were filled with quill-cutting, the occasional cut finger and resulting curse (at least they learned the healing spell raapeyna), and too many blots of ink as new pens scratched out unfamiliar formulae.

To Cait, two hours of pen-and-ink work felt like recess after concentrating so hard on understanding Melendez. She sent a million mental thanks to her old art class for teaching her how to use a crowquill pen. As she wrote, Cait deliberated between giving Melendez a "B" and a "C" for being half-understandable.

Finally, it was time to grab swimsuits from the dorm and join the cluster of students gathering at the archway under the Commons. Cait could plainly hear Loud Voice as she joined the group. "....your swimsuit? No? Boh-ee swimsuit!" Loud Voice waved her wand, a blur appeared in midair, and a swimsuit appeared in the surprised girl's hands as she went on to the next student. "Have you yours? Excellent!"

Many more students needed to have their suits summoned from home than had theirs in hand. Cait giggled as she jostled Penny. "Don't you think they'd have figured out that Salem's on the water when they were packing?"

Penny shook her head. "Nah, let's skinny-dip. I vote to skinny-dip!" Then her expression fell as she looked once more at the teacher. "That's her, that's the lady who left her roses behind in my mom's shop. Hope she doesn't remember me. I'd like to ask her what Germany's like," and she bit her lip as she watched the teacher.

Once everyone had swimsuits, Loud Voice appeared to count off silently, then began. "Good afternoon, firstyears. Your attention before we go to the pool. Any selkies present?" A girl with huge brown eyes and the build of a gymnast put up her hand.

Selkie ... the word sounded familiar to Cait, but she could not remember what it meant. "Any students who have never swum before?" Three hands. Loud Voice whispered into a shell which hung on a green cord around her neck. "Any certified lifeguards? Swim-team members? What do you call it, YMCA shark level?" Six hands, Cait included. More whispering into the shell. Penny bit her lip harder as she watched hands go up. "OK, let's go get evaluated and see how you all do in the water. I am Master Weatherworker of Witches' Academy. My full name is Alathanalo...." And here followed a stream of liquidy sound, followed by something like German. "And so, since Ms. Vom Brunnenwaldecke is a bit long for most people to remember, and since only loreleien are able to pronounce my first name correctly, I go by Lori Brunner here at Salem." Loreleien? Cait wondered if loreleis really did live all alone. Who had those roses been for? Was Ms. Brunner still with whoever-it-was?

Brunner continued. "For reasons of safety, we allow no students here to study weatherworking unless they demonstrate the ability to swim without magical aid. After all, if you call up the wrong kind of wind and your boat flips over, you won't exactly have time to spellcast. Not to worry, beginners, you will not need to equal lifeguards and selkies. I am sure that you'll all be together in Weatherworking when the time comes. Let's go!" And she led them through a door that blended into the Commons arch so perfectly that it was nearly invisible. The teacher had a slight accent which reminded Cait of Uncle Rude.

Down a flight of stairs, they entered a large and airy cavern with a perfectly round pool in the middle. Clusters of stalagmites surrounded it, forming alcoves large enough

95

to hide a person in each one. A general glow filled the cavern's roof and reflected gently off the water's surface. There was also the sound of rushing water. Cait groaned. How was she going to understand anybody above that?

To one side of the cavern, to the left of the stairs, a smaller chamber contained an old-looking stone well, complete with a softly glowing canopy over it.

To her right, Penny was saying something. "...never gonna pass," she moaned, "... dogpaddle. Selkies!"

"At least you're ahead of the real beginners," offered Cait, as she wondered again what selkies were, while watching Brunner to make sure she didn't miss any important information. "I'll paddle with you."

"Those of you who can swim ... get a shell ..." bellowed Brunner. A shell? wondered Cait. What were they supposed to do with that? "... across the pool ... many as you can ... short or long, doesn't matter .... Beginners ... here with me," and she waved at a smaller pool which Cait had not noticed at first. A "B" for this teacher, Cait thought as she looked for a good spot to change after collecting a pink and white shell that hung from a cord around her neck. Even with that running water, she didn't seem to miss too much of what Brunner was saying. But nobody else had needed to stare and concentrate just to know what to do next.

Out the corner of her eye, Cait saw Brunner motion the selkie girl aside for a moment. She then took off running up the stairs while the teacher waited at the small pool.

After about four laps, Penny's dogpaddle began to look more like real swimming strokes. She pulled herself out of the pool to rest and watch the stronger swimmers. Cait lasted another five laps across the full width of the pool, then left the water. Her shell gave a "peep" and turned completely pink once the water drained out of it. It felt great to do something physical and nonmagical for a while.

But what was she supposed to do with that shell? Looking around the room, she could see that the other girls who had finished swimming kept the shells around their necks, so Cait left her shell alone, leaned against a stalagmite and waited.

Over at the smaller pool, the three beginners took turns being pulled through the water, their hands on the back of a doe-eyed harbor seal. Something tugged at Cait's memory as she watched. Those eyes, something about those big eyes.

The last swimmer to complete her circuits was Crow Girl. "Clearly, I'm the best swimmer here," she bragged loudly as she pulled herself out of the pool.

Cait watched Claire beam and high-five her friend. "Way to go, Amanda!"

Now that the pool was empty of swimmers, Brunner went over to a girl in a bright-pink suit, took the shell from her neck, and put it to her ear. Then she pointed Pink Suit to the left, where a short, rounded stalagmite stood. Then a girl wearing blue was pointed towards a double stalagmite on the right, near where Cait stood. Claire was next; she was pointed to a third stalagmite just beyond the group. Then it was Amanda's turn; she was pointed in Claire's direction. High fives between them, and sympathetic waves at Blue Suit, who waved back.

Then it was Cait's turn. Brunner took the pink shell, listened, and pointed in Claire's direction. Ugh. Cait tried to look confident as Amanda scowled and Claire smirked. What was Claire up to? Why would she smile like that?

Penny was pointed towards Blue Suit, who didn't scowl or smirk, but sounded like she was introducing herself. Ella Beth? Elsa?

Also in Penny's group was Meg, who squirmed and mumbled as she caught Cait's eye. Cait eyed Meg warily as she leaned in to hear her. Was she about to start teasing, or laugh at her again?

"Sorry about laughing at you on the boat," she said sheepishly. "I forget not everyone here has a magical family."

Cait bristled, thinking of Aunt May and Aunt Joyce. "Who says I don't have a magical family? My great-aunts just never went to any fancy school for it."

"Truce?" pleaded Meg. "My brother always says I'm too much of a blabbermouth. And I don't want you mad at me if I don't even know you yet." Surprise rippled through Cait. Meg was afraid of her? And here she was, being afraid of Meg giving her a hard time. Meg held out a hand and looked so truly sorry, that Cait's anger vanished as she took her hand and shook it.

"Okay. Truce."

After more practice laps, the class day was over, and an hour and a half remained to tackle homework assignments before dinner. Cait ran a mental tally of her teachers as she changed out of her swimsuit and back into her robe. Two "A"s, a "B", and a half-mumbler. So far, so good. At this rate, she might not have to ask for accommodations at all. Maybe she really could be just like everyone else for once.

As everyone trooped up the stairs, Cait accidently bumped into the student next to her and was startled to feel fur against her hand. Fur? Gymnast girl grinned at her. A piece of spotted fur lay draped over her arm, the exact same shade of gray as the seal in the beginners' pool. Cait's memory finally kicked in. Selkie. Seal people. They're not just a story. Then Cait remembered the seaweed at the banquet, and all that fish. Cait stared as the girl took the stairs two at a time and vanished into the busy courtyard.

Chapter 8 – To the Skies

The next day's classes went smoothly. Penny already knew many of the Greenwitchery plants because of her mom's shop, and helped Cait with her homework. The five spells Corwin assigned worked well for Cait, except for shalhevet!, which made a small and wavery light travel from a lit lamp to their wandtips ("your emergency night light"). Cait decided to send home for her flashlight instead.

And at suppertime, a crow flew in, carrying a note from her mom: "Have you requested accommodations yet? Hope you like this school and are making friends. Please write! Love Mom." She flipped the paper over and wrote: "Dear Mom: my roommate's the best! But there's some real snobs here, too. Yes, I can understand the teachers fine. And can you send my flashlight? Love, Cait."

Wednesday's scroll was brought to Cait by a bright-eyed chipmunk, which kept bumping her nose with its own until she woke up. As soon as she saw that Broomwork was the first class of the day, Cait didn't know whether to be glad or worried. A multitude of thoughts whirled about her brain. What if she fell off? Whoever heard of a witch who couldn't fly? Well, how many witches had messed-up ears? But if she could ride a bicycle, she could probably do this, too.

Cait fumbled the scroll while rolling it back up, dropped her hearing aid while changing its battery, and by the time the wand fell out of her hand while she put it into her pocket, Penny looked worried. "Are you afraid of heights or something? If it's airsickness you're afraid of, they'll have something for that." Cait shook her head and kept walking towards the Commons.

Once Cait and Penny sat down with their breakfast, Cait swallowed her nerves, glad that the Commons was relatively quiet in the morning. That made it so much easier to understand what people were saying. She leaned over towards Penny. "So, tell me about broomwork. Is it like riding a bike where enough practice will make it work? Or do you need amazing balance to do it at all?" Penny shrugged as she took a bite of toast. "I've never flown before, Mom wouldn't let me. But almost everyone in the magical world can fly, so I don't think you have to be a super gymnast or anything."

From across their table, Meg turned aside from her conversation with Bracelet Girl. "Flying's lots of fun. I bet you'll be better than you think." Her voice carried easily across the table. "I've never heard of anybody who can't fly. The spell's put right into the broom, and all you do is tell it where to go. Piece of cake."

"So, what's flying like?" Cait asked as she picked up her muffin and began to eat.

Meg's eyes shone. "Think of the longest, snowiest sledding hill you've ever been on. And your sled is flying right down it without flipping or swerving or skidding on ice or anything. It's even better than that."

"That sounds great," replied Cait. She liked sledding. Maybe it really would be all right. Next to Meg, Bracelet Girl leaned back and scowled.

"It is great," said Meg. "I'm still trying to convert Violet, here." Violet smiled thinly and began to spin a silver bangle around her wrist. "And in May, we'll each get to fly across Salem Harbor at midnight to demonstrate that we're good enough to go on to secondyear. I can't wait for my turn."

101

Midnight? Sweat broke out on Cait's forehead and she felt dizzy. She'd be in Salem Harbor, not over it, if broomriding were anything like bicycle-riding.

Penny jumped in. "But what about when you want to travel to really far places, like overseas? Do people really get over the Atlantic by broomriding?" In the margin of her Greenwitchery book, Penny's pen traced the outline of a tiny Eiffel tower. "It's the weatherworking I can't wait for. Like when we get to sail ships."

"But the flying's just plain fun. There's all these in-the-air sports I can't wait to try," said Meg.

"So tell me about broomball already, now that I know it's not the one on ice," nudged Cait, to get her mind off midnight flying.

Meg reddened. "Sorry for being stupid on the boat. Okay, in broomball, you have two teams, and the goal is to keep this stone in the air for as long as possible."

Violet frowned, scooped up her books, and proclaimed, "Sports are boring. I'm going to go ask Elsbeth about our Alchemy homework." Meg waved absently at her, and continued to explain broomball to Cait.

Finally, it was one o'clock, and Firstyear Group A stood in the courtyard, where a set of school brooms lay on the turf. Cait hoped they'd be old-fashioned twiggy things like in fairy-tale pictures, but these were ordinary, flat, long-bristled "corn brooms" like the one she swept the front steps with at home. A husky woman with big square hands wearing a plain workrobe paced back and forth alongside a flowerbed in front of Hypatia Hall as they assembled. She stopped once the group was complete. Today, the Magenta Trio wore silver and blue stripes on their robes and caps; Penny snorted as soon as she saw them. She poked Cait, speaking into her good ear. "There's the team the Tour de France forgot." Cait giggled and made a mental note to look up "Tour de France" later.

"Well and good, everyone's here," said the teacher in a booming voice, looking about for people's attention. An "A+" for her. "We have a lovely day for flying. I am Patricia Greengage, and I will be teaching you the basics of how to transport yourself from here to there safely via broom. The ability to fly both with and without daylight will be mandatory for secondyear enrollment." The teacher paused and resumed pacing along the flowerbed.

Without daylight. Salem Harbor at midnight. Quivering nerves became icy panic as Cait remembered Meg's words. Those broomsticks were skinnier than bike tires. Could she really do this?

Greengage stopped pacing and faced them. "Once you reach the upper classes, I'll also be teaching you flying spells and charms, as well the arts of concealment in the air, such as the use of Daydark powder. Not now." Pace, pace, pace, stop.

Cait took a deep breath to steady her nerves. Worry about night-flying later. It was daylight now, lots of light. She could do this.

Greengage's voice took on added force as she jabbed the air in emphasis. "Before we begin, I must stress that common sense and courtesy in the air come first. Safety is very important. This is not broom derby, and I don't want to go visiting you in the infirmary. Don't bother telling me all about how expert in flying you already are. Doesn't matter. Simple practice benefits everyone." She clasped her hands behind her, rocked from toe to heel back to toe, and surveyed the group of students. Then she went on. "Once you are in the air, you will one by one fly from here over to the library and wait there. Experienced flyers, concentrate on control and steadiness. Beginners, you will start by pushing down on the handle, and will stop by pulling up on it. Now, everyone, straddle your brooms. You with the braid, no sidesaddle is allowed! Your name, please?" This was addressed to the timid girl who couldn't say "kh".

"Minna, Ms. Greengage." She was blushing.

"Riding sidesaddle is dangerously unstable, and is for stunt riding only. We are not Victorians, and have never been Puritans, thank the stars. All ready?" Greengage looked about the group. "The word is shemayma."

"Shemayma!" echoed twenty-five voices – but only twenty-two students were now in the air, hovering at about four feet up. One petrified selkie, a puzzled Cait, and another girl Cait didn't yet know still remained on the ground. Cait could see the selkie shaking.

Overhead, hovering students cast curious glances at the three of them.

"No need to fear the air, girls." Greengage put a reassuring hand on the selkie's shoulder. "The air is strong enough to hold you up when a broom-spell's under you, and if you do anything fancy and fall off your brooms, this courtyard" – she patted the groundcover – "is very accommodating. As a matter of fact, try it right now, all of you." She addressed the students in the air. "Fall off your brooms."

Three bold students rolled off their brooms and bounced on the springy turf as if it were a trampoline. Surprised looks turned to grins as they reached for their brooms, and the other students followed.

"Okay, on your brooms, let's do this again. Listen sharp: 'she-ma-y'ma'."

Twenty-four brooms were now in the air; Caitlin still stood on the ground fuming. She was saying exactly what the teacher had said. Way to go ears, she thought. Of all the words to not be able to say properly, why did it have to be this one? She remembered her grade-school speech-therapy drills and tried again.

"Shemayma!" Still on the ground.

Greengage came over, first gesturing at everyone else to hold their hovers and to not start flying around yet. "Let me hear you."

"Shemayma!"

Greengage shook her head. "Almost. Sshemayma."

"Shemayma!" Cait couldn't figure out what was missing. Bye-bye, normalcy. A witch who can't fly. Great. And I'm holding up the class, besides.

Snorts and fidgeting broke out overhead. "Toss her back in public school till she knows how to talk," floated down one snarky voice to a chorus of snickers; Amanda's voice? The students silenced immediately as Greengage glared at them, and then addressed Cait again.

"Put your tongue a bit further back, say it again."

"Sshemayma!" Sounded the same to her, but whoosh, her broom filled with a charge like that of her wand, and she was up in the air with everyone else, wobbling to stay on like many of them. She did it! But could she do so again?

It seemed as if the air itself were holding her in place; it felt cushiony under her knees, her elbows, and where she had automatically tucked up her heels beneath her. Cait reached out her hand. Let's experiment, she thought. How far does this flying spell go? As her elbow straightened, her hand pushed down as if someone put a brick onto it. Quickly, Cait grabbed the broomstick so she wouldn't fall off and have to say that new "ssh" sound all over again.

The selkie, to her right, still looked scared at being so out of her element. Meg was grinning from ear to ear, and Penny's eyes shone with anticipation.

One by one, they each took off toward the other end of the courtyard, some more slowly, some quickly.

"Yeehah!" shouted Meg as she shot off towards the library, only to fall off while trying to pull off a showy turn in mid-flight.

Greengage frowned at her. "Be less of a daredevil, Miss Ainslee, and you'll be flying as well as your sister."

"Yes, Ms. Greengage," replied Meg politely, but Cait saw her grimace when Greengage's attention shifted.

Penny went next, flying slowly but precisely, her expression like that of Cait's dad when he was listening to the car motor to figure out if it was tuneup time yet or not.

Then it was Cait's turn. She pushed down the handle, and off she went. Oh, the wind in her hair felt great as the broom zoomed forward. Then she found herself bouncing on the turf, one hand still hanging onto the broom.

"Um, nice turf," she said while picking herself up. She heard giggles overhead. Her stomach flip-flopped with nerves. What if she couldn't remember how to make that new "ssh" sound? She tried to remember how she said it before.

"Shemayma!" Nothing.

No, the tongue had to be even further back, this way. "Sshemayma!" she said, and as she did so, the broom brought her back into the air. Whew. She could do this. Just like these other kids who had all their hearing and balance.

By the end of the class, and three falls later, Cait figured out that flying worked something like walking on a balance beam. Going fast and steady kept her aboard, but going slowly needed more concentration, and then she would find herself wobbling and land on the turf again.

As they returned their brooms to Greengage, and headed to Mindcasting class, Meg rushed up to Cait. "Hey, you went pretty fast once you learned to stay on. I bet you'll make the racing team next year."

Cait glowed with the praise, relieved to no longer be laughed at. "Wow, thanks." Even when I mess up, this is way better than public school ever was, she thought. And I did it without "accommodations", too.

The euphoria of her successful broom flight vanished as soon as Cait entered the Mindcasting classroom, replaced by a feeling of uneasy wariness. The ebony-skinned teacher from the term-begin banquet sat reading the class list, still wearing her elaborately-feathered hat. The usual bookcases, desks, and blackboard filled the ordinary-looking room, and plenty of light streamed in through the windows. So why did Cait feel instead as if she were in the darkest, creepiest corner of her family's cellar? Around her, other students frowned at each other as they chose desks and sat down cautiously. Even the girl with beaded braids, who smiled upon seeing Auclair as she entered, quickly wore a sober expression.

The one student who didn't stay frowning was Meg. As she found her desk, her eyes widened, and she grinned as she sat down. Cait frowned even more. What did Meg know that the rest of them didn't?

Without warning, a fit of giggles came over Cait, and a snort burst from Penny. The mood in the room brightened even as the surroundings remained the same. Wait – was the teacher now watching them, instead of reading her list?

Then Cait felt an enormous yawn coming on as she pulled the small Mindcasting textbook from her bag. For

107

no apparent reason, she remembered lying out on the lawn during the hottest day of summer, watching dragonflies zoom around overhead. She looked at the book in her hand. Study? Naah, more like naptime ...

Cait's feeling of laziness vanished abruptly as a mindtap pulled everyone's attention up front. The teacher now stood at her desk, list of names pushed to one side. Penny still looked wary; Meg sat up straight at her desk, attention on the teacher.

"Welcome to Mindcasting class, everyone. My name is Ms. Auclair. How many of you now think that moods are private?"

Did that question make sense? Cait cast a confused glance at Penny, who shrugged. Claire's hand shot into the air with confidence; a couple of other students put theirs up hesitantly. Meg shook her head, still grinning.

Auclair nodded and said something with syllables all blurred together. Va zalor what? How many languages did people speak in this school? At least she continued in English. "... what this class is for. By the end of this semester, you will all agree on what the answer to that question will be. Bon. Wands out ... choose a partner ... a little of what you have just experienced." Auclair spoke quickly, words running together. She pulled a pack of cards out of a pocket, and began slapping groups of them down onto desks, while Penny turned her desk towards Cait's.

"Don't look yet!" Auclair held up a warning hand to Meg, who hastily put back the card she began to read.

Where was this teacher from? Auclair's accent was unfamiliar to Cait, and it took serious concentratration to catch all of what she was saying. Cait gave her a "B", and was glad that Auclair hadn't begun her class with the same long lectures that Corwin and Melendez had.

108

"No looking ... tell you when. Take out your wands ... six cards. Now one of you ... up a card, and feel the mood on it. Feeeel it. The other ... eyes closed, wand out ... antenna. Find the mood. One, two, three, allons." Auclair sat her bulk behind her desk with a look of satisfaction as the feathers on her hat bobbed up and down.

Penny reached towards her stack of cards, eyebrows up; Cait motioned at her to go ahead, took out her wand, and closed her eyes. Here goes nothing. How do I know what we're doing here? She held out the wand before her. Nothing. Moving it a little to the right, a tingly tremor ran up the wand, bubbly like birthday presents and parades and fireworks. Further to the right. Waves of jitteriness ran up the wand into her gut, butterflies of nervousness flapping around for all they were worth. "Nervousness," Cait said out loud to Penny as she opened her eyes.

Penny sat there scowling. "No, it was happiness. Let's try that again."

But no matter which mood Penny projected, it was soon overwhelmed by waves of nervousness and worry edging over from the right. Then there was a burst of anger that simmered for the next ten minutes as the worry vanished.

While Penny shuffled their cue cards, Cait looked around her. Beyond Penny, Meg looked like she was having the time of her life, guessing moods in quick succession, as Minna held up card after card. Definitely not where the worry was coming from.

The Magenta Trio were in the right spot, however, over to her right and one row back, with those silver-striped robes reflecting the afternoon light. Elsbeth looked absorbed in the exercise, while Amanda leaned back in her chair with an attitude of studied indifference and a few flecks of annoyance, while her crow played with a bit of yellow fluff stuck to her bookbag.

Claire was the one who was radiating the simmering anger. What's up with her? wondered Cait.

As the bell rang and everyone walked out the door, Cait scowled in Claire's direction. She held up one hand, palm facing out, and flicked her second finger out from behind her thumb in the direction of those silver-trimmed robes.

"What was that about?" asked Penny.

"Sign language," answered Cait. "It's lots better than note-passing. This sign means 'she's a pain'. I don't know what she's all mad at, but it killed my concentration in class. So --" Cait did the sign again while sticking out her tongue.

Penny giggled. "How do I sign, 'Homework's nasty?' Or tell my brother 'bug off'?"

"For 'nasty homework', same sign. Plus 'home' is like this" – Cait brought her fingertips together and touched corner of her mouth, then her cheek – "and work is like this." Her right fist tapped the wrist of her left fist. "'Bug off' wasn't in my book, so maybe we can invent something. The book I had in fourth grade was really boring and didn't have enough interesting words. We can pretend we're spies."

Cait didn't let on that her minimal Sign came from a resource-room tutor who had been lined up expressly for her and an ancient book she was encouraged to keep. The class hardly ever made sense to her though, because it took serious concentration to follow the huge long sentences Ms. Pencker was signing. It was a slow and clumsy way to speak English, words and signs together. One sign per word, sometimes two, bounce, bounce, bounce, boring.

Here was a language invented just for deaf people and Cait couldn't even understand it. What good was that? But that "I hate this" sign was a great way to let off steam when she needed to.

As everyone entered the next classroom, a thin and angular witch finished writing "Ms. Graycliff, firstyear Zoomorphia, Fall semester 2007" at the top of the blackboard, balancing on tiptoe as she did so. She turned to watch them find their seats. "Good afternoon, class, and welcome to Zoomorphia. I am Ms. Graycliff," and she turned to gesture towards the blackboard.

She glanced back at the class, and paused. "I see that four of you already have familiars. Good. You'll have a head start on observation. Don't worry if you and your animal do not yet know what their purpose will be. By secondyear, most of you will have figured it out."

Penny gave a smug smile and sat up straighter as she stroked Nicky, who sat right in the middle of her textbook.

Looking for the other three animals, Cait saw Amanda scowling at her crow as usual, while he pulled at the strap of her bookbag. Cait wondered the bird's "purpose" was, and why Amanda didn't seem to want him around. A small green snake curled around one girl's ink bottle two rows back, and a set of white whiskers poked out from another girl's sleeve, but Cait couldn't tell if they belonged to a rat, a ferret, or something else.

Then Graycliff turned to the blackboard and continued to write. It sounded like she talked as she wrote, but it was muffled by her facing the wrong way. So Cait took in the classroom instead of listening, noticing a mountain-shaped muddy heap in the back of the room, three logs in a corner, and an assortment of birdhouses on a shelf near the ceiling.

Finally, Graycliff stood away from the blackboard which now read: "Zoomorphia. The art of observing and understanding animals well enough to see the world through their eyes, first metaphorically, and then literally."

She gazed at the firstyears as she took off her glasses, swinging them by the temples as she said, "So you see, that is why we ride brooms rather than going into bird form whenever we want to travel. Did you all understand that?" Heads nodded all around the class. Cait looked around with a sense of dismay. Did everyone else actually hear all of what Graycliff told them while she was writing on that board?

Cait slowly put up her hand. "I didn't get all the details, Ms. Graycliff."

The teacher nodded, put her glasses back on, and began. "The risks of a transformation becoming permanent are considerable. That is why we spend a good deal of time at this level –" Graycliff turned to point at the word "metaphorically", mumbled something, then pointed at the word "literally", before turning around again. "Which of course, you all will be doing by your third year. All clear?"

Out the corner of her eye, Cait could see Penny doodling in her notebook, Meg staring into space, and the Magenta Trio passing notes. Swing, swing, swing. The glasses dangled once more from Graycliff's fingers. Why do so many teachers talk to chalkboards? She gets a "C", Cait decided, as she answered, "Yes, thank you, Ms. Graycliff." Yay ears.

Graycliff went on with her lecture, adding a set of columns labelled "land", "water", "air", and listing animal names beneath them, while Cait transcribed everything from the board into her notebook, and hoped that the textbook would explain whatever Graycliff was telling the blackboard.

Only gradually did the meaning of Graycliff's definition of "zoomorphia" filter through to Cait. She stared at her transcription of its last word. "Literally." Her mind buzzed with possibility. If people really could learn how to turn into animals here, literally, then why couldn't they make my ears work like everyone else's? If that were this school's accommodations, she'd take it in a heartbeat.

Graycliff's voice paused, and Cait looked up to see her once again facing the class, glasses in hand, asking "All clear?" Cait froze in the midst of her note-taking as her new hopes came crashing down. Glasses. This teacher had glasses. That meant whatever's wrong with her eyes couldn't be fixed with magic. Then they probably wouldn't be able to fix her ears, either. So then she'd be stuck doing what she did back home. Study the text, study the blackboard notes. And pray to not need any "special classes," especially now that she was beginning to make friends. There she was, still a square peg trying to fit into a round hole. Shave, shave, whittle, whittle.

Panic made Cait's hands go cold. And night flying. What was she going to do about night-flying if they couldn't fix her balance? Would they really hold her back if she couldn't night-fly? She remembered riding her bike one day at sunset, how the ground dipped and rose beneath her as the daylight faded, making her fall off her bike three times before she gave up and finally walked home.

This train of thought was interrupted as Graycliff assigned them an hour of "real-time observation." The mountain-like shape she'd noticed earlier turned out to be a giant anthill, and they were all supposed to pick one ant and follow it, using their shalhevet spell when needed. The very one she couldn't do. She looked around at all the students gathered around the anthill, with their wands out. She could feel a fit of giggles coming on. It was just like a movie she once saw of wild chimps at a termite mound, all fishing for a snack.

"Hey Penny," she whispered, "you ever hear of chimps fishing for termites?"

Penny nodded. "Hoo hoo, dinnertime!" she answered, making Cait laugh so hard that the girls nearly got themselves detentions from their annoyed teacher. Fortunately, the bell for dinner rang just then. Cait and Penny cheered as they ran off to the Commons.

As muddled conversation swirled about her, Cait watched Meg gab away with some secondyears as her hands mimed gripping a broom-handle. Must be talking about sports. To her right, Penny and Minna were in some sort of discussion, while the girl with the beads in her many braids listened in.

Well, Cait wasn't going to be odd one out this time. She pulled out her mini sketchpad and began to draw a series of ants with teeny tiny wands and hats. Out of the corner of her eye, she saw Penny pause, giggle, and point at the sketch, while Minna and the other girl leaned over. Then Penny motioned for the pencil and added a looming toad looking down on the ants, and Minna added an anthill castle with turrets. Lastly, the other girl drew an Auclair-style feathered hat on the toad, and introduced herself as what, "Eisha"? At Cait's puzzled look, she wrote "Keisha" on one corner of the page, then added another feather to the hat.

They were still giggling as they left for Astronologia. By this time, it was dark outside, and there were no lights at all within the Academy courtyard. Only a dim glow came from the pathway around its edges. Despite this, most of the Group A students cut straight across the courtyard to Hypatia Hall.

Cait worried as she watched them. How was she going to manage walking over there in the dark without stumbling and falling all over the place? Why didn't they have more lights around here? Cait started walking carefully along the glowing path, every little dip and rise in the ground making her wobble and put out her hands to catch her balance.

Penny started out across the courtyard, but stopped when she noticed Cait on the path instead. "This way's faster. C'mon over!"

Cait shook her head. A brief pang of homesickness hit her. Whenever it was dark at home, somebody was always nearby, offering an arm to steady her. Yay again, ears. Wimpy vestibular system and all. Well if she was going to fit in here, she wasn't going to run around asking brand new friends for help just to get to class. "I like the way this path glows. Do you think there's a spell on it?"

Penny now stood at her side. "You'll be the last one there. You sure you want to poke along the path?"

"That's right," said Cait as she stepped cautiously along the path, nearly turning an ankle on a sudden dip.

"You're stubborn," replied Penny with a shake of her head as she continued across the courtyard with the other students.

A witch with an unruly afro and an impatient air met Cait at the door to Hypatia Hall, and brought her around to the side of the building, talking away from Cait as she went. Only random words filtered through. "Up-Chute ... non-Hypatia ... Observatory Dome." The teacher stopped and faced Cait, apparently waiting for Cait to do something. But what?

At Cait's confused look, Unruly pointed to a flat round stone set in the ground. "Stand on this, and say the spell, mazal-yaa."

"Mazal-yaa!" repeated Cait. As soon the word was said, she flew straight up the side of the building, as if via invisible elevator, and found herself within the clear globe she'd seen yesterday atop the dorm. Why couldn't the flying spell be this easy? she thought. Then she looked up and the breath caught in her throat. She had never in her life seen so many stars in such a dark sky all at once. No buildings, tree branches, or street lamps interfered with the view, an unbroken sweep of brightly-spangled blackness.

"Hey Cait." Cait looked around at the shout to see Penny waving from a desk near the front and pointing to an empty chair next to her. As Cait walked across the room, Meg grinned and waved from her tipped-back chair, mouthed "Awesome," and pointed up.

Once the teacher had introduced herself as Ms. Pitts and confirmed that all students were present, she began the evening's lecture, and her voice dropped to a blurry mumble which Cait could only decipher with a lot of concentration, provided none of the other students decided to rustle their notes or flip through their text. "D", decided Cait. Definitely "D".

Then Ms. Pitts turned away from the students to point at a cluster of stars at the far edge of the dome, and her speech became completely incomprehensible. Cait could tell that she was still talking, but barely. Grade revision, thought Cait. "D minus."

The mumbled lecture went on, complete with more random pointing by Ms. Pitts here and there at the sky. Cait kept an eye on her, trying to catch what she was saying, and wishing she would face the class more. After pointing out one particularly bright point near the horizon, Ms. Pitts whipped around to look directly at Cait with an expectant air. Oh, no, was that latest mumble a question?

"I'm sorry, I didn't get the question," said Cait.

Snickers and whispers traveled around the classroom. A few voices echoed "samaya, samaya" to more giggles, which Cait pretended to not hear. Was everyone going to keep teasing her about that flying class? May as well be in public school again. Cait poked dents into the end of her quill with her thumbnail. First the blackboard lecturer in Zoomorphia, and now this.

"Pay closer attention to the lecture, then," Ms. Pitts snapped, then loudly repeated the question, overenunciating the words. "If the star Antares, which we have just been observing, sets three minutes earlier every evening from now, what time will it set next Wednesday?"

Cait quickly gauged how high above the horizon that bright point now was and did the arithmetic. "Eight p.m., Ms. Pitts."

The teacher nodded and continued her lecture, dropping her voice to the same mumble it had been before, as Cait fervently prayed to not be called on again. Graycliff was at least nice about repeating herself when needed. Not like this. To her right, Cait could see Penny flipping pages in her textbook.

Once the lecture was finally over and they all sat studying copies of the autumn star chart, something bumped Cait's elbow. She reached over to find a note which read: "I've been following the text. Same as the lecture, exactly. Boring – Penny." Cait felt better immediately. If this was how Ms. Pitts taught, then all she had to do was study the book. She had passed classes this way before. But she wished that she didn't have to.

Friday's schedule flew in with the soft whirring of a pigeon as Cait groped for the birdseed drawer. It was a "Monday" Friday, meaning that there would be Greenwitchery, Spellwork, Alchemy and swim class; next week would be a "Wednesday" Friday. Two "A" teachers, a "B", and a semi-mumbler, thought Cait. It's going to be a good day, and then there's the weekend besides.

Even a breakfast-time note from her mother didn't dampen her mood. ("Do you still like your classes? What kind of listening accommodations did they give you? Don't forget to write.") At least she didn't have to worry about Ms. Pitts or Ms. Graycliff until next week. She'd go to the infirmary then. Maybe.

Rosa Broadleaf greeted everyone with a cheery smile as they walked into the Greenwitchery classroom. "Are you all ready for our first quiz?"

Alarm filled Cait. What quiz? She looked around the room. Meg chewed her nails, but didn't look surprised. Penny sat with her notebook closed, ready to begin. Minna skimmed her book hastily, while Claire smirked directly at her.

"Miss Leo, have you forgotten about our quiz? I announced it right at the end of last Tuesday's class," said the teacher with a steady gaze at Cait.

End of class. Among the scraping chairs and banging books and people's chatter. No wonder Cait never heard the announcement. "Sorry, Ms. Broadleaf, I never heard you say there'd be one."

"Better listen more carefully during all of classtime from now on. Everyone, this is what you need to do. I'll give each of you the name of a different plant. Then once you've located it in the Sophia Hall garden, bring it back here, and tell me about its properties. You'll be responsible for tending and observing your plant in your

dorm rooms for the next two weeks. Best of luck. "
Broadleaf moved over the the door and began handing out
slips of paper to exiting students. Good thing Nini's not
here, thought Cait. She'd have Nicky the toad for dinner
and my Greenwitchery plant for dessert.

As they all proceeded to the garden, Meg groaned as
she recited plant names. "Artemisia. Beebalm. Coltsfoot.
Damiana. Elfheart. What comes after Elfheart? I've got to
get a decent grade. How am I gonna pass this class? Fifty
plants, and the one on this slip just had to be number
forty-three. Nobody outside my genius brother can
possibly memorize fifty plants this fast. He looks at
something once, it's in his head for keeps. I can barely
remember the first ten. I'm gonna flunk."

Penny was the first one to leave the garden, carrying a
purple-bloomed vine carefully with both hands. As Cait
hunted for pointy mint shoots, Meg squatted before a
cluster of fuzzy leaves.

"Cait," Meg poked at Cait's knee for her attention. "Is
that plant toothed or lobed? I forget which is which."

Cait glanced at the fuzzy leaves. "Toothed," she
answered.

"That means it's sweet cicely. Thank you, you saved
my grade," crowed Meg as she picked up the plant and ran
into the classroom building.

Having successfully identified, described, and
relocated her Menthus Phosphorescens, Cait ran off to
Spellwork. They were now working on moving
progressively larger and heavier objects, and Cait decided
to use the mugful of water she'd brought with her. The
weather was still very warm, and she'd taken to refilling it
whenever she discovered another of the many fountains
tucked in around the school grounds.

119

Ms. Corwin paced before the class as she described a new spell to them. "This one sends things upward, think sky, think clouds." Cait mentally ran down the vocabulary list in the back of the spellwork book. Ever since the failure of the shalhevet spell, she'd been studying it in an attempt to ferret out difficult words before having to pronounce them in front of a whole classroom.

Then Corwin pronounced a word that sounded to Cait like mayim. The Hebrew word for 'water' was not what Cait was expecting to hear, but that was what it sounded like. She chose her landing spot, pronounced, "Mayim!", and aimed her wand at the mug. The water lifted itself in a crystalline mass, leaving the mug behind, and traveled towards her chosen shelf. But not only the water in her mug was in motion. A stream of water emerged from Corwin's teakettle as well, and a ring of water joined both of these from a plant on the windowsill.

Caitlin watched the triple masses of water with fascination as they headed for the shelf. Then a giant splash of water interrupted everything as the spell finished its work.

Oh no. The room was completely quiet now, except for the water dripping off the shelf to form a large puddle on the battered wooden floor.

With a smile tugging at the corner of her mouth, Corwin asked, "What on earth possessed you to attempt moving all that water?"

"Wasn't the spell mayim?" asked Cait, wishing for an invisibility spell and cursing her hearing.

"No it isn't, the word was shamayim me'aal, which is almost like the broomstick spell shemayma. Why don't I write it down." She turned to the board, waved her wand in a graceful right-to-left curve, and gently-glowing letters appeared in the Alef-Bet everyone had just learned.

Then she directed her wand at the still-dripping shelf and the puddle beneath it, proclaimed "Shuvah na!" and the water returned to Cait's mug, the plant pot, and the teakettle.

"Please be sure to study your assigned spells before class next time," reminded Corwin. "I will not expect you to perform any spells in class that have not already been learned from your books, useful as the word mayim may be." She waited until Cait successfully "sshamaya me'aal'd" her mug, with the water this time, to the shelf and back to her desk, before continuing the class.

Once class was over, Penny barraged Cait with questions. "Oh you have to tell me – what was that word? How do you say it? Where did you find it? I wonder if other liquids can be moved around that way?" Cait wasn't sure she liked the scheming look on Penny's face.

"I got it from the back of the book and decided to experiment," she blurted out.

"Wicked." Penny broke out into a grin at Cait's lie. Cait wished Corwin would write down all of the spells the way she'd put "shamayim me'aal" on the board.

Alchemy class was thankfully uneventful; they spent it mixing a basic Vanishing Ink, visible only to the intended recipient of whatever was written with it.

"This ink will be mandatory for all exams here at Witches' Academy," informed Melendez as she walked about the classroom eyeing all of the cauldrons in use, "so you must follow the formula most exactly."

Fortunately, these instructions were all clearly written down, so there were no chances for mishearing anything important. All the same, Penny kept casting hopeful glances towards Cait's cauldron. Cait only glared back.

That first Saturday at Salem was wonderful. Cait got to spend the whole of it with Penny and Meg. They spent all morning badgering their Big Sisters to escort them into town and back, which they finally condescended to do, with a quick review of how to work the front gate. The Peppermill fudge lived up to Greatwood's recommendation, and they spent the rest of that hot Indian-summer day paddling around during "open swim" in the blissfully cool pool under the Commons.

Cait woke up the next morning wondering if she could remember the front-gate spell well enough to go into town and get herself back on campus. She looked at the stack of books on her desk. Vocabulary to memorize for Corwin. Plants to memorize for Broadleaf. Planets and their correspondances to memorize for Pitts, and an essay for Melendez' class due tomorrow. She definitely needed fuel for this study session, and Peppermill would be just the place to get it. Which should she get? The peppermint candy with the long name? More fudge? Chocolate almond bark?

Cait walked out the front gate at the same time as a group of very dressed-up secondyears. Among them was Keisha, who waved at Cait, before they all ascended the steps of a large stone church one block from the Academy.

As she walked along the tree-lined streets to town, Cait reviewed plant names, forgetting only a few. As she carried her candy back along the shady street with its antique houses, she felt pretty sure of all those new spells for Corwin's class, too. Just as she began to work out what she'd write for Melendez' essay, she saw that she was only one block from the school. Cait skipped with happiness as she approached the brick pillars of the Academy and its neighboring house, and reached into the bookbag where she stashed her wand. If only there were some way to wear it when in Plain Sight, she mused, as her fingers closed around the slender piece of chestnut.

122

Wait, she reminded herself just before retrieving it. Are there any Plods nearby? After watching two teenagers and a stroller-pushing dad go by, Cait took out the wand, pronounced what she heard Luatha say yesterday, "batel!", and sent the energy directly into the center of the stone atop the left-hand pillar.

She felt a slight tugging, a pull as if a wave were pulling sand out from under her toes at the beach. The footpath beside the Plod house vanished abruptly, and Cait found herself gazing with horror at one single, solitary brick pillar with a flat stone on top.

Her mouth ran dry and she couldn't move for shock. What had she just done to the Academy? Could people come and go, or was everyone stuck inside now? Was there any such thing as an "undo" button for spellcasting? The phrase "shuvah na" from Corwin's first spellwork class floated into her mind. That meant "return", didn't it? Maybe it would return the pillars to the way they had been before.

Cait aimed her wand with a shaking arm, and with all her might, visualized the two brick pillars as they had just been a moment ago, as they were supposed to be. Then she pronounced "shuvah na!" in a voice that shook even more than her arm and sent the energy. Nothing happened.

She tried again. Nothing, except for feeling more tired than usual once she sent the energy. She slumped down onto the ground at the foot of the pillar, tears of panic running down her cheek. She truly didn't know what to do now. What do you do when you make your school's front gate vanish?

She felt a push of air nearby, and there was sudden blackness before her. She looked up to see an unfamiliar witch who wore a long black dress and a round cap not unlike that of the firstyears. She looked down at Cait, her slim face creased with concern. "Are you all right? Has something happened to you?" she asked.

"I b-broke the gate," croaked Cait, her throat tight with panic.

Slim Face's jaw dropped. "You did this? I must say that I'm impressed, even if we're not sure how we'll fix this. We're here from the Council of Witches, by the way."

We? Cait got shakily to her feet in time to see another shorter roundfaced witch in a gray suit show up out of nowhere with another push of air.

With a third push of air, Corwin stood there as well, in her Schoodic shirt and jeans. "Why Cait, here's a surprise. What on earth happened? Are you all right?"

Why was everyone asking if she was all right? "I broke the gate," she repeated. "I told it 'batel!' like I heard everyone else say and it did this." She waved at the remaining pillar as she felt her face flush crimson.

Gray Suit's eyes lit up as she looked at the pillar, waved Corwin and Long Face over, and they all talked in low voices. Cait couldn't catch anything of what they said, but she could see that a smile was trying to lift the corner of Corwin's mouth.

After several moments of discussion that felt like forever, Corwin turned and held out a white slip of paper to Cait. "Learn this by heart, and keep it in your hat at all times. P'tach! is the spell you really want; please do your best to forget the other one." The smile stilled tugged at her mouth, and her eyes twinkled as well. "Have no fear, we know exactly how we'll get the gate back. You haven't broken it for good. But please do not go teaching your mis-heard version to anyone. Too many people will want it for getting out of exams."

Corwin turned to talk some more with the other witches, as Cait studied the slip of paper, then tucked it into her hat lining. Yay once more, ears, she thought. All she did back home was make a bus tire go flat and crack a blackboard. And Mr. Seekins thought that untrained magic was dangerous?

Even after the twin pillars were restored, and Cait had demonstrated to the three witches that she could properly perform the gate-spell after all, she could barely meet Corwin's eye in class for the whole next week.

Chapter 9 - Broomracing

Wed, Oct. 3, 2007
Witches' Academy
Salem, MA
Dear Aunt May:
You're lucky to get all those "A"s in your Elementary Spellwork classes! I wish I were getting all As. Half the time Spellwork spells don't work and I don't know why. Maybe my ears mess it up. But the other half's good.
I love Broomwork and stargazing, although the Astronologia teacher's awful; everything she says is mumble mumble mumble. And the Alchemy teacher mumbles too, but only sometimes. And when Meg told this story at dinner that had everyone cracking up laughing, she forgot to tell it to me later so I could laugh too. Still can't hear at all in that dinner hall. Makes me want to growl and hiss like Nini.
Do you always get spells right the first time you say them? Seems like almost everyone does except me. Sometimes I have to say it six or seven times before it works. And sometimes it does't even work at all. And once it made a disaster.
Especially when Claire and Company make fun of how I say things, like the flying spell and the time I said "Mayim" instead of "Shamayim." The rocks on top of the Partridge Hall roof (it's flat, don't worry) jump really nice when I need to go blow off steam. Then Meg and I do our broom sprints and she fills me in on what I missed at lunch conversation. When she doesn't forget, that is.
We sprint together every night before supper, and then Penny comes up to the rooftop and we all hang out and talk. Meg and I practice lots so we can be on the Broomball team next year when they allow us.

Gotta stay out of Meg's way when she gets all daredevil, though. Means she's worried about not being as smart as her genius older sibs. The other day she got a bad grade on a Greenwitchery quiz, and she nearly crashed into the dovecote three times practicing sharp turns. I tell her she's way better than me at Zoomorphia and Mindcasting, but she won't believe me. Last week, though, after Auclair complimented her in front of the whole class, Meg told us all about how her sister got her flying canoe a whole year early, and how she can bespell rainstorms out of her way when she travels. There was some weather crisis going on, and they needed as many weatherworkers as possible, and so the Council of Witches recruited some students to help. And Louise was the youngest one they asked, so she's kind of famous now.

Penny's already saving up for a canoe like that so she can go to Paris and Rome and Brazil and Australia.

And Meg can even Mindcast chipmunks and squirrels and doves and tell us where they hide nuts or find grubs or when they're being summoned to carry a letter somewhere. Meg think's she's gonna flunk out if she stays on here beyond the first three "Hedge" years. I think she's wrong.

Gotta go now. Just saw the eagles fly over to ring the lunch bell, then there's Broomwork. Yay!

Lots of love – wish I were seeing you at Halfterm, but am glad that your Extension class has its own Halfterm celebration too. Yay for weird, witchy us!

Am I a half-witch if only half of my spells work??

Love,

Cait

Weed Haven

Northern Kingdom, VT

Thurs, October 4, 2007

Dearest Cait:

So wonderful that you're making some real friends down there in Salem! I'm sure you'll be getting along much better in your classes once you've gotten used to the new languages and vocabulary. Unlike an old thing like me, you'll have the basics down in no time and will be flying along wondering why it was so hard in the beginning. After all, you have always been such a bookworm, how can you possibly do anything but succeed? Maybe you will have to work a little harder than your classmates do, but I know you can do it. Didn't you always bring home good grades from your old school?

All the same, I'll be sure to Broom-Courier you another boxful of herbal remedies, especially the ones that help with studying. I do dream about training a hawk to carry larger bundles for me once I've learned more Zoomorphia; my sweet little pigeon can carry nothing heavier than letters, alas.

Isn't spellwork fun? Ask your teacher to write down all the spells as she teaches them to you. New spells generally do work for me on the first or second try, once I know what the words are.

Not that I don't have my own challenges, mind you. I am simply hopeless at Alchemy and Astronologia. There's a reason Cousin Joyce's elixers and potions have always been so much better than my own. Especially the anti-Mal-de-Mer one that enables me to travel. Despite its name I need it to fly, and am down to my last bottle, But if I ever succeed in concocting that recipe myself, then you can expect me to come and visit for Winter Solstice. Otherwise, you'll see me at summer reunion. Highway driving has become singularly unappealing since I've learned to properly fly. Who wouldn't prefer a broom to a car? But I sincerely hope to see you more often than only at summertime these days, my dear! I will of course let you know.

Fortunately for you, my "A" grades have all been in Greenwitchery, so there'll be no worry that you'll ever run out of your box of herbs. Perhaps that is the reason that I love this little corner of country so much, even if it is so far from you and the city and your wonderful new school. Far away from cellphone towers and cable services too, haha. So much room for forests and all the lovely plants and wild creatures to be found there. Not all the useful plants grow in gardens, after all.

You simply must visit Weed Haven this summer, and bring your friends. After family reunion, of course.

With love,

Your delightfully weird

Aunt May

Cait threw the letter down onto her desk. Aunt May was sweet and all, and never mumbled to Cait or talked away from her, but she still didn't get it about Cait's hearing. "Work a little harder." "Ask your teacher to write it down." What did she think Cait was doing now? Nobody else in class made Graycliff repeat her blackboard speeches or made Corwin transcribe her spells. Would Aunt May ever understand that Cait never got a break from working hard? Would anyone?

A rumble from Cait's stomach interrupted her sulk. Better go and get some lunch. Maybe food would help her mood, even if it was impossible to hear inside the Commons. Cait looked over at the windowsill where Nicky sat in a sun puddle, waiting for Penny to walk by so he could hop through the bird-hatch into her hood on her way from library to lunch. The toad's throat went pooch-pooch-pooch in and out, as those amber eyes stared across the courtyard.

"You never have to listen up to anything, lucky you," she told him, stroking his nubbly back with one finger. Then she hoisted her bag and left the room.

Cait's mood lifted when she saw Genoa salami on the lunch buffet; it was one of her favorite kinds of sandwich. And there was Meg, waving at her from a table under the middle window, while hauling textbooks off the seat she was saving. Nearby, Penny was yakking and giggling with some of their classmates. Cait grinned and waved back as she sat down with her sandwich. "You look like you have news," she told Meg, who nodded enthusiastically.

"Have I ever!" announced Meg. "... boy's coach ... Halfterm we get to ... at Winter ... " Cait struggled to understand among the chatter filling the hall. What did "winter" have to do with Halfterm? She put up the volume on her hearing aids, and turned her chair towards Meg, who continued to talk. "... Broomball demonstration before the clambake, by the ..."

"Twenty-nine detentions!" burst into Cait's good ear, from Penny's direction, followed by giggles all around.

"Who gets to demonstrate broomball?" Cait asked Meg, hitching her chair closer. "What about winter?"

"Happens every year, according to Merle," Meg answered. "at Winter Island, and the best flyers ..."

"... on the Schoodic, no less ..." intruded another voice, drowning out Meg.

"Even with teachers?" this surprised reply from Penny was equally loud and intrusive.

130

"What do the best flyers do?" Cait asked, leaning away from Penny some more, But Meg answered with a dismissive hand flap, mouthing at Cait "tell you later."

"But you always forget," Cait protested as Meg picked up her bag, waved at her, and headed out the door. Cait stared at her half-eaten sandwich and fumed. She had been watching Meg so intently, trying to understand her story, that she didn't even get to eat her own sandwich. This was not working. And how long were these new friends going to put up with her if she couldn't even understand their stories at lunchtime? Time to find out what kind of accommodations magical schools offered. Yes, Mom, you win.

Cait stomped all the way across the courtyard and up two floors of the library building and past the classrooms, bookbag swinging madly at her hip. Once at the infirmary's front counter, she stood watching Ms. Broadleaf fill a many-drawered wooden cabinet with all kinds of dried plants, while a very thin and spare witch in deep-blue robes checked them off on a list. Cait felt a dim mind-cast tap as the witch handed her list to Broadleaf, and came over. "What can I do for you?" she asked as the mindcast-tap turned into a shimmer that traveled from Cait's head down to her toes, pausing briefly at a bruise on her shin she'd gotten in Broomwork class.

"My ears can't sort out all the noise in the Commons like everyone else's can, and I'm sick of missing out on conversations," she said. "And these don't help nearly enough." Cait pointed to her hearing aids. "It also messes up classes because I get the spells wrong," she added.

Blue Robes nodded, then placed thin and cool hands gently over Cait's ears. A warm vibration traveled down each ear canal, into her inner ears, and buzzed around there while Blue Robes stood with her eyes closed. It felt almost like floating in the hot tub Cait once got to try during a water-park daytrip. "Your ears have always been this way," stated Blue Robes, opening her eyes and looking at Cait. A statement, not a question.

Cait nodded.

Blue Robes sighed. "Magical healing is very good at restoring a person's body to their original condition. Your leg, for example, knows that the bruise on your shin was not originally there, and I can read that. Let me demonstrate." Blue Robes turned to the cabinet, chose a shaggy leaf from one of the drawers, and passed her hand over the bruise. She then laid the leaf on the bruise, took out a wand, murmured some words too low for Cait to hear and sent the spell. Instantly the leaf vanished, leaving a minute trail of dust, and Cait felt a ferocious itching where the bruise was. It then turned yellow and green before vanishing, along with the itch.

"Wow, it's really gone," said Cait, staring at her leg.

Blue Robes nodded. "If a bone had grown too much and made your hearing change, I'd be able to read the original shape of your inner ear and put it back that way. But in this case, I have no map to go by, so to speak." She frowned, again put her hands over Cait's ears, and the warm buzz traveled around some more. Then she lowered her hands. "I can see where your inner ears are different, especially the cochlea. You can hear many high sounds, but not the low ones. And your sense of balance relies completely on your vision. But if I tried to reshape your inner ears more like somebody else's, it could make things even worse. You have so much hearing already, I don't want to risk it. And balance is even riskier; you could get stuck with permanent vertigo. Imagine a merry-go-round that won't stop."

"But you made the bruise go away so easily."

"Two days of bruise versus years and years of that spot being unbruised. Very easy to fix. Your cochlea has been the same for your whole life. If I do the bruise-healing spell on your ears, nothing would happen. And if I try to reshape your cochlea like a hearing person's, the rest of your hearing could change as well. You have too much hearing to risk it."

Cait scowled. Great. No help here. "Yeah, they told me that a lot back home. Too much hearing for this, too much hearing for that." She remembered sitting in the doctor's office with her parents as he gazed at her audiogram and informed her parents that no, he did not recommend that Cait enroll in the deaf-outreach program her dad had just heard about. "Keep her in public school," he'd said, "She'll have much better academics there. She has too much hearing to really need deaf outreach anyway. She'll be fine." And he smiled unconvincingly at Cait.

As Cait got up to go, Blue Robes put up a hand. "That doesn't mean I can't help you out, though. I do have something you might want to try." She disappeared into a back room, returning with what looked like a single golden blossom on a long and leafless golden vine. "This trumpetvine knows what to do. You wear it necklace style. Whenever you want to listen to something in particular, the blossom end will take itself over to the sound you want to hear."

Cait stifled a groan at the thought of having to lug around some object even at this magical school, but couldn't help reaching out for the bloom. It truly was beautiful, with its bright gently-curving petals, and it curled itself onto Cait's shoulders very much like a cat settling onto a lap.

133

On her way out the door, Cait was dismayed to see Claire coming down the hallway. She paused as she saw Cait, and her eyes flicked to the golden blossom.

"What a beautiful necklace," she said. Her tone was pure friendliness. "It looks handmade. Is it designer?"

"It's custom," replied Cait. Now, why can't more "accommodations" be pretty like this one? she thought as she smiled at Claire, and they walked out to where Greengage awaited her Broomwork students. As they went, Cait snuck glances at the shimmering sleeves of Claire's robes, which changed from cobalt to midnight blue and back again. That's no cheap polyester, either, Cait realized. The shine was exactly like that of the expensive silk lining of her own dress robes. Noticing Cait's glances, Claire smirked and started to strut.

Once she was in the courtyard picking out her broom, Cait began to worry. What if I fall off my broom and break this? Besides, Greengage was pretty easy to understand. She tucked the trumpetvine into her bag, where it curled up snugly into one of the inner pockets. It lay there forgotten during a wordless Mindcasting class and a whole hour and a half of Zoomorphia animal-track drills.

As everyone headed to the Commons for supper, Cait remembered the trumpetvine with a thrill of excitement, and draped it once more about her shoulders, none the worse for its ride in her bookbag. As she settled into her place at table, she heard Meg gabbing about school sports and halfterm to Penny, Minna, and a couple other classmates, As soon as Cait leaned forward to get some of the details, the golden blossom snaked over to hover above Meg's plate. Her words now stood out clearly among the background chatter. "...and when you're secondyear, you get to try out for teams – what the heck is THAT?"

134

Cait jumped back at Meg"s surprised shout, then other voices chimed into her ear "Can I see?" "Oh that's pretty!" "I've never seen one of those. What's it do?" The trumpetvine became a zooming blur as it approached this person, now that one, now another. All eyes were now on Cait's new "jewelry".

Even Elsbeth leaned over from the next table, genuinely interested in the device. Claire, on the other hand, turned away with a toss of her hair, striking up a lively conversation with Amanda.

"This helps me hear better," began Cait. "The blossom end here picks up the sound-"

"Is that real gold? It looks like something to wear to parties," interrupted a townie.

"You could totally design a prom dress around that," remarked another girl.

Penny's voice cut through the babble. "Guys, it's just a trumpetvine. Can we get back to talking about Halfterm? Like do we really get to team up with the boys from BWIS?"

"Yeah, that's right, boys!" boomed Meg's overamplified voice as Cait yanked the vine's earpiece from her better ear. "My brother told me they're going to set up for racing and clambake and everything right in front of the boys' school." Cait let the earpiece settle back into place as Meg's voice returned to its normal volume.

"We get to see their school?" Even Minna's soft question carried across the table. And as long as Cait kept track of who talked when, the trumpetvine knew where to go, and the conversation swirling about her was understandable. She missed only one sentence when the selkie girl came up behind her and started talking before Cait realized she had joined the conversation. Cait's eyes shone as everyone got up to go to Astrolologia class.

"Maybe now I'll finally have a clue as to what Ms. Mumbler Pitts is saying," she told Penny.

But as soon as the vine snaked its way from Cait's second-row seat to the teacher during her incomprehensible lecture, Ms. Pitts squinted at it and frowned. "We cannot allow such bright objects to disturb the light levels in this room" were the only words that Cait heard clearly before the vine bounced back to her as if it had hit some invisible barrier. "Listen more closely." Cait fought the simmering anger at once again having to hear this phrase, just like in her old school.

"This is how I listen, Ms. Pitts," replied Cait.

"Then find a way to listen, Ms. Leo, that doesn't glitter or fly into people's faces," she answered, then returned to her mumbled lecture.

While Cait drew lightning zigzags in her Astronologia text, she consoled herself with the thought that at least the trumpetvine was bound to go over better in Graycliff's class the next day. No low light levels there to worry about, and it would be so nice to not have to ask her to repeat those blackboard speeches.

The first part of the lecture went well, trumpetvine resting lightly on Cait's shoulders as Graycliff described how to tell a real animal from a person disguised with a glamour spell. "Their tracks will look different," continued Graycliff as she reached for a piece of chalk. "If it's a human in disguise, you will see a shape like this –" Graycliff turned towards the blackboard and began drawing a paw-shaped set of ovals. She mumbled something as she drew, and the trumpetvine obediently sailed off towards her. A shriek blasted into Cait's ear as the bright blossom came within Graycliff's line of sight. "Unspell that creeper now!" she demanded as she turned to face the class. "Oh, it's yours." Her eyes traced the vine back to Cait. "Kindly explain what this is and why it's here."

"I'm hard of hearing, and this helps me understand what you're saying," Cait said. Graycliff raised her glasses and gazed at the trumpetvine for a long moment and gave a slow nod.

"Ah, well, let's continue with our tracks then." But as Graycliff continued at the blackboard, her drawings were shaky, and she kept looking back over her shoulder as if a whole crowd of trumpetvines were about to follow the first one.

The trumpetvine worked best of all in Melendez' class, bringing her soft voice up to where Cait could reliably hear it. "Well, what have we now?" said Melendez with a small smile as the trumpetvine made its appearance during Alchemy. "Our own botanical version of the dancing cobras of Cairo?" And as she continued her lecture on the three forms of mercury, Cait was delighted to notice that she wasn't missing a single word. She leaned back in her chair, noticing that the vine was still able to reach from her chair to Melendez' desk when she did so. That alone was a treat. With a shock, she realized how much of her day was spent leaning forward in her chair, trying to not miss too many words from across a table or classroom. Even better, there was no receiver falling out of her pocket, no wires getting caught, no batteries winding down.

After class, she sent off a joyful note to her mom, telling her how pretty and nice the "hearing accommodations" at this school were. Her mom's reply was brief: "Good girl, I knew they'd have something worthwhile. Now don't you wish you hadn't waited so long?"

137

With or without the trumpetvine, Broomwork class remained Cait's favorite, next to Spellwork. The courtyard began to feel very small and confining as the whole class practiced sprints and turns, and Greengage reminded them again that there would be firstyear participation in the halfterm broomwork demonstration. Meg and Cait redoubled their rooftop efforts, while the Magenta Trio walked about with insufferable smirks.

"Don't forget that there'll be boys at Halfterm." Meg's eyes glowed as she reminded Cait.

On the morning of October 10th, Cait looked up from reading her schedule scroll to see Penny staring at her own scroll with a frown.

"Why would Broomwork class be at the pool?" she asked Cait.

"Maybe people really do fly over oceans," replied Cait. "and you won't have to save up for your boat after all."

Penny wrinkled her nose. "Ha ha. Actually, I have heard of games being held over the water sometimes. I've just never seen them because our Solstice races are always held over a hayfield."

"Meg will know. C'mon," Cait pulled at Penny's arm as she took off down the dorm hallway. "Hey Meg!"

To her surprise, Meg stood at her open doorway as the duo approached. "I don't know everything about brooms, you know," she grumbled, fiddling with her sleeves as if she'd just pulled the robe on over her head.

"You Mindcasted our question," Penny blurted out. "How do you do that?"

"Nosy big sibs," Meg answered with a shrug. "I have no idea why Broomwork's at the pool today, by the way."

"Water landings, maybe?" guessed Cait. "What if you fly really far and have to land on a lake or something?"

"I bet some of Mom's customers fly over the bay to get to her shop," mused Penny. "That would explain why she keeps these weird until-midnight summer hours. It gives people a way to get to her shop by broom without breaking Plain Sight."

"Or maybe they'll teach us Broomball so we can be ready to join the teams next year," Meg said, bouncing on her toes in excitement. "Broomball is always played over water."

As it turned out, they were wrong on all counts.

Greengage led them to a passageway on the far side of the pool, and the rushing-water sound became quite a bit louder, as Cait reached for the trumpetvine and draped it about her. The cavern floor pitched down, and then they were at the bank of a furiously-rushing underground river. It was like no river that Cait had ever seen before. It flowed in two directions at once, the near side flowing to the right, the far side flowing to the left. A set of canoe-like double-ended boats with four seats apiece hovered just above the water, awaiting their passengers. The furthest one on the left was already loaded with brooms, and each boat had its own glow-globe hovering above it.

"Step in ... step in!" bellowed Greengage above the water noise. The trumpetvine hovered in the air halfway between Cait and the teacher, straining at its full length, catching only some of her words above the rush of water. "Four to a boat ... go! Last boat ... five, step it up!" Cait, Penny, and Meg eyed the boat nearest them: step into a boat that was in midair?

Cait felt a pushing and jostling behind her; the selkie smiled up at her. "You'll need a fourth person for your boat," she announced while beaming at Cait. She stepped nimbly into the boat, which held itself as firmly as if she were stepping onto a dock. She then nodded and waved the other three girls in after her. As Cait watched her friends climb in, she wondered why the selkie wanted so much to be in her boat. There was a tap on her arm; Meg leaned back in the boat and mouthed, "plenty of room", while the selkie beamed and motioned at Cait to get in.

Greengage continued shouting once everyone was in their boats, now too far away for the vine to reach, which Cait packed away safely in her bag. The words were nothing but incomprehensible babble against the competing sound of the water, and Cait could catch only bits and pieces: "... elbows IN ... sitting, ... NO standing, ... wands AWAY...." Greengage stepped into the boat with the brooms, sat down, and said one more thing which must have been a spell, because all seven boats lowered themselves in unison and shot off down the river as soon as they touched water.

One bookbag fell overboard, and Greengage fished it out with a quick spell. Caitlin guessed that she must have been keeping an eye out for boating novices who didn't know to stow their stuff properly. Another set of shouts came from Greengage, which must have been further reminders about boating etiquette.

The river's course took them through caverns of all sizes, and at one point, the walls unexpectedly closed in on the river.

"Ouch!" yelped Cait. Her elbow had been further out of the boat than she'd realized, and she now had a scrape from that rock wall. No wonder Greengage had mentioned "elbows in".

After about ten minutes, the boats all lifted and hovered. A green-filtered light glowed overhead, and the walls widened around them. Greengage's boat flew up to the ceiling, where the light filtered in, until they could see only the bottom of her boat. After a moment, the empty boat floated down to hover above the river, and Greengage's face appeared among the tall grass that edged a narrow opening in the cavern roof. "... boat ... up here ... out as soon as you get up here, no dawdling."

Two boats went ahead of them, and then it was time for Cait's boat. The rush of air as the boat lifted up was better than a Ferris wheel. All too soon, they were in the open air, and surrounded by tall grass. "Step out, step out," prodded Greengage beside them.

As before, the boat held steady as they all stepped out. Once empty, it sank out of sight. The students in the first two boats were selecting their brooms from where they were piled nearby, and Cait, Meg, Penny, and the selkie hurried to do likewise.

"What's your name, by the way?" Cait asked the selkie "I hope broomriding's a lot less scary for you now."

The brown-eyed girl answered something like "Andy", "Drey", "Andrea"?

Cait frowned and began to think that maybe she should wear the vine in Broomwork class after all, even if she did risk breaking it. "How do you spell that? No, wait, I've got paper here –" she rummaged in her pocket for mini-sketchbook and pencil. Better to see the name and get it right, than to guess and get it wrong, she thought. Then to be on the safe side, she pulled out the trumpetvine, which glittered in the sun as it settled around her neck. Cait wrote "And-" then paused, looking at those big brown eyes.

"I'll write it, it's spelled with a 'y'. Spelled that way to honor Andre, a famous relative of mine from Rockport. The one in Maine." She took the sketchbook from Cait, wrote "Andreya," and handed it back. "And yes, I still don't really like flying, but at least I don't shake all afternoon

141

anymore. You're lucky you like the air so much." Andreya sighed at the end of this speech, her doe eyes huge.

"But you get to be a seal sometimes," Cait pointed out. "That's pretty amazing."

"You're the selkie?" interrupted Meg. "Are you the one who eats all the seaweed in the Commons? Weird."

"And what about you eating mustard on toast for breakfast?" countered Cait. "That's pretty weird, too."

Meg raised her hands in mock surrender. "Guilty. Learned from my hungry omnivore brother."

Cait turned back to Andreya. "Graycliff is taking forever to let us do our first transformations in Zoomorphia. So, what's it like to be a seal sometimes and a person sometimes?"

Andreya shrugged. "How can I tell you? I don't know what it's like to only be a person. But I sure don't ever want to swim the ocean around here in person form. Way too cold."

Soon, all twenty-five students were out of their boats and equipped with brooms. They stood on the edge of a golf course, where a sign hung on a weathered split-rail fence. "Closed due to soggy ground conditions. Apologies, The Management."

"Welcome to the Salem town golf course," boomed Greengage's voice, much clearer without the water noise. Everyone stopped their chatter to listen, as Cait moved over within trumpetvine range. "This is where we will hold tryouts to find out which of you will represent the firstyear class at the broomwork demonstration at Halfterm. We will also hold practices here occasionally, where you will note that there's much more space than our courtyard. Your schedules will tell you when that's the case. There will eventually be night flying next semester when you are more solid on your brooms."

142

Panic gripped Caitlin's gut. Again, the night-flying.

"I'm gonna fail night-flying, I know it," she said to Meg, while putting the trumpetvine safely away.

Nearby, Claire paused from fussing with the golden fringes that decorated her robes. She shot Cait a look of disdain and turned to Amanda, saying "... so many other ways to fly."

Amanda's eyes lit up. "My parents ... maybe a flying carpet ... graduation ..." And the two girls were off and running with their conversation.

Meg tapped Cait's shoulder. "She's lying. Nobody can afford flying carpets."

"Time to warm up," boomed Greengage. "Let's fly!" The teacher swung her arm in the direction of the golf course, and twenty-five whooping and hollering firstyears dropped their bookbags onto the manicured grass and were swooping and racing in the open air. Once everyone had settled down a bit, Greengage signaled them all over to an ancient and very tall oak, and had each of them fly their fastest from that oak over to a jagged-topped spruce. Cait wondered if it had been struck by lightning.

As each student reached the spruce, Cait saw a flash of blue. Then it was her turn, and she hovered beside the teacher. "Not until I give the signal. When you see my left arm drop, go." Greengage pointed the wand in her right hand at the spruce as she held her left arm up, drew a small circle with the wand, and a shimmering pale-blue circle appeared at the spruce, slightly to the right of its trunk.

Greengage's arm dropped and Cait was off. She felt the glory of open air and wind rushing past her, with no nearby buildings to avoid as she sped towards the circle. Then the flash of bright blue light surrounded her, making her slow down in surprise. Cait curved the path of her broom-flight around to face the oak before dismounting, pleased to finally be able to do so without falling off. To her right, Andreya beamed at her.

Then it was Meg's turn. She reached the flashing hoop in barely any time at all.

"I don't think I've ever seen you go so fast. You look great," said Cait.

"Just wait 'till we're all allowed to race for the school," bragged Meg.

Soon, Greengage was reading off everyone's 500-broomlength times, Cait straining to hear what hers would be, while wishing her bookbag weren't all the way over by the fence. Meg let out a huge whoop and high-fived Cait. "We're gooood. The three halfterm flyers are you, me, and Amanda. Woohoo!"

Amanda lifted her chin coolly as she regarded the jubilant pair nearby. "Dream on. I'm still going to win the real race." She drifted over to Claire, who high-fived her, and Elsbeth, who looked pleased but exasperated. The words "Plod-raised dork" and "wish I had some real competition" floated back on the breeze as the Trio's golden fringes flashed in the sun. Amanda's crow zoomed back and forth overhead, occasionally daring to land on the broomstick she held.

"What's she going to do, bewitch the judges?" Cait eyed the strutting blonde.

"Nah, athletic judges are hexproof," answered Meg. "They've been really strict ever since this guy bought himself a trophy last year. With pixie Adels, no less. We'll show her. We know how to work hard."

Cait could tell that it was going to take some really hard work to top Amanda. During the rest of that day's practice, she kept an eye on the haughty girl. Amanda's confidence was not unearned. Her turns were neat, her

144

swift landings precise, and she never fell off. Probably learned to fly from that crow of hers, thought Cait.

As everyone headed back to the boats, Meg elbowed Cait. "Meet me on the rooftop tomorrow after breakfast. We need lots more sprints."

"You're on," replied Cait. "Team Stubborn in training." And she grinned all the way back to the Academy.

Chapter 10 – A Small Difference

Fwoosh!

The bag full of spellbooks went flying onto Cait's bed, followed by her hat. Nick jumped off the windowsill where he had been blissfully sunning himself, and dove into the safety of his terrarium next to Penny's bed. Cait's wand very nearly went flying too, but she stopped herself. One didn't just throw wands around. Besides, if she broke it, where would she be? But then again, if her spells only worked half of the time, what kind of witch would she be? She threw herself on the bed, and stared at the crackled old ceiling plaster.

After today's miserable Spellwork class, Cait thought that Alchemy would never end. She was looking forward to burning off some good old muscle energy in swim class. And it felt great to be in the water, butterflying away. But then, in the periphery of her sight, there was Brunner madly running alongside her yelling, "No spellwork! No spellwork!" As she pulled up at the side of the pool to find out what the yelling was about, several disappointed swimmers also got out; they had been riding the current that Cait's fury had inadvertently created.

Then there were the spells that worked, but not the way she wanted them to. That disastrous front-gate spell, for example. And the time she said "mayim" instead of "shamayma".

And now today's class.

She couldn't get the spell to work at all, not even once! They were practicing a spell that was meant to put things away in their designated places. It was a simple spell, really, with one single word: sader. For everyone else in the class, that is, it was simple. Her own paper, quill, and ink, sat right there on her desk. They wouldn't budge even once, no matter how many times Corwin coached her in how to say it, no matter how clearly she could hear Corwin's voice through the trumpetvine, no matter how many different ways she tried to pronounce it. It all sounded exactly the same.

Sitting up on the bed, she aimed her wand. "Sader!" she told the books which had fallen out of the bag and lay scattered about. "Sader!"

They remained immobile.

A flash of insight burst upon her. It had to be the "s" sound. She had always had trouble pronouncing "s", the one sound she couldn't properly hear. And when she tallied up in her mind the spells that didn't work, they always seemed to involve some variety of "s".

But she had learned to do the flying spell, shemayma reliably, and she was going to learn how to do this one, too.

"Sader!." She tried once more with the books, turning her tongue a little bit towards the roof of her mouth. Nothing.

Her stomach rumbled, and she remembered the apple that was supposed to be in her pocket for a mid-morning snack. There it sat, on her table by the window. She didn't feel like getting up to get it, and who knew, maybe the spell would work if she tried another object. She aimed her wand at it.

"Sader!"

It sat.

"Ssader!" Still nothing. Her temper flared.

"So sit there then." Wand still pointed, her annoyance flashed along the wandlength as her fingers did the "I hate this" flick. The apple exploded.

Cait blinked. Damn, she had wanted to eat that apple. Too much temper.

But wait a minute. She had just exploded the apple without using any words at all. Her fingers formed the sign again as she mulled the idea over. Was there any such thing as signing a spell? She wished she knew more signs. What if there were a whole wizard signing vocabulary, the way so many spoken languages were used in regular spellwork? And if there were such a thing, would one form the sign and wand out the energy with the same hand? Or would it be better to sign with one hand while wanding with the other?

She had to find out more. Stowing her wand in her robe's wand-pocket, Cait tore out of the dorm to the library, only to stand immobile before the ranges of books. Where to begin looking?

The roomful of books, four levels high, stood before her. Three-fourths of the room was filled with elaborately-carved wooden shelves full of books of all sizes and kinds. Lacy iron-filigree spiral staircases linked the four levels of bookshelves. She was the only student in the quiet room. The weather was sunny and warm, and most of the students spent the hour before supper hanging out in the courtyard.

Just inside the library's front door stood a line of stone arches. She had thought they were decoration at first, but the school librarian, Ms. Fletcher, had explained the use of these arches during the first-years' library orientation.

Now, she stood under an arch and considered. Spells had to come from somewhere. Spellwork, spellmaking -- "Spellwriting," she told the arch. A flash of light went up from a range of books to her left, and one level up. But the arch filled with a red-tinted glow that restrained her momentarily: that was an advanced-level subject. She ran up to that range anyway, tripping over some of the spiral steps in her hurry.

148

She sat down on the floor and opened up the first book to its first page. "Many intermediate spellcasters find that once they have mastered the first of the semipemanent forms of transformation, that is, those which shift the molecular affinities of the substance in question, prewritten formulae no longer suffice, and one must begin to make use of their adductive capacities, for which a heuristic method is most highly recommended." This must be where Greatwood gets her speech style, Cait decided as she put the book back.

The next book had the intriguing word "Panglossolalia" for its title, but when its contents pages went from "Guide to enunciation" to "Glossaria Hellenika" to "Codex sapentiae latinae" to entries in alphabets that curled like ribbons or hung suspended as from a line or sat in the neat blocks of Chinese script, she decided it wouldn't help her either.

The third one appeared to be a dictionary, complete with pronunciation guides throughout. No help there.

She went back to the stone portal and said, "Sign language." One book in the basic-reference area lit up, and a white glow emanated from the portal: that was an entry-level book. As soon as she opened it, she could tell it was useless; it was an elementary guide to Plod languages for loreleien, dwarves, and other magical peoples who had their own indigenous languages. Now what?

Think. Did a formal spell always have to be spoken?

Her teachers all used spoken spells in class, and on the Schoodic they did as well. Hold on. What had Corwin said about the dorm's front-door spell? They could have used a spoken-word spell for the dorm door. But because it might be overheard by other people, they'd decided to make it more secure by using a different spell, one that didn't need to be said out loud.

Cait ran back to the portal, shaking with excitement. "Silent spells," she told it. Brightness appeared two shelves over from the original books she'd consulted, and the portal now glowed rose, indicating that it was an upper-level subject. She hurried to the shelf. Of the five luminous books before her, two carried "For teachers only" red bands around them. Remembering her bookstore experience, she left those ones alone, and took the other three from the shelf.

Nonverbal Spells for Healing Practitioners read the first title; it went right back onto the shelf after one look at the text: "The median response rate of the average clinical patient indicates that an empathetic response to full restoration of disrupted function is important..." It reminded her too much of those boring audiological offices where there was lots of sitting and listening to strange noises and repeating the same list of words as always, while wearing those same horrible heavy headphones that hurt.

The next book was more promising: Peace in the House: Quiet Spells for Canny Parents. Did Penny know about this book? Cait was going to have to ask her how often magical parents used strategic spells to keep unruly kids in line, and if Penny's brother was often the target.

That left The Unvoiced Spell: A Brief Introduction. It had a whole chapter on how to form mental images, which Cait found rather boring, since this was one of the easiest parts of Spellwork class for her. Although some of the vocabulary and techniques were beyond her, this book looked like it might help.

Flipping to the index, she looked up "hands", "handshapes", and "signs". No luck there. Then she looked up "Gestures" which did appear in this book. But that was about wand movements, not hand movements. Annoyed,

150

she shoved this last book onto the shelf with more noise than she should have, earning an inquisitive glance from Ms. Fletcher, who was marking up an issue of Spellcraft Today with notes about new books the library should purchase.

Think. Think.

She was very sure that the apple wouldn't have exploded without the hand-motion she had done, any more than the rocks at her house would have moved without the finger-flick, or the bus tire would have gone flat without that fist. Why was there nothing in the books about this?

Think. Gesture ... signs ... deaf. She had to look that up.

Back at the portal, she said, "Deaf."

A white light went up from the portal, and one book glowed off to the right: The Pedagogy of Wizardcraft. The index showed one single page-reference for "deaf". Flipping to that page, she read: "The education of deaf children of magical ability is generally regarded as impossible unless they are able to acquire excellent speech skills."

Great. So this was as good as it got? She threw the book down, earning a glare from Ms. Fletcher, and blushed as she put it back quietly. So much for the library. She longed for the family computer back home. Magical energies made electronic circuits go haywire, according to Meg. Fortunately, they didn't disrupt her hearing aids too much, except for making a funny fluttering noise whenever she cast a spell.

As Cait headed for the door, Fletcher didn't look at all mad, only sympathetic. "It looks like you could use some help," she offered, her voice clear in the quiet room.

All Cait wanted to do was to go back to her room and sulk, but she figured she'd better answer. "Nothing here on what I want," she grumbled.

"Don't be so sure," Fletcher assured her. "Just because we don't have it in this library doesn't mean we can't get it."

Cait sighed. "I'm trying to find out if there's any such thing as spells that are signed, instead of spoken. Do spells have to be all spoken, or set up special, like the dorm doors? Can a sign that is done with your hands" – she gestured automatically – "be the spell, the way words are?"

Fletcher thought for a moment. "It is true that we belong to a very logocentric tradition of magicworking here at Witches' Academy, and at BWIS as well. But there are, as you know, many magical traditions, with many different methods. You might want to browse A World Guide to Magical Traditions, over here." She waved her wand, and a book lit up to her right in the reference area. "In the meanwhile, I'll search the periodical literature for what I can find." She nodded toward the back of the room, where Cait could hear something which sounded like a hundred birds flying around. Fletcher regarded the issue of Spellcraft Today which she still held. "Unfortunately, much of the periodical literature is also quite heavily logocentric. If I do find anything useful, the library fox will bring it to you." She now motioned over to a nearby table. Under it, a fox was napping, but it now opened its eyes and regarded Cait and Ms. Fletcher.

Cait was surprised at how much calmer she now felt as she browsed World Guide to Magical Traditions, even though it didn't offer anything to help her.

Thanking Ms. Fletcher, she made her way back to her dorm room while still thinking things over.

If she did the signs she knew, but changed the handshapes so that she could still hold the wand, would they work? After all, signing, writing, and wandwork were all done with the same hand, one just didn't swap off. And why was spellwork always done in other languages? If spellwork wasn't done in the plain English they spoke, maybe she shouldn't borrow ASL signs for spellwork, either. But on the other hand, nobody used sign language at Witches' Academy besides her, so maybe that wouldn't matter.

Well, she was going to try it anyway.

Cait's mind ran through the possible spells for which she might know an appropriate sign from her slim vocabulary.

Maybe she could begin with that spell that Corwin used for the teacup on their first day of class. Cait grabbed her Spellwork text from the bed. There it was: Boh-ee kos!. Looking up its translation, she realized there was one equivalent sign she could remember from that fourth-grade class, "to come over." Two hands pointed away from the signer, bring the hands up towards the face. Simple enough.

Excitement filled her. Pointing her index finger away from her while clasping the wand, she directed it toward a quill that had fallen out of her bag, formed the intention in her mind, made the sign rather awkwardly while trying to decide exactly when and how to direct the energy, and sent it through the wand. The quill gave a hop and made it halfway down the bed to her. Not much of an effect, but the spell had worked using the sign instead of speaking the word.

She tried again, forming the sign with her left hand as she did the usual wandwork with her right. Better. The quill travelled a bit further this time, but fell back when she wasn't quick enough to catch it with the left hand, still in the handshape from making the sign.

Her hands shook a little as she rubbed off the sweat that popped up. This could just work.

Now, to try a signed version of that dratted sader spell her tongue refused to do right.

Again, time to consult the Spellwork glossary: it meant to "put in order". The sign for "nice and neat," perhaps? Thankfully, that was another sign she still recalled from fourth grade. Left hand, fingers together, facing up. Right hand, fingers together, facing down. Slide the right hand against the left travelling outward.

She concentrated on the books scattered on her bed, which really belonged on the shelf above her desk. Cait visualized the books traveling there, slid one palm against the other as best she could while holding the wand, then aimed the wand at the books while sending the energy through it. Sure enough, they began to move themselves over to the desk.

Exactly then, the room door opened. Books crashed to the floor as Penny took in the scene: the apple mess, Cait's hands in midair, the scattered books.

"Girl, are you possessed or something? The way you were swimming, I didn't dare ask. And what is that?" She cast a glance and a grimace toward the exploded apple.

"I've got this really exciting idea," babbled Cait, "but I wouldn't have had it if it weren't for that horrible spellwork class, and Ms. Fletcher is going to send me a fox if she finds out anything, and you know how I've been having a really hard time with some of the spells not working at all."

Penny's bewildered face made it clear that Cait wasn't making one bit of sense.

154

Cait took a big breath. "You remember the spell I couldn't do in today's class?"

Penny nodded.

"Well, it works if I sign it instead of saying it. Watch."

Cait turned to the books on the floor, concentrated, slid palm against palm, pointed her wand, and sent the energy. This time, the books completed their journey, and lined themselves up on the shelf.

With a huge grin, Cait turned to Penny. "Ta dah!"

Penny's eyes were round with awe. "Only advanced students can make spells. You're scary good if you can do that in your first year. But what in Hecate's name is this mess?" She grimaced again as she waved at the apple.

"Uh, I lost my temper while trying to do the sader spell in here," answered Cait. "How come they haven't taught us any cleaning-up spells yet?"

Before going to dinner, Cait sent a crow to her parents, asking them to get out her old sign-language book which had been gathering dust in the living-room bookcase for the last year, and explained that a Broomcourier would stop by the house soon to pick it up.

The beat-up old paperback was in her hands at suppertime the next day, and Cait showed it off to her friends over dessert, trumpetvine in place. "We should learn these signs anyways. They'll give us a way to gab when it's too noisy to hear or when we have to be quiet," she told them.

"C'mon, where are the dirty words and the swears?" demanded Penny as she perused the well-worn book.

"Maybe we can get some cute Deaf guys to teach us more," said Meg.

The next morning, Cait awoke at dawn, too excited to sleep in. How could she get this signed-spell idea to work better? Holding a wand while signing was awkward. There had to be a solution.

Noticing that Penny was still fast asleep, Cait sat up and looked at the objects on her desk for something to experiment with. Books would be too noisy. Her cap was right on the edge, easy to see, and it won't be noisy if it fell down.

What would happen if she didn't use a wand at all? She focused on the hat, formed her intention, and made the "come-over-here" sign with both hands, and then sent the energy through her wandless hands. The hat gave a little hop.

Getting out of bed, she retrieved her wand. Maybe she could attach it to her hand somehow. Looking about the room, the hat again drew her attention; there was a ribbon right on it. Removing the ribbon, she now wrapped it around the wand and her right hand, then spent about ten minutes trying to tie it with her left hand while holding the other ribbon-end with her teeth.

There, success. Test-drive time.

She walked a few steps away from the hat, and raised her hands to make the sign.

Ka-lunk – the wand slid out of the ribbon onto the floor.

Take two. If she tied the ribbon around the wand first, and then her hand, would that work? Again, there was the ordeal of one-handed knot tying. There.

Intention – sign – aim. The wand wobbled, and the energy dissipated. Not enough control over the wand.

If the wand hung from her wrist, maybe she could make the sign, then flip the wand into her hand to hold it as usual, and direct the energy as it should go. Would that work?

Cait retied the ribbon.

Take three. Intention – sign – ouch. The wand had whipped around with her hand motion and hit her on the forehead, barely missing her eye.

Not an option.

Think, think, Cait told herself while trying to undo the knot with her left hand. Maybe if the wand were on her head, she could use a head-nod to direct the energy. Would that work?

The ribbon, wand still tied into it, went back onto her hat. Now wearing it, Cait looked around for a new object to practice on. Something light, that wouldn't make noise if she dropped it.

A writing quill. Perfect.

Intention – sign – aim – Ugh. A little of the energy got to the wand and moved the quill about an inch, but the rest of it gave her an instant headache.

What was she going to have to do? Glue that wand to her hand?

Cait flopped back onto her bed. Glue. Maybe there was a spell to make things stick to you. Maybe it could be installed into her wand the way flying spells are installed in brooms.

Grabbing her spellbook, she flipped through it. Nothing there.

In the meanwhile, maybe the ribbon idea could be improved. Cait removed the wand from her hat and retied the ribbon as it had originally been. Elastic perhaps, something she could slide on and off easily. Or maybe that magical dressmaker in the underground shop would have something even better.

In the meanwhile, she needed as many signs as she could learn. When breakfast time rolled around, Penny awoke to find Cait still immersed in her old signing book with its red and blue "ABC" on the cover.

157

Chapter 11 -- A Visual Kinetic

Monday morning, as class began, Cait proudly showed off her version of sader to Ms. Corwin, her wand held in place by a wide elastic band.

"Oh my," said Corwin, running the hem of her wide sleeve through shaky fingers as she took in the orderly desk before her. "What an unusual solution you have devised. I believe our director will be very interested in this."

Dismayed, Caitlin lowered her wand. No praise?

"That was very well done," Corwin quickly added. "It just happened to be rather unexpected. Usually, firstyear students don't have the magical power to pull off something like this. Tell me, where did you get these signs you're using?"

"From my old school. They're the ones deaf people use for talking."

Corwin went pale. "All the more reason for caution. Haven't you wondered why people use languages other than their everyday ones for spellcasting?"

"But wouldn't that be easier?"

Corwin shook her head. "Easier is not always a good idea. There are some very real dangers to having things be too easy sometimes."

The rest of the class had now arrived, and many of the students crowded nearby, trying to eavesdrop. Corwin looked around and cleared her throat. "Page 55, everyone; please review the spells listed there for tomorrow's quiz."

She faced Cait again. "Please go demonstrate your discovery to Director Lumen, exactly the way you just showed it to me. Her office is on the first floor of Old House. You have a strong gift, and she'll want to see it firsthand." As Cait closed the classroom door behind her, she saw Corwin hand a scroll to a chipmunk, who immediately raced off with it.

As she walked across the courtyard and under the Commons towards Old House, Cait couldn't help feeling nervous. Would she have to go off to some other school to study now? Would they forbid her use of sign language and make her use only spoken words? Corwin said she had a gift. Were there more classes that the firstyears hadn't yet been told about? Would she be stuck in with older students if she was already doing something firstyears weren't supposed to be able to do?

All too soon, the Director's office was before her. As soon as the door opened, Lumen's sharp gaze caught Caitlin's eye, making her feel as if she were under her aunt's old-fashioned round magnifying glass, analyzing and measuring her up in an instant. The office itself was a plain but comfortable space. Its walls were of white-painted plaster and pale pine tongue-in-groove paneling. A ship's compass stood alone in its own rosewood stand, waist-high; a large and flawless crystal ball lay cradled in shining brass in the midst of a broad oak desk. A glass-fronted bookcase of ancient-looking leather-bound tomes occupied the wall behind her desk, and a beautiful carpet in vivid reds and blues lay underfoot. Cait wondered if it could fly.

Lumen motioned Cait towards the ladderback chair in front of her desk. Cait wasn't sure who was supposed to talk first, and so she waited. It was a bright and windy day; tree branches swayed on the other side of the diamond-paned windows.

Lumen finally spoke. "So, it appears that we have a visual kinetic among us," she stated. Her voice was clear in the quiet room, and the trumpetvine remained

159

motionless on Cait's shoulders. "How did your gift become apparent?"

Cait tried not to squirm as she wondered what 'visual kinetic' meant. "I was trying to do a spell from Ms. Corwin's class."

Lumen shook her head, gave a negative hand-wave. "How was it discovered that you have magic?"

"I made a bus tire go flat."

Lumen's gaze was unrelenting. "Exactly how did you do that?"

"I got mad. A bunch of kids were teasing me" – Cait's fist clenched at the memory – "and it went pop as soon as I did this." Cait demonstrated the fist to Lumen.

"I see." A pause. The gaze. "Other times you inadvertently did magic?"

Cait supposed that she ought to tell Lumen about those leaves in fourth grade, but didn't really want to. Such a good memory, tainted. Then there was that math-class blackboard she cracked. Embarrassing. Cait looked up. "There was one time when I wanted to get a songbird away from Nini. That's my cat at home; my mom's cat really. But I was too far away, and so I did this –" Cait made a shooing motion in front of her with one hand, fingers together. "And the bird slipped out of Nini's paws, and Nini kept looking for it, but I could see that the bird was safe." Cait smiled at the memory, and then remembered where she was. Wait, was that a hint of a smile from Lumen?

"Very kinetic. Always with gesture," Lumen mused. "These things didn't happen with voice? You didn't shout or sing?"

Cait shook her head.

Lumen continued. "Most of our students use voice before they're trained, and only sometimes gesture. That's

very strong kinetics if you've not used voice, very strong."
Lumen's gaze never wavered.

After a pause, she spoke again.

"Visual-Kinetic spellwork has its own methods. Whether to bring them into an ordinary class is a complicated issue, and you will later be receiving word about how to proceed. In the meanwhile, keep on with the ordinary class."

Lumen's gaze locked with Cait's.

"I understand that you sign a little," she said.

How did she know that? Cait wondered.

"Please do not use your conversational signs for magic. It would risk trouble."

More trouble than misunderstood and mispronounced spells? Cait forced herself to nod politely while resisting the urge to blurt out her question; Lumen's stern expression left no room for discussion. Maybe Cait could ask Corwin about it later.

"Now I believe the rest of your spellwork class awaits."

Recognizing the dismissal, Cait thanked the Director and left the office with a sinking feeling. So, what was to happen now? What were these "other methods"? Would she now get more lessons and more to study? And why couldn't she even use all those signs that she had just relearned? Cait remembered how those fourth-grade Signed-English classes ate into her afterschool time, and hoped the Visual-Kinetic stuff wouldn't mess up broomsprints with Meg. Whatever "visual kinetic" meant.

As Cait walked into the classroom, she heard nineteen voices rehearsing a new spell written on the board, accompanied by the click of tapping wands.

A handful of black walnuts lay on each desk; at almost every wand tap, a perfectly split shell and a whole, naked

161

nutmeat would result. Cait was surprised at how many nuts sat on people's desks, uneaten.

"We're gonna use this spell for the halfterm clambake," Penny informed Cait as she took her seat and the trumpetvine snaked over to pick up Penny's voice among the competing sounds of wand-taps and other students' voices. "Imagine how much easier it'll be to eat lobster, and how much fun this'll be to show off. Bratty Bro will have to ask me very nicely if he wants me to shell his food."

Corwin frowned as she read a small scroll at her desk; a chipmunk nearby stuffed one of the newly shelled walnuts into its cheeks.

As she looked up and met Cait's eyes, Corwin's expression cleared. "Hello, Cait. Let me teach you this spell everyone's practicing, which is most useful for hard nuts, lobsters if you eat them, and jewelry boxes with lost keys."

As she taught the spell, Corwin sounded out the words with more than her usual care. She appeared to want to say more, but only shook her head to Cait's inquiring look.

All week long, chipmunks ran to and from the spellwork classroom, and Corwin went about with an exasperated expression. It seemed like every time Cait looked down, another chipmunk went zooming out the door. Despite the trumpetvine and the spells written on the blackboard, Corwin continued to overenunciate the new spells as she taught them. Helpful but embarrassing.

On the Monday before halfterm, as Melendez drilled them on silicates versus clay, Cait felt something nudge her foot. A chipmunk stood there waiting, with a scroll. Her pockets were still full of the black walnuts she loved; many of her classmates disliked the nut's distinctive flavor. She now gave the diminutive animal a shelled-out nut, and unrolled the scroll to read: "Please meet me at the spellwork classroom for your first Visual-Kinetic tutorial, 6 pm tonight, L.Corwin."

As the chipmunk dashed off, excitement and hope fluttered inside Cait. Would that mean that she'd no longer be stuck trying to say things she couldn't? Would Corwin finally stop over-pronouncing new spells?

Cait flew through her swimming with enough extra speed to garner scowls from Amanda and grins from Penny, who no longer dogpaddled half her circuits.

As soon as she was back in her ordinary robes, she ran across the courtyard to the Spellwork classroom. Corwin sat at her desk, two books with shimmering green covers before her, and a triumphant look on her face.

"Shall we begin?" Corwin smiled broadly at Cait. "You'll probably find these lessons quite a bit more enjoyable than fighting the letter "s" all the time. You'll spend these lessons learning the kinetic equivalents of spells we've learned thus far in class. After that, you'll be attending only the regular spellwork class, but will be learning the kinetic versions of the spells at the same time everyone else is learning the spoken versions. You were particularly needing help with 'sader'; its kinetic version is like this," and Corwin's wand traced a sort of reversing double loop and aimed it at a dropped nut, which bounced back into a bowl on her desk.

Corwin continued her explanation. "What I just did was to write the Hebraic word in the air with the Rashi script, instead of saying it out loud. So, your first step will be to visualize the word, trace it with your wand, then send the energy as usual. It's very fortunate that you've learned the script version of the aleph-bet so quickly."

Cait's hopeful mood plummeted. She was supposed to remember how all these words were spelled? When to use the sound-alike Ayin versus Aleph? Samekh versus Sin versus Shin? On the other hand, if she didn't have to pronounce them any more, maybe it would be easier to concentrate on remembering how each word looked when written. Wasn't that what she already did with English? Cait thought of all her books at home, and the spelling tests she'd aced.

Cait looked at Corwin, whose eyes were bright with hope and encouragement as she held the green book open to the sader spell and tapped the page, then nodded towards another nut which had escaped the bowl. Cait forced a smile and picked up her wand.

As they practiced, Cait had to concede that the spells were indeed more reliable with this method, even if spelling them out in full was a nuisance.

At the same time, she could not shake a creeping sense of annoyance. What good was having this kinetic gift, if it made her -- once more -- different from everyone else? The trumpetvine made her different enough. Fortunately, her new friends didn't seem to care too much. So far.

The words 'lechu na' now stood on the board in square letters, as Corwin nodded in the direction of her tea set, which sat on a desk in the middle of the room. Cait visualized her intent and then the script version of the phrase, wrote the words with her wand, sent the energy, and felt an accomplished thrill as the whole set arrived at its shelf without spilling a drop.

Corwin grinned and gestured at a tipped-over vase of flowers; a square-lettered 'sader' now stood on the board. Water seeped out from the vase and petals lay scattered on the floor. This one was going to be more complicated. Cait envisioned petals, stems, and flowers all returning to the vase, and then vase to windowsill, held that image as she saw the word 'sader' in script, traced it with her wand quickly while she could still hold the image, and sent the energy. Whew. The "tik" of vase on windowsill made Cait drop her shoulders in relief. It might be easier getting to see the spells rather than having to listen to them, but this method was going to demand every bit as much work as the regular one.

"So much better, Cait, brava!" The twinkle was back in Corwin's eye, and Cait felt as proud as she did during that perfect "lech na" spell of her first spellwork class. "That's plenty for today, I'll see you again tomorrow at 6:00."

Cait skipped all the way across the courtyard and up the Partridge Hall stairs to meet Meg. There was indeed plenty of time left for broomwork practice.

Chapter 12 – Halfterm at Last

The rest of the week flew by, the only glitch being during the next day's Spellwork class. Quahog shells floated in midair as everyone practiced a new hovering charm which was written on the board. This phrase was full of sibilant "s"s and "sh"s, and Cait celebrated inwardly at not having to say it out loud. She decided to send a second shell aloft. The first shell wobbled as she cast the spell again, but it didn't fall. Two in the air at once.

From across the room, Claire did a double-take. Her hand shot up into the air, and her voice rang out with indignation. "Wait a minute, how come she's not doing this spell the normal way?"

Shells clattered to the floor as students lost their concentration, and looked around for the cause of the disruption.

Cait's wand hand flicked downward in the sign for "stay", pinkie and thumb extended, then sent the energy to rescue her plummeting shells. Oops, had Corwin seen that? Then she lowered her wand to glare at Claire's pointed finger.

Corwin sighed as she looked at Claire, then everyone else. She gave no sign of having noticed Cait's use of Sign. "Miss Delphine's rudeness aside, spoken-word isn't the only, or even necessarily the best way to spellcast. Our dorm doors, which you know so well, are an example of that. Most witches have a strong affinity for words, therefore our spoken-word spells are the standard. Some witches, however, have stronger affinities for image and kinetics. The Visual-Kinetic technique which you see here is no lesser and no greater than the spoken spells, only different."

The teacher's gaze returned to Claire. "A one-page essay on Visual Kinetics, please. Be prepared to read it to us next class."

Looking up again, she continued. "Speaking of images, shall we practice the visualization exercise on page sixty-one?" Leftover walnut shells were soon tracing elaborate patterns in the air, as students paired off and sketched each others' flight paths.

Friday's classes seemed to take forever. Even the grownups weren't quite their usual selves as Broadleaf postponed a pop quiz in favor of telling wood-nymph stories, and Corwin made a game of everyone showing off their favorite spells. Everyone was distracted by thoughts of the night's clambake at the boys' school, the flying demonstration, tomorrow's broomball game, and the chance for students to finally see their families.

Alchemy class was the last one before the halfterm events began, and as Cait concentrated on measuring the correct number of pokeberries into her cauldron of ink, Meg babbled away. "Just wait till you see my new dress robes. The old robes were so little-kid, it's embarrassing; it's so nice to finally get something that doesn't look dorky. You should see the things I left back in the house. Frills! Pink sparkle! This one's really beautiful, real changeable silk."

Penny snorted and put down the ink-vanishing spell she was reading. "Dress robes to a clambake? They'll get full of sand and smell like fish. Save them for Saturday's banquet. Besides, I've figured out a way to shorten up our regular robes so we can still look cute and show off the last of our suntans," she said as she examined her ankles.

As soon as the bell rang, they were free to go; there was no swimming class that day.

Books flew into bags and chairs banged against desks as a torrent of students headed outside. The first magical families had already arrived, and were socializing in the October sun while classes for the day finished up. From the direction of Old House, Ms. Greatwood appeared, leading a cluster of people wearing Plain-Sight clothes.

Meg dashed out the front door to an animated tall-hatted group of two grown-ups and a muscular boy who made a face and began mock-wrestling with her. Her roommate Violet joined the group, chatting politely with the Ainslees while looking about for her own folks.

Cait and Penny remained by the door, surveying the courtyard full of strangers.

Amanda sailed up to a cluster of crisp-robed stately blondes who flashed overbright teeth and held their heads as if they were surrounded by cameras. Even a plump baby in miniature robes looked like she should be in a commercial.

Then there was Claire, picking nervously at the bright trim on her robe as she talked to a cluster of hatless grownups who shared her square jaw and wavy hair. Their robes were more brightly colored than most, and Cait wondered if they were brand new. Were those fold lines? A tall boy with hair that hung to his shoulders scowled and poked at the groundcover with the toes of his very shiny formal laceup shoes.

Where was the other third of the Magenta Trio? Cait caught sight of Elsbeth over by a quince tree. Her family wore plain black robes that hung just right and made the Delphines' robes look garish.

Then Cait saw what she was looking for.

"There's my folks," she yelled, as she ran across the courtyard. "C'mon, Penny, you can meet my parents. I'm sure your Mom'll be here soon, no matter what Stu's messed up." Cait glanced back, then paused. Was Penny crying?

"I'm okay," said Penny as she wiped her eyes, gave a small smile, and toyed with her wand. Her grandmother's wand, Cait remembered. Penny must really miss her.

But what was Cait's dad carrying? The old-fashioned domed wooden carrier topped with screening could only be one thing. "You brought Nini!" Cait squealed as she threw her arms around her parents.

"Please take this cat off our hands," said her dad with a broad grin. "She's been making it very clear for weeks that she wants to be with you."

A deep sigh came from her mom. "Screen door replaced three times. Front hall thoroughly scratched up, cat in the car whenever either of us needs to go anywhere, yowling all night long. Figured at first that she missed you and would get over it in a couple of weeks. No such luck." But she smiled as she looked down at Cait and Nini.

"Listen to that animal. She's purring right through the carrier," her dad said, shaking his head as Cait opened the door and cuddled the cat.

"Mom, Dad, this is Penny, my roommate. She has a toad for a familiar, right there in her hood. Nini, don't you dare even think of sampling toad, you hear me?"

Cait felt a gentle bump against her elbow, and turned to see a hovering tray piled high with spun-sugar-topped cookies. She reached for one, and a gentle voice announced "Cobweb cookies." The tray then floated upward to offer itself to Cait's parents and Penny. Cait stood up just as her dad accepted a glass of "Avalon Ale", and the cookies made their way to the Delphine family.

As Penny took the last piece of "Pumpkin brie" from yet another tray, Cait watched it fly off to a half-open gray door that blended in with the granite of the Commons' first floor. There, a witch in a short, pointed red hat sent the tray in through the door, peered inside, and with a flick of her wand, summoned out a new tray of cheese, keeping its path even and smooth as it floated out towards the crowd. Must be a dull job, thought Cait, hoping she wouldn't have to be stuck with it someday.

A familiar voice boomed above the chatter. "Broomracers ... at the pool ... all broomracers!" Greengage stood under the archway of the Commons with hands on hips, regarding the crowd as new families continued to arrive.

"Hey, there's my mom now. Nice to meet you, Mr. and Mrs. Leo," said Penny as she took off.

Meg appeared at Cait's side, swinging a light punch at her arm to get her attention, and motioning towards Greengage.

"Gotta run, but you'll see me soon," Cait told her parents. "I'm one of the broomracers, even with my balance. You'll see." Cait handed Nini to her mom, then sprinted to her dorm, threw her bookbag on the bed, and ran back out to the courtyard, waving to her parents on her way to the pool room. They were now in conversation with Greatwood, and Cait wondered how everyone was going to get to the clambake. Were there enough underground-river boats for everyone? Or more busses like the one that brought them to the Academy from the Schoodic?

Twenty students stood near the pool when Cait arrived. The usual boats awaited them on the double-currented river, but this time they traveled in the other direction and the trip was shorter. As the boats lifted up to the cavern ceiling, everyone stepped out onto the edge of a manicured lawn that swept up to a green-painted two-story mansion. Rusty-leaved oaks surrounded it, and the ocean shimmered to their right. The clear sky and calm air were so perfect for flying that Cait wondered if the weatherworkers had been busy making it so.

As they collected their brooms and flew over the lawn towards the water, Meg bubbled with excitement. "My brother has no idea that we've been practicing broomracing, and I haven't even told him we're in the demonstration. Bet we'll top that Amanda yet."

A crew of plain-robed people were setting up the beach for the clambake. There were driftwood logs the right size for sitting, lots of cushions, and small tables everywhere. Smoke drifted up from a dark weedy pile in the middle of the beach, and Cait's stomach rumbled at the aroma. She could tell that all kinds of wonderful food lay under that seaweed, cooking atop a bed of coals.

Off in the water, a kayaker wanded out a hovering red line that enclosed the cove.

"Your race courses will run from the dock over there parallel to the beach," announced Greengage as the group of broomriders landed around her. Meg rolled her eyes as Cait pushed her way closer to the teacher, but then followed. Halfterm was important; Cait wasn't about to risk missing any of what Greengage had to say. "We will go in order of your classes, firstyears, then secondyears, then thirdyears. Take your places, wait for the kayakers to finish setting up your race lanes, and then watch for my signal. Remember, cheating and jinxing will not be tolerated."

Greengage rocked on her heels as she surveyed the group of racers, then led them to the dock. As they went, Cait recognized the beach where they'd picnicked after disembarking the Schoodic. So this was where the boys' school was.

171

Meg elbowed her. "Teachers are such sneaks! We were looking at the boys school on our very first day and didn't even know it." Meg started to scan the grounds.

"You have ten minutes for warm-up sprints," announced Greengage. "Please keep within the red lines. Everyone land when I give the signal."

By the time they were back on dock, the beach was full of people, and small boats crowded the cove. There were going to be a lot of people watching them. Cait's stomach flip-flopped and her hands broke out into a sweat. As the upperclassers arrived and began their own warm-ups, Cait calmed her nerves by looking at them instead, and trying to figure out how high they were flying. Fear gripped her stomach as Cait remembered the end-of-year requirement to fly over Salem Harbor at midnight. Would this cove be where they'd set out? How soon would Cait be off her broom and in the harbor instead?

Out the corner of her eye she could see students from the boys' school filling the end of the dock, brooms in hand. More audience. She wished her nerves would calm down. Meg eyed them and stood taller as she held her broom.

"Upperclassers, take formation." Greengage's voice rang out.

Cait looked up to see all twelve of the upperclass students hovering in a long line. They took off in perfect unison to form a giant circle that stretched up into the sky, perpendicular to the beach. It completed three full revolutions without wobbling or breaking formation.

On cue, they split into two groups of six flyers each. A ball appeared from nowhere, and they began a series of giddy spins and turns as they kept the ball in midair. Or was it a ball? It fell too fast --- Cait then remembered Meg's broomball description and realized that it was a stone they were keeping aloft. A stone! Cait marvelled at the upperclassers' skill. They flew around in every direction imaginable as they kept the stone in volley by swatting it with the brush ends of the brooms they rode, making them look like a cross between trapeze artists and hockey players.

Ten of the students now flew off, five to each side, hovering as two seniors continued the volley, flying and volleying faster and faster until the stone became nothing but a blur. Then the blur became a burst of rainbow fireworks as the seniors joined the other flyers, and they all formed their huge circle once more before landing on the dock.

Everybody applauded loudly. Cait was pleased to note how impressed the boys were with the demonstration. So this was what broomball looked like. No wonder Meg loved it so much. How did they do all those twists and turns without falling off?

Greengage shook hands with a curly-haired man with a deep tan, then she stood aside. He waved for their attention.

"Everyone ... on the dock," he announced to all the broomriders, "the program ... soon as we have our audience." Sure enough, the beach was even more packed than it had been before. Parents, siblings, and students from both schools chattered away as they adjusted their seats for the best view.

The water became a mixed shade of lavender, bottle-green, and periwinkle, and the golden glow of late-afternoon sun slanted from behind the trees. Holding a hand to the sky, Cait gauged that there was about an hour and a half of daylight left. A rush of alarm filled her. What if the boys went first, and there wasn't enough sunlight left for girls' races? Would she have to race in the

173

dark? Would she even be able to fly at all? Please let the girls go first, please, she pleaded silently as she watched her surroundings.

A very thin man with a short white beard stood talking to the crowd as his hands waved in punctuation. Then he turned to the right and stepped off the rock that was his podium. Would they get to fly now, while there was still plenty of light?

With disappointment, Cait saw Lumen step up onto the rock and address the crowd as well. Cait couldn't understand either speech. At last, both speakers took their seats, and the crowd turned to watch the dock.

Greengage nudged the Witches' Academy flyers to their feet. Applause rose from the audience as Amanda, Cait, and Meg walked down the dock and took their places. Cait's legs shook as she went. Would she even be able to fly? She had never felt so shaky before. But at least it was still light out.

She sent her broom aloft and hovered. To her right, Meg gave her a thumbs-up, which she returned. Definitely enough light for her balance to hold steady on the broom, but her hands still quivered with nerves. You know what to do, she told herself. And you know how to do it.

Two kayakers out in the water finished creating bright-green race lanes which floated five feet above the water. They raised their arms in unison, and a shimmering red finish line hovered at the end of the lanes.

Greengage's voice rang out clearly as she raised her arm for the start signal. "On the count of three, are you ready? One ... two ... three."

And Cait was off with the others, as surely as if she'd never had a moment of trouble flying.

A quick movement flickered to her left. Amanda's sleeve fluttered, Cait's vision blurred, and she found herself immersed in the frigid waves, spitting out salt water and clutching her broom. A kayaker zipped over and pulled her aboard.

"What happened?" sputtered Cait. "I was flying just fine."

"Daydark powder," answered the kayaker through tight lips, looking furious. "The girl's claiming she forgot the stuff was in her sleeve pocket."

Overhead, Cait could see Amanda flying back to dock with an insufferable smirk. Too mad to speak, Cait signed "I hate you" double-handed. With shock, she felt the familiar spellcasting energy flow down her arm and watched as Amanda started, yelped, "Ow!" lost her balance and tumbled into the water.

The kayaker who rescued Cait raised her eyebrows and whistled. "Don't ever do that in competition; it'll get you disqualified." She signaled to the other kayaker to retrieve the surprised and seething Amanda.

During the ride back to the dock, chill fear gripped Cait's gut and her head swam. She hadn't meant to spellcast that, she didn't intend to push Amanda off her broom by signing "I hate you". She remembered Corwin's advice that "easier is not always better." And that things could and did get mixed up when the same words were using for speaking and spellwork. What if her wand had been in her hand? Visions of the exploding apple arose in her mind, and she shivered. Corwin and Lumen's advice to not use her conversational Sign for spellwork made sudden, terrible sense. What would have happened to Amanda if Cait's wand had been in her hand?

Cait shivered and shook as she climbed out of the kayak and accepted the blanket which the boys' coach threw over her shoulders with a worried look. Greengage glanced over from where she was pep-talking the secondyear racers. Cait made an "I'm OK" wave in the direction of both coach and Greengage as she sat at the beach end of the dock to huddle under the blanket and gather her wits about her. Meg also hung back with a concerned look; Cait waved at her, "Go on ahead."

Who was really going to understand this? Did other Visual-Kinetics even know how to sign? It wasn't fair – her lovely signs that worked so well. Too well. Leaving her stuck with misheard words and clumsy Visual-Kinetic longhand spelling. Square peg, round hole, whittle, whittle, shave. Why was she always the one that didn't fit? Why was it the peg that always have to be carved down? Why not change the hole instead?

She pushed the fear to the back of her mind, and waited until the shivering stopped. Then she put down the blanket, and stood up to go enjoy the clambake. Maybe food would help take her mind off her troubles.

But as Cait regarded the crowd, she felt tired and overwhelmed. How was she going to find her folks?

Then she felt something bump her shin.

"Maow – woo." Cait knew that loud voice very well. Nini looked up at the still-soggy Cait, then trotted among the crowded beach, tail high, leading Cait to where her parents pushed through the crowd towards her. Cait felt her dad's jacket being dropped onto her shoulders as her mom embraced her, then sat her down with a plate of hot food.

"Really, this isn't how she usually flies," said Penny to the Leos, pausing to give Cait a worried look. "I haven't seen Cait fall off her broom since the first week of class. There's a really good reason she was one of the three people picked out of our whole firstyear class, and it stinks that you didn't get to see it."

Ms. Dingle surveyed Cait's wet robe, and with a quick word and wandwave, removed the cold water from the fabric.

It felt wonderful to sit, warm up, admire everyone else's broomwork, and to pretend that she was as normal as the other students. Once the boys began their own broomwork demonstrations, Meg was at her side as well, poking Cait and pointing out the best broomwork and the cutest boys.

In an attempt to erase exploding-apple thoughts from her mind, Cait ate more than her share of the corn, lobsters, clams, mackerel, and baked potatoes which emerged from under that heap of seaweed. There were even pots of bean-hole beans emerging from the pit, bottoms of the pots glowing red in the dark as they floated around the beach, offering themselves to anybody still hungry. They were then followed by a series of pies: apple, squash, mincemeat, custard.

This time, their plates were white with flashing bits of blue and purple. Cait guessed that they might be shell, and was proven right when her surprised dad went to pick his plate up for a second piece of pie and found only a mussel shell where his plate had been.

"Hey Dad, watch Mom's plate when she puts it down," said Cait. As soon as her mom let go of it, the plate shimmered and became a mussel shell with glowing mother-of-pearl inside, and a trickle of sand.

Once everyone was stuffed full of clambake and pie, it was fully dark, and a spectacular set of fireworks crowned the evening's events.

Exploding apples and tumbling broomriders were far from Cait's mind by next night's Halfterm banquet. The Commons was full of crystal-cased candle flames, silver streamers that snaked themselves around the room,

177

catching flashes of light along the way, and lengths of blue and black silk draped through the rafters. By now, all of the firstyear students were radiant in their dress robes, whose bright silks blended with the formal wear of the non-magical guests.

Halfway through some of the best roast beef and new potatoes Cait had ever tasted, Penny nudged her, a conspiratorial look on her face. A cupped hand at her mouth, she signed to Cait, "Your glass – over here!" Cait leaned in and pulled her hovering trumpetvine to a less obvious spot. "Shh," said Penny through the trumpetvine, "I've been waiting to show this off." She pulled a small bottle from her pocket and poured a pale gold liquid into Cait's glass, then some into her own.

Checking that their parents were still deep in conversation with each other, then keeping eye contact with Cait, Penny raised her glass slightly, and said, "To the class of 2014! Don't you dare stop at hedge level – I plan to do all seven years and want you there. Oh, Meg," Penny kicked under the table to get Meg's attention, "You too. Let's toast ... seven years at Witches' Academy."

Meg shook her head. "I'll toast to Hedge, not seven."

Penny turned her hopeful gaze to Cait.

"I'll keep you company." Guilt prickled at Cait. What business did she have, promising to finish all seven years, if she didn't even know that she could make it to secondyear? If only there weren't that night-flying requirement. Nobody believed that she really couldn't balance in the dark. On the other hand, she wanted to complete all seven, so that part was honest. "Here's to earning those tall, pointy seven-year hats," Cait said.

Penny smiled and downed her glass, and Cait followed with caution. It tasted like plain grape juice, and she looked at Penny in puzzlement.

Penny shrugged. "That first Greenwitchery class –
remember the mess? That was Broadleaf's self-fermenting
grape. Good news: your accidental 'mayim' spell works on
these grapes, and that's how I got the juice. Bad news: it
won't ferment outside the grape. Over-smart teacher."
Penny scowled at her glass.
"You're bad," admired Cait.

Sunday, October 28, 2007
Partridge Hall, Witches' Academy,
Salem MA

Dear Aunt May:
I hope your halfterm was great! Mine was, mostly.
We spent all of Saturday afternoon watching our first real
broomball game. We got to ride the Schoodic out there
because it was played over the ocean, and all these people
got to watch it from flying canoes, but we were on floating
bleachers. The team we played against came all the way
from Quebec City, and their ship was this huge thing with
square sails that looked exactly like a pirate ship. Yo ho
ahoy!
And because my ears messed up on Saturday, we get to go
to a pro broomball game. We're all sitting around, Penny
and Meg and me and our families. Even Nini, who's been
following me around everywhere. Meg and her brother
Merle are yakking about broomball, and then I think he's
talking about "Seattle Signers". What?? Nope, it's really
the "Seattle Spiders", but he's going to buy us tickets, and
we'll all get to go out to Fitchburg in November and see a
real professional broomball game. Yay!
And Penny's all worried that her senior year's going to be
ruined, because it turns out her brother has the Gift, too.
This little kid told somebody's broom "shemayma," and up

179

it went on the very first try. Lucky kid. Must be nice to have normal ears. So Penny was all grumpy, until I pointed out how lucky we are that our school's all girls, and that the boys are all stuck out on Winter Island.

Meg's still all down on herself about studies and thinks she'll quit after Hedge. I wish she wouldn't. Do most people finish all seven years? Does your teacher know?

Speaking of flying, I saw this kind of flying that people at the Academy never even heard of. It was late on Saturday night, when the magical families were all flying home. (Mom and Dad stayed at a hotel in Salem and drove home this morning.) Most everyone had taken off, and I was on my way to the dorm, when I see Amanda's friend Claire off to one side of the courtyard, with her family. This is the girl with the fancy robes that change all the time. Well, there she was, having this fight with her family; I notice it because she's got this flashy trim on her robes, and she was waving her arms around, and it really showed up. Then I hear her yell "I'm happy here, OK?" and they all talk quieter, but still waving arms and looking ticked off. And I'm wondering where else would she be? She's got a French last name; maybe she's supposed to be up at the Quebec school or something? Then this longhaired guy who looks like he could be her big brother pulls the shoes right off his feet and throws them on the ground and yells "you can have your white-man shoes." But that's not even the weird part.

At this point, everyone stands still for a moment and stares at each other. I'm at the Partridge Hall door and about to go in. Then I realize that they haven't got any brooms! How are they going to get home? Then Claire's family forms this little circle, and everyone reaches into some little pocket or pouch by their waist, takes out something pinched in their fingers, holds it up in their

180

palms, and I see the wind carry off this little bit of smokey something. Next thing, they're all taking out feathers, these big long grand feathers, just a bit larger than our very best writing quills. Each of them is holding up one feather in their wand hand, up to the sky, and I hear a bit of chanting. Then up they go, everybody lifting up into the sky with their feathers.

Have you ever heard of this feather-flying? I hope you have, because neither Penny or Meg knows a thing about it. You think they would, with all the magical tourists that visit Penny's mom's shop from everywhere. Or Meg's weatherworking sister who's in Europe this week and China next week and Mexico last week and so on. And Meg of course, knows almost everything about broomsports and flying. So how come they don't know about this? I bet I could night-fly this way, if I could learn it. Then I won't have to worry about being stuck at firstyear anymore. And if you tell me it was all some weirdo dream, I won't write to you anymore.

OK, I have to go do homework now. Write back soon!

Love, your onliest niece,

Cait

Cait awoke abruptly the next morning, as ten pounds of surprised cat landed on her. She opened her eyes to see Penny glaring furiously at her in the semidarkness of dawn, something cradled in her hands.

"You keep that cat away from my Nicky," she growled. "I caught her right on the terrarium, trying to open the lid. Real familiars don't do things like that. If Nicky's panic hadn't woken me up, he'd probably be gone by now. So learn how to control her. If she's even a real familiar, that is." And with that, Penny wheeled about, threw on her robes, and left with a slam of the door.

181

Cait looked at Nini, who was still standing big-eyed where she'd landed. "Oh Nini, you've ruined everything. You want to get shipped back to Central Massachusetts? You can't hunt other people's animals." She tried to glare at the cat, but couldn't stay mad at those big eyes. As she patted Nini, she wondered, how did people keep all the animals on this campus from eating each other? Could Penny be right? If Nini weren't a real familiar, would she be even allowed to stay here? Would Cait have to watch this cat every minute?

"Leash time," she declared, and reached for the leash clipped to the handle of Nini's carrier. Nini began a low growl that thrummed through Cait's fingers as she attached the harness around Nini. "Stop growling. You were a bad girl. You'll only get to hunt when I say it's okay."

Nini sulked and belly-crawled halfway to the Commons, but was walking normally by the time they entered the room, where Penny sat in the furthest corner. Whenever Cait sent a Mindcast her way, it ricocheted as if off a steel wall, and it stayed that way all through Greenwitchery class.

While Ms. Broadleaf illustrated plant-drying techniques on the blackboard, Cait looked around the room to see what other people's familiars were up to. A plump black cat napped under one chair. Amanda's crow rearranged some gravel that had fallen off the potting bench, and the green snake sat coiled up on her owner's desk. To her relief, there was one other animal on a leash, a golden-brown and white ferret that darted out of a bookbag to retrieve a nearby dropped quill, then put it in the bag and curled up inside, chin resting on the edge. Cait hoped the ferret was returning the girl's own quill and not stealing somebody else's.

182

By the time they arrived in Spellwork class, Cait decided to try one more Mindcast to Penny. Steel wall. Cait sighed. Maybe this really was a Zoomorphia question, but she couldn't stand the thought of having to wait until Wednesday's class to ask Graycliff. Her hand went up as the last of the students trickled into the room and took their seats. "Ms. Corwin, what keeps all the animals in this room from hunting each other?" With her other hand, she held Nini on her lap.

"A fine question, excellent question," answered Corwin, "and one that gets asked by somebody every semester, guaranteed." Penny looked up with interest, but still avoided eye contact with Cait. "In some fortunate cases, the mind-link between animal and person is so strong, that there is no need for the person to have to explain out loud to the animal what to do and not to do, so to speak."

Mind-link? Was this something like Mindcasting? Cait wished she knew what Corwin was talking about. To her right, Penny nodded in understanding as Corwin went on. "In other cases, however, like in so many magical arts, person and animal both need to learn how to do this, which takes time and practice. And strategic use of leashes and carriers." Cait double-checked Nini's harness with relief.

"What about all those messenger chipmunks running around?" asked the townie with the snake. "Tulia hasn't even been interested in them, which is really weird for her."

"It's a simple glamour spell," answered Corwin. "It's in the Zoomorphia curriculum, so you'll be learning it soon. We can't perceive it, but to other animals, those chipmunks have a hideous and very unappetizing smell. Shall we continue with today's lesson? Who had trouble with the weekend practice set?"

Cait sighed as she stroked Nini, then took out her spellbook. It was going to be a very long two days until Zoomorphia class.

Chapter 13 – Extended family

"Wow, I want to fly like those Maenads," said Cait as she and Meg sat down to breakfast the following Wednesday. "That halfterm game was great. I'm sure glad the weather wasn't this cold then." An iron pot swung her way from the kitchen and hovered at her shoulder. Cait blinked in surprise. "How come we get flying food today? It's not even a holiday yet."

"Real Irish porridge like this gets nasty if it sits on a buffet getting cold, so they don't let it," said Meg. "It's good. Have some."

Even though Penny was still mad at her, Cait thanked the stars there was Meg. Take that, old public school. No more eating alone while other cliques gave her strange looks and gossiped behind their hands.

Cait looked over to where Penny, Minna, and Keisha sat talking. Penny didn't seem to be so mad any more, but when was she going to start talking to her again? Every night, Cait locked Nini into her carrier at bedtime, where she stayed until Penny and Nicky had left the room the next morning. The rest of the time Nini was on a leash attached to Cait's hand. And maybe today Graycliff would teach them that anti-predation glamour, so that Nicky would be safe from Nini once and for all.

Cait decided to try sending one more Mindcast of apology. To her surprise, instead of hitting a steel wall, it felt more like pushing on a heavy door. And Penny actually turned and looked at her before going back to her conversation with Minna.

Cait turned back to Meg. "You remember the volley where the Maenads got a dozen points before dropping the stone and flew just like this?" – whip, whip, whip, she demonstrated with a zigzag motion of her spoon.

185

"Stop, you're throwing oatmeal," said Meg, putting her hands over her face. "Yeah, that was a good game. Just wait until you see the pros play."

Cait dug into her oats, made a face, then reached for the butter. At her feet, Nini head-butted Cait's shin for her share. As Cait put a saucer of buttered oats onto the floor for her cat, a thought struck her. "Do broomracers have to be broomball players too? I don't think I'd be too good at broomball."

Meg shook her head as she sectioned her neatly Shell-out bespelled orange. "Not really possible to do both. Broomball and racing both go on all year, and it's really hard to get enough practice space for both teams, so whenever the space can be found, they double up the teams on it. It's really crazy how they arrange it so that the racers and the players don't collide during practice."

"And we have to wait all year till we get to do any of it," grumped Cait as she finished off her oatmeal, then watched Meg polish off her orange and begin nibbling the empty peel.

"You're way too hungry."

Meg shrugged. "They put the peels into marmalade, don't they? Why not eat it?"

Cait toyed some more with her oatmeal. "They'd better not hold me back for not being able to night-fly, either. I hope Greengage has something to help."

"They're not going to hold you back," said Meg. "Everybody night-flies. Now as for me, I'll be lucky to not flunk Greenwitchery. I'm going to be outta here as soon as I hit Hedge."

"Don't you dare," said Cait. "If I survive night-flying, you can survive hitting the books more. I'm not going to be stuck all alone putting up with Amanda Almighty."

"And you're too obsessed with night-flying," said Meg. "Relax. This school knows what it's doing."

Cait poked at her cooling oatmeal. "Yeah, we'll see. And what if Greengage doesn't figure out a way for me to night-fly after all? Like the other things they don't get. What's it going to take to get people to stop calling me 'Molasses' in Spellwork class?"

"Maybe your kinetic method's not so fast, but at least you don't get the spells wrong anymore," offered Meg. "You'll still get an A and I won't."

"How do you know? You're too gloomy," answered Cait. And the meal was finished in cold silence.

Back in her dorm room, Cait laid her spellwork book on her desk and scanned the list of words before her, while Nini curled up at the foot of her bed, still attached to the leash, just in case Nicky or a messenger bird showed up. Shalhevet, shemayma, shamayim me'aal. All these words which she kept misspelling in class. Making her slower than slow as voices echoed around her, and the occasional note landed on her desk. "Molasses, slower than cold molasses." "Caity Molasses. Cait the speeding flood of molasses."

Shamayim me'aal reminded Cait of the mistake with all the water in Corwin's class. That might be a useful skill. Could she do it on purpose? Her glance fell on the plant on her windowsill. It was her Greenwitchery homework, and she had again forgotten to water it. Penny told her that mints were greedy when it came to water, and this one was no exception. The leaves were curled up into sharp little daggery shapes, which whenever the plant got thirsty. Cait checked the mug on her desk, finding water inside.

But first, she needed to get the spelling right. Leaving her wand in its pocket, Cait traced the word "mayim" with fingertip, following the spelling in her book. Mem, Yod, final Mem. Then she took out her wand, concentrated on the water in the mug as well as the path it should take, and began to trace the word. Mem, Ayin ...

Stop. There's no Ayin in this word.

Again. Concentrate. Mem, Yod, Mem, aim. Her concentration dissipated; had she used the right form of Mem, the final one? Impatience filled her. Why couldn't she use the ASL sign for "water"? So much simpler, one handshape, tap her chin, finished. How could she possibly harm anyone with the sign for "water"? It wasn't like the "I hate you" sign which was obviously dangerous.

Slipping the elastic band onto her hand, she put the wand into place and gathered her intent. Then she signed the "w" handshape with pinkie tucked under thumb, tapped her chin twice, and aimed.

As she watched, the water picked itself up, a crystalline globe in the sunlight, and poured itself right into the thirsty soil. After a moment, the plant's sharp leaves unfolded into harmless flat ovals, and Cait could almost hear it scolding her. "About time you did that, missy." She hadn't realized that one could Mindread a plant. Could one? All the same, this spell was a keeper.

On their way to the Hallowe'en banquet that night, Cait and Meg rigged up wreaths of flaming maple leaves to wear on their student caps as they decided to not talk about grades or night-flying until, say, February. Even Nini's collar and leash were garlanded with miniature Japanese-maple leaves. Cait wasn't about to let her off leash until she knew that the new Zoomorphia spell really worked.

As they walked into all the chatter and bustle of the Commons, something small and dark fluttered in front of Cait and then swooped into the rafters. Looking up, she could see that the air was full of motion; every bat in the school was flapping its way about the rafters of the Commons. Cait loved watching the bats' erratic flight, but wasn't as fond of the jack o'lanterns that lit the hall. As one of them swooped right over Cait's head, the shifting light made her feel as if the floor had swayed suddenly, and she had to grab a chairback to regain her balance.

As Cait and Meg took their seats, more pumpkins appeared, only to hover at their tables. These contained pumpkin-apple soup, accompanied by colorful gourd ladles for serving it. And to Cait's surprise, Penny came over from across the hall and sat with them.

"Are we friends again?" offered Cait.

Penny made a noncommittal wave. The trumpetvine flew over as she said, "Let's just say Nini's on probation until forever." Then she started toying with silverware and napkin, reaching up into her hood from time to time to stroke Nicky, while glancing over at Nini.

Cait gave herself and Nini some soup and decided to sign to Meg, "Want some, yes? No?" Something dark plummeted in front of her, and she found herself returning the gaze of a small brown bat which sat with folded wings beside a bowl of toasted pumpkin seeds, blinking at her. Cait looked at Meg, who shrugged.

Penny raised her eyebrows pointedly at Cait.

Exam time for Nini and Cait. Were all these bats Graycliff's way of testing if they'd learned that anti-predation glamour properly in class?

Cait pulled out her wand, formed her intent, and wrote the spell V-K style as small as she could manage, so as to not startle the bat. Then she sent the energy.

Nini looked up at Cait's glance, sniffed the air, and lost interest. Then she yapped and pawed Cait's leg for her share of the soup. "Of course, of course," said Cait with relief, as she put the saucer before her cat.

At that moment, Andreya walked by and saw the bat. "Oh, how cute!" She leaned over to pet it, but it only hissed at her, while continuing to watch Cait. With a shrug and a smile she sat at the next table.

The bat sat there until dessert, watching Cait through furled-up wings, picking up its head every time Cait or Meg picked up their hands to fingerspell some word gone missing in all the noise, or to describe a broomball move, or the way birds flitted around during Zoomorphia observation.

Just like the bat, Penny remained completely quiet and didn't make even one joke about Broadleaf's frazzlement or Graycliff's glasses. Too weird. Cait was glad to have her nearby, but this total silence? Enough was enough.

Cait began to balance pumpkin seeds on the edge of Penny's plate. Wand out, Lech na! spelled out in tiny motions, energy sent. Seed number one. No reaction. Another one, tottering atop the first. Penny still spooned up soup, oblivious, even though everyone else was now digging into lasagna, Nini included. Another seed. By the time eight seeds sat wobbling one atop the other, Penny finally noticed them, looked up and put her face in her hands. Then uncovered her eyes and took a deep breath.

"Gotcha," said Cait. "Are you back with us?" The trumpetvine floated over to catch Penny's reply as the pumpkin-seed tower toppled over.

"It's the annual Thin-Veil Social tonight, after dinner. And I've been stupid about my own friends. And I don't want to feel stupid when I visit Gramma."

"I'm lost here."

"We get to talk with the dead." Penny said, momentarily interrupted as pies and hot cider began their rounds of the Commons. One tear ran down her cheek. Cait's mind reeled during the pause. Talk with dead people – and they call it a social? Did Penny really say that? According to Aunt May, it was always the ghosts who approached the living, never the other way around. And their stories were always unhappy, involving murder, illness, or betrayal. Why go talking to ghosts on purpose?

Once pecan pie and cider were before her, Cait asked, "Did I hear you right? You go have a social with the dead? On purpose?"

Penny sniffled and nodded. "It's an upper-level mindcasting technique, but easiest to do on Hallowe'en. My mom always visits the great-aunts and uncles and her own gramma then, and she told me all about how Witches' Academy does it too. But I really wish I had someone to come along with me. Ghosts like meeting new people, and they hate it when everyone just sits and cries. They like to meet new people too, but Minna's not the kind of person who's up for that. And Keisha's got her own reunion tonight. I shouldn't have stayed so mad at you, Cait."

Meg became very interested in her pie, snagging a second piece when the pie plates made another circuit around the hall.

Cait could feel her heart pounding. This was the first time she'd lost a friend ... and then got her back after all. But socializing with ghosts? Was this what it took to put a friendship back together? What was she getting into? Cait remembered how Aunt May finished all of her ghost stories with the same warning: "Ghosts envy life, but the otherworld is where they really belong. May you never become haunted, and don't go seeking out ghosts."

Then Cait remembered that it hadn't been very long since Penny's grandmother had died, only last summer. There was only one answer Cait could give to Penny now.

"I'll go with you," Cait said.

Penny looked up in surprise. "No way."

Cait signed "true", then crossed her heart.

Flames crackled in both of the Commons fireplaces and the smell of wood-smoke filled the room. As people finished their desserts, some left for the dorms, while others began to congregate at the warm hearths.

"I haaate my homework," said Meg as she got up to go. "You'll find me back at the dorm. Welcome back, Penny. Good luck with the social."

The bat at Cait's place looked up at her one final time, yawned, stretched its wings and fluttered up to the rafters. From the chair Meg had just vacated, Nini paused from washing one leg to cheep in frustration at the fluttering bat overhead. But she did not go into sharp-eyed hunting mode. "You're a very good girl, Nini," said Cait, as she scooped up the cat.

Penny scanned the clusters of people heading towards the two fireplaces. "Mom told me to look for orange hats," she said. Sure enough, some of the upperclass students and several teachers wore orange versions of their usual caps and tall hats and now stood at the two fireplaces, awaiting the beginning of the Thin-Veil Social.

Penny and Cait got up and headed over to the less-crowded of the two fireplaces. Ms. Auclair stood nearby, supervising the proceedings. Around them, people were clustering in twos and threes with the orange-capped mediums. Soon, the clusters contained three, four or even five figures, the newcomers silver and blurry as if seen through a scrim.

An alabaster-complexioned upperclasser now caught their eye, and the girls walked over to her. Her hat had the slightly-flared brim that those beyond Hedge level earned; it was half the height of the seniors' hats. "Who do you want to call over?"

"My grandmother, Penelope White," said Penny in a low, nervous voice. She looked pale and trembly. Cait put a hand on her arm, although she herself had no idea what to expect, and Nick gave a reassuring ribbit from his usual spot within the folds of Penny's hood.

The orange-hatted girl smiled. "I'll call over Penelope White, then." She closed her eyes, and began singing a chant which Penny apparently knew, as she joined in after a few notes. Soon, another silvery figure took form before them, gaining shape and details gradually, like watching a rainbow stretch itself across the sky. A smiling, short, round woman in a voluminous cloak stood before them. Penny gasped and choked down a sob.

Cait could see a dim glint of something with a familiar shape at the old woman's throat – a trumpetvine! No wonder Penny was so good at not mumbling and always remembered to face Cait when she talked. It had taken lots of nudging to get Meg to understand those things.

The woman glanced around, and nodded. "So, the Commons still looks just as it did when I was here. Well, Penny, how do you like Witches' Academy? Are you happy here? And you look like they feed you enough. Growing like a weed as always, just like you should."

"Oh, Gramma, I'm so glad I can see you! School is going great, I like my classes so much, and this is my roommate, Cait." Cait waved at her, supposing a handshake might not work. Penny continued, "Cait's never visited with ghosts before, and we get along great, although she has a cat and we just had a scare with

193

Nicky. But we've figured all that out now." She shot Cait a brief glare.

"It sounds like magical life agrees with you." The old witch chuckled.

"Oh, and your wand is working just fine for me, no problem at all ..." and as Penny continued her conversation with her Gramma, Cait abandoned the effort to understand their speech among the hubbub of all the chattering voices. At first, she simply enjoyed watching the bats swooping and fluttering overhead, while Nini completed her bath.

Then Cait looked around at the rest of the room. The Commons was now as full of people as it had been during the banquet, only half of them were silvery shimmering shades. The ocean of indecipherable babble washed over her, along with the lights of the still wandering jack o'lanterns. It wasn't creepy or scary at all; it was just another kind of family reunion. She was going to have to ask Aunt May if she were learning about thin-veil socials, too. It was time to send her another note. Especially since Aunt May hadn't yet answered Cait's question about feather-flying.

A raised voice to Cait's right cut through the conversational hum.

"What do you mean, you can't bring him over?" Cait had to grab her trumpetvine, which swung over to this new noise, to keep it from making her look like a blatant eavesdropper. "But he's my dad and I miss him!" shouted an upperclass girl as tears flowed down her face.

"I'm sorry," said the orange-hatted girl with her, as Auclair hurried over. "Not all spirits want to be pulled back ... should not force them to if they don't want it."

"But doesn't he miss us? How could he not want to come over?" whimpered the girl as Auclair took her off to a quieter corner. Cait felt a chill that reminded her of Aunt May's grimmest ghost stories. What if someday Cait wanted one more moment with someone and couldn't get it? She shivered and went back to watching the people around her.

As she watched the round silvery ghost nearby, Cait couldn't help but wonder if Penny were friends with her just because she was hard-of-hearing, and Penny knew what to do around hard-of-hearing people. No, Cait thought. Sorry-for-you folks didn't sit around giggling about Broadleaf's runaway vines being just like her frazzly hair, or swap stories about stupid summer tourists, or take turns inventing pompous speeches for Greatwood.

And after this misadventure with Nini, why would Penny ever even want to talk to her again? What made her come back? How did Cait get that kind of luck?

"Pardonnez-moi." The trumpetvine lifted and Cait looked up to see Ms. Auclair at her side. "You have learned well with that new spell in class today. But you and your familiar should have more of a mind-link by now. Remember that we do not allow mere pets at this Academy." And Auclair was off again with a Mindcast of warning, as another orange-hatted girl waved her down from across the room.

Cait remembered Penny's angry words on Monday morning. What if Nini weren't a real familiar after all? But then why would the cat have wanted so badly to be with her in Salem?

Cait realized that many of the shades were now noticeably dimmer and more blurred. She turned her attention back to Penny and Penelope; the alabaster-complexioned girl had long ago gone to call up shades for other students. Penelope, too, was becoming dim and blurry.

195

"The otherworld is pulling me back now, dear," she told Penny. "Don't worry, and don't cry! We will have other visits, so bye for now!"

"G'bye, love you, Gramma!" shouted Penny as the old woman vanished; she was smiling, but Cait could also see tears on her face.

Weed Haven
Northern Kingdom VT
November 1, 2007
My dearest Cait:
What a lot of surprises the magical world holds for us! Who knew that there would be such a thing as a thin-veil social? Not for me, I'm afraid, even though I'm glad that you enjoyed your social in Salem. Perhaps next year I shall try it with Joyce. But I shall have to ask her very, very politely. Knowing how I feel about humans contacting ghosts, she very well may think I've lost my mind and refuse to socialize.

You do have an exceptional ability to find out about unusual things! Most of the folks up here have never heard of this feather-flying you describe. One gentleman I know claims to not know anything about it, but I doubt that he is telling the truth; there is fogginess when I Mindcast him. What a delightful skill Mindcasting is turning out to be.

My herb patch is growing up to the sky, and a pair of redtail hawks have started to hang out around that red oak that you have always wished you could climb.

Perhaps they heard me wishing for another letter-carrying bird?

Keep up with your good studies, and all the best to your new friends.

With love,

Your weirdly witchy Auntie May

Chapter 14 -- A Broomball Surprise

Classes continued as usual until the morning of November 16th, when a crow flew into the dorm-room window to land on Cait and Penny's pillows and deliver the day's schedules. This time, however, both girls woke up remembering the Fitchburg game, and jumped up from bed, yelling, "Game day!" "Field trip!" "Woohoo!" The startled bird, accustomed to sleepy protests, flew frantically around the room, dropping their scrolls on the floor before escaping via the window birdflap.

Cait noticed with alarm that Nini sat with perked-up ears, wide alert eyes, and her tail swishing back and forth. Had somebody forgotten to put the anti-predation glamour on that bird? Or was that supposed to be their responsibility now that they knew how? Then Nini began to wiggle her rear in preparation to pounce, even though the bird was already outside.

"Nini, no!" shouted Cait, as her right hand flew out in the sign for "stay", thumb and pinky out. The cat turned her gaze to Cait and meowed in protest.

"You'll get to go hunting soon, promise," Cait told her.

Despite the fact that it was a Wednesday-Friday schedule, and they were stuck on campus until Astronologia, the buoyant mood continued. Broomwork was especially fun. When Greengage gave them a ten-minute break, there was a tap on Cait's shoulder.

"Hey Cait, watch this," said Meg. Her broom climbed the air in a series of fishtail shimmys before she zoomed back down to stop exactly six inches from the end of Cait's broom."That's the Brindisi maneuver. He used to rack up so many points with it before the other teams all learned to copy him. Took me six months of practice before I could pull that off without falling. Wait till you see Brindisi, too. Cutest player on the Flitters team."

At long last, Astronologia class was over, and they could hand in their star charts, grab bags and familiars, and head for the Partridge Hall roof. It was a clear, calm night, but chilly. The three girls shivered as they huddled in their cloaks and hoped Louise wouldn't be late. From Penny's hood came a soft burbling sound. "Nicky's telling us it's gonna be great flying weather," announced Penny as she reached back to stroke the toad. What's it like to have a mind-link with an animal? Cait longed to ask her. But then Penny might start accusing Nini all over again of not being a real familiar, and that would ruin everything. So Cait kept quiet.

Cait saw it first: a movement in the air, a sort of ripple, no more than a shimmer in the dark sky, darkness against darkness. There was no object there that they could see. But a definite and deliberate motion approached them all the same. As the amorphous dark-against-dark shimmer crossed the boundary of the school's airspace, the darkness peeled away, and a canoe emerged onto the rooftop, steered by a willowy blonde who had one hand on the boom of a pale gray sail. Nini arose from where she'd sat in front of Cait, bristled and backed up, mashing herself against Cait's ankles. Cait could feel her growling. "It's okay, Nini, it's like cars, just another way to get around." As she patted and spoke, Cait could feel Nini's growl diminish even as the cat stayed pressed against her.

Louise set the canoe down lightly on the roof, jumped out of it, and embraced Meg. "Baby sis, you're a real witch now. How do you like Salem? Sorry I couldn't get away to see you at halfterm. Hello, you must be Penny and Cait, yes? So good to meet you, I'm Louise."

Meg looked disappointed. "We don't get to broomride?" Cait was amazed that Meg didn't protest being called "baby sis."

"Meggie, you're still a newbie. Can't have you pitching overboard halfway there because you've never flown so far, can we? Besides, you haven't even learned night-flying yet. Do you all have your stuff? Be sure to hold on tight while we're in the air, bags go under the seats. And remember that we can't talk – wind carries voices a long ways, and we can't break Plain Sight." Nini had cautiously crept forward while Louise was talking, and now sniffed all around the edges of the canoe, with whiskers quivering.

Cait waited until Nini had finished her examination of the canoe before picking her up and stepping in. As she did so, the cat growled again and clung to her, claws digging into Cait's lap. Cait held her firmly with both hands as she spoke into her ear, "It's okay, this is how we travel here." She wished she knew for sure if Nini were really a familiar or not. When would she know? How would she know?

"Shemayma!" called Louise, and the canoe lifted up into the night. She then spoke an unfamiliar spell, full of fluid syllables, and a breeze filled the sail, sending them westward over roofs and roads. Almost immediately, Louise began pitching Daydark powder around them, making the view momentarily go blurry and dim. Cait remembered the moving dark on dark of her arrival, and wondered if that was what the boat now looked like to the nonmagicals below.

Once away from town, however, Louise put aside the pouch of Daydark powder, and a moonlit landscape unfurled below them. Rolling hills stretched out, with shimmering rivers twisting in between them. A bright line of highway carrying its mechanical rivers of cars cut through masses of lacy treetops.

Every so often, a bird or bat would flutter past the canoe, while Cait tightened her grip on the cat in her lap. Nini sat with ears swiveled, eyes focused, and legs tensed as if to jump, but Cait could also feel her shake, and knew that she was nervous about being so high up in the air.

"It's all right, Nini," she whispered into the cat's ear.

In front of her, Cait saw Meg turn around with a bright smile. "Isn't this great? Wait 'till we're over Salem Harbor – "

"Shhh! Can't talk now," hissed a voice behind her, and Cait turned to see Louise glaring at her sister, finger to lips. Meg mimed zipping her lips, then hunched down in her seat, staring at the view below.

Cait's nerves jangled. Night-flying. Salem Harbor. Worry about that next semester, she told herself. This view's too beautiful to ruin by worrying. Not having to listen to anything for a while is great, too. A bright flash to her left caught her eye, and Cait looked down to see a shimmering "s"-shaped pool reflecting bright trails of moonlight, and immersed herself once more in the passing landscape.

Then a burst of Daydark powder obliterated the view, startling Cait. They were there already? She wished the trip were longer. The canoe begin to descend, and landed in a backyard ringed with trees. A river shone just beyond the trees, and a lit-up house full of Ainslees awaited their arrival, ushering them inside, taking cloaks, dishing out hot soup, and showing them to their room.

The skies were gray and overcast the next morning as everyone boarded the Ainslee canoes at their tiny backyard dock.

201

"What if the game gets rained out?" asked Cait as she untangled the trumpetvine from her cloak fastenings.

"No way," said Penny, as she stroked Nicky, who sat on her palm. "This one disappears into my deepest, darkest pockets whenever the weather's bad. We'll be fine."

"Our games don't get rained out," said Meg, as she stepped into the front of her canoe and put a rolled-up bundle of red fabric by her feet. "We did get hail one time, but that turned out to be a weather hex gone wrong because one witch tried to make a snow flurry happen whenever the Flitters got points. Only she got the spell wrong. And whenever the weather's iffy, the town's wizard Council sends two weatherworkers to divert the worst of it downriver. They haven't had to cancel a game since I was little."

Under a giant maple to the left of the house, Cait saw something coming her way. Nini held the plume of her tail high as she marched across the lawn, carrying what? She dropped a deep-gray object at Cait's feet, looked up, and yapped at Cait. Oh gross, a mole. Cait made herself smile. "Good girl, Nini."

With a flurry of her ruffled cloak, Mrs. Ainslee stood beside Cait. "Oh, what a good hunter your cat is, so talented as well as beautiful. Will she let me pat her?"

"Of course."

For the next few moments, Mrs. Ainslee bent over the cat, chucking her chin, scratching behind her ears, and gabbing constantly. "... yes, excellently good cat you are ... hunt all you like ... beautiful and you know it ... garden eaten up ... whole family of woodchucks ... fat ones ..." Then she gave Nini one more pat, winked at Cait, and headed off to her own boat, as Nini trotted back to the maple, tail high, to settle into the grass, and see them off.

202

Cait figured that Nini was going to have her own version of a great day.

Cait now stepped into the canoe behind Meg, Penny following. Merle already sat in the back to steer. Louise, her parents, and a wizard friend from two houses over shared another canoe, steered by Mrs. Ainslee. Cait looked about the inside of the canoe as they settled in; there was no sign of the sail which had propelled them to Fitchburg last night. As Merle and Mrs. Ainslee raised their paddles in unison, a current began to flow under their canoes and carry them against the river's natural flow – the game's location was upstream. Meg looked back from the front of the canoe. "You two do have to paddle, even with this spell. Still gotta Hide in Plain Sight. Just follow me. Cait, you paddle on the left whenever I paddle on the right and vice versa. Penny, you copy me exactly."

For about ten minutes, the ride was pleasantly uneventful, with other canoes, rowboats, and kayaks joining them from time to time in their upstream journey.

Then a white wall of water arose before them. A waterfall? How were they going to paddle over that? Cait glanced over her shoulder towards the back of the canoe. Merle, however, only grinned at Cait's look of dismay. With a quick look around to make sure no Plods were nearby, he turned the canoe sideways to the current, intoned a quick spell, and the canoe lifted itself to the top of the falls, and the other Ainslee canoe followed.

Two waterfalls later, the river became much more crowded, and traffic slowed to a stop. There were not only the usual canoes and kayaks, but also rafts, jetskis, and a swanboat apparently filched from the Boston public garden. Meg turned around again. "This is it, we're here."

Cait looked at the riverbanks where people were gathered in large clusters; around them were only weeds, with a couple of shabby warehouses. The Ainslees paddled towards the lefthand bank and pulled up to a tiny unpainted wooden dock where an attendant awaited them. A neon-green sign hanging from the dock announced "Parking: 2 Quillers per boat." Then glowing orange letters appeared, "Latecomers pay 4 Quillers and a Summon spell."

Merle and Mrs. Ainslee received glowing bracelets for their Quillers, and matching glowing circles were slapped onto the front end of each canoe. As soon as everyone stepped out, the canoes whisked themselves under a large rock. As the Ainslees pushed their way into the crowd standing on the riverbank, Cait kept watching that rock, only to see the swan boat, a raft, and three more canoes vanish under it. How did they all fit in there? Then Meg pulled at her elbow, and Cait lost sight of the parking rock as she scrambled up the bank to join the Ainslees.

The crowd was oddly quiet as boaters climbed up the riverbank, and pedestrians filtered down to join them from the street. Nobody was babbling about broomball moves or boat traffic or parking rates, Meg included. When it seemed their part of the riverbank could hold no more people, Cait realized everyone around her was staring in the direction of a nearby building with peeling gray siding. A husky bearded man with a Boston Athletic Association jacket stood there facing them, one hand signaling everyone to "hold on". A blue ribbon-like line hovered just beyond him. He looked across the river, seeming to await some signal from the other bank.

Cait felt something being pushed into her hand. Meg leaned in, saying, "Gotta have your ticket in hand, or you can't get through that blue line over there." Then she saw Meg go over to Penny, who nodded in return. Cait returned her attention to Bearded Guy who then pulled out a wand and spoke something inaudible. The weeds and rocks of the riverbank vanished, replaced by stadium seats on both sides of the river.

"Bye bye, Red Sox," Cait heard Merle say to her right. He spoke a spell Cait didn't recognize, wanded himself, and his Red Sox jacket and grungy jeans melted away to reveal a gold-trimmed Flitters robe. The crowd about them now began to chatter and laugh as Plain-Sight garb became robes and tall hats, and people headed for the blue line and the stadium beyond. The Ainslees climbed up to one of the higher rows.

Once Meg unfurled her Brindisi banner and laid it across her lap, Cait asked, "How do they get away with having a whole stadium here in the middle of a town full of Plods?"

"You saw how they hide it," replied Meg.

Merle leaned in as the trumpetvine snaked over to him. "The real way they keep the Plods out is that the Council struck a deal with a couple of ghosts that haunt these two buildings. The ghosts can stay there all they like, provided that whenever developers begin nosing around, the ghosts put on a real poltergeistery spook show and make the developers think the buildings aren't worth going for after all."

Wouldn't Aunt May like that, thought Cait.

Then the Seattle Spiders flew into the stadium, making a couple of circuits over the water as people cheered, mostly on the opposite bank. Now six riders with fluttering red and gold robes skimmed over the water, climbed the air, and were making their own circuits of the space.

"That's our Flitters," shouted Meg into Cait's trumpetvine. "That last one in line is Brindisi – number six – and he's the BEST!" Meg shouted this last word at the players as she unfurled her banner and held it overhead.

Then the crowd quieted and sat as all twelve players flew to the center of the playing space to begin the game. They hovered for a moment in formation, waiting, sizing each other up. Then the point stone flew into the air, and the game was on, players zooming and gyrating over the water. Cait and Meg whooped and vigorously waved the Brindisi banner each time player number six made a particularly spectacular point-stone save. All the while, Cait watched the virtuoso flying with fascination and envy. Even the Academy seniors looked like stumbling beginners compared to the seemingly effortless dives and swoops of these players. Would she herself ever be able to do anything fancier than plain racing sprints?

"Ooh, I think he was smiling at us that time! Gorgeous," sighed Meg.

Penny was also impressed. "I could start to get into sports if all the players looked like that," she admitted.

Meg grinned at her. "Now you're catching on. Being at a game with you guys is so much more fun than sitting here with just big bro and pro sis. Hey, look over there at that brilliant flying. Everything about the guy is gorgeous. Woohoo, there he goes again!" and the banner fluttered with extra energy.

Cait grinned as she looked at the cheering girls beside her. It was so much fun to finally have real friends, and Cait hoped that she, Penny, and Meg would stay so for a long time. What if Penny got mad at her again? nagged a little voice inside her. What if Meg drops out in two years? Or if you get held back? Cait pushed these thoughts aside.

An image of the Magenta trio with their fancy robes popped into her mind. Them, she couldn't figure out. Elsbeth seemed nice, there was always a crowd around her. Maybe she was too nice. Didn't she ever get mad at anyone? Why would she hang around a snobby cheater like Amanda? Now Claire's attitude was a perfect match to Amanda's snobbery. But on the other hand, it was fun to see what flashy variation of the school robes Claire would come up with next. But who'd want to be around that attitude all day?

Cait pulled her attention back to the game. Both of the teams were strong ones, matching each other point for point, giving Cait lots of time to admire the oversized spiders on the hats of the fans on the opposite bank. Whenever the Seattle Spiders scored, the spiders jumped up and did a victory dance in the air above the fans' heads.

"Poor Jeffries looks just awful," said Meg. "He's number four. I don't know what's happened to him, but he should get way more points than he is right now. It's lucky the rest of the team's having a good day. Carlisle especially, she's newest on the team, strongest point-server I've ever seen. Her number's three. Everybody thinks Jeffries should retire; I was hoping they'd be wrong, but maybe they really are right."

The trumpetvine swung around to Cait's other side; Penny looked irked as she scanned the stadium. "I wonder how Miss Steeple managed to get away to see this game," she snorted. "Mom's always complaining about how Steeple's way too busy to help Mom out in the store on Saturdays."

"How many people here do you know?" Cait was impressed. She hadn't expected that Penny, like Meg, would know some of the people at this game.

"Oh, not many, she's the only one I recognized, and I'm not supposed to worry about the store anyway," Penny huffed, turning back to the game. "Hey, they're selling

Salem Baked Beans down there. I'll treat ya." She jumped up and ran down the stairs after the candy vendor.

For a while, they chucked beans back and forth at each other in between glances at the whirling, speeding broomball players. Then Penny spoke again. "The magical community gets kind of small. There's only a couple of towns outside of Salem that have enough magical people to set up Councils and stuff, and people will travel miles and miles to get to games like this. See those people in gold robes over there? They're Council members."

"How many magical people do you know back home?"

"Lots. I have to so I can help out with Mom's business. But I'm sure not gonna take over the shop when I graduate, even though she wants me to. Be stuck in a shop all day? Ick. I wanna travel."

Cait wondered if there were any magical people in her own town. Poor Aunt May and Aunt Joyce had lived for all this time not even knowing that so many other people had the "Gift".

Just then, the point stone plopped into the river, and a roar went up from the crowd. "Flitters just got themselves 14 points, guys," Meg elbowed Cait, then Penny. "They're in a tie with the Spiders. What a wicked awesome game. Halftime show better be good, too."

A school of green-haired girls with long fins ("They're nixies," said Meg, grabbing Cait's trumpetvine blossom) swam into the playing area, and gave a choreographed performance with lots of gravity-defying leaps out of the water.

They were followed by a team of seven broomriders who demonstrated something that seemed to have no rules, as they unseated each other while zooming at unbelievable speeds above the stadium space, then popping back onto their brooms in midair.

208

"That's pro broom-derby," said Meg, beaming as she watched Cait's confused look. "Aren't they amazing? It's a new West-Coast invention."

Cait nodded. "I want to see more of that. Lots more."

As the gray-and-green-clad broom-derby team finished their demonstration and flew towards the bleachers opposite them, a flicker of motion caught Cait's eye. That derby player was signing! One hand gripped his broom while the other one formed signs with the rhythm of conversation. Holding her breath, she kept her gaze on the player and the person he was signing to, only to see the other player answer with signs of her own. As the rest of the team settled into their seats, she watched them. They were all signing among themselves, with fingers flying, and faces animated.

Cait stared at them openly. So that's what signing's really like. The language that's for really deaf people. The language Cait had too much hearing to need, or so she'd been told by all those teachers and doctors. As conversation flew effortlessly from derby player to derby player, Cait watched with growing envy. No hunkering forward to concentrate on fugitive syllables. No frown lines from staring at ever-so-slight and ever-so-fleeting mouth movements. No fragile vines to look out for while flying. No interruptions of "What? What?"

Cait felt torn. Why am I envying them? she asked herself. I'm the one with so much hearing that I can stay in regular school and not need to learn sign language.

But her eye kept returning to the derby players whose sentences flowed so quickly from person to person. Cait remembered her Signed English class from fourth grade, sitting in the Resource Room with Ms. Pencker who mouthed each word on an expressionless face, as her hand bounced from sign to sign. And for one embarrassing semester afterwards, Ms. Pencker stood beside her teacher in every single one of Cait's classes, hands going bounce, bounce, bounce with every word the teacher said. Watching it all was tiring, and making sense of it was more tiring still. It was actually a relief to go back to using the school's FM system after that, even if she did have to worry about battery power and teachers who forgot to talk into the microphone.

But Pencker's bouncing signs were nothing at all like these swiftly-flowing thoughts. This, this was a whole beautiful language waiting for her to learn it, even more beautiful and tempting than all those posters on Corwin's walls, all those mysterious scripts in the underground bookstore. Cait longed for the fluency to know what these derby players were saying to each other as their fingers flew.

"Meg, who's that team? Where are they from?" demanded Cait.

"Whoa, chill. That's what all the pro broom-derby teams look like," Meg answered.

Cait shook her head. "Do they all gab in Sign? Look!" She pointed across the river, where conversation continued to flow from hand to hand among the team.

"There was an announcement earlier about who they were, but I wasn't really paying attention," Meg admitted sheepishly.

Penny now watched them as well. "Wow, is that what signing really looks like? They're fast. Maybe we could find out who they are from their team colors."

Now Cait noticed that not all the gray-and-green-clad broom-derby players were in their seats yet; some stood, still holding their brooms. From time to time, they tossed glances to where their coach stood conversing with one of the Council members. The Council member nodded, the coach turned towards the team, and signed "OK, go." Each of them grabbed a small pouch, and got back in the air for another circuit around the stadium.

Without warning, the air filled with tiny flashing silver birds with green wings. Cait caught one gently and saw that it wasn't a bird at all, but a silvery sheet of paper lettered in green ink: "Seattle Eagles – See us in New York City – February 2008". As soon as she finished reading it, the paper folded in on itself, and a small bird again sat in her hand.

If only she had a broom. Cait was dying to fly right across the water to this team, but the game was beginning again, and gold-robed officials were making sure that everyone stayed within the seating area.

The Eagles were settled again on their bleacher – all of them this time – and the last of the foil birds disappeared into the eager hands of spectators.

The Flitters and the Spiders now played with redoubled energy, and Brindisi had barely a glance to spare for adoring fans as the players drove the point stone back and forth with extra determination.

As Penny and Meg watched the game, completely absorbed, Cait kept looking across the river at the derby players, who continued to converse as they, too, watched the game overhead. Why had all those teachers and her doctor acted as if signing were such a horrible, last-resort way to communicate? Those players over there looked so relaxed, so happy. Effortless, that was the word she wanted. Effortless. Cait stroked the petals of the trumpetvine as she watched the signers, with occasional glances overhead to keep up with the broomball game. Did any of those derby players have to spend all day "listening up"?

211

A jostle in her ribs interrupted Cait's thoughts. Meg was biting her nails and motioning at Cait to look up, now. Just as it looked like the Spiders were about to score the last point of the game, leaving them in tie, Brindisi swooped in with impossible speed, rescuing the point-stone inches before hitting the water, but not sending it high enough for the Spiders to score another point of their own.

"They did it again, a completely undefeated season -- Whoo!" Meg yelled, hugging everyone around her. The whole stadium on their side of the river was now on their feet and cheering for all they were worth. Another shower of glittering things filled the air: metallic red maple–seed-shaped wings, with gold writing announcing the Flitters' next game.

As everyone poured out of the stadium, Cait tried to catch the attention of those broom-derby players, but the crowd was too thick. Hordes of people gathered around the triumphant Flitters, hoping for autographs, while everyone else tried to arrive first at the boat parking or up the bank to the street.

A flash of green and silver-gray flickered overhead. Cait looked up as the derby team coasted into "V" formation on their brooms over the river. There was a moment of simultaneous eye-contact, and a synchronized wand-wave as they hovered. Then as they flew off, they blurred up and vanished.

Cait gasped with amazement. "What did they just do?" she asked, making sure the trumpetvine hadn't gotten blocked when she pulled her cloak tighter around her.

"Advanced weatherworking," answered Louise. "There's a way to call up winds to bring you from coast to coast quickly, but you have to be a very good magician and an

212

extremely good broomrider to pull it off. Can't blame them for showing off. They're amazing flyers."

As chatter surrounded Cait on the way back to the Ainslee's house, she could only daydream of what she had just seen: a whole team of signing magicworkers. Were they all Deaf? Some of them? Was there a Deaf magical school the way there was a school for Asian magic and another for Native-American magic? She just had to meet this signing team. Her new friends were great, and the trumpetvine did make things a whole lot easier, but the way these people signed looked so much easier and much more fun. How much time did it take to learn this language?

After an enormous supper of the Ainslees' excellent cooking, everybody stood in the riverside back yard to see Meg, Penny, and Cait off to Salem. Nini had received a heroine's welcome -- a neighbor of the Ainslees reported a whole family of woodchucks running down the street "right in the middle of daylight." As Louise readied the sail on their canoe, Cait studied the enchanted craft. "How hard is it to fly a canoe for just one person, versus flying a broom?"

Louise shrugged as she tested the rigging. "It's actually easier in some ways. Better for balance, especially if you have to drag along a lot of stuff. But it doesn't go as fast as a broom, and it needs stronger magic to keep it aloft. It's that much bigger, after all. You'll get to try it out for yourself once you're thirdyear."

"How come we have to wait so long?"

Louise frowned as she untied a knot, pulled its rope more snugly, and retied it. "You seem awfully interested in these boats. You won't have the magical strength to power one for at least another year."

213

"But what if I can't night-fly? I'll be stuck in firstyear forever. I fall off when it's dark."

"No such thing. Everyone figures out night-flying before first year is out."

Before Cait could protest Louise's optimism, Mrs. Ainslee swept Cait up in a hug and pressed a packet of cookies in her hand. Penny shook Merle's hand goodbye, thanking him for the broomball tutorial he'd given her during the previous night's supper, and Nini sat bolt upright in the middle of the canoe as if to say, "Let's get going already." As they sat down and the canoe lifted off, Nicky burbled in Meg's hood, and Nini hardly shook at all beneath Cait's hands.

Thoughts spun around and around in Cait's head. Won't be able to see the Eagles until their February game ... she had to meet this signing team. Maybe there would be an East Coast game sooner than February. Or practices. And where? And how would she get there? Could she pull off sneaking out of classes if she had to? One way or another, Cait was going to find these signers.

Chapter 15 - Snohomish

Something sat outside their dormroom door. A dog? The one who guarded Partridge Hall? From where Nini rode on her shoulder, Cait could feel, then hear, a growl beginning to build. No, the shape wasn't quite doglike. As they got closer, she and Penny could see the library fox waiting for them, a black-bound book between its paws, which it presented to Cait. Nini jumped down and watched from the other side of the hallway. A thin red ribbon extended from the book's pages and waved about like a snake tongue.

"Awright, I told you she'd send a fox," said Cait as she accepted the book and watched the fox trot down the hallway and out of the dorm. Nini raised her hackles as it went by, and dashed through their door as soon as Penny opened it.

Cait looked at the title: A Night-Rider's Guide to Team Flying. Inside the front cover, a picture of a rambling mansion surrounded by pines filled a bookplate which read, "Snohomish Magical Academy" in neat letters. Below the bookplate was a message in glowing red ink: "PLEASE NOTE that after 14 days, this book will fly back to Snohomish." Cait had never seen a name like that, "Snohomish." What an exotic word. What kind of language was it from? How far had this book travelled? What would it say about signing? More importantly, could it help her night-fly?

Cait fought a yawn as she scanned the page while following Penny into their room. "Am I glad tomorrow's Sunday. Where's Snohomish?"

Penny shrugged as she tossed her bag onto her desk and put Nick in his terrarium. "No idea. Gotta sleep anyway. Now." She curled up under her covers without even brushing her teeth.

Cait looked again inside the book's front cover. "After 14 days" ... from when? On the fluttering red slip was written: "Checked out on 11/16/07 SMA-WAS." She fought her tiredness to remember what date that was – oh yeah, Friday. It must have arrived just after she'd left for Fitchburg. So, she didn't have to give it back for a while. Plenty of time to learn whatever was inside. If only she weren't so tired.

Sunday morning found Cait up early, reading the night-flying book before breakfast, as Nini remained curled up on her bed. Penny gave her a surprised look as she padded to the bathroom, but said nothing. Most of the techniques the book described were very much like what she was already learning with the V-K method, including a description of how to wand 'shemayma' instead of saying it out loud. There was a chapter on "How to communicate in the dark when silence is essential," but to Cait's disappointment, its basic vocabulary of signs for "up," "down," "right," "left," and such included no spells. There was one spell written out in the back of the book, but it was on how to make glow-globes. "Once you have established a thriving colony of fireflies, you may begin creating your first small glow-globe ..."

A blur of brown landed on the page, and Nick's amber eyes looked up at her. Penny laughed as she scooped up her familiar. "Hey Cait, since when do you risk missing breakfast?"

Nini stretched, yawned, and jumped down from Cait's bed to gaze at her.

"I surrender," said Cait, shoving the book into a pocket. Her stomach growled. "Food!"

They arrived at the Commons to find Meg already in line at the buffet, glaring at the bread assortment.

216

"Hey Meg, where's Snohomish?" Cait asked as she picked up a plate and joined her friend.

"Should have grabbed a loaf of Mom's homebaked before leaving Fitchburg," she grumped. "Good morning to you, too. What's up with Snohomish? You planning to go play for the Spiders? You can't go pro before you're over the Hedge anyways."

"So you do know Snohomish. It's on the West Coast?"

"Somewhere around Seattle. A lot of broom athletes come from there." Meg picked up an English muffin and sighed. "Sooo -- ?"

Cait showed Meg the book. "That's where this book came from."

"Whoa, I wanna read that," said Meg. She put down her plate and flipped through the pages. "Can I have this next? You know how great some of these techniques will be once we're allowed to join the sports teams?"

"Hey, it's still mine for now," protested Cait. "Hand it over."

"You're holding up the line. We're starving back here," wailed somebody behind them. The book went back into its pocket, and food went onto plates. The rest of the meal was spent analyzing yesterday's game and trying to decipher the Alchemy homework they'd procrastinated on until now.

Going home for Thanksgiving turned out to be lonelier than Cait expected. She poked at her turkey as a tableful of chattering Leo aunts and uncles and cousins surrounded her. Uncle Phil was telling some story about golfing in Florida, but Cait could only hear about every other sentence. "An eighty-pointer at the nineteenth hole," he said. "Plonk!" Everyone burst out laughing.

A spoon reached across the table and rapped on her plate as the golf talk continued. Cait looked over to see

Aunt Marsha with her old-fashioned giant glasses looking at her. "Didn't ... school in Salem?" she asked.

"Oh, yes, the school's right in the middle of town. And Salem's on the ocean, so we get to go there by schooner from Boston," said Cait.

"Delightful," Aunt Marsha answered. "Your uncle ... boat-building you know ... next year ... interested."

"Salt, please," interrupted eight-year-old Kent, jostling Cait in the ribs. "Salt!"

"Kent, don't bellow," Aunt Marsha scolded as she handed him the shaker. "So Cait ... Portsmouth next year ... what do you think about that?"

"You'll have to tell me again, please, I missed too much of what you said." Cait longed for the trumpetvine tucked away in her bookbag and cursed the need for Plain Sight. She did have an FM system for times like this, but its batteries just ran down, and it took too long to recharge.

In her mind's eye, she saw the fluid signing of the Eagles team, how it flowed from person to person to person so seamlessly, how everyone understood each other so easily.

As pies were brought out and another indecipherable joke sent laughter rippling around the table, she recalled going to the theater last summer, where a pair of sign-language interpreters stood on one corner of the stage. Why didn't they capture her attention the way the Eagles had? She couldn't wait to be back at school with her friends, trumpetvine and all.

Once she was back in Salem, watching sparrow-flocking patterns in Zoomorphia class, Cait realized that she did – just maybe – have a way to get to Seattle and to find those signing derby players. The book was supposed to fly to Snohomish. Could she fly there with it?

218

With her mind full of signing, Snohomish, and broom derby, Cait got snapped at more than the usual number of times in that day's Astronologia class, especially after she answered a question about orbits with "west wind."

"We are studying the stars, not weatherworking, Miss Leo," growled Ms. Pitts, raising her voice in annoyance. "You are making even more mistakes than Miss Ainslee."

Ouch. She threw a sympathetic glance to her friend when Ms. Pitts turned to mumble something about those orbits.

After class, Cait waved Meg over. "Can we broomsprint after class tonight?" she asked.

Meg paused and frowned. "You really want to fly in the dark? They'll teach it to us soon enough. My big sister wasn't scaring you with her stories of weatherworking dangers, was she?"

"Of course I'm nervous about flying in the dark, and it's nothing to do with Louise. What if I wipe out in front of the whole firstyear class? What if I flunk night-flying and have to stay back while you all get to go on to secondyear? It's been scaring me all semester. Besides, I can really go for some flying after putting up with Ms. Pitts."

"Suit yourself," Meg shrugged. "Sure, let's try it."

As Cait stepped onto the rooftop and reached for a broom, she felt the familiar brush of fur against ankle as Nini strolled out to sit in her usual spot next to the aviary, where she liked to watch Meg and Cait's broomsprints.

"Hey, your cat's actually purring over there," said Meg "Remember how she puffed up huge that first time she saw you go up in the air?"

Cait nodded. "She hasn't missed a single broomsprint since that first one. I can't believe how fast she got used to flying. How did you get her so calmed down that first time? She was really spooked out."

"Just a bit of mindcasting. Same thing Auclair taught everyone. But hey, she's your familiar, not mine. How come you don't just calm her down via mind-link?"

"Uh, we haven't got the hang of that yet," lied Cait. "C'mon, let's fly."

"Sure." Meg shrugged. "You ready? Shemayma!"

Cait swallowed her nerves. "Shemayma. Um. Sshemayma!" The broom rose as usual. So far, so good. She pushed down cautiously, sped forward a couple of feet, and then she could feel herself veer over too much to the right and as she tried to steady herself, the rooftop dipped up towards her on the left, and she landed onto the roof with a heavy thud, smack onto her left arm.

"You okay?" asked Meg from overhead.

"Yeah, new bruise, nothing broken. I'm doing this again." Cait got back on the broom with gritted teeth. I have to do this. Sweat broke out on her forehead. What if I really can't? No, I have to do this. What if I hunker down more like this and go more slowly ... "Sshemayma!" But once more, the rooftop rolled and dipped below her as she set out, and Cait fell onto the roof again.

After about ten tries, several scrapes, and a goose egg on her head, Cait flumped down in a black mood and pushed her broom aside. Nini came over, sniffed the broom, and curled up in Cait's lap with a huge purr. Meg finished her circuit of the rooftop, then landed next to her.

"Greengage will figure out something to help you. I've really never heard of someone who couldn't night-fly."

"Ha. I'll be the first one. Does it have to be with brooms? What if I learned how to do that feather-flying I saw at Half-term?"

"Sure you didn't dream that? I've never seen that anywhere. But I saw a flying carpet once. Now there's one high-class way to travel. I'd love to try out one of those."

"People do that? Like Aladdin?" Hope flared up within Cait. "I wonder if I could stay on one of those in the dark."

"You have to be filthy rich, Persian, or both. My dad says they cost three years' salary and then some. They make them by hand in some tiny village in Iran and there's a ginormous waiting line."

"I wish I could at least fly a canoe instead," fumed Cait. "Are you sure there isn't some kind of balancing spell I could use?"

Meg shook her head. "There's a reason broomcouriers use backpacks and carry-straps. You can't fly and run a spell at the same time unless you've got two heads."

"Hey, you know, there was this TV show I saw at home about these conjoined twin girls," said Cait, her gloom momentarily lifted. "Two heads, but they have to share one body. I bet they could do some pretty incredible stuff, if they turn out to be magical."

"They'd be famous," speculated Meg. "One of them could run illusions while the other one hangs on and steers. They'd be able to get away with almost anything."

Two days later, on the morning the night-flying book was due back in Snohomish, Cait woke up with a thrill of excitement, but also a bit of worry. What if the Eagles weren't in town this weekend? How would she find out what they were up to? Showing up would be pointless if they weren't even there. Merle and Meg had mentioned some broomsports quarterly during the Flitters game, but of course Cait couldn't remember its name. The sound of birdwings came to mind. Right – the library had a periodicals section. And there was plenty of time to look, since there wasn't a class until one o'clock.

"I'm off to the library," she announced, as Penny glared at the Alchemy assignment she'd been cursing since they'd received it on Tuesday. From her bed, Nini stretched, looked at her, curled up tighter, and went back to sleep.

"I'll follow you there," answered Penny, picking up her own bookbag, and renewing Nicky's anti-predation glamour as he jumped into his terrarium. "I have no idea how I'm going to learn all these rocks. Clear quartz for lucidity, rose quartz for love, at least those I know. Smoky quartz ... what do you do with smoky quartz?" She grinned suddenly. "Hey Cait, speaking of love, have you been noticing all the soppy looks Andreya's been giving you lately? I bet you've got yourself a fan."

Cait frowned as they crossed the courtyard. A fan? Her? Since when? There had to be some mixup, or a cruel joke. But a quick Mindcast in Penny's direction revealed not a whiff of deception, only amusement. Huh. Andreya. The selkie girl who was so scared of flying at first. And she did always seem to be right beside Cait in broomwork class, but didn't she make those puppydog eyes at everyone? On the other hand, that was one big smile she'd given Cait when the halfterm broomracers were announced.

"Nah, she's cute with everyone. People don't follow me around." Cait replied to Penny with a shrug.

Penny snorted. "Uh-uh. For somebody who sees so much, you better look around you more in Broomwork class. OK – Amethyst ... tourmaline ... I have no idea. Make sure I don't forget to look those up."

Once at the library, Penny ran to the nearest stone arch and announced "Amethyst," then ran over to the white-glowing Reference book it showed her.

Cait went over to Ms. Fletcher's desk. "Um, thanks for the night-flying book, Ms. Fletcher, I'm almost done reading it. Do we have newspapers and stuff for outside New England?" Cait was ashamed to realize that she had not read a single newspaper since arriving at Salem. Her parents were always on her case to read more about the outside world, now that she was in middle school.

"Is there any particular area you're researching?" prodded the librarian.

"Well, I've got a favorite broom-derby team that's in Seattle, and I want to know more about them," replied Cait.

Ms. Fletcher smiled. "Better a sportswoman's interest in news than no interest at all. Let me show you how the periodicals room works." Leading Cait to a door behind the desk, Fletcher continued, one hand resting on the doorknob. "Everyone is completely welcome to use this room. You'll see why we keep the door closed in a moment. The stone archways over there work the same way as the ones you already use, but you also need to be sure to specify the date you want when making your request. And don't forget to close the door behind you." Fletcher took her hand off the knob and went back to her desk.

Cait turned the knob and went in, remembering to close the door. Cubbyholes filled with rolled-up booklets of all sizes lined the tall room, running all the way up the walls, making the place feel more like an aviary than a library. The middle of the room was open and airy, while the shelves looked just like the messenger-birds' coop on the Partridge-Hall roof. A flurry of motion in one corner caught her eye. "New Arrivals" announced a sign in that corner. Sure enough, more pamphlets were flapping themselves in through a special pane of the tall window opposite the door and arranging themselves along a long table underneath the sign. In the opposite corner, periodicals were winging themselves out a window labeled "Outdated ephemera."

Walking under the closest archway, Cait spoke aloud: "Seattle." A rustling and fluttering erupted from a nearby shelf, but nothing else happened. "Seattle, November 23," she added, remembering that she needed a date.

There was now only a little rustling as a single roll of paper unfurled itself, spread out its pages, and flew down to Cait, hovering just outside the archway. As Cait stepped out from under the arch, the paper dropped into her hand, pages flat and ready to be read.

Broomsports was the last section of the paper. International racing. US racing. Broomball. Spidernet-ball. Finally, at the end of the section, there was derby. Gold! The Eagles had a Saturday home game. Did that mean that they would be there on Friday, too? Cait could find out nothing further about the team. She put the paper down. Once it hit the wood of the tabletop, it opened up its pages and flew back to its original compartment.

In the meanwhile, Cait felt a buzz coming from one of her pockets. It was the book. What was it going to do? And when was it going to do it? If it decided to fly home after sundown, swiping one of the faculty-staff brooms would be pointless, given her balance. Her mind raced. What other options were there?

It dawned on her that one of the school boats might do the trick. Hadn't Louise said they'd be easier to balance? And they had a flying spell built right in.

On the way to the door, she paused. Should she tell Penny her plans? She'd figured on taking off solo, whenever the book did whatever it was going to do. She was used to doing things on her own and looked forward to an adventure that would be all hers.

On the other hand, Penny knew a lot more about magical things and how they behaved than Cait did. And it would be pretty unfair to disappear without letting at least one of her friends know what she was up to. Penny had also been spending a lot of time with Minna and company lately, gabbing away at lunch and supper, and here was something Cait could offer which those hearing girls couldn't. After all, Penny had been dying to travel to other places since forever. Cait made up her mind.

Bolting out of the periodicals room, she ran towards Penny, but a handwave and an arched eyebrow from Fletcher stopped her. The door. Cait felt a twinge of guilt as one periodical flapped its way over Fletcher's head towards the stacks.

Closing the door, Cait went up to Penny, whispering, "I found them. The Eagles have a home game on Saturday, and I have an idea."

Penny looked up from her guide to crystals. "Home game?" Her face was blank for a moment. "Aren't they from Seattle or something?" Cait nodded briskly and waited.

A gleam came into Penny's eye and she looked down at the book before her, then back at Cait. "I'm studied out anyway. Let's take off, and you tell me your idea. Is it against rules?"

Once they were in the courtyard, Cait said, "This book is supposed to fly to Snohomish tonight. Do you know what kind of spells can do that?"

Penny considered. "I don't, but I bet Meg does. Bet it uses wind and stuff." Cait began to wish she'd taken off alone after all. How many people were going to be in on this?

Penny continued. "My mom has a spell she uses to send potions to people when they're needed in a hurry. It's a really tough one though, and she gets together with a weatherworker for it. This spell calls up a really fast wind to zip the thing there --" Comprehension dawned on her.

225

"So that's why you want to know about Snohomish. Whoa, an adventure!" She paused. "But the spell won't be strong enough for a book and a person."

Cait nodded agreement. "That's why I'm heading to the Commons. Will that spell pull a flying boat?"

Penny flashed her a wicked grin. "Let's go. We don't have nearly enough adventures around here. It's almost as boring as public school."

They were now at Partridge Hall.

"Let's ditch the bags while we're here. They'll be too heavy to take along," suggested Penny.

"Yeah, you're right," agreed Cait. Stowing their stuff in the room, Cait made sure she had her wand in its pocket, plus some money, plus her mini sketchpad and pencil. Checking Nini's box and opening up a bag of kibbles Mom sent her "just in case", Cait told the cat, "Now be good while I'm out." But Nini jumped onto her shoulder, digging her claws into Cait's heavy winter cloak and refusing to budge. "You win," sighed Cait. Would a "mere pet" be this stubborn? But where was that mind-link that everyone else knew about?

Penny reached one hand back to her hood while pulling out her wand with the other, as Cait heard her renew the anti-predation spell for Nicky.

At the doorway Penny stopped. "Meg really should be in on this. She knows more than we do about flying, weatherworking, and how to find teams at practice."

"Go ahead", said Cait, conceding defeat. Five minutes later, Penny returned with a beaming Meg, and they all ran to the Commons together.

To her enormous relief, the pool-room door wasn't locked, and they ran downstairs to the double-currented river and its boats. So far, so good, Cait thought as they crossed the pool room. Nobody here at lunchtime. A splash to their right interrupted that hopeful notion, and she saw a blur of motion. A harbor seal watched them from the edge of the large pool. It disappeared below the surface of the water for a moment, then there was another splash. A sealskin lay at the edge of the pool, where Andreya gazed at them quizzically, arms crossed before her.

Cait made a "shhh" motion to her lips.

Andreya tipped her head and raised her eyebrows. "Are you on teacher-sent business?" she asked softly, leaning out of the pool.

Cait shook her head "no."

Andreya's eyes sparkled. "Is it secret? I'll keep anything secret for you." She kicked happily in the water.

Beside Cait, Penny snorted as she suppressed a giggle. Cait growled at her, "Okay, you were right, you were right." Meg's expression made it clear that she had just put two and two together, and wasn't quite sure she liked the conclusion. Cait motioned her friends into a huddle before anybody started any teasing or worse. "Okay, what do you think, can we trust her?" Cait whispered.

Meg hesitated, but then did a quick Mindcast, and she and Penny both nodded. The book buzzed ever more insistently in Cait's pocket.

Cait approached the selkie. "Well, I have a library book to return. And I'm going with it. To Snohomish on the West Coast."

Andreya squealed with joy. "That's a great secret. Teachers will have a fit if they find out, but they won't, not ever, not from me." She paused. "That's near Seattle, right?" Meg nodded, and Andreya thought for a moment. "If you get into any trouble out there, ask for the Orcas Clan of selkies. They're my mom's cousins. I've told them all about your flying, Cait." Andreya now did a stunning

227

backflip into the water as Penny did the twohanded ASL "sweetheart" sign with a snort of laughter.

Meg's face was red as she scuffed her feet and stared at the floor, muttering something about "weird seaweed eaters."

Cait fervently wished she'd done this trip solo after all. She was curious about one thing, and now asked Andreya, "Are you officially supposed to be here?"

Andreya nodded. "Selkie privilege. I have to spend a certain amount of time in seal form, overnight included, or I'll outgrow my pelt. And that would be a real disaster. But your secret's safe with me. Good luck." She grabbed the pelt, vanished under the water, and a harbor seal swam once more in the Academy's main pool.

"Time for the boats," announced Meg as she bolted from the pool room, with Cait and Penny following.

Cait stopped and held up a hand just as they were about to step into the nearest boat. "I won't be able to hear you once we're over the river. Do either of you know the spell to get these boats going?"

Meg nodded. "Yeah, I recognized the spell Greengage says because it's the same one we use for our family canoes. I'll tell it to go to our practice golf course so we'll be in open air and not in the middle of town or the boy's school."

"You're on," said Cait, and they all piled into the lead boat, which took off as soon as Meg pronounced the spell. The book's buzzing become more forceful. Pulling it out, Cait could see that it now glowed as well. Sweat popped out on Cait's palms. Too late to back out now. More quickly than she'd expected, they were rising up to the grass-lined fissure in the cavern roof, and now hovered in the afternoon air at the Salem town golf course.

The book began to flash.

Nini dove for the floor of the boat. "Brace yourselves. Hold on tight," yelled Cait, as she clung to the book with both hands.

Without warning, it felt as if somebody turned on a giant vacuum cleaner, and their boat was the dust bunny pulled inside. No sun, no sky, no grass, only a bright blended breathless everythingness and nothingness as they were pulled by the spellworked wind from coast to coast in an airless limbo that might have been five minutes or five hours, and Cait's hands ached from holding the book, but she could not move them had she wanted to, and her lungs ached, as did her legs from bracing them against the sides of the boat, and just as she felt she couldn't hang on for a moment longer – there was a change in the wind and the pressure. Then came the sound of voices sorting themselves out into words.

"Here comes the book now. Let's see who wanted to hang onto it so badly."

"More than one somebody, seems like."

With a spine-rattling thump, the boat hit the ground.

Light surrounded them. There was no more blur, and they could breathe.

"Is this the Snohomish Library?" gasped Cait, the book still in her outstretched hands. "Here's your book."

But another voice was drowning out hers, "Aha. We caught a whole pack of book thieves." A sternfaced witch hovered above Cait and snatched up the book.

"I had no idea that one book could bring along three people with it," said a young blond wizard in an awestruck tone, as he reached out a hand to the stunned travelers. Cait winced as she stood up, hoping she hadn't broken her tailbone or anything else. Nini shook herself, looked about briefly, and jumped onto Cait's shoulders, seeming none the worse for wear.

"But we did get the book back on time, didn't we? You are Circulation staff, right?" Cait continued. She, Penny, Meg, Sternface, and the blond wizard were the only people in a quiet, long, and airy room. The place reminded Cait more of some of the big old beach houses she had seen on Cape Cod vacations than of any school she'd ever seen. Bookcases along the walls alternated with large windows looking out at a white-capped gray-ridged mountaintop which shone in the distance.

"Nice try," snarled Sternface. "We hear all the excuses, all day long. Thought you could escape the return spell, eh?" She turned to the young man. "Detain them in Classroom B and contact their school."

"No, really, the book's all yours, we're not stealing it," protested Cait. "Really, we wanted to follow the book here because there's people in Seattle we've got to meet, and it's near Snohomish. I'm looking for the Eagles team, they play out of Seattle. I've got to."

"You and a million other fans," scoffed the witch, and waved at the young man to proceed.

"And the Orcas Clan," added Penny. "Don't forget we're supposed to look them up too."

Sternface's eyes still flashed, but the blond wizard's grip on Cait's arm let up a bit.

"Who sent you to the Orcas Clan?" His voice reflected genuine interest.

"Andreya –" began Cait, embarrassed at the crush, and at suddenly not even being able to remember the selkie's last name.

"Andreya Goode," added Penny.

"You still have to be detained until we contact them," barked Sternface, and the young man motioned them to pick up the boat and follow him down a short hallway. Their arms ached as he ushered them into a room filled with darkwood desks. Built-in shelves and cupboards lined the pale-painted walls. He cast a spell that filled the classroom doorway with a web of brightly-glowing orange threads, and left.

Cait flumped to the floor in a black mood, Nini purring against her cheek in an attempt to cheer her up. So here they were, stuck in a Snohomish classroom and about to be sent back to Salem in disgrace. How would she ever meet this team now? "We're stuck before we've even started," she moaned.

"Girl, you're the one who wanted adventure, weren't you? Don't be a wuss," said Penny, turning towards the door to examine the bright crisscrossing threads.

"Well I thought they'd be fine with the book being back, not jail us up as book thieves," retorted Cait.

"Stop fighting! I'm trying to concentrate over here," bellowed Meg, who sat in the canoe. "I can't get this to fly. Shemayma won't work. My sister's travel spells won't work. Nothing works. I think this thing needs a river."

They were interrupted by the tremor of angry footsteps from the hallway, and the sound of a booming voice. "What lovesick young jock has Dez enticed out to Seattle this time? So help me, if I have to bail out her romantic messes one more time –" A solidly-built man with salt-and-pepper hair appeared glowering in the doorway. He broke off in surprise as the three firstyear girls looked up to meet his eyes.

"You're no boys." He blinked. "And you're way too young. What the hell has Dez dragged you into?"

"Who's Dez?" asked Cait.

There was a moment of blank silence.

"Dez didn't send for you," stated Salt-and-Pepper.

All three firstyears shook their heads.

"But you do know Andreya," he added.

231

"We're in her class," stated Cait. "I'm Caitlin Leo, this is Penny Dingle, and Meg Ainslee's in the boat over there."

"Aha," said Salt-and-Pepper, as his eyebrows momentarily unclenched from their scowl. "So you're Cait. You're the one who worked so hard at becoming such a strong broomrider. Andreya's very impressed with you." His expression darkened. "That means we're in for a whole new generation of rescuing impetuous jocks. Well, they'd better all start traveling to the east coast, instead of the west, because I've had more than my share of this stupidity. Well, c'mon, can't say I haven't had plenty of practice with bailing out surprise visitors. Although you are the first ones to actually bring along your own boat." He motioned at them to get up and follow him, as he released the Retaining spell with a quick wandflick.

All the way down the hallway, Cait could hear him muttering under his breath, but could only catch occasional words about "sister of mine" and "out East."

Leaving the library and the classroom corridor behind, they crossed an airy foyer with a sweeping blond-wood staircase, then walked out onto a lawn which rolled down from the front door. Students sprawled here and there on the grass, enjoying the fine weather.

"About time the sun finally showed itself," growled Salt-and-Pepper. "You have no idea how lucky you are to even see this mountain at all. We hardly get to see it ourselves."

As they followed Salt-and-Pepper's long strides, the trio of girls struggled to carry the canoe with aching muscles. Salt-and-Pepper stopped at the edge of the lawn, and they let the boat down with groans of relief, while Nini nibbled at the grass, then rolled aroud happily. He now turned to face them, catching them all in his gaze. What a beautiful shade of brown his eyes are, thought Cait. How come he has to be such an old grownup?

"While we're still on school grounds, better tell me why you're here."

Meg was also gazing at those eyes in an odd way; Penny elbowed them both. "Not the time to go moony-eyed," she hissed. Then she answered Salt-and-Pepper. "We want to meet the Seattle Eagles team."

"I am not a ticket agent," he said with a huff. "But I can get you to where their games and practices happen. I suppose that none of you know how to charm the wind to carry you all back home."

They shook their heads, chagrined. True, none of them had thought to figure that out.

He sighed. "I'll help you on one condition, for Andreya's sake." He gave a thin smile. "A spellbound promise from Cait."

A what? Cait frowned. Nini picked up her head, then sat up, alert.

Penny nodded. "I know those. It's something my mom's customers do when they owe her more than they can pay at once. Break one of those and you feel like you've got flu until you make good on it. Barfing and all."

Salt-and-Pepper nodded. "For a firstyear she knows something. Now you three, how's your Mindcasting?"

Penny pointed at a squirming Meg as Cait nodded. "Top in class."

"Good. You, then, stand there and read our intentions. Got your wand? OK. Now Cait, you put your right hand up like this, no wand needed. Hold it there." Salt-and-Pepper raised his own hand, as a band of yellow light extended from his palm to hers. "Ready, now –"

"But I don't even know what I'm promising," said Cait, dropping her hand. "Shouldn't I know that first?"

"Nothing unattainable," answered Salt-and-Pepper. "Perfectly within your powers. Do you want to meet this team of yours or not?"

"Don't go wuss on us," said Penny with a glare.

Meg made a "come on, come on" gesture.

A vision arose in Cait's mind of sitting at a table with people like the Eagles. Being able to chat across whole playing fields and rooms with no squinting, no "listening up", no batteries, no "huh, what". She set her chin and raised her hand once more. Once again, the band of light stretched from hand to hand, tingling warmly where it touched, while a Mindcast-tap came from Meg.

Salt-and-Pepper's eyes met hers. "Caitlin Leo, promise that whichever selkies you may meet from now on, whether Andreya Goode or anyone else, do not follow them out to the west coast, or send your friends to do so. Promise."

Cait swallowed. "I promise," she answered. At that moment, the yellow beam split in two and vanished, and she felt the warm shimmering tingle shoot up her arm and settle around her heart before fading.

"Good. Now to get going." He eyed their robes. "This charm will see you to the town dock without being noticed by Plods." He murmured a spell and made a triple wand-wave, and Meg, Cait, and Penny stood dressed in jeans and Seahawk sweatshirts. It was only illusion, however, as Cait could still feel the shape of her robes as she felt for her pockets.

"You'll pass," he nodded. "Now we're Plod daytrippers on their way to the town boatramp." He motioned for them to follow him down the sloping road before them, Nini bringing up the rear with her tail held high.

Beyond the tall pines surrounding the school mansion, they walked past block after block of wooden houses

234

whose long, sloping rooflines were nothing at all like the boxy and upright New England houses Cait knew. Beyond the houses, they could see the sparkling ocean.

Just when the girls thought they could carry the boat no longer, Salt-and-Pepper turned and saw their sagging grip. He flicked his wand their way, hiding it back in his sleeve, and the boat felt forty pounds lighter.

The houses soon gave way to a cluster of shops of all kinds: ice cream, secondhand books, antiques, an art gallery, and handmade jewelry. A sign to their right announced the best coffee in town, and so did one two doors down, and another one across the way.

Then the street ended right at the shore at a paved area that didn't quite look like a parking lot, since there were long lanes painted on the pavement, rather than parking spaces.

"Plods need ferries to get about." Salt-and-Pepper indicated the paved area. "We have our own ways of getting from here to there. Over this way." He now led them towards the far right corner of the ferryboat lot. There, a footpath led through a forest of pines which crowded up to the water in the fading light. Just beyond the path, a small cement boatramp could barely be seen. Salt-and-Pepper motioned for them to stop and put their boat down.

In the distance, a ferryboat made its way towards a barely-visible island.

Remembering the charm on their clothing, Cait looked down to see her Seahawks shirt getting blurry about the edges; she could see the outlines of Meg and Penny's robes beginning to take form as well.

Salt-and-Pepper now went up to a nearby tree trunk and nodded as he examined a squirrelhole just above his head. Speaking a quick spell, he reached inside and

235

retrieved a carefully-folded object from it. It took a moment before Cait realized what it was – a pelt, like Andreya's.

Holding it carefully, he turned to face the girls. "I will need a moment alone to get myself ready." His gaze was stern. "You three get yourselves in the boat, and be ready to push off and follow me as soon as I'm in seal form and ready to guide you. Watch that ferry in the meanwhile or something."

"But we don't have any paddles," squeaked Meg.

"What the hell do they teach you in magical school? We're out of Plain Sight now. What do you need paddles for?" The exasperation in his tone was obvious.

"We're firstyears. They haven't taught us any boat-propelling spells yet." Penny's arms were folded, chin held high.

"Besides, I only know river-boating spells, not ocean," added Meg.

He shook his head in annoyance. "I'll tow you then. Get the boat in the water and yourselves inside. And no staring." He performed some wandwork towards the bow of the boat, put the wand into the tree, then motioned at them to stop watching him.

Moments later, a seal's head bobbed in the water before the boat. As he swam forward, the boat followed after, gliding smoothly in the calm water. Silhouettes of tall pines arced over them to the right. Gulls swooped over the water to their left, looking for goodies tossed overboard by ferryboat passengers. The last light of sunset still glowed beyond the gulls, and Cait could feel herself beginning to relax for the first time in hours. Now this was an adventure.

Chapter 16 – Orcas and Eagles

All too soon, they pulled up to a cove with a smooth-pebbled beach. A small cedar-shingled cabin nestled beyond the tide line, among the piney roots of an embankment immediately behind it. The door stood open, and a faint glow emanated from within. The seal flumped up the beach towards the house, went in for a moment, then returned to vanish among the waves.

Meg, Penny, and Cait looked at each other. This must be their overnight housing. As they stepped out into the shallow water and pulled the boat up the pebbled beach, a woman with friendly eyes and fluid motions moved into the doorway and stood there watching them.

"So you're our surprise guests," she stated in a friendly voice. "You'll need to put that boat up further – up here." Leaving the doorway, she showed them a level area just beyond the cottage. "Come in, come in. There's not much, but at least you'll have a roof over your heads tonight and won't have to sleep out in the open."

As they entered the cottage, the smell of smoked fish surrounded them, and a fire burned on a small stone hearth. Penny barely restrained herself from grimacing. In contrast, Nini, who was on Cait's shoulders, picked up her head and sniffed the air, eyes wide, whiskers alert. Cait's stomach growled; she loved fish of all kinds. There was also the smell of homebaked bread, making Meg's eyes light up. A steaming loaf sat on a wooden table in the midst of the single room, accompanied by a plate of various kinds of fish, and settings for four. Yellow pine paneling surrounded them, and benches sat against each wall.

Overhead, the rafters were full of dried and drying fish and seaweed of all shapes and sizes. Nini chattered in frustration as she followed Cait's gaze upward.

The woman filled a brown teapot from a kettle over the small fire, as she gestured at them to all take places at the table. "You must be starving – please help yourselves. I'm Marnie Orcas. My less-than-polite husband Timo has probably not introduced himself to you at all; he's the one who brought you here. Am I right?" In the quiet cabin with only the crackle of the fire behind them, her voice was easy to hear.

She sighed as they all nodded, mouths already full of bread. Meg had cut herself an especially large piece, and she had an ecstatic look on her face. The flavor was not quite what Cait expected, but she could see why Meg liked it so much. This bread had heft and tasted a little like oatmeal.

Cait and Meg now reached towards the platter of fish, as Penny moved her chair away from them. At Cait's feet, Nini growled happily over her very own chub.

Marnie continued. "You'll have to forgive him. After a certain member of our clan got married, he was really looking forward to not bailing out lovesick pursuers and surprise guests anymore. Dez believed in having too much fun for most people's good."

Cait buttered one of the few remaining pieces of bread while trying to figure out which question to ask first. How long had there been a Eagles team? Was there a magical signing school in Seattle?

"So, what did this Dez do, anyway?" asked Penny, as Marnie poured tea all around.

Marnie shrugged. "Trouble is, Dez didn't have to do anything. People just fell for her, all the time, all sorts of folks, but she did have a thing for athletes, especially broomriders. And it was the kind of silly puppy love that made people do really stupid stuff." Penny smirked and signed "sweetheart" in Cait's direction, and got an elbow in her ribs.

"Like?" prodded Meg as she nabbed the last fish off the platter. Marnie gazed into the rafters, cradling a cup of tea between her hands. Cait could tell she'd lost her chance to ask questions for a while.

"Like the time a love-of-the-moment brought a whole broomball team along with him, which wasn't too bad, except that Dez happened to be at the game of their worst rival at the time. When the fans saw this other team show up, a bit of a brawl broke out. When you girls grow up, never try to down more than three double-fizz ciders at one go, especially at a game. For one thing, it makes people think brawling is great fun. Took us months to get the incitement fines paid off, not to mention physical damage repaired." She took a drink of tea, watching the girls. "Timo says you're firstyears, friends of Andreya's."

"Yeah, and we don't get to do any sports yet," complained Meg.

"But I really do have to meet that broom-derby team," added Cait. "They all talk in Sign, and I think they can help me."

"Just don't try falling in love with any of them." Marnie chuckled. "I have plenty more jocks-in-love stories, if you want to hear them."

"Yes, please," chorused Meg and Penny together.

More stories, more listening up. Cait dropped her concentration and let the storytelling blur into a half-understood stream of words. She watched her friends as she waited for a pause in the conversation. Penny looked particularly entranced, listening with her chin on her hands and a cold cup of tea forgotten beside her.

As the voice went on, describing one wild Solstice where all the right people were with the wrong dates, Cait wondered if she'd ever get a chance to change the topic. Images of the Eagles' signing filled her mind. Then the promise she'd just made with Timo made nerves jangle in her gut. Were selkies rare? Or were there lots of them around? Just how careful did she have to be? On the bench beside her Nini shifted in her sleep, curling tighter against Cait.

Finally, Marnie's voice stopped, and Cait jumped in. "This Eagles team that signs. Is there such a thing as a Deaf magical school? And also, if this is the Orcas Clan, where's everyone else?"

Marnie's brow creased into a frown. "I've never heard of any magical school just for deaf people. After all, most spells do have to be spoken. And there wasn't any broom derby at all before the solstice races this year, so this team must be brand new." Cait's heart sank as she heard this. All the more reason to go find these Eagles and learn what they did know, and how they knew it.

Marnie went on. "As for where everyone else is, most of us prefer to spend the night in seal form. We keep several cabins like this one for when we feel like being in human form instead. Or when surprise human guests show up."

Meg tried to stifle a huge yawn and Cait could see Penny's head begin to nod off to her right, even as she mumbled something about "more stories, please."

"Bed time," announced Marnie. Plates and teacups had reverted to shell, which Marnie scooped up and tossed out the door. Then she said, "Each of you, please take a seat against the wall so this table can move."

Bench legs scraped the floor as the girls moved out of the way, staring to see where in this cabin the table could possibly go.

240

Marnie said something that was lost among the noise of moving benches, and the table legs folded themselves up flat against the tabletop as it turned itself sideways, zoomed up to the rafters, and came to rest on two beams above all the drying fish and fronds of seaweed.With another spell and wandwave, three hard benches became beds with down comforters.

"Good night, until morning," said Marnie. She pushed the last bits of the diminishing fire together in a pile, then stood in the doorway to set a glow-globe by the door, and send another one to a nearby outhouse. Then she disappeared into the darkness outside and there was only the sound of waves on the beach and the occasional bark of a seal.

For a long time, Cait lay awake in a flurry of nervousness and anticipation. She knew so little Sign. How would she talk to this team? How did so many signers find each other? Or did they go to some gigantic school? If Cait were the only hard-of-hearie in the Salem Academy, would a school twice as big have two hard-of-hearing students? Or more? Were some of these derby players hard-of-hearing, too? Or were they all the very-deaf people who were "supposed" to sign? And could they all night-fly? If only it were tomorrow already. Cait glanced at the black window. No trace of dawn there. Then she stared at the eye of a glowing ember, not falling asleep until the fireplace was cold ash.

Early the next morning, while everyone enjoyed another loaf of brown bread and fresh-caught fish pan-fried by the still-grumpy Timo, Marnie slipped quietly out of the cottage. While they ate, Timo twice caught Cait's eye, and mouthed the word, "promise". Her palm prickled, and she nodded.

241

Then Marnie was back, together with a boy their own height, who had fuzz beginning to grow on his cheeks. He had a quick smile with a dimple and eyes as deep a brown as Timo's. Was there no such thing as a homely selkie? wondered Cait as she tried to not stare too much.

"Neil here is a very avid Broomball fan, but he also follows this new derby racing," said Marnie. "He tells me that chances are good that you can catch up with the Eagles during their practice today, before somebody from your school drags you back to Massachusetts." She took a cup of tea and sat down.

"Are you all ready?" Neil asked the girls. He sounded anxious. "Not to be rude, but we have to set out now if we're going to reach Seattle in time. We'll be stuck having to hide our magic because too many commuters can see us. So I've put some paddles in your boat. Can we go?" He flashed a smile that set off a gush of excited chatter from Meg, and an eye-roll from Penny although she also blushed and made a point of showing off her muscles as she helped carry their boat to the water.

Once settled in the boat, the three girls looked about in panic. Where did Neil go? A seal head popped up before the boat and gazed at them, then nodded his head towards a set of very hazy and distant skyscrapers. Seattle was that way. As he swam off in that direction, the boat followed; apparently the charm that Timo put on it last night still held.

Bit by bit, the skyscrapers and brick waterfront of Seattle came closer. Instead of continuing to the city, Neil guided them to a small cove overhung by forest, bringing the boat up to a rock just the right height for disembarking. The seal vanished. A moment later, a pelt lay draped over the side of their boat, where Neil now rested on crossed arms, gazing at them. Meg began to giggle madly, while Penny signed behind her hand to Cait, "Want to look doooown," making Cait blush furiously while cuffing her.

"The Eagles practice on a meadow up over that hill." He rose out of the water a bit as he turned away to point out a path twisting its way up the forested rise beyond the beach, making all three girls blush and giggle more.

He turned back to them, again resting his arms on the edge of the boat. "They like to practice out there first thing in the day, before all the Plod hikers hit the trail. It takes a while for the early-bird hikers to get to this part of Discovery Park. I hope you get a good visit in before your school catches up with you. Good luck." He flashed another dazzling smile that melted all three of them, before taking the pelt and vanishing into the water.

"I wanna marry a selkie when I'm out of school," said Meg as she goggled in Neil's direction. "Are there any selkies at BWIS? I've got to find out. Those regular guys suffer in comparison."

For the sake of her promise with Timo, Cait hoped there weren't any selkies at BWIS. Then she saw flashes of motion through the trees which immediately erased all thoughts of selkies, no matter how cute they were.

"C'mon," she told the others, as she set Nini on the rock, and jumped out. "We've got to get up there. The team's out there right now. Let's get this boat out of water." She began pulling at the boat's bow as soon as Penny and Meg were on land. Leaving the boat above the beach's high-tide line of seaweed, Cait clambered along the steep path up the slope, Nini running after her.

"Wait up, wait up," shouted Meg and Penny.

Now over the rise, the trees opened into a clearing, and Cait could see the entire team doing practice sprints and dodges, their coach signing comments up to them from

243

the ground. A white board stood propped up nearby, covered with squiggles that looked like game plans. When the coach caught sight of the three bedraggled girls appearing over the rise from the beach, his hands intersected in the sign for "breaktime," and all six fliers paused in the sky to look down at them.

"Hi," signed Cait self-consciously, hand at forehead. "Deaf – all of you?" she queried shakily in her rediscovered Sign, pointing to cheek and mouth, then at each of the fliers who were now landing nearby.

Of the seven signers, three fists – coach included – bobbed downward in the ASL sign meaning "Yes," while the other four players stood by.

"Deaf – you?" asked the coach of Cait.

She nodded, and as she had been taught in fourth grade, signed "I – am – Hard-of-Hearing, I – am – C-A-I-T-L-I-N", spelling the letters slowly and clumsily with her right hand. Oh yeah, better introduce my friends, she thought. Pointing at each girl in turn, she fingerspelled M-E-G, then P-E-N-N-Y."

Realizing that she didn't have nearly enough signs to ask all the things she really wanted to say, she held up a finger, "Wait a minute," while groping in her pocket for her sketchpad. Not finding the pencil to go with it, she signed, "Have --question. People – who – sign – where – do – you -- learn – M-A-G-I-C? How?" She mimed waving her wand while casting a spell, and dropping it. "How?" she signed again.

The coach saw her perplexity, and held up a hand. "Hold on." Picking up the board with the game plan on it, he tapped it with his wand, and the markings vanished, then he performed a spell Visual-Kinetic style and tapped it again. The board now hovered next to him, where Cait could easily see it. He nodded, fingerspelled, "OK – here –

244

team – E-a-g-l-e." and then stowed his wand into his robe. He paused and motioned to one longfingered girl with a flurry of signs as she nodded, signed, "Fine – of course," with her five fingers out and thumb tapping her chest. She sat down next to the whiteboard, and pointed her wand towards it.

The coach began signing fluidly, fist against chest, thumb-up, then his hand went to his shoulder, and next there was a flurry of fingerspelling. As he continued to sign, Long Fingers wrote on the board: "I'm Coach Joe. Am myself Deaf and have hearing parents. One aunt is Deaf, so I grew up knowing Sign. I made Hedge level at Snohomish two years ago with interpreter, and lots of speech therapy. Now I've escaped school – whew - and work at a garden center. We formed this team this summer and hope to go pro."

He pointed at a tall blonde girl who had the rosy coloring Cait's aunt called "peaches and cream," and began signing with another flurry of fingerspelling, more signs, some numbers. As before, Long Fingers translated his signing onto the whiteboard. "Lillian is also Deaf, and her parents are both Deaf. She began Snohomish during my second year there, people told me about another deaf person at school, wow, we became friends right away. She plans to finish all seven years." And the coach paused to applaud her by waving his hands in the air in a sort of shimmy as the Eagles joined in.

The coach now pointed out a short and lithe boy with laughing eyes and unruly dark hair. "Alberto here, also deaf, was supposed to go to school in Los Angeles. Then he heard there was a deaf student in Snohomish, and transferred here just to find her. Lucky that the Witches Council approved. No deafs in his family, grew up speechreading, mainstreamed, learned to sign from us. He plans to stop at Hedge."

Then the hearing Eagles were introduced. Tom, with a build like a lumberjack, had a deaf brother who was nonmagical; he was glad to meet other signers. Jake, with eyes the color of sky and hair so pale it was nearly colorless, loved derby, and learned to sign just so he could join the new team, as did Cara, a widehipped girl with deep brown skin and very long nails. Don't those fingernails get in the way when she signs? Cait wondered. Last was the girl sitting at the whiteboard. Her name was Diane, and she planned to become an ASL interpreter once she finished her seventh year.

Now the coach looked at Cait, eyebrows raised, and pointed at her. "And you?"

She began to sign "I – am – m-I ... m-a-i-n-t .. " No. Breathe. "m-a-i-n-s-t-r-e-a-m" Whew. "School – with – hearies –." Why are my fingers so jittery all of a sudden? Cait thought. These are exactly the people I'd wanted to be around. She tried again. "I – one –" pointed to her hearing aids, paused to collect her thoughts.

The coach waved for her attention and signed as Diane translated, "Calm down, you can use your voice if you want." Then he gestured at Diane, who mimed listening, with her hand held up to her ear.

"I have a lot of hearing." As Cait spoke, Diane's writing followed faithfully. "Went to public school, haven't met anyone deaf until now, although I've seen interpreters on stage a couple of times, and how did you keep the wand from falling from your hand when you were signing earlier?" It felt so good to ask exactly the question that was in her head, and still be understood by everyone, deaf and hearing. "And how do you do magic? Are there

246

special signs? Other than –" she dropped her sketchpad, and levitated it, using the Visual-Kinetic spell.

"We do the same," answered the coach, "we call it V-K", and he demonstrated it fingerspelled, with a little shake to each letter. Then he held up his wand and opened his hand wide – the wand clung to his palm, as if he still gripped it. Pointing to the board, the words appeared, "Clingspell. Your wandmaker will know how to install it for you."

"So there are no magical schools for people who sign? Only the regular hearing-person schools?" Cait asked.

As her questions appeared on the board, all the Eagles' faces showed looks of sympathy. Lillian reached for Cait's hand, and held it, then signed to Cait. As she did so, the board wrote out, "We persevered, and found each other. If you study and persevere as well, you too, will succeed. You can do it."

Coach Joe was now waving frantically for everyone's attention. "Plods will be here soon. We still need to practice. Into the air, everyone."

Lillian gave Cait a hug, and then Alberto threw his arms around her and took the green and silver cap off his head and put it on Cait, and then the Eagles were overhead again.

The coach wrote on the board himself. "Stuck in mainstream, yes hard. In Boston other Deaf, other mainstream, you will find, yes? We will look for you next game East Coast." He pressed something flat into Cait's hand as he turned to watch the Eagles maneuvering overhead. Cait slipped the object into her sleeve-pocket; she'd look at it later. Right now, she wanted to bask in the company of this team that flew, signed, looked like they were all such good friends, and were so welcoming to a stranger dropping in on them out of the blue. More and

247

more things looked so possible all the time. She couldn't wait to sign as well as they could. How many other magical signing people were out there on the East Coast struggling along just like Cait? Did the Quebec school have any mainstreamed "hearing-impaired" students?

A tap on Cait's shoulder broke the reverie. "We're busted," moaned Penny.

Sure enough, another set of broomriders approached them rapidly, a trio of riders in full, voluminous robes and tall hats. As they landed, Cait realized with dismay that they were the same three witches who had fixed the front gate when she had messed up the P'tach spell earlier that year.

Worst of all was seeing the disappointment on Corwin's face as she approached and addressed Cait in a soft voice. "I'd expected better of you, Caitlin. All of you, where's the boat? We'll discuss this further when we're back in Salem."

As they went down to the beach, settled into their boat, and listened to the teachers calling up the Speed-Wind spell, Cait replayed every bit of the encounter with the Eagles in her memory, and wondered how she was going to go about finding the ASL-signing magicworkers of the East Coast. She loved her family, she loved her friends, and she loved studying magic at Witches' Academy; but being around signers felt like home.

Chapter 17 - Ole Jim

"I am most disappointed," repeated Lumen.

Caitlin stood in Lumen's office. Lumen presided from behind her oak desk, flanked by Greatwood and Corwin. Penny and Meg had just been dismissed from the room; they were to be confined to campus for the rest of the semester.

As Cait's friends exited the room, casting worried backward glances, Greatwood laid a restraining hand on Cait's shoulder. Motion caught her eye. In the corner behind Lumen, a raven hopped and fluttered. It was playing with some small object, and Cait had to keep reminding herself to keep her eyes on the Director, not the bird.

"Why?" Lumen asked her.

Thoughts swirled about Cait's brain as she stared at the grain of the oak desktop before her. How was she going to explain it all to these teachers? It was those effortless words flowing from hand to hand, the language that nobody thought she really needed. They were what pulled her across the country without waiting to fill out request forms and get parental permission and possibly be turned down. She needed to be around that chatter which went so easily from hand to eye to brain, so different from depending upon batteries and quiet rooms and making people not talk all at once and not mumble and not talk away from her. How can a hearing person understand that?

Caitlin shrugged. Her voice felt tight, and tears were trying to form behind her eyes, but she swallowed them back with an effort.

"I don't know," she whispered, while unconsciously signing the phrase, right hand flicking out from her temple.

Lumen's voice now continued. "Leaving campus without notice or permission. Three missed classes. Stealing school property." Cait's head snapped up at this. That wasn't stealing, they were going to return the boat where it belonged. Greatwood put up her hand in warning: now was the time to listen, not speak. "Inducing fellow students to collaborate in this stunt. For the sake of a sports team whom you've never met." The trademark gaze met Cait's eyes, demanding explanation. "I presume this was not simply the escapade of a sports fan."

"They sign. They talk – really talk – with their hands. I had to go meet them. They don't have to listen up all day every day to people who mumble and talk to chalkboards and won't repeat themselves in noisy rooms." As Cait spoke, the words fell flat and limp, becoming flimsy and hollow. She looked down at the crimson wool of the carpet as tears of frustration began to spill out. Dimly, she could feel the gentle push of someone Mindcasting her.

Silence.

The raven fluttered in its corner; Cait watched it as she choked back her tears. Lumen signaled to Greatwood and Corwin, and all three of them gathered around the ship's compass. They took out their wands, and aimed them at the compass with closed eyes. They then opened their eyes, gazed at the compass for a long moment, and exchanged glances. Lumen nodded, then settled herself once more behind the oak desk. A decision had been made.

"You will remain on campus for the remainder of this semester, and will broomride only on campus, and only in the Academy courtyard," she pronounced. "When you are

250

not in class or at meals, you will be in your dorm room. You may visit the library, but must notify the dorm supervisor whenever you do so."

Lumen turned and signaled to the raven, which dropped its toy and strutted over to Cait, cocking its head to look at her with one eye, and then the other. Turning back to Cait, Lumen went on, "Poe will accompany you at all times. Of course, your parents have been notified of this weekend's events. Expect to receive word from them as well."

As Cait trudged back to her dorm room, the raven strutting officiously beside her, she passed a group of third-years practicing their weatherworking. A tiny cloud hovered over each girl. As they spoke and flourished their wands, a gentle shower descended from most of the clouds. One girl did her spell with too much vigor, however, and got herself drenched. My mood exactly, thought Cait.

A girl who was helping dry off her soggy classmate caught sight of Poe, and the whole group began whooping and laughing. "Woo! First probation of the year," drifted over one of the voices. Cait couldn't get into Partridge Hall fast enough.

Even her room was no haven. Nini bristled and hissed as soon as she saw Poe, and spent all evening glaring at him from the top of Cait's wardrobe. Penny snorted in surprise. "Wow, I didn't know they'd give you an escort. You got bad-girl cred. Gimme five!"

But Cait only flumped over to her bed. "They don't get it, they don't get it." Something in her sleeve poked at her. Pulling the flat object out of her robe, she finally looked at it. Tickets to the Eagles' game. Didn't matter; she was grounded. But having the tickets in hand brought back the vision of all those signers descending from the sky.

She knew that they would understand. Back into her sleeve pocket the tickets went, pocket buttoned shut. Didn't matter what the teachers thought. She had this. And she had some East Coast magicworkers to find. She pulled the Eagles cap more firmly on her head as she stared at the cracks in the ceiling and daydreamed herself back to Seattle.

December 2, 2007
Dear Cait:
Your father and I are very disappointed in you. What on earth were you thinking? You don't just take matters into your own hands. There are rules that have to be followed, and when you're different, you have to be even more careful to do everything the right way. You're supposed to be fitting in, remember? You have the chance to fit in and accomplish everything that normal people can. This magical world puts you in a small enough group already. You're not like people who have to be sent to signing schools because they can't do the regular academics. Don't go and ruin your chances. I know that you like this school and your new friends. I don't want to have to make you transfer back to public school.
Love,
Mom

Over the next two weeks, Cait trudged her way through classes and meals, hardly talking to anyone. Meg and Penny tried to nudge her into conversation, and Corwin gave her concerned looks during Spellwork class. Andreya clowned around in swim class whenever she was anywhere near Cait, and platefuls of cobweb cookies and muffins decorated with heart-enclosed "A.G."s appeared at Cait's dorm-room door. She did enjoy the treats, but they didn't do much to offset the snickers which followed her whenever people caught sight of the raven at her heels.

Poe flew alongside her every moment during Broomwork class, and the distraction made her wobblier than usual. And when she looked down at the ground, Nini would be hunkered up under a tree, hissing at the raven, rather than watching Cait with bright eyes and upright pose.

And with Poe on the scene, mornings became pure chaos. As soon as the schedule-bearing dove or crow or chipmunk arrived, Poe would jump on her pillow, and the smaller animal would usually drop the scroll and run off, leaving Cait to retrieve it from floor or sheets or under the bed. Then Nini would wake up to growl, swat, and hiss at the raven's intrusion, before retreating from the foot of Cait's bed to the top of her wardrobe.

Then there were the taunts from Claire when she walked into class, right where Cait could hear them. "Look, there's Molasses the Delinquent with her parole officer." And Amanda would snicker and answer, "Such a shame she can't race these days."

Not only that, but the bird would also imitate Corwin's spells in his gravelly voice, making Ms. Corwin eyes sparkle as she said, "See what happens when you don't have intention? That's why his spells won't work."

Even the sight of Yule preparations depressed her. They only reminded Cait that she was that much closer to being back home where there was no magic-working at all, and the other kids looked at her funny.

Why did she have to live so far away from her friends, out in the country where there weren't any busses or trains and you couldn't get anywhere without a driver's license? Well, maybe she could figure out a trip to

253

Fitchburg to see Meg, but the drive to Penny's part of Connecticut was a long one.

Even the weather matched those gloomy weeks, with the ground still bare. They had only one dusting of snow so far, and it was during class. By the time they got out, it had all melted.

Finals approached. It was Sunday night, and Cait and Penny sat studying in their dorm room for their first set of exams the next day. Instead of her badly-neglected Greenwitchery book, however, Cait reached for her old sign-language text with its red-and-blue ABC on the cover. Staring at the front of the book, Cait spoke out loud, "So where are all these other signers? The Eagles told me you're out there, but where?"

The round NAD logo at the bottom of the cover caught her eye as she threw the book down. NAD. She picked up the book again. What did that stand for? She flipped through the pages – there it was. National Association of the Deaf. This book was old, published before she was born. Were they a boring bunch of grownups? Were any of them even magical? The Academy library had so little about signing and deaf people. If only she had a computer so she could Google the NAD.

She thought for a moment. The National Geographic Society had a magazine. An interesting one too, with all those amazing pictures from all over the world. Maybe the NAD had a magazine? Library time.

"I'm going to see if I can go to the library," Cait announced to Penny, wishing she didn't have to ask permission. As Poe followed Cait to the door, Nini yawned and jumped down from the wardrobe to make herself comfortable on Cait's bed. From the depths of her alchemy notes, Penny groaned. "Good luck, hope you do better

254

The dorm-supervising dog got up from in front of the fireplace as Cait entered the lobby, and sniffed Cait's palm thoroughly as she made her request. Then she lay back down, tail thumping on rug; Cait was free to go. On the way to the library, Cait followed the glowing courtyard path carefully in the darkness, keeping close to the dorm walls in case she lost her balance. There must be other magicworkers with balance like mine, Cait thought. What do they do about night-flying? On Cait's left, Poe was only a black shadow as he coasted and paused, coasted and paused, sailing from branch to branch of the small trees which lined the courtyard's edges.

Once at the library, Cait went right to the periodicals room, remembering to close the door behind her. Turning around, she saw Poe winging into a frenzy of chasing the arriving and departing daily newsletters, ephemera charts, and evening newsflashes. Hoping the bird would stay distracted for a while, she stood under the stone arch and told it, "NAD".

Nothing.

"National Association of the Deaf." Still no response.

"Deaf!"

One scroll winged toward her, followed by a handful of others. Cait sat down on a nearby chair, and the scrolls hovered around her. Taking the first scroll, she could see the letters DAR written on its outside page. DAR? There was a DAR highway that her family took when driving to Great-Aunt May's house, but she doubted it had anything to do with this scroll. She opened it up to find that the acronym stood for "Deaf Alchemical Ring," and that it was located in Great Britain. Just a bit too far away. She set it down on the arm of the chair, and it winged away to its pigeonhole.

One by one, she looked at the other scrolls which hovered before her. All of them were DAR, except for the last one, which read WFDA.

It opened up to show the full title, Newsletter of the Wizarding Federation of Deaf Athletes. Pictures of athletes from all over the world smiled up at her with brooms in hand or posing with sailboats, some flashing the ILY sign or giving the thumbs-up, others using handshapes she'd never seen before. The captions described them being from Brazil, Cambodia, Nicaragua, Germany, Saudi Arabia. If only she had found this magazine back when she'd exploded that apple and was looking for deaf magicworking the first time. She browsed the pages full of broomriders and weatherworkers from places she'd never imagined would have either magical or Deaf communities.

The word "Washington" jumped at her as she flipped through. Washington state? Or Washington DC? Turning back to that page, she saw a picture of a large half-timbered building with a broomriding team standing before it, everybody signing "ILY." Below, the caption read: "The Belfry Bats of Ole Jim are pleased and proud to host the 2001 International Broomracing meet..."

2001? That was a while ago. What had happened to the WFDA since then? And who was Ole Jim? The caption continued, "Regrettably, the famous cherry blooms of Washington DC have already gone by, but we are sure the international teams will enjoy the Southern hospitality on the Potomac all the same."

DC. Three cheers, it was on the East Coast. But did this Ole Jim group still exist? Excitement bubbled within Cait, and she felt lighter than she had for days. She had to get to a computer to learn more. She had to find this group. And if they were still around, she had to go there. But how? During the school year, or after? By broom? By train?

As if he had the ability to Mindcast, Poe snatched the magazine from Cait's hands. Cait glared as the pamphlet reverted to scroll form. Then Poe began a game of flying up several feet, dropping the scroll, catching it; dropping and retrieving it again ... all while keeping a firm eye on Cait.

Being grounded stunk. Stink, stank, stunk.

How was she going to find out about this Jim guy? Maybe he was a really popular coach. Or some superstar athlete. Just wait till I get my hands on Google, she thought. Then her common sense kicked in. Hide in Plain Sight. Magical groups wouldn't be on her parents' computer, would they? At least she could find out more about groups like the NAD. If it was a big enough group, might some magical folks also belong to it? Even just a few?

As she stood up to go, the WFDA scroll zoomed back to its pigeonhole just as Poe dove to catch it. He landed with a squawk of protest and strutted towards Cait.

Back at the stone arch, she told it, "Washington DC, November –" but as she spoke the words, bells rang and lights flashed. Closing time. Poe was now flapping his wings against Cait's legs and adding his throaty "krrrk, krrk" to the general noise.

All the way back to the dorm, hope dispelled the gloom of the past two weeks. There really was an East Coast group of Deaf magicworkers. And as soon as this semester was finished, Cait was going to find them.

With a shock, she realized that there were only five more days of probation left. Finals had been so much on her mind that she hadn't realized how close they were to Yule Fest. The party was on the 21st – only five days away.

Only five more days of Poe patrol and being stuck on campus and not being able to broomsprint with Meg. Less than a week. Let the countdown begin.

Chapter 18 – One Old Book

The morning after finals ended, Cait was woken up by a schedule-bearing chipmunk, while Poe hopped over from the nightstand to the pillow to chase it away. The chipmunk dropped the schedule scroll and fled. Nini had just gotten up and was hissing at Poe when a squirrel came in the birdflap as well. Did the squirrel have an anti-predation glamour on it? Wand, where was her wand? Cait groped around her nightstand before remembering that the wand was still in her robe pocket, behind the wardrobe door.

At this new intruder, Nini bristled up to twice her usual size. "Stay," said Cait to the cat with both voice and Sign, while Poe hopped onto a bedpost. The squirrel dropped a note which said: "Please present yourself at the Director's Office, Old House, 10 am today. Director Penthesilia Lumen."

As Cait walked through the courtyard towards Old House, Poe flew to the next tree ahead of them with a ground-skimming swoop. Then he hung upside down from his branch to watch Cait approach before coasting to the next tree and repeating the stunt. Lumen actually smiled as the two entered her office, motioning for Cait to take a seat in the ladderback chair before her desk. As she did so, Poe marched back and forth between Cait and the desk as if on sentry duty.

"Congratulations on passing your first-semester exams," Lumen began. "The break from broomriding appears to have improved your studies. Corwin was quite concerned about your spellwork earlier in the semester, you know."

"Thank you," answered Cait. If Lumen wasn't even going to mention the Visual-Kinetic method, then Cait wouldn't either. Even if people still called her "molaaases" for having to write out all her spells in longhand, Cait knew that her grades wouldn't be nearly so good without it.

"You seem to have suffered no ill effects from missing three classes," Lumen continued. Her expression demanded explanation.

"People were really nice. They shared their notes," Cait said. As a matter of fact, while Poe had stared and strutted on her first class day of probation, Claire had come smiling up to her at the end of Greenwitchery class and hinted that Astronologia and Zoomorphia notes could be had for a price. Why would Claire need to sell anything to anyone? wondered Cait. She already had plenty of money. Cait held back giggles as she explained that she already had the notes she needed, "Thank you sooo much for asking."

"Concern, ha," Penny said as they went off to Spellwork. "Bet she put wrong stuff in those notes." Cait nodded agreement and thanked the stars that she'd taken the time to look at the booklet which Andreya had slipped her that morning. It had taken two all-night study sessions to fully absorb the contents of the booklet which contained detailed notes from all three of the classes that Meg, Penny and Cait had missed. It felt like a party as the trio studied those notes in the dorm lounge, while Andreya smiled from a nearby armchair "in case they couldn't read her writing." It had been the one bright spot in those weeks of Poe patrol.

Lumen appeared satisfied with Cait's answer and went on. "Next time you feel a need to go out of town during the school year, bring a proper request to Greatwood. We are a school, not a prison, and there is no need to jailbreak. We

260

do realize that there are occasional compelling reasons to be elsewhere while school is in session."

Again, she cast a steely look at Cait.

"I'll do that, Ms. Lumen," said Cait.

"Good." Lumen nodded in acceptance. "I believe that Poe is more than ready to enjoy some personal liberty, which you also will not mind. Yes?"

Cait nodded, and Lumen signaled to the bird. Poe gave a loud "krrrrk" and flew around the room before dropping into the corner where Cait had first seen him and retrieving the toy which still lay there.

"Much better," murmured Lumen, watching the bird then turning to Cait. "You are free to go. Happy Solstice and Glad Yule to you."

"Glad Yule to you, Director Lumen," answered Cait. She skipped out the hallway and into the courtyard feeling light with joy. Same air, same weather, but such a different mood. She wanted to grab a broom and do sprints all over the courtyard. At least there was broomwork class today at three. But she had free time right now, and decisions to make. What to do first? Go downtown for fudge? Have a browse in her favorite bookshop? Watch the boats at the town dock? Tease the shopkeepers by making the Christmas-display manikins move when nobody was looking? Time to find Penny and Meg.

They were both in the Partridge Hall lounge, grinning from ear to ear. "We just got a chipmunk telling us the grounding's off," babbled Meg. "I can't wait to go into town and check out the view at Peppermill. Boys!"

"So what did Lumen say to you?" asked Penny as Meg checked her robes for cat hairs and snags, adorning it with a holly twig from the mantelpiece arrangement.

"Not a lot," replied Cait. "Only a little lecture about getting permission to leave campus next time I need to. Hey Meg, what're you doing? We have to wear Plain Sight clothes downtown. It isn't Hallowe'en any more."

By noontime, they were at Peppermill flirting with BWIS students. Cait bought a thank-you box of fudge for Andreya for all the note-taking and the help with Seattle, hoping the selkie wouldn't get the wrong idea and develop an even bigger crush on her.

On their way to their other favorite nonmagical shops, Penny tossed a quick wandwave at a window full of plush-toy Santa's elves, then popped her wand back into her sleeve. One of the elves flipped upside-down and flew to the top of the window. Inside, the shopkeeper caught sight of the change in display, pointing and talking to a clerk, who now looked up at the window in complete confusion.

Exploding in giggles, the trio ran down the street to Cait's favorite bookstore, a place near Crowhame which had overflowing bookshelves and windows full of calendars with sunny beaches, cute pets, and swimsuited models of both genders.

As Meg and Penny ogled a calendar full of soccer stars, Cait wandered over to the part of the shop where the secondhand books were kept. As her gaze roved around the towering shelves of books, she wondered again just who "Jim" was and how she was going to find him. A shelf label caught her eye: "Travel – US". Of course. Tourists went to DC all the time. Maybe there would be books about the city with a picture of that building the Ole Jim team visited.

The travel books didn't seem to be in any particular order. A book about the Ohio Valley sat next to "A Guide to Seminole Folkways", with "Canyons of the Southwest" next to it. Think, think. Would the boh-ee spell work on a picture in a book? Cait looked around for nearby Plods. A few people on lunch break finished their purchases and hurried out the door. The coast was clear, but there wasn't much time. Cait retrieved her wand from the pocket she'd sewn into her Plain-Sight jacket, held it before her, and visualized the picture she'd seen in the WFDA newsletter, concentrating especially on the building in its background.

Then she wand-wrote 'boh-ee!' and sent the energy.

Much to her shock, there was a small motion at the top of the overloaded bookcase. A clothbound volume inched out from under a stack of books, as the books around it swayed precariously. Cait reached out to keep the books from falling, but wasn't quick enough – three hardcover volumes crashed to the floor. Heads turned her way. Penny's eyes widened as she and Meg looked up from their calendar. "Hide your wand," Penny signed madly.

A clerk rushed over, and Cait stashed her wand as he bent to pick up the fallen books. He then eyed the stack of books Cait still held steady with one hand. "Which book do you want?" he asked. "You really should ask for help with those upper shelves."

"That hardcover up there with the yellowish spine," replied Cait.

A hefty but not-too-thick book now sat in her hand, entitled History of the College for the Deaf, 1857-1907. 1907? What if this place weren't around any more? If Ole Jim went to school there, he must be really old. Time to find that building. She flipped through the pages. There it was on page 142, the entire building in its half-timbered glory with pale wooden beams contrasting against dark walls. Under the picture was a caption, "The gymnasium (Ole Jim) in 1880."

Ole Jim's the building? Not a person?

The gym – Ole Jim. Cait groaned at the pun and felt like an idiot.

Penny and Meg appeared at her side. "Look at the time. We have to go. We can't cut our last day of classes now that we're off the hook," nudged Penny.

"Wait'll you see this yummy calendar I got," said Meg, "I'll show you after classes. What's your book?" she asked, peering at the open volume. "Looks boring."

Thoughts of her new book barged in during all of Mindcasting class, prompting Minna to ask if Cait lived in the library or something because of all the book images she was sending.

Cait woke up the next day to a furry headbutt from Nini, who settled down purring on her chest. No more probation, no more Poe, no more chaotic waking up. She happily scratched the contented cat behind the ears. Tonight was the Solstice Banquet, complete with dress robes, and all day was free from classes. What could make this day any more perfect? There were rumors of ice sculpting in the courtyard, a Yule log right in the middle of the Commons, and pyrotechnic broomraces by the seniors.

A rustle of paper caught Cait's attention, and Nini's head swiveled around to the other side of the room. There was a blur in the air between desk and window. Then there was another blur. Cait followed the source of motion to see the last remaining library book atop Penny's desk lift up into the air. Its pages began to flap as if someone were flipping them, while bookmarks and scraps of paper fell out of the book. Then it zoomed spinefirst toward the window, becoming nothing but a blur which vanished just before hitting the glass of the windowpane.

The same thing then happened to the Mindcasting book Cait had forgotten to return after finals. It left scraps of notes all over the dorm-room floor before it, too, vanished. As another of her library books lifted itself from the desk and blurred itself out the window, Cait sat up to watch it go. But as soon as she looked out the window, she forgot all about the books.

Snow was everywhere. Beautiful, perfect, sparkling, bright-white snow, with a clear sky making it look even brighter. She got out of bed to have a better look. Footprints left crisp impressions; powder shook off the tree branches with every breeze; crystalline flakes reflected back the early-morning sun with dazzling sparkles. Powder snow, bone-dry, perfect powder snow. The kind that shoveled up easily and didn't turn slippery and treacherous underfoot. Sledding and skiing snow. This day was sugar-coated like the sparkling top of a cobweb cookie.

Cait looked over at her roommate; only her nose was visible between pillow and covers. She reached for her wand and boh'ee'd a few snowflakes through the birdflap to Nini, giggling as the surprised cat snapped at the falling flakes. Then she sent a few more onto Penny's nose. A hand arose from the covers, flapping as if at flies, then Penny sat up, suddenly awake. "What the heck?"

Cait sent over a few more flakes. "Look what the weather sent us. It's perfect perfect perfect out. And we're not grounded any more. Yay!"

But Penny just groaned and rolled back under the covers. "Wake me up after they've shoveled," she grumped, falling back asleep. On Cait's bed, Nini curled up tighter and flicked her tail up over her nose.

Cait couldn't believe Penny's reaction. Who would want to sleep through this? Then she thought of Meg. She would be up early. She'd been an athlete all through public school, complete with 5:00 a.m. practices, and the habit had stuck. Cait wanted nothing more that moment than to see what all this snow looked like from the air. Broomsprint time. Pulling on her heavy robe, boots, cloak and mittens, and making sure her wand was in its pocket, Cait took off for the dorm's front door, and walked around behind the dorm to Meg's window. Peering through the corner pane, Cait could see that Meg was already dressed and puttering at her desk. Perfect.

Cait lech-na'ed a few snowflakes through the birdflap to drift onto Meg's nose. Meg looked up at the ceiling in bewilderment, then caught sight of Cait at the window and shook a fist at her in mock anger. Cait stuck out her tongue, grinned, and signed, "US-two -- go upstairs – fly?"

Meg looked at her desk, considering. Then she signed "Yup," to Cait as she reached for cloak and boots.

Once on the roof, it was just as beautiful as Cait expected, and it felt wonderful to zoom back and forth as much as she wanted.

Meg waved for Cait's attention. "Awright, you've still got your speed," she proclaimed with a huge grin as they hovered over the center of campus and took in the view. It was still early in the day and the sun cast long blue shadows on half the courtyard below, while the other half shone diamond-dazzling bright. Some of the kitchen witches in their red hats were out and about, supervising the transport of crates and boxes while wanding scraps to Ms. Broadleaf's compost pile behind the garden at Circe Hall. A delicious smell of baked goodies wafted from the Commons' chimney: yeast bread, pies, cake.

"Hey Meg," asked Cait. "Do people who stop at Hedge really get stuck with those kitchen jobs?"

Meg shrugged. "Some do, but there's other jobs, too. Not everyone gets along with books as well as you and Penny. Wish I did."

266

"You do alright," said Cait. "I bet you could go above Hedge just fine."

Meg grimaced. "Don't start. Now you sound like my parents and my genius sibs. The only reason I haven't flunked so far is because I'm up with my books at four a.m. and still looking at them at midnight. You think I'm gonna survive more than three years of this kind of schedule? No way. Let's fly some more. Race you to the library!"

Cait thought this over as they took off. It never occurred to her that books might be difficult for some people. Written words had fascinated her ever since she was a toddler playing with alphabet blocks; her dad loved to tell stories about how she'd sit figuring out their letters, rather than building teetering towers. She especially enjoyed the challenge of learning new letters and watching them turn from nonsense to sense on the page. She couldn't wait for Ms. Corwin to teach those other alphabets that hung on the walls in Spellwork class. A new thought struck her. What if reading were as difficult for Meg as 'listening up' was for Cait?

By the time their growling stomachs drove them back to the dorm rooftop, upperclass ice-sculpture teams were setting up for the afternoon competition, and Penny waited at her usual spot to walk with them to brunch, with Nini hunkered down beside her.

Then it was time for everyone's families to arrive on campus. Cait's stomach flip-flopped with nerves as she stood waiting underneath an ice dragon whose outstretched wings flashed in the sun. Would her parents still be mad at her for running off to find the Eagles? Greatwood appeared under the Commons' archway with a crowd around her, and now Cait's parents were running up to her, embracing her as if everything were back to normal.

"Finished your very first away-from-home semester, eh? I knew you could." Her dad stepped back from their hug and beamed with pride.

There was something searching about her mom's gaze as she stepped back and asked Cait, "How are your new friends? Have you received your grades yet?" Nini wound herself around her mom's ankles, and was rewarded with a cuddle.

"Meg and I had the best time racing each other this morning, and Penny's doing good, too. Let's all sit together at banquet. Penny doesn't like being stuck with her brother for too long. Oh, and I got half As and half Bs, except for a C in Astronologia. One of the As was in Spellwork, where we get to use lots of languages. It's my favorite." Across the courtyard, Cait could see Penny pulling a struggling Stu away from a towering flock of ice birds that reached up to the sky.

Cait's mom wore her usual expression as she listened to Cait's replies, but still, Cait wondered if there would be talk about Seattle later. Should she Mindcast her parents? Was it okay to go around Mindcasting Plods? Cait could usually feel the gentle push at her mind when somebody was Mindcasting her, but had no idea if the same thing happened with nonmagical people. And Ms. Auclair had never said anything about not Mindcasting Plods.

"Let's see the other sculptures," said Cait.

"Lead on," answered her dad.

Cait sent a Mindcast toward her dad as he laughed at a giant ice crow looking at a crowd of miniature pointy-hatted and big-robed people. Nothing there but pure goodwill. And there was no reaction to the Mindcast at all. Then again, it was her mom who was most upset about

268

Seattle, wanting her to fit in, fit in, whittle, whittle, shave that square peg to fit its round hole. As her mom admired the birds-in-flight sculpture, Cait carefully sent a Mindcast her way. No anger there, but uncertainty. A little fear. And a lot of concern. Cait worried about the coming semester. Would her mom haul her out of this school if she flunked night-flying? She resolved to get the best grades possible in all her other classes. And to find out as soon as possible if the Ole Jim group were still around ... and could help her with night-flying.

For the Yule banquet, tables sat around the edges of the Commons, and an empty hollow dipped into the center of the floor. Had that always been there? Was it hidden during the rest of the year? Cait puzzled this over as a procession of brightly-robed faculty proceeded into the room and formed a circle around the hollow. All chatter ceased.

Lumen stepped forward and began to give a speech whose words, as usual, disappeared inaudibly into the large room, despite Cait's trumpetvine hovering as far as it could reach. Around her table, her parents, the Ainslees, and the Dingles all listened attentively, not seeming to miss anything. Well, Cait wasn't going to sit there pretending to understand this time. Nudging Penny, she signed, "I – go – there" and pointed behind a table that was much closer to Lumen. To her surprise, Penny got up and followed her. Then again, Stu had been kicking her chair.

Now the trumpetvine was getting much more of Lumen's speech as they stood and listened. Lumen was saying something about ... "Maccabees?" Cait listened with surprise as Lumen spoke of small lights in darkness, a small group of people who chose not to blend into the surrounding Greek culture. Cait remembered her brass menorah, her unlit box of candles with embarrassment. She'd completely forgotten to look up when Chanukah began. Now Lumen was talking about "roots" and going on about Christmas. The usual, ho-hum. "For those of you who are Wiccan ... later tonight." Oh, not the usual. What did she just miss?

Cait leaned forward to listen more closely. I am so sick of listening up so hard, she thought. Lumen paused as if startled. Cait held her breath. She must have sent an accidental Mindcast. For a moment, Lumen turned and looked right at Cait. Her forehead creased briefly, followed by a slow nod. Then Lumen looked around at the rest of the roomful of people, and put her voice up just a bit louder. Enough to make all the difference.

"So, you can see now the diversity among us ... like all diversity makes the tapestry of our world that much more beautiful ... celebrate the returning light in the darkest time of year ... magical and nonmagical, Christian and Hindu and Jewish and Wiccan and Muslim, let us celebrate light together." Lumen stepped back to join the circle of waiting faculty.

Fifteen voices began a soft and simple tune as Cait and Penny made their way back to their table. It grew in volume as the teachers' hands arose. With that motion, a giant log, a circle of lamps, and a wreath full of candles filled the hollow. The singers changed their tempo and the log, lamps, and candles all burst into bright flames, with their smoke drifting upward to a small hole in the very center of the the Commons' roof. The wreath then floated upward to adorn the rafters, while the lamps hovered in midair over each table, and the log stayed put.

With the flames came a burst of music as well; brass, strings, flute, drums. Where were the musicians? Penny grinned and pointed up; Cait's jaw dropped. Balanced on the rafters, a band of musicians sat suspended in air. She saw more drums and instruments than she could hear, and Cait laid her fingertips on the tabletop before her. There were the rest of the instruments: the beat of the bass drum pulsed through her fingers, as well as the buzz of tuba melody.

Yule banquet was as spectacular as Cait had hoped, complete with a flock of roast turkeys and geese which flew from table to table. Cait chose goose, which never showed up on regular Plod menus. Not in New England, anyhow. Ever since reading Dickens, she'd longed to try it.

The tune from the banquet still played in Cait's mind the next day as she packed her suitcase, exchanged addresses with Meg and Penny, and promised to write during January break. Cait dreaded all the time away from the Academy and her friends, but told herself that the vacation would give her plenty of time to read her new book and find out more about Ole Jim and this College for the Deaf to which it belonged.

As Cait and her parents walked down the sidewalk to their car, Cait remembered the Clingspell that Coach Joe had recommended.

"I've got one thing to get in town. May I? Please?" she asked.

"Walking distance?" asked her dad, while her mom glanced at her watch. "Parking's awfully scarce around here."

Cait nodded.

The witch at Crowhame stood as usual in her doorway as the family approached her shop, frowning as the nonmagical Leos were led to the concealed staircase. But she smiled as soon as she recognized Cait, and vanished into her touristy shop.

At the wandshop, Cait walked right up to the wandmaker, as he burnished a nearly-complete ebony wand. "How much does a Clingspell cost?"

He gave the ebony wand one more swipe with the chamois rag he held. "That will be one Adel to make a permanent Clingspell, good for the life of your wand."

A whole Adel? Where was Cait going to get that kind of money?

At her dismayed look, the wandmaker added, "Not all wands are worth that kind of investment, you know. I wouldn't put a permanent Clingspell on a Hedge-level wand, for example. Yours, however, is well worth putting the permanent spell on it. That chestnut should see you through all seven years and into adulthood. Even University, I daresay." He paused, stroking his red beard.

Behind her, Cait's dad cleared his throat, and her mom's eyebrow rose: Translation, please?

"That's about two hundred dollars," Cait explained. Her dad shook his head in disbelief, and her mom picked up her purse and Nini's cat-carrier.

"You can also have a six-month version of the spell put on," the wandmaker added quickly, "It's only one Orso to do that. It'll last until summer solstice."

"Can we do twenty dollars?" asked Cait. Her mom, who was halfway to the door, turned around.

"Isn't your book money supposed to cover things like this?" she asked.

Cait began to regret all the fudge runs to Peppermill. "I spent the last of it on a book about a college for deaf people in DC," she admitted, as she scuffed one toe on the shop's stone floor.

"That's right, there is this place in DC." The shopkeeper's voice startled them. "The last time I did a

Clingspell was for someone who was moving there, but I don't remember the name of the place."

Was this 'someone' another Deaf signer? Now Cait really couldn't wait to start in on her new book and get to the family computer. "Can we do the Clingspell? Mom? Dad?" she asked. "It will make the Visual-Kinetic thing so much easier to do. Visual-Kinetic is how come I got that A in Spellwork this semester."

Her parents sighed in defeat, and her mom handed over a twenty. "Thank you, thank you, be right back," shouted Cait as she ran down the alley to exchange it for an Orso.

By the time they reached central Massachusetts, Cait had read half the book and learned that President Lincoln had signed the college's charter, that it took twenty years before the first women were enrolled as students, and that it had the fanciest school gym around when Ole Jim was built.

As the car left the highway and approached town, she flipped through the rest of the book, looking for anything magical, but finding nothing. The wandmaker had said: "there is this place in DC", not "there was", so it must still be around. If it were a nonmagical school, then what were the broomracers doing at Ole Jim? Playing tourist? Or doing a very, very good job of Hiding in Plain Sight?

"We're here, scholar-girl," her dad proclaimed as the car pulled into their driveway. Beside Cait, Nini yowled from her carrier. Opening the car door, Cait stopped, spellbound, as she caught sight of the many tiny white lights twinkling from the front-yard maple and the bright tree right in the middle of the living-room's bay window.

"That's so beautiful," she sighed. Her parents beamed. With a pang, she again remembered missing Chanukah. Well, she had been a bit preoccupied at the time, with Poe following her around. She wondered if her mom felt lonely lighting candles with just her dad.

"Hey mom, can we have potato pancakes even though Hanukah's over? With sour cream?" Her mom hugged her as they walked into the twinkling-lit house.

Aunt May showed up after supper on Sunday night, knocking on the back door, broom in hand, grinning from ear to ear. "Success, my dear. You'll be seeing plenty of me now that I've brewed Mal-de-Mer-remedy twice in a row perfectly. No more highways. Isn't night-flying the loveliest invention of the magical world?"

Cait felt a bitter twist of envy and nerves as she hugged and congratulated her aunt. "But what if I can't night-fly?"

"They'll figure something out, my dear. After all, that school's three hundred years old, they're bound to have more tricks up their sleeve. Now, shall we compare our spellwork methods? I want to see this V-K business you keep complaining about in your letters."

"Watch what I can do with this Clingspell I just got. Makes V-K easier, even though it's still way pokey. They'll be calling me 'molasses' until I graduate." And with that, Cait sent her card to Aunt May up to the very highest branch of their glittering tree.

"Two can do that, you know," said Aunt May with a chuckle, as she took out her own wand and sent a tiny box marked "Cait" to perch among the branches of the living-room chandelier.

Cait's dad stood there shaking his head. "Just don't forget anything in the rafters, you two."

The Dingle's crow tapped on the Leo's kitchen window the next day, with a little box for Cait. Inside it sat a tiny bush with dark-green leaves that released chocolate drops at random times throughout the day. The day after that, the Ainslee falcon showed up with a long tube containing a poster of the Seattle Eagles flying in formation and throwing quick signed greetings at the viewer. Of course the birds didn't return empty-clawed. Cait didn't have anything magical to send, but she liked to bake, so she sent a large boxful of her prettiest cookies to each of her friends, wrapped up in plenty of plastic, duct-tape, a Shedwater spell, and a sturdy twine handle for the bird to carry it by.

After the Ainslee's falcon took off into the sky, Aunt May motioned at Cait to sit down with her at the kitchen table. "Where's your notebook and pen? Good. Once you know how to get a wild bird to carry letters for you, it's far better than email. You know that magic and machines don't mix. And phones, ugh. Wires, reception, phone bills, forget it. Do you remember the spell I use to summon my dove? Close, it goes like this. Let me write it down. You want to start training a dove, they're easy to work with. Crows are too smart and bratty. The way you show them where you want them to go works something like a Mindcast. Here, it's something like this ..."

Not until after New Year's celebrations were over and Aunt May had gone home did Cait remember all the things she wanted to find out about the Deaf college in DC, where the Deaf magicworkers were, and how she could learn to sign like the Eagles team. She fidgeted with her sketchpad all morning, filling it with pictures of broomriders, signing derby players, seals, letter-carrying birds and the Schoodic, waiting while her mom took forever to finish a manuscript that was under deadline. Finally, pages emerged from the printer. Her mom smiled as she flipped through the newly-printed sheaf and popped it into an envelope.

"I'm off to the post office. Have fun online, I know you've been waiting your turn for a while. Don't print anything until I get home. Toner's low, and it's expensive. Your dad's in the shop fixing the brown upright."

"Okay, Mom. See you soon." A thrill ran up Cait's spine as she sat at the computer. What to search first? College for the Deaf, Washington DC.

The first Google hit turned out to be the university's site itself. Yay, Cait. Give the girl two points. The top of this page was all about students, enrolling, academics, undergraduate, athletics, boring, for the grownups. Then there was another link: "Center for Deaf and Hard of Hearing Children."

Score, Cait gets two more points. If they included "hard of hearing", then this place wasn't just for kids who were too deaf for anything else. Was Cait's doctor wrong? Or ignorant? Or did he on purpose not want her to find out about places like this?

On to the link. Score again, a teen web-zine. Now, could they help her sign like the Eagles? Did any magicworking Deaf kids read it? Was this zine any good, or was it just some grown-up's lame attempt?

When Cait's mom returned, Cait was absorbed in reading, and jumped when her mom tapped her on the shoulder. "Looks like you had no trouble finding something interesting while I was out," she said with a smile.

"Mom, I want to read all of these zines. They're for deaf and hard-of-hearing kids."

Cait's mom looked down awkwardly and dithered a bit as she put down her handbag, pulled the ottoman closer to the computer, and sat down. "Um, well, I did want to show you something from Washington, DC. But your

276

Seattle adventure raised a lot of questions. Important questions."

Cait's throat went dry. Was her mom going to yank her out of school after all?

"Don't worry, I'm not dropping any big changes on you. I just want to tell you that sometimes your dad and I pay too much attention to the hearing you do have, and are too quick to ignore the hearing you don't have. And we have spent too much time taking doctors and teachers at their word and not trusting what we know about what you need. And that's been harder on you than we've realized up until now."

"Um, okay." Cait guessed there was an apology somewhere in that speech, although she wasn't really sure quite what Mom was trying to tell her.

"Also, I thought you might like to see this, especially since you seem to be making a lot of sketches lately." Her mom's voice was back to normal as she pulled a magazine out of the nearby bookcase, handed it to Cait, and went off towards her dad's piano workshop.

Cait turned directly to the page which had a yellow flag sticking out of it. "National Essay, Art, and Sign Contest. First prize: $1000." Really? That would put Clingspell on her wand for life and buy all her books through Hedge level. Then there wouldn't be any Sorcerers' Aid certificate for Claire to taunt her about. Then she read further. Shoot, that was only for ages 15-19. What about the other age ranges? There it was, prizes for ages 9-14. That first prize was only $100. Not fair. Still, that would pay for half of the permanent Clingspell. Further down the page, the announcement read: "Art entrants will have their work considered for display in the art gallery on campus in DC."

Something was clipped behind the page; Cait removed the paperclip to find an entry form.

There it was. She now had a ready-made reason to go to this Deaf campus in person. And maybe once she was actually there, find the Ole Jim witches and wizards. Provided that she was able to produce a piece of art worth giving one of those prizes to.

She had to do this. How much time did she have? The deadline was February 8. One whole month to create something. What could she draw that would get her that prize? It had to be something great. No, magnificient.

Chapter 19 – Derby Plans

Cait admired the final version of her drawing one more time before nervously putting it between sheets of cardboard, then into the padded envelope her mom had ready. The contest theme was "Yes, I Can!" Cait's first response was "Hokey, hokey, ick," but as she worked on the picture, she began to enjoy it more and more.

The picture portrayed Cait smiling and wearing the fanciest robes she could imagine, fancier than Lumen's dress robes. She stood atop an enormous stack of books, and held a wax-sealed scroll in one hand. She wished she could include the tall, pointed seventh-year hat, but she didn't want to risk the Plod judges thinking she'd misunderstood the theme. A star chart behind her had a big, red "A+" on it; maybe they'd think she was a budding astronomer. A botanical sketch beside it also bore a big "A", as did sheets marked "Essay" on its other side. Atop two more stacks of books stood smiling renditions of Penny, on her right, and Meg, on her left, each girl also with a wax-sealed scroll in hand. Meg's the one who really needs this theme, thought Cait, sorry that she couldn't at least include a broom in this picture. Behind the trio were three pairs of Grecian pillars in the background, labeled "College", "Advanced College", and "Doctoral Dissertation." Cait's mom always did a lot of complaining about her dissertation, so Cait decided it must be a really big "I can" sort of thing.

Cait slipped the picture out of the envelope to have one last look at it. Was it really ready? Anything else to add to it? Nini napped nearby in the quiet living room; random notes filtered through from her dad's studio as he played a waltz on a just-repaired piano as her mother listened. Cait listened to the music for a while, admired the way the sun

279

fell across Nini's chair, then looked once more at the picture. It was good. Then she pulled out her wand and put a good-luck charm on the picture. Now it was ready to travel.

And so was she. Tomorrow she'd be on her way back to the Academy. She couldn't wait to see her friends, and to find out what riding the train from Boston would be like.

Cait sealed the envelope and sat down by the front window. As she waited for the mail truck to show up, she remembered her tickets for the Eagles game in February. A thrill went through her as she recalled the swoops and turns of those expert flyers above their practice ground in Seattle and their effortless and fluid way of signing. She'd get to see a whole game of theirs at last. Not a ten-minute halftime demonstration. Not a snippet of time stolen from their practice session.

But if she was going to get to that game at all, her parents had to okay it. This time she was going to be good, good, good, and get off campus the official way. All the "i"s dotted, all the "t"s crossed. Come on, mail truck, hurry up. I can't forget to ask about this, she thought.

Neighbors' cars went by. A fuel truck. Three bikers. A dog walker. Finally, the boxy blue and white mail truck pulled up, and the envelope was swapped for the day's mail.

Cait raced to the studio door. "Mom, Dad, I need a note to go off campus during the first school weekend."

The music stopped in mid-phrase as her dad looked up from his score. Her mom stood up slowly from a nearby bench as one eyebrow rose higher than Cait had ever seen it. "Do you really think you're going anywhere after that stunt in November?" Her tone was chilly.

Donald laid a hand on Miriam's arm, glanced at her, then spoke to Cait. "She's right. We sent you to go to school in Salem, not Snohomish or to wherever else. Travel is a privilege, not a right. Your mother and I have to talk about this."

Talk about this. This was serious. Cait hadn't heard them use this phrase since she forgot to put her bike away the summer she was ten and it got run over. It had cost her three weeks allowance to fix it, and three more weeks of not being allowed to ride.

Cait's cheeks burned as she fled the studio, scooped up Nini, and ran for the refuge of her bedroom. She fought the urge to throw something as tears began to stream down her face. How could following that book to Snohomish have messed things up so much? That was way back in November. Why did they still have to punish her for it? Not fair. She bet that Penny and Meg had their permission slips all signed and ready to go.

Would writing to Aunt May help? Dad always listened to Aunt May, and Mom was the one who was more upset. And this would give her a chance to try out those new bird-handling spells she'd learned at Christmas. Cait retrieved her wand from the homemade holster she wore under her Plain Sight clothes. She then took out the extra cookie she'd saved from supper last night, broke off a small piece, and laid it on her windowsill. She shivered as she opened the window, pushed up the storm window behind it, and propped open the birdflap she'd cut into the screen. Nini's eyes were bright and alert as she noticed the outdoor smells, but a second gust of the cold air sent her running for the warmth of Cait's parents' bedroom.

It took three tries of Aunt May's bird-summoning spell before she was rewarded with the sight of a bird flying over from the front-yard maple. A crow landed on the

281

window sill, snapped up the bit of cookie and cawed for another. What about that mourning dove she'd really wanted? Up until now, it had never occurred to Cait to wonder where doves went in winter. Sticking another bit of cookie in the window frame to keep the crow busy, Cait scribbed a note to Aunt May, then remembered that this bird didn't know how to carry a letter. Ribbon, did she have any ribbon? Or string? Rummaging through her desk drawer, she pulled out a bit of twine, only to see the crow take off.

When she put out another bit of cookie, it came back. Cait reached out with the twine, only to see the crow take off and sit on a nearby branch, leaving the cookie behind, and warily looking at her with one eye, then the other. Cait tried the other half of Aunt May's spell, the one that told the bird where to go. But it fizzled out into nothingness as she sent it.

She put another piece of cookie on the windowsill, only to see the crow hunch up, spread its wings, and fly off. Great. Off to a stellar start in the bird-training business.

Was the computer free? Cait walked quietly down the stairs and peered into the living room. Her mom banged away at the keyboard, looking too grouchy to disturb.

Cait stole back up the stairs. That left the telephone; good thing she had enough hearing to use one. One ring, two rings. Ten rings later, she hung up the phone in frustration. Did Great-aunt May have to be so very retro? No voice-messaging even? How was that even possible?

Nobody talked at supper that night.

After an equally-quiet breakfast the next morning, just before leaving the house, Cait's mom held up a white envelope. "I'll be giving this to your Deputy Director Greatwood when you board today's train. I still think it's too soon for you to have full travel permission. But I also realize that you need to be around other hearing-impaired people, and I hesitate to deprive you of that chance. And so, your permission to travel is contingent upon three things. One, that you not miss a single class between tomorrow and that game. Two, that you write to me every day proving that you've done so, and that this note be sent from the school's administrative office. Three, that you remain on campus for the whole week." She handed Cait a piece of paper on which was printed, "Proof of Attendance 2/4/08", with four numbered blanks below. "Those blanks are for your teachers to sign. Every day. I only wish that your father and I were allowed to chaperone you and your friends ourselves."

Even though she was glad to be back on campus, Cait cursed the noisy Commons as she took her trumpetvine along to supper that evening. She wasn't about to risk losing conversational details when there was so little time to get their New York plans together. Chaperone. Why did finally seeing the Eagles again have to depend on having some grown-up member of the magical community chaperone them? Making all these teachers write their names on that "Proof of Attendance" sheet was going to be bad enough.

"So, can your sister help us out?" asked Cait, but Meg shook her head. "No way. She really wants to go, but she's stuck in Mexico, something about a mudslide. I'm waiting for word from big-bro Merle, maybe he can go with us."

The trumpetvine shifted over to Penny, on Cait's other side. "Maybe one of us could disguise ourselves as an of-age person and pretend our real self is visiting home for the weekend while the other two of us go to New York. No, better yet, I'll say that Mom needs me at her shop to fill in. It'll be the perfect excuse."

Meg's eyes lit up. "You know how to do that? Can you really hold a glamour that long? I can't get one to stay put for more than ten minutes in Zoomorphia observation. I get so tired of animals spooking when the glamour drops. What've you been up to all January?"

"We can't risk it." Cait's heart thumped. What if they got in trouble again, and she never got to see Ole Jim and find out if other Deaf magical groups got to go there, like the team from the WFDA? "I can't get grounded again. There's this other school I have to get to. I think they've got signing Deaf wizards there."

Penny sighed. "But it was such a great adventure last time. I bet we could pull it off."

"Yeah, well you didn't have Poe shadowing you everywhere for weeks," retorted Cait.

They ate their chowder in silence.

As they were finishing their dessert, the Ainslee's falcon winged into the Commons, barely missing Meg's bowl of chocolate-mint pudding as he landed on the table. The trio held their breath as Meg unrolled and read the note from BWIS. "Sorry guys, I've got a really important meet then. Be sure to tell Bosso he's a good bird before you send him back, and give him plenty of treats. Love, your big bro Merle."

Cait pushed her dessert aside and put her head down with a groan, while Meg pounded the tabletop, then had to soothe a ruffled Bosso. Who else could they ask? Penny's mom had a shop to run. Cait's great-aunt was hardly "fully fledged" but still a student herself. Would they have to start asking teachers? Staff?

Penny broke the silence. The trumpetvine swung over as she said, "I know we can figure out something, I know it."

284

"No grown-up disguise glamours," said Cait. "Too dangerous, it'll get me grounded for life. Being grounded for this week is bad enough. There's this art contest I have to get to. I sent them a picture that has all three of us in it, and if it wins the contest, then I'll have enough money to put Clingspell on my wand 'till I'm over the Hedge. Best part is, the college that's putting on this contest is all Deaf people, and I know that magical people are there too, and I've got to find them. Meg, have you ever heard of the Wizarding Federation of Deaf Athletes?" Meg shook her head. "A bunch of their broomracers posed for a picture at this campus back in 2001, right in Plain Sight. So where are they now?"

Penny tapped her spoon on the table. "First things first. Eagles game. Let's figure out how to get to that college later." She tapped some more. "Maybe Greengage can chaperone us. You're two of her best fliers, after all."

But the chipmunk they sent came back with an apologetic note explaining that Greengage spent her Sundays advising amateur racing teams and could not get away.

As they bundled up to return to the dorm, Penny's eyes lit up. "The chaperone can be an adult magicworker from anywhere, right?" As Cait nodded, she went on. "What if we could get ourselves to the city? What if somebody in Connecticut or New York can chaperone us? I know we can't fly ourselves there yet, but there are these really cheap busses that go to the city. And my mom knows lots of people who could help us."

"Coach Joe!" Cait exclaimed. "He's the one who invited us to go to this New York game in the first place. I'll write to him. Penny, can our aviary birds go cross country? How long would they take?"

"We don't have enough time," she said. "Not even an eagle can get across country and back fast enough. Broomcourier can do it, though, and I think it won't cost too much. And I'll send a crow to my mom to see if she knows anybody."

During Monday's Greenwitchery class, Broadleaf glanced at the "Proof of Attendance" sheet and signed it right away. Cait sighed with relief. Maybe other parents had made students do something like this before.

But in the following class, Corwin gave her a searching gaze that seemed like an eternity before finally setting quill to paper. "We have high hopes for you, Cait, don't forget that," she said as she handed it back.

Fortunately in Alchemy class, Melendez signed the slip without hesitation, while in Swimming class, Brunner gave a wry smile when she saw it. "Not unlike the first school where I taught. Ein Stempel fuer Alles, that may as well have been their motto. Very well, I will sign it."

When Cait went to Old House to present Greatwood with her list of signatures, she was dismayed to see Poe strutting before the deputy-director's desk. The silver-haired witch perused the names and nodded. "I'll be glad to see you enjoy an out-of-town expedition with full and proper permissions this time. Please don't forget to find your chaperone as soon as possible. Any Hedge-certified responsible adult will do." She paused. "May I also remind you that below-Hedge students are also not permitted solo out-of-town broom flights. If your chaperone can't provide transportation, then we will consider loaning you one of the school boats, for a fee. But we must know this as soon as possible. Good day, and see you tomorrow." Greatwood handed Cait a new slip with the heading, "Proof of Attendance 2/5/08", and turned her attention to a rustling stack of papers which had lain silent during her conversation with Cait.

Cait walked towards the school's front gate to see what would happen. Did Greatwood and Lumen know that she was supposed to stay on campus? A burst of black feathers appeared out of nowhere. There was Poe right in front of her, beating his wings against her legs to shepherd her away from the gate.

5 Feb 2008
Maguire House
7 Pines Point
Snohomish WA
Dear Caitlin:
Yes, am delighted you and friends will come to New York. You say you need chaperone, full grownup, full magicworker, please give my name, OK. If they question, can talk to the Greater Snohomish Mages' Council, I have good record there. I will make sure you safe, safe from Salem to New York and back. OK.
Your friend,
Joseph P Maguire
Snohomish Magical Academy, Hedge 2005
Broomsports Coach for the Eagles Derby Team

As Cait finished unrolling the letter, she could feel that there was a second sheet rolled up with it. This one read:
PS from Maguire House, 7 Pines Point, Snohomish.
Dear Cait and friends:
I understand teachers love paperwork, signatures, ya ya ya. Other letter is for them, this letter is for you. Can you get from Boston to New York? If yes, is easier for us. Then you look for signing people in red t-shirts in Penn station.

If stuck in Salem, we can come get you OK, but long trip from West Coast, understand. Tell me soon, OK.

Take care,

Coach Joe

Cait skipped all the way to Old House as she brought the letter to Greatwood first thing on Wednesday morning, and exchanged her slip of signatures for "Proof of Attendance 2/6/08". Greatwood looked pleased as she read Coach Joe's note, then frowned slightly. "Mr. Maguire's grasp of grammar isn't quite the usual skill level for a Hedge graduate, is it?"

"English isn't his best language, Ms. Greatwood." Cait's pulse pounded. Would they think he wasn't a capable person because of his writing skills?

"And he has to bring himself all the way across country and pick you up besides. You really do have your transportation all arranged?"

Cait nodded. "He – and his whole team, actually – are very adept with the Speedwind Spell. Seven broomriders all at once." She crossed her fingers and glanced out the door where Penny waited to go into town to buy bus tickets, as soon as Cait gave the okay.

"Ah, a team Speedwind should be quite safe, I can accept that. Going by boat would have been preferable, but I will accept Speedwind if you ride tandem. Make sure Ms. Greengage puts extra stability spells on your brooms."

As Cait tucked the new attendance list into her bookbag, she dreaded having to present it to a whole new batch of teachers. Would her whole class have to hear her explain why she was getting all these signatures?

Greengage took one look at the slip, shook her head, and said, "You are the very last student I would imagine ever missing a broomwork class." She signed it in a swift scrawl. "Don't forget that next week's class will be after Astronologia instead of at our usual time. Into the air now, let me see if you've kept your flying skills over winter break."

Auclair sighed and signed it right away, while saying, "Helicopter parents, we make them happy, make life happy, here you are, bon."

Graycliff merely shrugged, signed it right away, and wanted to know how many redtail hawks Cait observed over winter break. "You live in a wonderful area for birdwatching, never forget to advantage of it."

Ms. Pitts read it through slowly, and picked up her pen. Cait relaxed as she stood before the teacher's desk. This New York trip was going to happen after all. Then Ms. Pitts put her pen down again while giving Cait a long and searching look. "I'd like to have you fully here in my classes, Miss Leo, before I put my name to this slip. You've neglected to do one of the things I asked you early last semester. Until you have done so, I will not consider you as fully present in this room." Ms. Pitts folded her hands and looked at Cait.

The pulse pounded in Cait's throat as she broke out into a sweat. What could she have possibly forgotten to do? There was no "incomplete" in her grade record. "I don't understand, Ms. Pitts."

"Corwin tells me that you're quite accomplished in spellwork. A simple glamour can darken a bright object, and hover spells are quite basic. I'm sure you can do a competent job of either one of them."

"I can, Ms. Pitts." But what did this have to do with Astronologia? wondered Cait.

Pitts made a steeple with her index fingers. "So you did forget my original request to you. Very well, I shall repeat it. This is about your listening vine device. I'd asked you to find a way to listen to my lectures in a way that will not glitter nor fly into people's faces. Unfortunately, I'm still waiting for that to happen. When it does, I shall sign your paper." She pushed the slip back at Cait and announced to the class, "Everyone, take out your star charts and sketch out tonight's correspondances and orbits."

Cait pulled out her trumpetvine with shaky fingers as she sat down. Meg's and Penny's eyes were wide with disbelief, and Cait wasn't sure she believed it herself. For all this time, Pitts had actually wanted her to use the trumpetvine, so long as it wasn't in the way. But how would she ever be able to concentrate on lectures and questions, if she had to run both a hover charm and a glamour on it? For a whole hour and three-fourths? She caught Penny's eye and mimed looking over her shoulder to read her notes, then signed "Yes?" with raised eyebrows, "may I?"

Penny looked at her as if she were nuts to even ask. "Study party after class," she wrote on a corner of the page. "Run your glamour."

Cait cast a glamour that turned the bright gold of the trumpetvine into a dull gray, then sent it to hang over Pitt's desk as if it were a ceiling lamp. But she was barely able to listen to Pitt's comments on erratic orbits because the glamour and the hover spell demanded so much concentration from her. At least Pitts' voice was no longer a blurry mumble, so long as the teacher stayed at her desk.

Pitts nodded as she signed the "Proof of attendance" at the end of class. "Good illusion, but make it darker next time. Have Ms. Corwin give you a binding spell for these charms so you can concentrate on listening to my lectures rather than spellcasting."

By Sunday morning, the weather was bitterly cold, and Penny scowled as she watched Cait top off Nini's water and kibble bowls and double-check the cat pan. "A real familiar would never consider being so far away from their person all day like this."

"Nini can't stand cold. Back home she never leaves the house between December and March. Is she supposed to sit there freezing all day because I want to go to a derby match?"

"Up to you. I'll never rat you out. But what if someone else sees Nini hanging around the dorm while you're out? How do you know they won't go to Greatwood? Let's go, we can't miss the early train to Boston."

But when Cait put on her Plain Sight coat and boots, Nini stood at the door ready to accompany her. "You crazy cat, it's really cold out there!" But the cat only yapped and purred and curled up inside Cait's hood as soon as she picked her up. Cait grabbed an extra scarf from her wardrobe as Penny raised her eyebrows, then smiled.

Meg poked her face in the door. "You two are so slooow in the morning. I've eaten breakfast already. You know there's a chipmunk heading your way?"

Cait stepped into the hallway as the chipmunk ran up to her, whiskers quivering at the smell of cat. The scroll it carried said: "Hello Cait: three brooms with stabilization spells are waiting for you by the the pool-room river; I hope Mr. Maguire has a safe trip to Salem. Enjoy the game in New York! All the best, Patricia Greengage."

Cait's stomach flopped. "I'd better go get these brooms. We've got to stick to our story if we're going to get away with this."

"We don't have time," said Penny.

"I'll sprint," said Cait.

"I'll get you some breakfast, meet up at the front gate," said Meg.

"Deal. Penny, make sure she doesn't give me mustard toast," said Cait, as she put down Nini and high-fived Meg who stuck out her tongue.

Cait ran out the dorm to the pool room for all she was worth, with Nini following. There were the brooms, just as described. Good, where should she stash them? The Partridge-Hall roof – that should work. Right behind the aviary.

Once in the courtyard, Cait told Nini "stay", grabbed all three brooms, and said, "sshemayma". Whoosh – she was three times higher in the air than usual. And wobblier. As she steered for the rooftop, one broom handle slid away from the others, and Cait had to pull up sharp to avoid getting stuck in a crabapple tree. Then a little to the right; there, she'd landed.

Cait deposited the brooms in the narrow space between aviary and roof edge. Then she raced downstairs and through the courtyard just in time to see Meg and Penny walk towards the front gate, while Nini waited for her under the Commons archway.

"Way to go sprint-champ Cait," said Meg.

"You're disgustingly lucky," said Penny. "Let's get to the station. Good thing Meg and I already know Boston transit."

Two trains and a bus ride later, Cait found herself looking at more buildings than she had ever imagined one city could contain, as the "Fung Wah" bus made its way to New York's Chinatown. She gave up trying to calculate how many hundreds of people were inside all those apartment towers. She had truly never seen so many people in her life.

Then there was the noise. Blaring car horns, jackhammers, shouting, talking, loud music, sirens. Nini pinned her ears back and shrank against Cait's neck as they got off the bus. Penny unfolded a map and began talking, but what was she saying? Cait tapped her, and signed, "Don't understand," shaking her head with an index finger popping upward from her temple.

Penny pointed at the map where "Penn Station" was circled in red, then pointed to another circle labeled "Fung Wah". Her finger traced a line on the map going from the one to the other, then she shouted, "Let's march." She looked around her, looked at the map, looked up again, and pointed. "That way."

After twenty minutes of fighting all the crowds just to stay together, being swept up by mobs of pedestrians at light changes, and nearly being run over by two bicyclists and a speeding red Jetta, Cait pulled Penny aside, noticing that Meg looked as glazy-eyed and overwhelmed as Cait felt. "How far?" she asked.

Penny looked at a nearby street sign that said, "Houston" and answered "32 blocks", holding up three fingers on one hand, and two on the other.

Cait's eyes widened as she pulled out her pocket sketchbook and pencil and wrote "Game's at two. We'll be late." She could feel Nini shiver on her shoulders, and she pulled her hood up around the cat, glad that it was a nice broad one.

Penny shook her head, and took the sketchbook to write "we just walked 9 blocks, 20 mins."

"Need cab," wrote Cait, while Meg grabbed the pencil and sketchbook and wrote "yes yes yes." How much money did she have that wasn't in Quillers and Blatt? Cait pulled out a ten dollar bill and some ones. She fingerspelled "c-a-b" to emphasize her point.

293

Penny put up her hands in surrender. Ten dollars later, the cabdriver announced "Penn Station," and pulled over to a sidewalk full of people pulling suitcases to and fro.

They followed all the suitcases to a big round room below street level and looked around for signers in red shirts. Penny walked ahead with confidence, while Cait fought panic. How would they find anybody in these masses of people?

Meg saw them first, bouncing on her toes with excitement as she pointed out a flurry of motion between a coffeeshop and a newsstand. A cluster of people stood there talking in Sign, and half of them were indeed wearing red t-shirts with a logo that said "NYMDC". Both she and Penny looked at Cait.

"What, I'm the leader? Okay, here goes." Cait's mouth went dry as her mind went blank. What was the sign for "look for", "search"? Then she remembered. Catching the eye of a red-shirted girl about their age, she signed, "I seek E-a-g-l-e-s, you know?"

The girl broke out into a broad smile, formed her hand into a fist to sign, "yes, yes," and waved at all three of them to join the group. "Cute", she signed, as she reached over to pat Nini, who lay draped over Cait's shoulders.

Cait pointed at the logo on the girl's shirt. "N-Y-M-D-C, meaning what?" she signed.

The girl answered with a flurry of signs Cait didn't even recognize, but she stopped at Cait's look of confusion, and reached for one of the coffeeshop's napkins. But Cait already had her sketchbook and pencil at the ready, so Red-shirt Girl wrote, "New York Magical Deaf Club. My great-great grandparents helped found it. Hosted their first broomrace in 1902!"

As Cait finished reading the note and showing it to Meg and Penny, she felt more pushing and shoving around her than ever. She looked around to see that many more people had joined their crowd.

Red-shirt Girl held up one finger, looked around, and a lively conversation among the NYMDC members ensued. Cait stared at the signing with envy, wishing she could understand what they were all saying. Red-shirt Girl then returned her attention to the three girls, waved good-bye, and gently pushed them towards a tall man who led the crowd out of Penn Station to street level, while six people in NYMDC shirts stayed behind at the coffeeshop/newsstand area.

After walking a few blocks this way and another few blocks that way, Tall Man stopped in front of a shabby white facade and waved them into what looked like an ordinary office-building lobby.

He guided them around a corner to an elevator where everybody crowded in, but there were no doors and no ceiling. In front of it stretched a blue line that looked familiar.

Cait felt a poke at her arm. "Our tickets?" said Meg, with her hand out. "Need 'em to get through that." She pointed at the blue line.

"Right," answered Cait, remembering a similar barrier at the Fitchburg game, and quickly handing her friends their tickets.

As they stepped in, they all saw a brass plaque that read, "Mazal-yaa". All around Cait, people were saying the word and flying upwards. Some were wanding it instead, V-K style. Other Deafs? Cait wondered with a thrill of excitement. Then it occurred to her that other people, too, might be using the game as a way to find magical signing-Deaf people. Cait smiled as she grabbed Meg and Penny's hands, made eye contact, and they all three said "mazal-yaa" and zoomed upward.

The girls found themselves in the middle of a rooftop stadium where glowing numbers hovered above their seats, disappearing once they sat down. In the center of the stadium, a pink haze covered a field full of the same plushy plant that filled the Witches' Academy courtyard.

Happiness filled Cait as she sat in the middle of a noisy crowd in the midst of a very noisy city, debating with Meg about whether pretzels or hot chestnuts were better for cold days, while broomriding food vendors hovered overhead. Nini purred away, curled up on Cait's lap, under her coat.

Cait had never tasted roasted chestnuts before, but she now proclaimed them to be "Best, the best," with her hand sweeping thumbs-up from her chin. Finally, she could really enjoy not having to "listen up" in all this noise.

In return, Meg did a so-so hand in the direction of the chestnuts, pointed to her pretzel, and signed thumbs-up.

During this, Penny rolled her eyes and counted out coins for the cup that was being wanded her way from a vendor whose sign read "Snowbane hot chocolate."

Blurs of motion surrounded them. There were people settling into seats; the sweeping motion of food descending to customers, and money ascending in return; broad swoops of people flying overhead. It was so much fun to not be shouting above the honking horns and loud engines of the city. She remembered the doctor with the thin smile back home telling her parents Cait "didn't need" the local signing-Deaf outreach program. How could he have been so wrong? Take that, Dr. Thin Smile.

As Cait picked up her hands to fingerspell "snowbane" to Penny and ask "what's that", the gaze of a skinny-faced man two seats over caught her attention. He was following their conversation. She put her hands down, and Penny turned her head to see what Cait was looking at. The man ducked his head a little and slowly signed, "Sorry – you two – think I'm rude – myself Deaf." Then he was fingerspelling "J-e-r-r-y" and signing a "J" on his bicep – must be his namesign -- and introducing his family. Then he began pointing out other members of the Deaf magical community whom he knew in the audience.

Sure enough, as soon as he began pointing out other Deaf people, flurries of signing appeared throughout the stadium, and Cait began to wonder how she could possibly have missed the motion of all those conversing hands. Exhilaration filled her at the thought of so many magical signing people. Even though she couldn't understand most of the conversations she saw, just watching them felt festive.

Should she be staring at their conversations? She had never heard well enough for eavesdropping on spoken conversation to become an issue. How much eavesdropping did signing people allow? She brought her attention back to Jerry, but was distracted by a blur of bright red. A witch wearing a sweatshirt saying "Ole Jim 4ever" and pointy hat pushed her way to a seat two rows below Cait. Ole Jim – the picture from the WFDA newsletter sprang before her mind's eye. Where's the team from that picture? Might this woman know?

Turning to Jerry, Cait signed, "Her – you know?" pointing to the woman in the Ole Jim shirt who sat frantically writing in a tablet she held.

He looked, shrugged, and asked Cait, "You want – you-two – chat?" and asked someone in the row below to get the woman's attention before Cait could tell him, "That's OK, don't bother."

She turned around, and signs flew back and forth between her and Jerry. Her face glowed with excitement as she pointed several times towards the playing field. How could people understand signing when it was that fast? Cait wondered.

She then gave her attention to Cait. "Student – you?" she asked, signing much more slowly and clearly.

Cait could barely sit still for excitement. Two rows away, and here she was, easily having a conversation, with no trumpetvine and no guessing. She signed back, "People – m-a-g-i-c-a-l – study -- at – deaf – college – O-l-e J-i-m?"

Her eyes lit up in a smile very much like Corwin's as her fist nodded, "Yup." Then she took off her tall hat, fished around inside it, and wanded a pitch-black card with gold letters up to Cait. Or it looked as if she did the spell – but did she have a wand? Cait wasn't sure if she'd seen one. But as soon as she saw the card all other thoughts vanished. It read: Jessica Stern, Signspell mentor, Belfry Bats.

Belfry Bats. Hadn't she seen that name before? There was a blur of motion in Cait's peripheral vision. Jessica motioned at Cait to turn the card over. As she did so, new letters appeared: "For full information about Belfry Bats' support of mainstreamed witches and wizards, send a crow to 3rd floor, Ole Jim, DC."

Cait grinned and nodded her fist in return. "Yes – yes." This day was getting better and better. Then a thought struck her. "E-a-g-l-e-s," she fingerspelled as Jessica read the word, nodded and waited for her to go on, "not – know – about" she signed, and then pointed at the Belfry-Bat card in her hand.

Jessica's face showed dismay as she signed, "True? Seven Deaf not know about us?" Then a flow of signs followed, of which Cait caught the signs "how" and "miss." Cait held up a hand. Wow, she actually knew something this grownup didn't, but should. "Three Deaf," she signed, "four Hearing. S-n-o-h-o-m-i-s-h school. Deaf -- people – are – h-e-d-g-e -- h-e-d-g-e -- seven-year." She watched Jessica write away on her tablet even more frantically than before.

"Thank you, thank you," Jessica signed back at Cait.

Then Meg was poking Cait; it was time for the game to begin. Cait put the Belfry card safely in her sleeve pocket and watched the Eagles swoop into playing space with their team banner hovering above them. Coach Joe, Lillian, Alberto, Jake, Tom, Cara, Diane. Cait cheered and waved until her voice ached and Meg held her hands over her ears and made faces at her, but was grinning all the while.

Then the home team came into the stadium to even louder cheering. Their bronze and black banner read "Palisade Pounders". Cait hoped they wouldn't be too literal about the "pounder" part of their name.

Meg motioned for Cait's sketchbook and wrote, "You get to see real derby now. Ten races. It'll be great." She rubbed her hands in anticipation and hunkered down to watch.

What did Meg mean? And then Cait remembered that the derby she'd seen in Fitchburg was only a demonstration, not a full match.

The teams now faced each other, each player shaking hands with an opponent. Then they backed away from each other, and something like a whiteboard materialized above them. And the insults began.

A square-faced Pounder shouted something. The whole Eagles team scowled and pointed to the floating whiteboard. Square Face paused, then smacked his forehead as his face went red. He pulled out his wand, and the words "grass-eater" appeared on the whiteboard as the audience laughed and applauded.

An Eagle – Diane -- signed something that began at her nose and travelled in a bobbing and weaving pattern. Then she took out her wand, and the words "fizz-breath" appeard on the board as the crowd laughed even more.

The insults continued in turn, except for when another Pounder forgot to transcribe his shouted insult. Whole clusters of audience members, not just the Eagles team, protested and pointed to the whiteboard that time. Once everybody had swapped an insult, the first race began, with all the pushing, gyrating, and lawlessness that Cait remembered from November.

Then it was time for more heated insults, and race number two.

By the fourth race, Cait had learned to tell, in the jumble of arms, legs, and broomsticks at the finish line, who was the actual winner.

By the last race, Cait imagined that she'd just seen enough insults to last her a lifetime of dark alleys and skeevy pervs ... if she could only remember how to sign them all.

"Lost by ONE broomlength?! Down with Pounders." Meg scribbled in Cait's sketchbook as the racers left the field, and spectators began to leave.

Cait shrugged, and began to fingerspell "E-a-g-l-", but Meg shook her head with a glazed look, so Cait wrote: "Eagles have the best insults. They'll win the next one," before pocketing the sketchbook.

Cait felt a jab from Penny, who pointed at her watch while saying and signing "Hurry! B-u-s!"

But first, there was one thing Cait needed to do. She could see the Eagles team still on the field with fans crowded around them, and Coach Joe right in the middle. Good. Cait concentrated with all her might and sent a Mindcast of thanks to him. He paused in his conversation, looked around, saw Cait, beamed, and waved.

February 10, 2008
Partridge Hall
Witches' Academy of Salem
 Dear Jessica Stern:
Please sign me up for Belfry-Bat outreach. I would like to learn how to sign much better. Also, is Visual-Kinetic the only way to work magic without using spoken words? It is so slow, that I sometimes use a sign instead when I need to spellcast quickly. But that gets dangerous sometimes.
I'm so glad to have met you at the derby meet, and wish I knew about the Bats a long, long time ago. What if the Eagles team had your cards, and dropped them into the crowd, the way they do with their game announcements?
Sincerely,
Caitlin Leo

Chapter 20 – Eye and Hand

With the new semester came changes in some of their classwork.

The weather had turned unseasonably mild, and Ms. Broadleaf sent the Greenwitchery class to the corner garden to find the first greening sprouts of Snowbane, which was sturdier than horseradish and hotter than habanero peppers. It was so hot that little circles of melted snow puddled around each of the sprouts. "Collect no more than one seedling apiece, and wear gloves," were Broadleaf's exact instructions.

They were finally allowed to perform their first transformations in Spellwork, turning eggshells into seashells, and back.

Graycliff encouraged everyone to find their own pairs of nesting animals to observe for Zoomorphia class as spring migrations began.

And their broomwork class now included night flying.

That first class was a disaster. Every time Cait got into the air, the ground pitched and rolled beneath her and she'd fall onto the turf. Then Nini would come over and head-butt her as if trying to make her feel better.

"Let me add a stabilization charm to that broom," said Greengage after Cait's fifth tumble. She uttered a phrase, sent the spell, and the broom quivered slightly. When Cait went into the air this time, it felt as if the broom were going in slow motion. But the ground still dipped up as fast as ever, and Cait went overboard again, while the other students flew around the courtyard, getting better and better by the minute.

"Hey Amanda, Molasses is out of the running for night races," said Claire from directly overhead as she gave Cait a smug look. Then she high-fived her friend and set off in a showy climbing spiral.

Greengage sent the other students on a set of short relay races, then called Cait aside, while Nini watched from nearby. "Let's see you try again. In the air, over to that apple tree."

And every time Cait tried her hardest to correct her course when the ground went reeling and swaying beneath her, but landed on the turf all the same. Greengage's frown grew deeper and deeper every time Cait looked at her. Great, thought Cait with a sinking heart. Bye-bye seventh-year tall hat and all those languages. Hello, permanent kitchen job, sending pots and trays around dining rooms. What kind of jobs do you get when you're not even Hedge level? Nini draped herself over the broomstick Cait still held and leaned against Cait's leg, purring.

"I don't know what to tell you," Greengage said at last, while watching Cait pat Nini. "I'd like to offer you a flying carpet. That could work well for you, and I suspect the Council will back me up on this. But first we have to locate a carpet whose owner is willing to let you borrow it. They are very rare and quite expensive." She paused and looked at the cat beside Cait. "Your cat's gotten quite used to brooms, hasn't she? That reminds me of someone I once knew on Council. Do you know your cat's purpose yet?" Cait shook her head as Greengage began to pace back and forth, throwing thoughtful glances at the pair. "Don't worry about it. Some familiars and their people don't figure it out until secondyear, or even third." She continued to pace, deep in thought.

The other students had finished their relays, and some had landed and were chattering among themselves while others coasted overhead.

Cait remembered what she had seen during Half-term and hope filled her. "What about feather-flying, Ms. Greengage? Would the Council consider that?"

Greengage frowned and paced back and forth for a moment. "I can't remember having seen any kind of flight in human form involving feathers. Where did you come across that idea?"

"I saw somebody fly with a single feather once. They held it up like this," Cait reached her right hand upward, "and off into the air they went."

"New to me, but interesting," said Greengage. "That could have real potential."

"She dreamed it up, Ms. Greengage." Claire stepped into view. Her voice was glacial. "There is no such thing here as flying with a feather." She glared at Cait, who glared back.

"I don't lie," said Cait. How dare she? Cait felt her face go hot.

"Hallucinate, then," said Claire. Cait wanted to slug her. Why was Claire lying?

"Girls, enough." Greengage laid a hand on Cait's shoulder. "Cait, you keep on with daylight practice. I promise to find some way to get you to secondyear successfully. Everyone else, speed laps, three times around the courtyard."

Cait was still upset the next morning. "Stuck at below Hedge and being called a liar besides. How much worse can a class get?"

"Maybe they'll let you have a boat early," offered Meg. "A really small one that a firstyear can power."

Something white fluttered above Cait. A dove? It dropped a small red box into Cait's lap and sailed out of the Commons again. Grumpiness vanished as Cait opened the box. Fudge, she loved fudge. "Chocolate pecan from

The Peppermill," read the writing on the box. But who outside of Cait's family knew to get her fudge that had no walnuts in it? A slip of airy rice paper lay nestled between the pieces of fudge. On it was a series of three red-inked hearts and the sentence, "To the best daylight-flyer in the class of 2014. A.G."

Penny whooped and signed "sweetheart" at her as Cait's face grew hot. Meg grimaced, tipped her chair back, and muttered something about "weird selkies." Cait remembered that it was Feb 14th today. Duh.

She looked around the Commons and saw that there were more bird couriers winging around than usual, dropping cards and candies into people's laps. To her surprise, a small hawk coasted through the hall directly toward her, leaving a flat, oval package at Cait's place as it perched on the back of a nearby chair. In the return address was inked, "Belfry Bats, Ole Jim, DC". As she picked it up, Cait's fingers sank into thick padding.

At that same moment, the school eagles flew past a nearby window to ring the bell for class, and those who had morning classes left.

As the room cleared out, Cait untied the twine around the package and removed the layers of paper and padding. An oval piece of glass in a dull-bronze frame lay inside. Some sort of mirror? But it was far too dark to be a mirror, and gave no reflection when she looked into it. Why would the Bats send her a mirror, or a picture frame, or whatever this was? A book was with it as well, but she couldn't read it; its script was none of the ones on Corwin's walls. It reminded her of Egyptian hieroglyphs. Excitement filled her as she perused. Would she get to learn how to read this script, too? Cait couldn't wait to start.

A note fluttered from the book's pages.

"Dear Caitlin Leo:

Thank you for your excellent suggestion concerning Belfry-Bat outreach. We will definitely contact the Eagles about this idea. Please set this dark glass up in a convenient spot in your dorm room – on your desk would be ideal – and be in front of it this Sunday at 3:00 pm. Barring conflict, you will be learning Signspell-casting on Sundays at 3:00 pm, and ASL on Wednesdays at 11:00 am. With power of eye and hand,

Jessica Stern."

All three girls gazed at the smooth, dark surface of the object.

"My mom has one of these," ventured Penny, "but I've hardly ever seen her use it. It was really for Gramma since Mom would rather just send a crow to people."

"But what is it?" asked Cait.

"It's to talk with, long distance, face to face," said Meg, touching the frame delicately with one finger. "I've heard of one, but have never seen one before. They're really pricey and it takes a lot of spellwork to set it up right. Can we be there on Sunday when it does whatever it does?"

"Sure," said Cait. "That's what friends do, right?"

Then conversation turned to the snow-rabbit observations that were due the next day in Zoomorphia. Nobody had liked the idea of having to watch white rabbits against white snow, and the whole class had been near mutiny when the assignment was announced. As Penny and Cait complained about the homework, Meg smirked as she polished off the last of her pumpkin muffin.

"How come you're not complaining about the homework? Did you cheat?" asked Cait.

Meg broke into the guffaws she'd been containing. "It was easy. All I had to do was Mindcast, and there's the bunnies. I wondered if you two would ever figure it out. C'mon, let's go observe some rabbits."

Sunday afternoon, Cait sat at her desk, fidgeting as she checked for the tenth time that the dark glass was securely propped up before her. Penny had pulled over her own desk chair and sat on it backwards, chin resting on the chairback, while Meg perched on the corner of Cait's bed. Nini napped on Cait's pillow, oblivious to their excitement. Cait set her clock nearby. As the minute hand slid onto "twelve", a swirl of motion began within the dark surface, black on black, a gentle shifting. Then Jessica's face gradually became visible, white on gray on black, with colors filtering in slowly along with details of both face and background. This time she wasn't wearing a hat, and her dark, wavy shoulder-length hair was tied back in a ponytail.

Jessica waved a cheery hello at Cait, but then peered around with a questioning look, and signed, "All three-of-you – deaf?"

Cait answered, "My friends – M-e-g – there – P-e-n-n-y – there. Hearing – hearing. Curious – this mirror."

Jessica leaned back, chewing her lip and frowning slightly.

"My good-friends," signed Cait, stressing their close friendship by tightening the handshapes of the sign for "friendship" close to each other, making her index-finger knuckles ache. "Two-of-them want learn sign," she added.

Jessica now shrugged and leaned forward again. She waved at a board beside her which read, "Lesson One;" it contained some of the mysterious writing Cait had seen in her new book.

"Your book?" queried Jessica, looking about as if trying to see Cait's room. Cait grabbed the new book from her desk shelf as Jessica nodded. A wand was now in

Jessica's hand, and she pointed out a quill which lay on a table before her. The board displayed the word "boh-ee" and a squiggle of the new script. Jessica made a gesture which looked like the sign "to come here," but with a different handshape than ASL. The quill flew smoothly from tabletop to Jessica's hand. Jessica then demonstrated that unfamiliar handshape to Cait, and showed how to read the squiggly writing, which indicated exactly what fingers to hold where and which motion to use. Once she pointed it out, Cait could see that the writing was almost like a picture of a hand.

Three signspells later, Penny remembered a paper she needed to rewrite and pushed her chair back to her own desk. A moment later, Meg decided to go practice her Zoomorphia homework.

Cait, still fascinated with watching this new spellcasting method, didn't at all mind waving them off. This looked better than the Visual-Kinetic method. No clunky pause between writing the word and sending the energy. Here, the sign and the energy looked like they were all one piece as Jessica's hand formed the spells. Sometimes, when Jessica signed too quickly for Cait or used a sign she didn't understand, Jessica would catch the confusion in Cait's eyes and pause. Then the English translation would show up in one corner of the board.

Cait couldn't wait to try this method out for herself. Finally, after showing Cait a fifth spell, Jessica swept an "L" handshape off her chest and in Cait's direction. "Your turn." Then she added, "Number one," and gestured at the board with its list of five signs.

Looking around her desk, Cait picked up a cat toy which Nini had batted onto her notebook, and placed it before her. Making the new handshape, she performed the signspell, and the toy flew right into her hand. It felt as easy and fluid as using the ASL sign itself. This was what she'd been wanting to do all along. And there wasn't any danger of repeating the "I hate Amanda" broom-tumble, since this method kept conversational signs and magical signs completely separate and different. V-K couldn't hold a candle to this. She couldn't wait to use this in class, if Corwin allowed it. There'd be no reason for anyone to call her "Molasses" any more.

Jessica grinned at the obvious delight on Cait's face and pointed to the next sign on the list. The rest of the hour flew by all too quickly, and the color began to fade from the glass as Jessica hastily signed, "See you – Wednesday."

And the glass now showed only blank darkness.

After five minutes of copying the new signspells into her notebook, Cait wondered if she was supposed to use them in Spellwork or if she'd be stuck with the V-K method. Glancing once more at the blank glass before her, she spoke, "Hey Penny, how does your mom work this thing?"

Penny turned from her paper. "There's a spell to catch the other person's attention, but I don't know what it is."

Dang. I'd better send a crow. Or go ask Corwin. Nah, I'll send a crow to Ole Jim.

But Corwin beat her to the punch. "I'm so glad to learn about this Belfry Outreach," she said with a radiant smile, as Cait stepped into the Spellwork classroom five minutes early the next day. "I don't know why I've never heard of it before, but their method looks like a very promising way to perform visually-based spellwork. If you're ready, why don't you show us the Belfry Bats' version of the 'boh-ee' spell? I'm sure it's quite different from the Visual-Kinetic one."

At Cait's look of surprise, she added, "Farsight mirrors don't get sent around to just anybody, let alone to students. Ms. Stern was thoughtful enough to inform the administration well in advance that she had plans to send you one. And I for one heartily approve. So, let's see your new spell."

As Cait demonstrated, the rest of the class arrived and settled into their desks. Corwin nodded at Cait to take her seat, and announced, "Let's play, everyone. The ice-water-ice spell on page 97, please."

Despite the ease of the spellwork, something felt wrong in the classroom that day. People were whispering behind their hands, and Cait could see quick looks being tossed her way. Oh no, was this going to be "weirdo Carrie" all over again? Or did she have a big, giant D for "deaf" on her forehead now? But there were no teases and no taunts, and the rest of the day's classes were completely uneventful.

After supper, Cait sat down with her Belfry-Bat and her Witches'-Academy spellbooks propped up side by side. She began to make a list of all the spells Corwin had ever taught them. Boh-ee. Gamarnu, lech na. Lechu na. Shalhevet.

There was a knock on the door. Cait wanded it open to see Meg's roommate Violet, toying with her bracelets. "Can I come in? I hear there's a Farsight Mirror in here."

Cait shrugged. "Sure, come on in. It's not doing anything right now, but here it is."

"What a pretty frame! Weird, it's like a black hole. Does having no reflection weird you out? Really, it doesn't? Thanks for letting me look," and Violet took off as if afraid to ask too much.

Back to work. Cait sat down, and went back to her list. Where was she? Shalhevet. Got that. What next? She consulted the Academy text. Shamayim me'aal. She remembered spashing water all over the spellwork classroom, and wrote, "not to be confused with mayim". Then she thought of the broomwork spell that sounded so much like it, too. As she finished writing shemayma, there was another knock.

Minna stood there this time. "Hi Penny, hi Cait. I hear there's a Farsight Mirror here. Is that true?" She stood shyly inside the doorway, hands clasped together before her.

"Come on in, Minna, you heard right," said Penny.

Cait put down her quill and wondered how long it would take to finish her list. She picked up the glass with both hands and held it towards Minna. "This is the mirror, but it's not doing anything interesting right now."

"Ooh, that darkness is spooky, no reflection like that. Does the other person look like a ghost when you talk to them, all silvery?"

"Nope, the silvery part's only at the beginning and end of the talk time. They look totally normal the rest of the time."

"Who do you get to talk to with it?"

"You know how I'm using a new method in Spellworking class? I learn it through this mirror because my teacher's in Washington DC."

"Ooh, thank you for showing me, Cait. You're lucky. I'm going to save up for one of those some day. See you tomorrow, Penny," and Minna was off.

When Cait sat back down, her quill was missing. Did she put it someplace strange while talking to Minna? Good thing she had a nice, large batch of new ones freshly cut. She took a new quill and used a quick boh-ee spell, Belfry style, to fill it with ink. That was right, one Belfry spell she knew cold. She could check it off her new list list of Academy spells already.

If nobody else stopped by, maybe she could get all the Academy spells written down tonight. That front-door spell for example. P'tach. And she'd better put down the word she got wrong, too. Cait blushed at the memory of the vanishing gate as she wrote batel.

Three-fourths of the way through her list, Cait had the feeling she was being watched, and she looked over to see Nini sitting in the middle of the floor, staring at her. Just like she did at home when Cait stayed up too late. "You win, Nini," Cait said as she closed her books, cleaned her pen, looked at the time, and gasped. Was it really 1:00 am? As Cait stood up, Nini jumped onto the bed, kneading the covers with a loud purr.

The next night, as Cait sat down to finish her list, there was again no quill on her desk. Must have left it in the bookbag, she thought as she reached for another quill. Then she remembered a hex Meg had showed her, learned from her older sister Louise. It was meant to catch thieves, but why not practice it on the rest of her quills? Then, if anybody down the road did steal her quills, they'd break out into pink spots. There was one ferret familiar in her class after all, and it was always swiping small objects. Cait giggled to imagine the slender brown-and-white animal with pink spots on its fur. She cast the hex.

Now, to work. Cait sat down and began transcribing more of Corwin's spells.

By the time the list was done and Cait began cross-checking it against the Belfry spells she'd just learned, somebody knocked on the door. More Farsight-Mirror gawkers? She opened the door to see Andreya, smiling, with a crowd of firstyears around her.

312

"You don't mind us stopping by, do you?" Andreya asked with a tip of her head. "Rumors are flying about your Fairsight Mirror. Can we see it?"

"Sure, come on in," said Cait. By the time she'd answered all their questions, and everybody had filed out, Cait turned to her desk. Once again, the quill was missing. This time she knew that it had been right next to her spellbook when Andreya and company showed up.

But a motion from the doorway distracted Cait from thoughts of lost quills, and she looked up to see a secondyear girl with green eyes and cinnamon skin standing there. It took a moment to remember the "Big Sister" from Term-begin back in September.

"Your name's Luatha, right?" asked Cait. "Let me guess. You've heard a rumor about a Farsight Mirror."

"I sure have. I hope you don't my stopping by. I've never known anyone who had a Farsight Mirror before. Do you get to use it a lot?"

By the time Luatha had left, Cait saw that Penny was hunkered down over her books, trying not to giggle. "Girl, you sure know how to be popular. And look at your cat!"

Cait spun around to look where Penny pointed. Nini's pink-spotted face poked out from under her bed, with a chewed-up feather dangling from her mouth. "Nini, you little brat! Why didn't anyone warn me that I'd have to put the anti-predation spell on my writing quills, too?"

As she put away her books at midnight, cued by Nini's bedtime stare, Cait remembered the conversation she and Meg had during that glorious broomflight at the end of probation. Hadn't Meg herself talked about always staying up late and getting up early in order to study? Hadn't they enjoyed those study parties back in November with Andreya's notes? What on earth were they poking around in their rooms solo for, when they could be hanging out together?

I bet Meg's still up, thought Cait, and she sent out a tentative Mindcast query. Almost immediately, a Mindcast of surprise came back from Meg's direction, and Cait opened her door to see Meg peering out her door, pointing at Cait and the spellwork book she still held, and whispering "You too?!"

Cait nodded her fist, "yup", mouthed "every night", then mimed reading the book, and falling asleep in it. Then signed, "two-of-us study together?"

Meg signed a big, dramatic "yes" in reply, then "tomorrow", then mouthed, "bed now!"

During Friday's Spellwork classes, the glares continued, and Cait could still see gossip going on behind people's hands. All the while, Corwin beamed at everything Cait did in class. During broomsprints, Meg reported that they were all calling her "teacher's pet" and talking about some "unfair advantage."

By the time the Magenta Trio appeared in Cait's doorway to see the Farsight Mirror for themselves, Cait felt uneasy. Why did Amanda look so disapproving? And Claire looked like she was up to something. Only Elsbeth seemed truly interested in learning how Cait used the mirror and why.

Cait figured that the dark glass probably had a few protection charms on it already, but decided to add a couple of spells from the back of her spellbook just to be on the safe side. For good measure, she put on the same spot hex that had identified her quill thief. Wrapping the glass in her extra winter scarf, Cait slid it in among her textbooks. Nobody could accuse her of being a show-off now.

But the following Sunday, when Cait sat at her desk ready for her next lesson with Jessica and reached for the Farsight mirror, there was nothing inside the neatly-folded scarf. Panic gripped her gut; she sat for a moment in shock. Did she move it somewhere else and forget? She felt disoriented. Unmoored. Adrift. How could losing this link to her new community rattle her so?

"Penny," she asked, pulse jumping at her throat, "Did you borrow the Farsight mirror to talk to your mom or something?"

Penny shook her head. "I don't know if you can use a mirror set up for someone else," she answered with a worried tone.

Anger began to rumble inside Cait. She resisted the urge to pitch a fit and start throwing things. Who would take the mirror? Somebody jealous? Somebody greedy? Somebody who thought that Sorcerers'-Aid girls shouldn't own such high-end things?

The Magenta Trio certainly didn't need to steal anything from anybody; they had enough money to buy whatever they wanted.

Maybe it was somebody who was trying to impress the Magenta Trio, somebody who couldn't afford such things. Meg's roommate – she was always hanging around the Trio. Cait tore out of the room with Penny following, and raced to Meg and Violet's room. The door was open, and they looked up in surprise as Cait burst in. There was no sign of the mirror, no sign of spots on anyone.

"What are you doing?" Meg asked.

"I can't find my Farsight mirror, and I need it," said Cait.

"Well I didn't take it," Violet blurted out.

The room fell silent as all eyes turned on her. "Why would you?" asked Meg.

"Well, that's why I wanted to go see yours," said Violet to Cait. "It impresses people, they think you're rich if you have a Farsight mirror. But I didn't touch yours."

"I believe you," said Cait. So who did this? Elsbeth had no reason to. Amanda? She hated being in the same school with "no-talent plebs", but would she actually take the mirror? After all, there was that Daydark stunt. But she only got that way with sports, she didn't seem to care about classwork so much.

Claire. It had to be her. She was always mouthing off in Spellwork, and thought she deserved better grades. Maybe Claire was jealous of Cait's good Spellwork grades, jealous enough to do something about it.

"Is Claire around?" Cait asked.

Violet looked like she wanted to vanish. "Yeah. We were going to go downtown, but not till later."

As soon as Claire's door opened to their knock, Meg burst into guffaws and Penny into snorts. Spots!

Claire's face was covered with them, bright pink and obviously hexed, as she sat with a surprised look at her desk, wand still in hand from opening her door.

Cait stormed up to Claire and grabbed for the mirror propped up in the middle of Claire's desk. But Claire moved with equal speed, turning and keeping a firm grip on the mirror's frame.

"I'm bringing this back to you, promise," Claire pleaded. "I needed to learn how it works. See, it's already beginning to work for me." Sure enough, swirls were gently winding their way within the surface of the dark glass.

"It's not working because of you, it's working because somebody is trying to contact me right now," growled Cait. "Haven't you wondered why you have those spots?"

"Spots?" said Claire, puzzled. She looked at the mirror built into the wardrobe door, and shrieked at the sight of her face. As she let go of the dark glass in surprise, Cait gasped and rescued it with a quick signed boh-ee! The glass arced upward just in time to keep from smashing on the wooden floor, and headed toward Cait. Before it was in Cait's hands, however, Claire grabbed one edge of its frame, and a tug of war ensued, Cait's spell against Claire's grip. Within the glass, Jessica's confused face was now visible, craning her neck in an attempt to find out what on earth was going on.

Then the screen went blank.

"Must have broken," huffed Claire as she let go and the mirror smacked into Cait's chest with the full force of her spell.

Cait clasped her arms about it protectively as she asked Claire, "Why? I'm not going to remove that hex until you tell me why. You're rich. You can probably bribe yourself a set of good grades. Stealing this mirror so I can't study would be really stupid."

Claire stomped to her door and closed it, facing Meg, Cait, and Penny defiantly.

"That's not why. That's not even close. And if you breathe a word of the truth to anybody, you're dead." Claire glared at them from the doorway and squared her shoulders. "And I'd rather not pretend that this is chickenpox." A loud snort erupted from Penny, which Cait ignored.

"The truth," answered Cait. "Hex to be removed after I hear it." Claire continued to glare, and then nodded slightly.

Meg did a Mindcast in Claire's direction and nodded. "Go."

"I don't have the money to bribe anybody for anything," said Claire.

"Excuuuse me?" Penny giggled. "With clothes like that?" She pointed at Claire's robes, which were trimmed with winter-white cashmere that day, with silk sewn into the sleeve lining.

Claire's chin rose proudly as she silently strode to her wardrobe and flung the door open. "My own sewing, all of it." The cabinet glowed with all sorts of sumptuous fabrics in brilliant colors, cut and pieced onto school robes, and sewn into tops for Plain-Sight wear with jeans. "It's fashion-fabric remnants. And reading all the magazines people leave behind in Mom's shop. She sells pricey things there. And then I get to watch the people who can afford this stuff, how they act, what they wear. And I knew how to sew since I was six because kids learn how to make their own regalia in my tradition. It's a lot more fun to make your own things and pretend they're designer than it is to be stuck sewing them for somebody else. And when I'm done with school, I'm never going to be stuck with some old seamstress job, magical or not. And you're not going to mess with that." Again the glare. "People think I buy all these" -- she tossed a head-nod at her wardrobe – "in fancy places like New York and Paris. So I let them. And people who wear clothes like this" – she flapped her silk-lined sleeves in emphasis – "also know how to use things like that." Claire pointed at the Farsight mirror which Cait still clutched to her chest.

"So pretend that you have one, it broke, and come ask me in person, instead of just taking mine," retorted Cait. "Ask, for once. And don't ever touch my stuff without asking, or I'll make that hex on your face permanent. This is the sign for 'spots' and I'm not afraid to use it."

The bluff worked; Claire flinched. Cait didn't actually know what would happen if she did the spell in ASL, but couldn't help thinking of Amanda and the "hate you" sign. She continued, "And tell Amanda to not do any more Daydark stunts or any other kind of cheating during our races."

"Agree," replied Claire. "Promise." Her voice was flat, but steady.

Cait brought her wand downward in a shimmering motion, and the spots faded from Claire's face. Cait, Meg, and Penny all turned to leave. As Penny reached for the doorknob, Claire's plaintive voice sounded from behind them; Cait turned and raised an eyebrow.

Claire repeated her question, "Can't I borrow it sometime? Just to practice?

Cait paused. "Maybe. If you behave." Then she thought of that horrible night-flying class. Now that Cait and her friends were alone with Claire, would she stop lying? "I do have a question for you. Truth about that feather-flying. Can anybody learn how to do it?"

Claire lifted her chin as she answered; there was pride in her eyes. "Only if you happen to be Grand Bay Abenaki. That's my tribe. Up in Vermont."

"Thank you," said Cait, hiding her disappointment. Again walking to the door, she added, "Remember – spots." Forming the sign in ASL, she turned and marched out of the room with her friends.

Chapter 21 - In DC

As Cait strode back to her room with the Farsight mirror hugged to her chest, Meg and Penny continued to snort and giggle.

"Chickenpox. Yeah, right. Bratty baby bro with paintbrush, more like," Penny said as they entered the room. Before Cait could put it down, the mirror began to vibrate, and a glow went up around it.

The glow caught Penny's attention. "Somebody wants to talk to you," she said as she straddled her desk chair, arms leaning on the chair back. She kept her gaze fixed on Cait's desk as Cait propped the mirror up once more in its original spot. While Meg sat down at the foot of Cait's bed, Nini flicked her tail in annoyance and relocated herself to the pillow.

Silvery white swirls filled the mirror's surface, and the outline of Jessica's questioning face gradually took form. She was making only one sign, eyebrows drawn together, index fingers pointing at the trio, palms up, and then turning her hands over in unison. "What happened?"

Cait's retelling of the mirror theft and the spot hex set Meg and Penny off into a fresh round of hysterical giggles. Once Jessica vanished to go inform the Belfry Bats of this incident, Meg burst out in a torrent of chatter. "I can't wait to see other people's faces when they hear about this. She was going to pretend those spots were chicken pox? Ha. No way! I bet's she's never seen anybody have chicken pox in real life. But that stuff in her closet's wicked great; I can't believe she really made all that! She'd probably invent something to put over her face to hide the spots, or a hat or something and then pretend she's discovered a new fashion and then everyone in school would copy it and wish they knew where she got all her clothes. Hoo boy, but we'll make sure everybody knows it's really 'cuz she got hexed." Meg paused for breath.

"We can't tell anyone," Cait fired back. "We have a secret over her head, remember? A big secret." Cait smiled. "Us three will just happen to have a tiny little joke about chicken pox. You know, this is the first time I've ever been in on a private joke?" And Cait's smile grew broader.

During supper that evening, a crow flew into the Commons with a note from the Belfry Bats. Cait was to bring the Farsight mirror to the library every week on Thursday, where it would now be housed until Sunday, when she would retrieve it again. The following morning, there was an extra note on everyone's schedules as well: "A Farsight mirror has been installed in the circulation area of the library for use of the Witches'-Academy community Thursday through Saturday. Please be aware that it is set up to convey visuals only, no sound. Remember to check its schedule when reserving time at this mirror." Cait missed having the dark glass always right on her desk, but at least people weren't staring into her doorway and interrupting her studies any more.

It was now late March, and weather had warmed up. Snowmelt and mushy mud lay in all the places the firstyears were instructed to watch for garter snakes emerging from hibernation. If they were lucky, said Ms. Graycliff, they might see the rare and magical Ourobouros which cartwheeled with its tail in its mouth, instead of slithering like other snakes. And they were reminded once more to not forget to look for nest-building examples.

"Zoomorphia, my eye," grumbled Penny as she got up to head to the Commons for lunch. "All we've done this year is look at animals. When are they ever gonna let us start transforming? And did see how Amanda's always smirking in class? She's up to something. Maybe that bird of hers is helping her cheat. Wish I had a drying spell for these soggy shoes." She scuffed at the gravel underfoot, earning a nip from a hungry snake who mistook the movement for prey.

A motion in the sky caught Cait's attention; a gray dove whirred and fluttered towards her, carrying a letter with her mom's scrawl across the preprinted envelope: "Hope it's good news! Love, Mom."

Inside it was a "certificate of congratulations" upon the entry of Cait's artwork into the Essay, Art, and ASL contest.

"But I want to know if I won or not," grumped Cait.

"Hey, at least we know it got there alright," replied Meg.

"They're blind if they don't give you some kind of prize," added Penny. "All those doodles up and down your class notes look pretty darn good to me."

"How come you were looking at my notes?"

Penny shrugged. "Looked like you were doing something different, that's all."

"Doodling's just a way to keep me from being nervous about all those spellwork contests going on. Ours. The one at BWIS. Even people in town have one. And my aunt's extension class. How come they only gave us two weeks to get ready? Okay, closer to three weeks, but it's still not enough. I don't even know whether I'm supposed to do the spells VK-style or spoken or Belfry-Bat style or what."

Beside them, Meg scowled. "Never mind those old contests. They're just a trick to get us to study. Let's run. I'm starved!"

"You'd win a Mindcasting contest easy," protested Cait. "You're the best Mindcaster in class."

Meg flapped her hand dismissively and crouched, ready to sprint. "Race you to the Commons!"

When Cait sat down to her next lesson with Jessica, not one, but two faces beamed back at her. "Lesson – aside for the moment ," signed Jessica, as she turned slightly towards a round-faced older women who sat to her right. "Announcement special – for you."

Round Face began signing with fluid and easy motions, while words appeared on the nearby whiteboard. Was Jessica translating for her? Cait was too busy reading the whiteboard to tell. "Allow me to introduce myself. I am Myrna Felder, head of the Belfry Bats, and I am pleased to invite you to the annual Signed Spellwork competition at Ole Jim on April 5th. You will be one of four firstyear competitors."

A wave of dizziness hit Cait as Myrna continued with contest and travel details. Was there some mistake? Was she really that good at signed spellwork already? After all, she hadn't even learned all the Belfry versions of the spells from Corwin's class yet. Then it dawned on her that whether this was a mistake or not, she now had her way to get to Ole Jim. She didn't need that art contest to get there.

Cait grinned and signed, "Ready, ready. I accept!"

Felder smiled and signed, "April 5th —see you." Then she swept an L-hand in Jessica's direction, "over to you," waved at Cait, and was gone, as Jessica and Cait delved into the lesson with extra energy.

As the lesson finished up, Cait realized with alarm that she had no idea how she was supposed to travel to Ole Jim. "Felder – told me – arrive how? When? What-to-do? If I don't understand people? All sign – fluent, fluent?"

Jessica answered, "Calm down – OK – that whole list of things – we think you'll remember? No! You'll get a note

– all written down. Your parents – get one themselves. Understand signing – don't worry. Our Wednesday ASL lessons – for what? This. You'll be fine."

Sure enough, as Cait finished her supper, a small, dark shape fluttered in the fringe of her vision, and a bat carrying a golden scroll now perched on the edge of her cup of hot cider. As it landed, Cait felt paws on her lap, and had to send a "stay" spell to the saucer-eyed Nini, who yapped in protest as she sat back down on the floor, still staring at the bat.

She unrolled the scroll. Golden letters in flowing script read:

"Belfry Outreach is pleased to request the presence of Caitlin Leo in the Class of 2014 Division of the 127th annual Spellcasting Competion on April 5, 2008, at the Belfry Outreach Headquarters, Washington DC."

Then there was a section in smaller writing: "Festive dinner on April 4, overnight housing with board, and an aerial tour of campus will all be included. Transportation for all under-Hedge competitors will be provided via portal, pending proper permissions."

"Woo, congratulations, you wicked smart spellcaster!" exclaimed Meg, leaning over Cait's shoulder as she read the note. "Getting to travel to someone else's contest is a huge honor."

"This bat's almost as cute as Nicky," admired Penny as she fed it a piece of her gingerbread.

Cait nodded agreement. "Well, mice are cute, and bats are sort of mice with wings, aren't they? What's this portal permission they're talking about here?"

Penny leaned in to read the scroll as well. "That means you won't have to fly to get there, or take all day sitting on a train or dealing with airports. Only schools and town councils have portals, though – it takes a whole team of magicworkers to set one up. Better get your parents' okay right away, so you can tell us all about portal travel."

Cait put the scroll in her sleeve pocket as Nini curled up on her lap, and wondered what her parents would think about portal travel. Did Aunt May know anything about it? Cait didn't care how she got to Ole Jim. She'd take a bus or train if she had to. Learn to sail. Hitchhike disguised as a big, tough grownup.

She watched the bat, now stuffed with gingerbread, flutter its way towards the nearest window, only to settle on the ledge and fall asleep.

"Penny, what if you fed him too much? The Belfry Bats will think I stole their messenger."

"Nah, he'll be fine in ten minutes and ready to head back to DC. One of my mom's customers likes sending her orders by bat, and it pigs out like crazy when there's cookies in the shop. C'mon, we both gotta study. We have some contests to win."

Cait felt a pang as she realized what else was on April 5th; the Witches' Academy competition. "You know, I won't even get to see you compete."

Penny tossed her head. "We'd hate each other by competition time anyway. Your grades are getting too close to mine these days. Maybe it's good that we'll be in two different places." But her glance didn't quite meet Cait's.

Spellwork class had been pure chaos ever since Corwin announced the upcoming contests. "Everyone's welcome to enter the town contest, but only the top four students will represent the class of 2014 in our own Academy contest," said Corwin, as she walked about the room, offering memorization advice to one student, and reminding another that, "no, hexes are never allowed during any competition." The classroom copy of The Grand

Encyclopedia of Firstyear Spellwork was in constant motion from desk to desk, sometimes caught in tug-of-wars similar to that which Cait's Farsight mirror had recently undergone.

Cait sat with her Belfry book before her, cross-checking it against her classroom notes. She had finally learned the Belfry version of every spell which had been taught in Corwin's class up until now. That was worth every night that she had stayed up until one am during the past week.

Her fingers tingled with the urge to race through every Belfry spell and wow a whole stadium full of people with how well she could do them. And in the next instant her flip-flopping stomach would try to persuade her to summon a crow and say "no thanks" to the contest. After all, she hadn't even been using those brand-new Belfry spells for two months yet. How was she going to know them well enough to actually compete against the other signing students? For all she knew, the other students might have been using Belfry spells all along. And she was so new to speaking in Sign besides. Jessica promised that she'd be all right, but how was she going to understand everyone else?

And then there was that letter from Aunt May to live up to. Cait pulled out the note from her dad which had just arrived that morning. "Congrats, scholar-girl! Your great-aunt May is very proud of you, took her five pages of letter to tell us. Do us proud in DC. Here are your signed permission papers. Love, Dad. PS – your mother thinks you're taking a train there, so don't tell her otherwise."

Cait heard a snicker to her right, and looked up to see Amanda peering at Cait's Belfry spellbook. "That one has her own special competition," she said to Claire while rolling her eyes at Cait. "Not even the town contest is good enough for her."

Claire narrowed her eyes as if she were going to mouth off, but then changed her mind as Cait stared back and began to form the "spots" handshape. "Yeah, they probably had to send her off to another competition because everyone knows she'd win this one. I hafta practice. Let's do the Transformation spell again. Rocks into glass on the count of three."

Cait allowed herself a smug smile and decided to browse the parts of the Belfry spellbook she'd not really looked at before. As she read, it dawned on her that not all of the squiggles illustrated spells. Some of them looked a lot like the ASL signs she'd learned from her old NAD book, and from her lessons with Jessica. She turned to the front of the Belfry book to look at the title page. There was the title in English, but before it was another page full of squiggles, which she'd always ignored before. Looking more closely, she realized that one squiggle looked like a hand holding up one finger in the sign for "one." To its left, was a pair of squiggles that looked like two sideways hands moving apart, each bent at the knuckles. Was that the sign for "level"? "Level one". She actually understood that! And there was that same shape that looked like a "one" hand up at the top of the page, but there were two of them, with some arrows. Must mean that they both move. Maybe that was the sign for "signing"? Cait flipped to the English title page to check. Yes, it was in the same place as the phrase "Signed Spellwork", so it had to be.

She then turned to the first full page of text, which looked more like ASL than Belfry spells. Was this this entire section in ASL? It had never occurred to Cait that people could put Sign down into writing, let alone fill whole books with it.

What if a book like this one had been in the Academy's library last semester, when she needed so badly to find out about Sign and magicworking? Not even Ms. Fletcher knew about books like this. How many books were written in ASL? Could she write a book like this herself? Once she got good enough at Sign, that is. There should be books like this in every magic school, not just at the Belfry Bats' Ole Jim. And what about people who don't use ASL? Were there other signed languages? How many? Were there books in these languages too?

A hand swiped the cap off her head as the end-of-class bell rang.

"Aren't you going to come to lunch? I'm starving. You're clearly possessed by your own spellbook." Meg plopped the cap back on Cait's head, as she stood waiting with bookbag on shoulder.

"If I fail night-flying, I'm going to move in with the Belfry Bats and write books like this," Cait said.

"If you say so," Meg replied, "but I know you'll be racing for Witches' Academy. Nobody fails night-flying."

Before joining Meg and Penny for lunch, Cait ran off to Old House to present the permission forms to Greatwood, flipping through them nervously as she went. Had she forgotten anything? Were there any extra details, like needing a chaperone last February to go to the Eagles' game?

But Greatwood actually smiled as Cait handed over the papers. "Most meritorious of you to properly observe school rules and regulations this time," she said. "You are setting a much better precedent than you did last semester. And you will, no doubt, convey the best of Witches' Academy scholarship at this competiton at Belfry Outreach. I do not doubt that you will be an outstanding representative of this school after all."

To all this, Cait could only reply, "Thank you. I hope so," while wondering if Greatwood ever talked like a regular person.

All too soon, it was the afternoon of April 4th, and Cait felt like her brain would burst if she sat and studied any more. She wasn't supposed to go to the school's portal until sundown, but decided to find it now so that she knew where to go when it was time to be there. She reached for the travel cloak draped over her wardrobe door. From atop Cait's pillow, Nini picked up her head, gave a "mrrp," and ran over to Cait's door, fluffy gray tail held high.

"Sure, let's have a walk," Cait told her, as she patted the cat. A light breeze tugged at her robes and fluffed Nini's fur as she set out across the courtyard. Pulling the portal directions out of her sleeve pocket, Cait read, "The Witches' Academy portal is located in the pool room under the Commons, Southern Alcove." Finding the usual pool-room door unlocked, she went through it and descended the stairs, noticing as always, the lack of the river noise that used to greet her. It had been like this all semester. Sure, having a new door blocking off the boat area made it a lot easier to hear Brunner during class. But Cait still felt guilty for being the reason that door was there.

As she neared the foot of the staircase, she heard a splash. Andreya maybe? She looked at the directions again. "Southern Alcove" must be that stone wishing-well near the pool. Easy enough to find.

Nini's ears swivelled in the direction of the pool, and Cait heard the soft, muddied murmur of two voices in conversation. And neither of them were Andreya's. The tone was playful and the voices were of grownups, not kids. And they were giggling.

Now she was curious. Who were these two? Mind your own beeswax, girl, prodded her conscience. But her curiosity was too strong.

Cait walked cautiously over to the nearest stalagmite and sent out a tentative Mindcast, with Nini hunkered down beside her. Cait's ears told her true for once, there really were two people here. Peering carefully around the stone column, she could see a flash of bright hair. That could only be Lori Brunner. And who was the other person? Cait remembered Penny's story from last fall about the roses that Brunner had left behind in the shop. Might that be the person the flowers were for?

Cait watched some more. There was a rhythmic motion nearby; Brunner ran a comb through her hair as she talked. The rise and fall of her hand was a soothing motion, a homelike motion, a motion of calmness. It felt like being at home, that rise and fall, stroke after stroke. Bits of light reflected from water to ceiling and sometimes off that hair. Rise and fall, feels like home ...

With the portal no longer in her thoughts, Cait now wanted a better view of Lori Brunner. She took a step closer to the pool, and then another. Then she tripped over a budding stalagmite.

The voices stopped.

So did the comb.

Cait felt a push of air which felt like the "boom" of a very large firework; it came from the direction of the pool. She then sent out another Mindcast; Brunner was now the only other person there.

The teacher got up and walked briskly towards Cait. Her face glowed red, and she fumbled as she tried to stuff her comb into a pocket that was still buttoned. "So, Cait, you're early! Ohn' Fleiss, kein Preis. Na, gut. Good thing the Portal is ready in advance, ja ja, good thing. Nothing wrong with promptness, nothing at all." Cait had never heard Brunner talk so breathlessly before, nor look so flustered. And Cait never heard her mix up German and English like this before. "Why not get there early, nothing wrong with that at all. Unlike travelling by broom, you don't need the darkness, and if you've never been to a place before, so much better to figure it out in the daylight. Oh yes. I hear that this is your first time going to DC."

Brunner waved at Cait to follow her over to the canopied object she'd noticed during the first swimming class; the stone "wishing well" was indeed the portal. As they walked around behind the "well" with Nini following, Cait could see a break in the wall just large enough so that one could walk through and stand under the stone canopy.

Brunner continued to speak, her voice sounding more like her usual self. "Now, you stand on that stone in the center, and when I start the spell, you'll be on your way. This is also where you'll arrive when you return to Salem. I guarantee it'll be much more comfortable than your book-led trip west."

Does everyone in this whole school know all about my trip to Snohomish? Cait shook off her annoyance and concentrated on going to the Deaf college she'd read so much about. A thrill of excitement made her feet feel light. A whole campus for people like her, and she'd get all this extra time to explore it on her own. She hardly got to explore anything by herself any more. If Brunner hadn't realized that Cait wasn't supposed to be there this early, why correct her?

Then she felt Nini lean against her ankle. Cait frowned at her cat. "Penny will take care of you, remember? Go on back to the dorm." But Nini sprang to Cait's shoulder

331

instead, twenty claws digging into the cloak fabric. Just like Snohomish. "Cat, you're stubborn." But a little thrill fluttered in her chest as she patted her. Maybe this cat was more of a real familiar than even Penny knew.

"Are you ready? Have everything?"

Corwin's voice rang in Cait's memory: "Always have your wand on you," and Cait sent a million mental thanks for this advice. Wand, yes. Billfold, yes. Hat, yes. Then her stomach twisted as she remembered the Belfry spellbook that lay on her desk. Should she run back and get it? Would she lose her chance to get there early if she did? With a deep breath, Cait made her decision, and pulled Nini down from her shoulders to hold her tight in her arms. "I'm ready now, Ms. Brunner."

"Good. Do us proud in the competition. Bon voyage!"

With a sweep of Brunner's wand, and a word Cait didn't catch, she was off, hurtling through the same breathless darkness as before, but now it was more like a pleasant underwater glide than the nervewracking trip of last November.

Just as the breathlessness became unbearable, Cait realized that she was in regular, three-dimensional space again. As Nini jumped down, Cait reached out to feel cool cement walls on either side. A staircase rose up before her, and sunlight streamed in from the top of the stairs.

Now what was it that Jessica had told her to do? She had told Cait to go up the stairs. But before doing that, she had to make sure that she would be Hidden in Plain Sight. This was, after all, a nonmagical campus. At sundown, there would be a path, a bench, and a person there to guide her. Cait rubbed the hem of her robe between her fingers as she thought. What sort of glamour could she maintain while roaming around a campus she'd never seen before? A blue-jean dress could sort of look like robes, that would be a relatively easy illusion to keep up.

And what about Nini? Animals weren't usually allowed at regular schools. Did colleges allow them? "Nini, you make problems, you know that?" Cait sat down on a step to think, while scratching behind the cat's ears.

Now, if Nini were a dog, she could go as a guide dog in training. And there was this guy with epilepsy on her block, back in Central Massachusetts. He had a special dog to tell him when an attack could happen, with a little yellow vest saying "service dog at work". Why couldn't a cat do something like that too?

Cait cast the charm. Nini stood before her in a little yellow vest with red letters on it saying "service animal". Cait cast another charm to make her robes look like a denim dress, double-checked the effect, and then ran up the stairs together with Nini.

Boring – she was in a parking lot. That couldn't be right. A path sloped up a small hill before her, leading to a group of low brick buildings with fieldstone foundations, and black-mesh-enclosed walkways surrounding them. Cait ran up the path with Nini beside her, only to stand still before the cluster of buildings. The path now split off to the right and left. Which way should she go? To the right, was only more of that low brick complex. On her left, the hill sloped downward, and there were many more buildings over that way. That must be the rest of campus. And just up ahead there, was that a bench? The one Jessica described?

As Cait approached the apparently empty bench, she watched Nini, who padded along with nary a whisker twitch or ear-flick. No guide yet; she had the campus to herself for now. At least now she knew where to be at sundown.

333

Time to go exploring. For the first time, Cait was glad to be tall for her age. Could she pass for a college student? There had to be a library here, a bookstore. What if they had books written in Sign, like her Belfry book? Could she find them? But first, how much time did she have? Holding one hand up to the horizon, she gauged how high the sun was, using a trick her dad had taught her. Four fingers high times two. Fifteen minutes per finger equalled two hours. Time to start walking.

She followed the paved path with its buckled-up pieces of old, uneven, yellowed pavement as it sloped its way down the hill. A cement plaza with brick towers around it – some yellow, some red -- opened up below her. A shallow, stone-filled depression in the middle of it looked like it might be a pool or a fountain, had there been any water in it.

A two-story building stood on the right, and through its huge picture windows, Cait could see people sitting at round tables, signing away over plates of food. Cait watched with fascination. Even the Eagles game in New York didn't have this many signers. The festive hubbub of flying fingers and expressive faces was everywhere in this large room.

A bright blue light in the middle of the ceiling began to flash, and the diners finished their conversations, picked up their trays and shouldered their book bags. Cait tried to people-watch some more, but the blue light kept pulling her eye to the ceiling. Ugh what a nuisance. No wonder people were all leaving. Then a wide smile grew on her face. Of course this place would know how to get a crowd of deaf people to go on to classes or whatever on time. No bells, no alarms. Here was a whole campus where she wouldn't have to "listen up" to anything. She liked this place already.

Cait turned away from the dining room and continued walking. Time to find the library. Time to find the bookstore. Time to find those fancy, pointy-windowed old buildings she saw in her "College for the Deaf" book, not to mention Ole Jim.

By the time Cait had eavesdropped on videophone users in the Student Union, daydreamed about broomsprints over the football field, found out that the library held only one book written in Sign (an ASL dictionary) and speculated on how many ghosts Aunt May would find in the fancy building with the pointy windows, the sun was nearing the horizon.

Cait looked about her with alarm. Which way was that bench she needed to find? It was almost sunset already. She stood on a grassy lawn in the center of campus, next to a statue of a man who looked potbellied in his voluminous academic robes. In the distance, she could see something that looked like a yellow brick tower, and decided to start walking that way.

Nearby, a cluster of hackysack players bounced a ball around while a white-haired woman with a round face watched from a small bench. Cait thought they looked familiar, but first things first. She had an appointment to keep.

She felt the brush of someone's consciousness over the edge of her mind. Cait jumped as if stung. Who had Mindcasted her? Looking around the green, she saw that the cluster of hackysack players now stood still, a tousle-haired fellow holding the ball as everyone exchanged glances with the round-faced woman who now nodded, arose, and began to approach Cait.

But the tousle-haired boy got there first; Cait knew that quick grin. It was Alberto from the Eagles, and there was Diane, signing hello with those long, long fingers, and

Cara with those unbelievable fingernails, and Coach Joe, thumping her on the back, and thanking her.

Thanking her?

Coach clarified, signing slowly with a broad smile, while making sure Cait could follow him. "You told the Bats about us – we all got in touch." He put an arm around Alberto's shoulder while signing one-handedly: "Two-of-us -- what are we doing?" Then he continued with both hands: "Go to school again – four more years – become full seven-year wizards. How come? You."

Cait couldn't imagine feeling any happier. Even so, once the greetings slowed down, the roundfaced witch introduced herself as Myrna Felder, and then Cait remembered her from the Farsight mirror. Felder gave her a lecture for showing up so early that there was no one ready to make sure she got from the portal to Ole Jim without breaking Plain Sight. Many of the signs flew over Cait's head, but Felder's pulled-up stance, firm gaze, and emphatic signing left no doubt.

Lecture done, she eyed Cait's "denim dress", which was getting blurry around the edges, and renewed the illusion for her, while chuckling at the "vest" which Nini wore.

She waved at the whole group to follow. They all walked between a pair of boxy brick buildings. Then Cait saw Ole Jim. It was just as beautiful and grand as it had been in the picture, only now she could see that it was painted a beautiful, deep red, with two stories of multi-paned windows.

They caught a glimpse of a busy office beyond the foyer as they entered the building. A blonde wooden staircase inside the door led up to the second floor, but Felder guided them right past it, while rambling away as if she were a tour guide. "This lovely building was built in

1880 and was the most highly-equipped gymnasium of its time. Please note the exquisite woodwork ..." Some of the office workers looked over their way, then lost interest.

Felder rapped on the paneling under the staircase with her wand. A segment of woodwork vanished to reveal another staircase within.

"Up, up" she waved them all on, reminding Cait of Corwin at those underground shops on that first day at Salem. This staircase was a long one; Cait was sure that she had walked more than one story by the time the stairs finally bent to the left, and a lofty, light-filled room with thin metal rafters high in the eaves opened before them. Tall windows let in the coppery glow of pre-sunset light which bounced off the glossy, varnished wooden floor, while a light of a different sort drew her eye to the right. There, a brick chimney traveled up to the roof, covered in the flickering, flashing signatures and class years of countless Belfry-Bat alums.

"Stories – how many?" she signed to Felder.

"Illusion!" was the answer. A whiteboard floated over, spelling out Felder's explanation. Yes, Ole Jim was really a three-story building. During construction, it was designed to have only two stories. A master spellcaster had then added a secret third story accessible only to magicworkers. After all, finding future Deaf magicworkers was important work, and the Belfry Bats needed a permanent home base.

But in recent years, so many deaf students were scattered among the mainstream schools, that it became harder and harder to locate Deaf magical kids The Belfry Bats were still figuring out how best to do outreach, and many of them wished to be back in the days when they could simply visit local Deaf schools and look for magic.

"But enough history for now," signed Felder as she looked around. "Who's hungry?"

Hands went up all around the room. Cait now realized that there were many more people here than just herself and the Eagles. Snacks were summoned up, restrooms pointed out, and people's bookbags and cloaks stowed. The room filled with the festive hubbub of flying hands as people recognized each other and began conversations. Everyone seemed to know each other.

Cait stroked Nini as she watched. Then, even Nini strolled over to touch noses with a shaggy gray dog in a guide-dog harness. Some of the students brought their familiars as well; one girl had a green parrot on her shoulder, while a brown snake curled up in one boy's hood, reminding Cait of Nicky.

For one brief moment, it felt like being back at public school where she was always the odd one out, with no friends.

Then Cait noticed with relief that some of the Eagles still chatted nearby, keeping Cait within their line of vision. As she caught their eye and picked up her hands, their conversation paused. "Everyone here – know each other? How?" she asked.

"Deaf world – small, very small!" Cara shrugged, and then began pointing out people she knew from broomball games and her own Hedge-level years.

Older people filtered in, some carrying boxes, others summoning up tables and decorations. Across the room, a familiar face hurried towards Cait, hands flying, "Sorry – arrive so late. No – early you! You – plans messed up – I waited, waited, waited at the portal for you. Shame! -- Whatever – whatever – great to see you." and Jessica stood before Cait, hands on hips, her mock-stern face dissolving into a bear hug.

Just like at Witches' Academy, there was a proper banquet with lots of food, some of which Cait had never seen before. The sweet-potato pie was her favorite, and Nini's as well.

Least favorite were the greens. They were an overcooked glop with nearly all the color gone out of them, and Cait could not bring herself to eat a second forkful. She suspected that somebody might be in trouble down in the kitchen for overcooking them. The rest of the food was so good, how could they have overlooked these? Looking around, she could see that some of the students were slinging down those greens as if they were absolutely wonderful.

From across the table, Alberto saw her line of sight, grinned, poked at his own greens, and pulled a face. Cara and Jake nodded in agreement, and by the time Coach Joe pretended to bury his greens with his napkin, it was quite clear that most of the Eagles had the same opinion as Cait. They struggled to not burst out laughing because then they'd have to explain why, and what if they offended a local? After all, the menu called them "true Southern-style collards."

Once Nini had polished off the plateful of food Cait put down for her, she swaggered across the room to once again spend time nose to nose with the shaggy gray dog from earlier. Then her ears relaxed and his tail wagged slowly, and the two sat together as their people finished dinner.

A thin-faced girl opposite Cait caught her eye, then asked her name in signs that hesitated and stumbled. Why, she was no more fluent than Cait herself had been half a year ago.

"My name – C-A-I-T-L-I-N" she spelled back, being sure to keep her tempo slow.

"L-U-I-S-A," spelled back the other girl.

Cait asked, "Mainstream – you?"

Luisa looked confused as her hands copied Cait's sign. One of the Thoughtwrite boards zoomed over to them and displayed the words, "Were you mainstreamed?"

Cait blinked with surprise and looked at Diane. "You, just interpret that for me, did you?" she signed.

Diane grinned as she signed back, "Nope. These Thoughtwriters show your own thoughts, written, while you sign them. Me, I can relax, goof off, tonight no interpreting." Diane resumed conversation with her neighbor.

Cait repeated her question to Luisa, and soon, they were chattering away as easily as everyone else in the room.

A flurry of motion erupted around her, and all the Thoughtwriters zoomed towards the front of the room. They combined there to form a large screen, while waving hands throughout the room directed people's attention to Myrna Felder, who stood waiting for conversations to finish and all eyes to be directed forward. One cluster of signers persisted in their chatter. The room went dark as all the glow-globes hovering in the rafters doused themselves in unison and re-lit themselves after a couple of seconds. That stopped the chatter.

Speech time.

Cait was quickly lost among Felder's fluid signing, but it didn't matter. The words of formal welcome showed up plainly on the giant Thoughtwriter behind her. As Felder launched into a history of Belfry-Bat outreach, Cait's thoughts began to drift. This is so boring, why do I have to sit through all this academic yak yak yak? She leaned her chin on one hand and began to push pie-crust crumbs into decorative shapes on her plate. Then she put down the fork and grinned. This was the first time she'd zoned out because the speech itself was boring, not because it was too much work to decipher.

Soon the next day's schedule was being announced; the firstyears would be first to compete. Nervousness gripped Cait. Did she truly know the Belfry-style spells well enough to compete? What if she forgot the newer ones? And without her book, how would she even know which ones she might forget?

Once the speeches finished up, the banquet tables morphed into study carrels, couches, and coffeetables. The giant Thoughtwriter broke apart and the small Thoughtwrite boards scattered throughout the room as conversations resumed.

But Cait could not stop worrying about what she might have forgotten from the spellwork book sitting back in her room at Salem. She sat at a carrel, pulled out her mini-sketchbook, and tried to list all the spells she knew, but felt like she kept getting the spelling wrong, or not knowing which handshape to use. And her writing was all sloppy, and did her palms have to be so clammy? It was making the pencil slide around too much.

Cait tore out that sheet of paper and stared at the clean one beneath it. Take two. If she could remember the list Meg recited during their study parties, she'd be all right. Cait began writing, but flubbed up halfway through and lost track of what came next.

Then she thought of Jessica, and hope flashed within her. Would Jessica have a copy of the Belfry spellbook? Or a list of the spells they'd learned together? Cait jumped up and looked around the room, only to see Jessica deep in discussion with Felder. Probably too important to interrupt. Cait chewed at her lip as she flumped back down in her seat and poked holes into her half-written scribbled-out list.

Somebody pushed her cap over her eyes. Cait looked up to see Alberto looking at her with laughing eyes, flanked by Coach Joe and Diane. "No worry, you'll be fine. You will r-o-c-k! Go sleep now." And all seven Eagles hugged her good-bye and left the room, as the hovering glow-globes dimmed to amber, and Belfry Bats shooed remaining visitors towards the door.

Something else was going on. The lights became brighter, and Myrna Felder stood in the center of the room watching Jessica, who held a wand and gazed straight ahead, lips clenched in concentration. She nodded, then Felder signed, "Girls here – right; boys there – left!" and then nodded to Jessica, whose wand danced a series of arcs. Suddenly, hammocks hung throughout the room, all suspended from the rafters at varying heights. With another sweep of the wand, a shimmering silver partition divided the room.

Felder waved for everyone's attention. "Brooms there – for everyone – choose a hammock. Sleep well, good night," and both she and Jessica vanished. Some students flew up immediately to the rafters to look more closely at the hammocks and settle in. As the rest queued up for the two small restrooms, Cait picked up a nearby broom and looked about for a hammock that wasn't too far off the ground. *What if I fall out of this thing? How am I going to sleep up there? And what about Nini? Am I supposed to haul her up there with me?* Cait looked around for the cat; there she was, curled up asleep on her cloak by the chimney. Nini opened one eye, gazed at Cait, then stretched and went back to sleep.

There was a tap on her shoulder; Cait turned to see an older student, a girl with angular hands and an eyebrow ring. "Not to worry – can't fall out – safety spell." She signed at the perfect tempo for a beginner to understand, without the barely-disguised impatience of many of the other fluent signers. Then she paused, and the eyebrow with the ring formed a perfect arc as she signed, "You OK? More questions?" This girl was gorgeous as well as kind.

Cait shook her head, too shy to ask the girl her name as she thanked her, and flew up to the nearest hammock. Cautiously rolling into the hammock, Cait felt embraced; that was the only word for the feeling of well-being that enveloped her as the hammock rocked gently beneath her. Even the flapping butterflies in her stomach were calm, and she fell asleep dreaming of lots of new friends and lots of conversation where nobody missed out or got confused or couldn't keep up.

Chapter 22 – Curtain Up.

A cool breeze tapped her cheek, and a burst of light surrounded her. Cait opened her eyes to see the room full of sunlight. Or was it? This light flashed and twinkled. Mirrors filled the room, flashing morning sunlight at her and the other hammocks which swayed in the cool breeze. But the windows were closed, Cait thought. Duh – it's a spell. A Deaf wake-up spell. Cait's stomach growled. Grabbing her things and pulling her cap on her head, Cait rode the broom back to the floor, where tables were set, and Nini sat waiting in the middle of the room for Cait to bring her some breakfast.

As soon as the last hammock was vacated, the breeze stopped and the mirrors faded into nothingness. Once Jessica's wand danced a reverse set of arcs, the room looked as it did before. But chatter was not flying about as it had during dinner. Everybody was nervously searching spellbooks, perusing notes, and practicing Belfry-style spells.

Cait longed for her Belfry spellbook as Nini scarfed down scrambled eggs. But how much would she really learn so close to competition? she told herself. She'd done plenty of studying back at Salem. But her nerves still jangled.

She nibbled at a biscuit, then put it back on her plate. Practice time for her Belfry spells. "Lech na!" Back into the bread basket it went, then "Boh-ee!" brought it back onto her plate. With. "Shamayim me-aal!" Nini watched the hovering biscuit with wide eyes. Another "Boh-ee!" brought over a hard-boiled egg, and the Shell-out spell put it neatly on her plate, ready to eat. The eggshell transformed into a periwinkle just as she wanted it to, and she got the corn, water and cheese in her grits to divvy out in different parts of the bowl, and to reunite again.

She took a deep breath. She really could do this. Now she felt ready. Better stop playing with this stuff and start eating it, or she'll be starving later. She took a bite of biscuit, but could eat no more.

Across the table, Luisa stared at her own notes, then pushed both plate and notebook aside with a flourish that got Cait's attention. At the same exact moment, they both mimed nail-biting nervousness, and broke out into giggles, as Cait abandoned her own breakfast.

How easy it was to understand each other here, in this place that really was designed for her, for all of them. Worlds away from FM systems and hearing aids and trumpetvines and all those promises of "fitting in".

Two black-robed Belfry Bats now strode along the sides of the room. Stadium seating rose from the floor as the breakfast tables vanished and dishes were whisked away. As Cait stood up to get out of the way, Nini jumped to her shoulder and purred against her cheek. Cait tried to not count how many seats were in those bleachers, how many pairs of eyes were about to be staring at her and the other competitors.

Other Bats wanded banners into place, set green plants here and there around the room, and sent glittering streamers to snake their way through the rafters in elaborate patterns.

People in fancy robes filed into the room and took their seats: stately alums, boisterous fellow students, beaming parents. The Eagles burst into the hall in a cluster, all heading for Cait, thumping her on the back and sticking a grandiose plume in her cap before sitting down.

And there were three more figures heading her way, one short and rotund, another tall and lanky, the third,

345

her own height and curvy. Cait's jaw dropped as she ran to embrace them. "Mom, Dad, I didn't know you could come! But Aunt May, what about your own competition?"

"But my dear, Sunday is when we compete. I'm no longer stuck with highways now, remember? Plenty of time for me to fly back and forth, unlike your poor parents here."

"That's quite all right, May, I'll stick with vehicles, thank you," replied Miriam. "Caitlin, we know you'll do us proud. Just be yourself."

Eyebrow Ring laid a hand on Cait's shoulder and pointed to the far end of the room. It was time for competitors to take their places. Cait grinned as she waved back at her and signed, "Thank you – true, the bed rock, rock, but not fall out!" and earned a brilliant smile in return.

Felder stood at a podium directly opposite the staircase where spectators filtered in. Behind her were eleven seats, and over them floated numbers which looked as if they were made out of blown glass in all colors of the spectrum. Cait was pointed towards the "'14" on the far left, which glowed in a fiery shade of red-orange.

As she sat, Nini jumped from her shoulder to stroll over to the nearest bleacher, and parked herself next to a marmalade tabby cat who was twice her size.

A pale-faced boy already under the "'14" popped his knuckles and fidgeted with his cap. Don't get scared, Cait told herself. As she looked at the spectators, the festive flutter of all their conversing hands filled her with an effervescent happiness, and an unexpected calm. I really like being here, thought Cait. Doesn't even matter if I win, lose, or totally fluff this competition. It's so easy to just be here, be myself. This place was meant for her. How could she be scared? She felt a Mindcast tap from the bleachers to the left. Lillian smiled at her, and then all seven Eagles gave her thumbs up. Pride filled Cait as she grinned and waved at the team. With a pang, she wished Meg and Penny were there in the stands with them.

The blur that filled the stands calmed down as conversations ceased and all eyes turned to the staircase. A group of six colorfully-robed and tall-hatted witches and wizards stood there. In unison, the judges filed into the room and took their seats at a table which stood before the left-hand bank of spectator seats.

Butterflies flapped around in Cait's stomach in full force. Felder stepped forward; time for another speech, which was transcribed onto three large Thoughtwriters. One hovered above each bank of spectator seats, and the third one hovered over the staircase, where the competitors could read it. After what seemed like an age, Felder put down her hands, then stepped back and gestured towards the row of competitor seats.

"Class of 2014," she signed, and waved for the firstyears to stand. Too nervous to decipher Felder's signing, Cait read the Thoughtwriter instead. "Let's find out which of you is to go first. Each of you think of a number between 10 and 50, and when I do this" – Cait's eyes flicked back to Felder in time to see her arm make a grand sweep downward – "project it out for everyone to see, about this size." Felder checked to see that the competitors' eyes were on her and had finished reading the Thoughtwriter before her hands described a square the size of her face. "Use whatever color you like best. They don't have to be as perfect as the ones overhead, don't worry. Ready?" Felder's gaze swept over them, eyebrows high in inquiry. They all nodded, shifted, and tried to settle their nerves.

Felder's arm arose – get ready.

Cait chose her number and visualized her favorite shade of green, that vibrant neon shade of brand-new leaves, right after budding. She held the image of her number firmly in her mind, extended her wand at the ready, and fixed her eyes on Felder.

The arm dropped.

Four numbers flashed before judges and spectators. Cait was very pleased that her chartreuse "36" held steady, even though it lost a bit of yellowness when her concentration dropped. The pumpkin-orange "42" from the boy next to her wavered at its edges, and the purple "28" from the girl on her other side kept trying to fade to lavender. A yellow "14" at the far end of the group held remarkably steady. Wow, even that wobbly "42" is better than what the other folks in Corwin's class can do, marveled Cait. Maybe image-casting is easier for deaf people, the way speech is easier when you have all your hearing.

"Numbers 14 and 28, you are Team One; numbers 36 and 42, Team Two," announced Felder.

A cauldron now hovered before the Team One firstyears.

"The two of you will jointly pull out one slip from the cauldron," explained Felder. "Your task is to do what it says, using your spellwork skills and the objects which are in plain view in this room. Do not transport objects into the room from elsewhere, and do not use items belonging to spectators. These rules apply to everyone in today's competition. Break them, and you will be immediately disqualified from competing. Are you ready? Now choose – but eyes closed." The two students closed their eyes, reached into the cauldron, and pulled out a slip which Felder allowed them to read. Then she took the slip and signed to the rest of the room what it said.

The Thoughtwrite boards displayed the words: "Oops, two tables are left over from breakfast. Please relocate them to the back of the hall." And sure enough, a white-draped table stood before each of the two students, laden with china, silverware, food, and one vase of flowers apiece.

Lavender Girl's table successfully traveled the length of the room with only one dropped spoon and a shake of its flower vase. Wavery-Pumpkin's table traveled in stages. First the dishes flew to the floor, then the table zoomed to the other end of the room, tablecloth still fluttering as it landed, and the dishes flocked after it.

The judges sat in a football-style huddle so that nobody could see what they were signing. After several long moments, they took their places at the table, and directed their gaze at Cait and her partner. The tables vanished from where they had stood near the staircase.

Time for Team Two.

Cait thanked the stars for the ClingSpell on her wand as her hands popped out in sweat. The cauldron hovered before them, and they reached into it in unison. As their fingers bumped among the slips of paper, an instantaneous tactile conversation emerged. "Nah, not that one, how about over here?" "Or maybe this one over here?"

Then their fingers landed on the same slip at the same time, and they drew it out in perfect unison. "Water the plants on the rafters," was all it said.

Plants? On the rafters? Cait looked up. Sure enough, among the glittering streamers and twining vines were two large terracotta pots containing palm trees, balanced where the rafters intersected above each bank of spectator seats. Near the stairs where the breakfast tables had last been, were two large copper watering cans.

All the eyes in the room were on Cait and her team-mate.

Trying to ignore the judges' piercing scrutiny, Cait levitated her watering can slightly, gauging how much water was inside. She could tell that bringing the palm tree down from its perch would be awkward, with the heavy terracotta pot and the ungainly foliage. Maneuvering the large watering can with its long nozzle would be equally tricky. It wasn't light, and holding a steady hover-spell while also keeping the nozzle where it needed to be would be difficult. Her Mayim spell would be easier than either of these options, but she had never used it for quite this much water before.

Here goes.

Visualizing the mass of water and the path it needed to travel, Cait gathered her intention and made the sign. The mass of water sparkled in the sunlight as it traveled upward on the path she'd visualized. Just as Cait allowed the water to begin flowing into the soil, there was a slight slip in her concentration as she became aware of how long she'd have to hold onto that water to maintain that gentle cascade. If only she could just let the water go! No, she could do it, just hang on a little bit longer and all the water would be there. She kept the remaining water in place by sheer willpower as it finished pouring into the soil, then dropped her wand arm with a sigh of relief, legs trembling beneath her.

Was that a flurry of conversation among the stands? Cait wondered, as the motion caught her eye. Were people yakking like that with the first team? With surprise, she noticed that some hands were waving applause in the air. Her partner's empty watering can now floated down to the floor as he heaved a huge sigh. He looked tired, and Cait was glad to have chosen her own method for getting the water to her plant.

The judges were in a huddle again. Cait's nerves revved into gear. What if she was supposed to transport the water and the watering can? Would they disqualify her for moving only the water?

The judges returned to their places, and the Thoughtwrite boards read: "Team One, now you water the plants." Whew, guess I'm still in, thought Cait.

And if they're doing our plants, I guess we get to move breakfast tables next. Cait began to mentally rehearse how she'd move the loaded table with its fragile objects. Remembering Lavender Girl's wobbling vase, Cait tried to figure out why none of the things in Corwin's tea set ever wobbled. Then it dawned on her. The lechu-na spell was addressed to all of the objects on the tray, versus the lech-na version, which was for a single object. Lavender Girl must have told only the table to move.

Green leaves and flashing copper vanished from Cait's field of vision, interrupting her train of thought. The other team had finished, and the relieved competitors sat down as the judges deliberated.

New confidence filled Cait as the tables with their dishes and vases reappeared, and the judges directed their attention to her and her team-mate once more. She could do this. The table was larger than Corwin's tea tray, but not by much. Standing before her table, she formed the intended path in her mind, being sure to include every object before her: the tall vase with its top-heavy flowers, the spoon balanced across the top of a small bowl of berries, the narrow coffeepot which wouldn't need much encouragement to topple over. With a quick prayer, Cait sent the energy out to the table and watched it travel smoothly to the other end of the hall. Wow, nothing tipped, nothing fell. Were they done? Cait fervently hoped the firstyear competition was finished. She felt wiped out.

Thankfully, the secondyears were now being called up. Cait plopped into her seat to watch the more advanced students. Nini got up from her spot next to the orange tabby cat and settled onto Cait's lap. For a while, Cait tried to figure out how the students were doing such rapid Transformations, and getting them to stay put for so long.

A bark-covered branch stood before each of two secondyears. Faster than Cait would have thought, they were transformed into thin sheets of colored paper that floated into the rafters and then fell back down as a shower of tiny brass coins. As she picked up one of the coins and wondered how soon it would revert back to wood, a Mindcast-tap pulled Cait's attention to the bleachers to meet Lillian's gaze. "Next-year, you will-do same," she signed.

"Doubt-it," replied Cait.

"True, rock-solid true, you'll see," she answered, and turned back to the competition.

As the spellwork became more complex, with water becoming crackling flames and airy cobwebs turning into granite blocks, Cait gave up figuring out the spells, and simply enjoyed watching them. But what if you're stuck on the ground in night-flying and don't get to go on to secondyear? nagged a little voice in the back of her mind.

As Cait's nerves jangled once more, she felt a Mindcast-tap of support and love, from Aunt May this time. Cait looked her way to see her parents and aunt all give her thumbs-up. She smiled back, and hoped she could live up to a fraction of whatever they imagined she'd do next year.

352

Once the thirdyears had finished, it was lunchtime, and Cait was surrounded by hugging and cheering Eagles, parents and aunt.

Then it was time for the Above-Hedge competition, which she and the other below-Hedgies got to watch from the lowest bank of stadium seats, opposite the judges. These tasks were even more stunning.

Unlike the below-Hedge transformations which reverted back to their original forms ten or twenty minutes later, these transformations stayed in their new forms. And they were much more complex as well, such as buckets of water that became bonfires that left ashes on the floor that were still there at the end of competition. Brick walls turned into teacup-sized houseplants.

Then she realized with a start that not all of the competitors had wands. Where were their wands? Were they really doing all that spellwork without wands? Cait's mind reeled at what she was seeing, while at the same time she longed to learn how to do the same.

A pair of wandless sixthyears with a handful of seeds covered the rafters with seedlings which grew into trees covered with pink flowers, which then dropped off into the audience. As the petals brushed Cait's cheek, she realized that this was no illusionary glamour, but a true growing season compressed into ten minutes. Then the branches filled with red cherries as everyone's arms lifted in applause, and were rewarded by the ripe fruit dropping right into the audience. Cait could only imagine how exhausted those students must be.

The trees reminded her of the wand shop in Salem and the chestnut wand which was supposed to see her through all seven years of study. If Meg thought the Witches' Academy curricula was scary, she ought to get a look at these students. Classes at Salem looked like a piece of cake in comparison. Not even the teachers went wandless at the Academy.

The last of the seniors sat down. What now?

Names began to appear on the Thoughtwrite boards, and hands were waving all over the room. Was that her name up there? Cait stared in disbelief as a judge motioned her up towards their table where a set of crystal trophies sat.

"Firstyear First Place: Caitlin Leo," was indeed what it said. This was some wonderfully unbelievable dream, and she was going to wake up at the Salem Academy, saying some spell the wrong way as she fell off her broom. But no – the hands pushing her towards the table were all too real. Cait grinned as she shook the judges' hands and accepted her trophy. That old Erin McGowan could keep all those elementary-school awards and honors, thought Cait, remembering public school. And it wouldn't even matter if Amanda won all the races at Witches' Academy. Cait had this.

Now a portly judge in a maroon hat was signing something to her. A Thoughtwrite board zoomed over to display, "Your innovation with the water was remarkable. We will be watching for you in future competitions. Congratulations!"

But she couldn't escape just yet. The judge laid a hand on her arm and pointed to a waiting photographer.

Finally, all the prizes were awarded. People drifted out of the hall, shaking hands, admiring trophies, and hugging goodbye.

And were Cait's parents ever going to stop hugging her? She had never seen her mom so weepy, nor her dad smile so broadly before, as they introduced themselves to each of the Eagles, to Jessica, and to Ms. Felder, as they all came by to congratulate Cait. Aunt May only stood there with her broom in hand and beamed. Then she too hugged Cait and sent a proud Mindcast, as she pretended to sweep Cait's parents out the room and to their car.

Not to be outdone, the Eagles swiped a tablecloth from one of the breakfast tables, and blanket-tossed Cait innumerable times up to the rafters to check on "her" plant, letting up only when the spectators and judges had left.

As they lowered the blanket and let Cait step off, she could see people around her tapping shoulders and pointing to the front of the hall. Myrna Felder stood there, a row of brooms before her. She announced, with signs large enough to be seen throughout the room, "Tour of campus before departure. Please choose a broom and be ready to follow me."

Sunset colors streaked the sky through Ole Jim's windows, and sweat broke out on Cait's forehead. There would be too little light for her to fly properly out there. Did nobody else here have daylight-dependent balance?

Felder, however, was not yet finished with her announcement. She pointed off to one side, where stadium seats had just been. "Boats are reserved for those who cannot broomride after dark." Surprise and relief made Cait loosen shoulders she hadn't realized were hunched up, and to stand a bit taller. Trust. She could trust these Belfry folks to look out for what she needed, all of it. This was no longer some mainstreamed school where she had to do all the work herself. To tell the teacher "I can't hear you", to bring that FM unit or trumpetvine with her, to make sure it worked, to sit up front, to pay extra attention, over and over and over.

Cait grinned as she headed to the nearest boat, and waved to an angular long-limbed boy who already sat

355

there, folding up a candy-apple red walker and putting it aside.

But there was no Nini hopping into the canoe along with Cait. That was really odd. Now that the weather was warmer and the snow had gone, Nini was always there watching while Cait did broomsprints, and was in the boat whenever they had off-campus practices. She could swear that the cat developed a taste for flying. Cait scanned the room. Was Nini visiting with the dog from last night's dinner? Or checking out that orange tabby cat from the competition?

Then Cait spotted Nini right in the center of the room. She was parked atop a broom and staring right at Cait as if to say, "You're in the wrong place." Just beyond Nini, Cait could see the motions of Ms. Felder's and Jessica's chatter as they waited for everyone to choose brooms and get into boats.

"Over here, Nini," said Cait, patting the side of the boat. "It's getting too dark out there for me to fly." Cait saw Nini meow in reply, but the cat didn't budge from her spot. Cait scowled and patted the side of the boat again, harder. "Over here, Nini."

Ms. Felder and Jessica paused in their signing. They looked at Nini, and then over to Cait. Jessica frowned and said something to Felder, whose own forehead creased thoughtfully as she gazed at the cat once more.

Why was Nini being so stubborn? Cait sighed as she got up and headed towards the brooms. As she approached, Nini sprang up and yapped as she rubbed against Cait's leg, then stood by a broom, front paws kneading the floor, gazing at Cait.

"Fly in the dark, you crazy cat? How?" Cait said and signed as she reached down to pick up Nini, who jumped from her grasp and once again stood by the broom. As

Cait stood up, she saw Ms. Fletcher signing at a rapid clip as Jessica's face lit up, and a whiteboard zoomed over to follow her. And they were coming Cait's way.

As Jessica aimed a flurry of fingerspelling at Ms. Felder "Alwilda and Mog!" showed up on the whiteboard, and Ms. Felder nodded. Who were "Alwilda" and "Mog"? Then Felder began signing to Cait, and the whiteboard displayed the question: "Does this cat usually accompany you in the air?"

"In boats, sure. But never on a broom. I can barely keep myself onboard during daylight, never mind in the dark. How could I take Nini along? But she always watches me practice."

"Let's experiment. Let's find out what happens if you do take your cat on broomstick with you," answered Ms. Felder. She paused to announce in sweeping signs to the whole room, "Campus tour in ten minutes," then turned her attention back to Cait. "Your cat seems to have chosen a broom for you already."

Cait glanced around the room as she picked up the broom with chilly and nervous fingers. Was everyone going to be staring at her? Was the extra ten pounds of cat aboard going to throw off her flying? But the well-lit room was full of blurring fingers, as people took advantage of the break to catch up on chatter. Cait held the broom at the ready, and Nini sprang onto her shoulders with a deep rumble of a purr that thrummed through Cait's neck and shoulder.

"You can do this," signed Jessica, as Cait hesitated. "We'll stay right here with you."

Sink or swim. At the "Shemayma!" command, the broom hovered in air as usual, but Nini now descended from Cait's shoulder to perch on the broomstick itself, front paws resting against Cait's clenched hands, and the vibration of her purr travelling along the broomstick.

Then something like a Mindcast tapped at Cait's brain, and the purr grew stronger under Cait's fingertips. Was that Mindcast Nini? As the surprised thought made Cait lose her concentration and the broom wobbled, something from outside her own consciousness righted the broom as the Mindcast touch grew stronger, then lessened. And the purr continued uninterrupted.

Cait looked down to see that Jessica wore a broad grin, and Ms. Felder now smiled as she signed something to Jessica. Cait looked over at the whiteboard to see: "Exactly like Alwilda Thornwhistle, that witch in the Maryland Council who never, ever flew without her cat Mog. Think of the difference this could make. After all, fully one third of all deaf people have damaged balance and we've only been able to offer them boats or carpets up until now. Cait, how about going up a bit higher, then flying over to that chimney and back?"

Without daring to loosen her grip to sign back to Ms. Felder, Cait nodded, and pushed down on the broomstick as the purr continued under her fingers. As the broom set off, it felt as if she were riding a friendly current while floating on water, rather than struggling to run along some balance beam, with the constant shifting and adjusting that kept her from falling off. Now she was at the brick chimney with its glowing names. It was time to turn around, but where was that wobble that always happened at the crest of her turns? Gone entirely. She had never completed such a perfect turn before.

Cait glowed with happiness as she returned to Ms. Fletcher and Jessica. Nini jumped off the broomstick ahead of her, rubbing and headbutting everyone's legs, then jumping back on Cait's shoulders to purr against her cheek. "Nini, you are one unbelievable cat," Cait told her while scratching under the cat's chin. "How does she know what to do? How?" Cait signed to Ms. Fletcher.

"Some familiars have very good intuition," was the answer. "Nini must have studied your flying lessons as well as you did, and figured that her own good balance was what you needed. This is a very exciting discovery; we thought Alwilda and Mog were one of a kind. Do you know how many people this will help? We would like to have the name of your flying instructor. Jessica tells me that you have some night-flying to learn, and this could well be the key. But for now, we have a tour to lead. Be ready in five minutes."

This time, when Cait walked over to her place in the waiting boat, Nini trotted along right at her heels, with her gray-plumed tail held proudly aloft.

Felder now took her broom and flew up to a section of ceiling which opened up skylight-style. Red and black streamers flowed from the back of her broom, making her easier for everyone to follow.

As boats and brooms lifted up after the fluttering streamers through the roof into the open air, Cait's mood floated with them. If she and Nini really could night-fly as a team, then there'd be nothing to stop her from going through every single level of study that the Academy had to offer. No more Hedge-level jobs for Cait. No being stuck at firstyear in disgrace. No needing to save up and borrow for some unaffordable carpet or having to beg some rich person for a loaner. Cait reached forward and hugged Nini, who sat staring at a passing bat.

Below the canoes and under each broom, Cait could see dim outlines of outstretched wings and long necks, and guessed that a glamour kept them from being visible to Plods. They hovered over a green lawn while Felder waved everyone into a circle and began to point out buildings, their names hanging in the air, written in glowing light which faded as soon as everyone had read them. "The library. The Founder's house. The original classroom building from the 1860s." Now they were on the move, up and over the old buildings, counting the eaves, admiring fancy roof-tiles, and circling the pointy clock tower. People are going to think we're the weirdest geese they've ever seen, Cait thought as she tried to imagine what their group must look like from the ground.

Several buildings later, Felder announced, "This is our middle and high school," and Cait looked down to recognize the building she first saw when leaving the portal. She wondered what it would be like to go to school here, to be around Deaf kids all the time, to never again have to "listen up" to anything. But then, she'd miss Penny and Meg. And would they miss her, too? And would the teachers here be as good as Corwin? As patient as Greengage? And she'd have to spend the whole day hiding in Plain Sight besides.

All too soon, they were following Felder's streamers back into the skylight-hatch of Ole Jim's roof.

Once Felder assigned departure portals and times to the Under-Hedge students, Cait found herself reluctantly following Jessica out to a building on the edge of campus which looked like a miniature brick house, complete with white-painted gingerbread trim. She clutched her new trophy in one hand while Nini followed, once again wearing the glamour of an assistive-animal's vest.

"This place – I miss now!" she complained as Jessica held the door open for her. "Again put-up-with teachers - think I understand mumble mumble mumble?" Cait wrinkled her nose as her fingers fluttered in the sign for "incomprehensible speech."

Jessica shook her head. "Worry, no. You'll come b-a-c-k". She fingerspelled that last word for emphasis, then began listing things on her left hand. "Socials. Sports. Contests. Maybe art – your picture nice, sorry no prize this year."

Oh. "Thank you," Cait replied quickly. The excitement of the competition had put the art contest completely out of her mind.

Jessica waved Cait towards a flagstone in the center of the room. Cait scooped up Nini, whose blue "vest" made her smile despite her regrets on leaving campus. That vest is more than just a glamour now, thought Cait. What'll Greengage think of how Nini helps my flying?

"Ready?" Jessica signed a double "R" at Cait.

"No," Cait grumped with thumb and two fingers of her free hand closing emphatically. Then she clutched cat and trophy tighter and thought of how much fun she'd have showing off to Meg, Penny, and Ms. Corwin. And Greengage. "OK – anyway -- I'll go," she signed awkwardly with one hand.

"See you, see you," signed Jessica.

And the breathlessness carried her back to Salem.

Chapter 23 – Nestlings

As soon as the glow of the pool room surrounded her, Cait burst out of the portal, ran up the stairs to the courtyard and took the steps leading to the Commons two at a time, with Nini racing alongside her. As she entered, the room full of diners looked strangely subdued. Faces were static and no hands flew about in chatter. Almost as odd was the wave of vocal babble which made Nini pin her ears flat against her head.

Cait looked around for her friends. Meg caught her eye and nudged Penny. Holding the trophy aloft, Cait wore a huge smile as she skipped to their table. The hubbub of voices calmed as people turned to see what was going on.

Cait handed the trophy to Penny. "Firstyear division, first prize!" she signed, then spoke. They all admired how it reflected the lights of the Commons, and the tiny holograph of Cait that stood within its center.

There was an imperious wave from the faculty table. Lumen wanted to see the trophy, and it was soon traveling the length of the table as Cait explained Belfry-Bat outreach and the national Deaf-wizarding school-age competition. Corwin's eyes shone as she told everyone how good a Spellwork student Cait was from the very first class. Cait shifted her weight from foot to foot, wishing she could sit down and be out of the spotlight.

As soon as she sat back down, the Commons broke out in chatter all over again, and Cait wished she were back among the Belfry-Bat signers and their Thoughtwrite tablets. She was dying to find out how the Academy competition turned out, but the babble of voices around her was too loud, and she didn't have her trumpetvine with her. After all, what would have been the point of bringing that to a signing school?

A crowd of curious students stood around her table, all asking her ... what? Bits of questions surfaced through the swirling sound while Penny tried to help out by interpreting what people said into the signs she'd learned out of Cait's NAD book. Through it all, Meg scowled and tipped her chair back, trying to balance it on one leg.

Too much chatter, too much noise! What good was getting to go to that Deaf college for a weekend, thought Cait, if I have to be stuck trying to understand all this noise back home? Not fair.

Cait's foot hit the floor with a loud thud. Meg's chair fell to the floor with a bang, Penny's hands stopped in mid-sign, and the surrounding chatter ceased abruptly. Cait looked at the surprised faces around her, then pointed at random.

"You first. One at a time."

Minna blinked at the end of Cait's finger. She paused only for a moment before asking, "Did they make you night-fly all the way to DC?"

"Nope, they've got this other way for us to travel long-distance and it's right in the pool room. It's called a Portal, but not many places have them."

"Did you get to use open-book?" This came from the girl whose brown and white ferret sat on her shoulder.

"No, how could we? Our hands were too busy signing to hold anything else. But here's what's really incredible. Some upperclassers didn't even use wands."

"Get out! That's impossible."

"Nobody can do that."

"No way."

Cait let the hubbub of reactions subsite before replying, "I saw it myself."

"How many tasks ..." "Any upperclassers..." A pair of secondyears started talking at the same time.

363

"No," Cait shook her head, hands over her ears, "One at a time or I can't answer. You first."

Finally, she was back in her own quiet room, where she could ask Penny how the Academy competition had gone. Penny beamed and pulled a silver trophy down from the top shelf of her desk. "Transformations, second place," she bragged. "And we didn't even have to worry about any dirty tricks from the Magentas, since Elsbeth was the only one to even qualify, and she'd never cheat. You should have seen Claire stomping around when the finalists were announced. She earned herself an essay on the seven levels of Transformation for muttering something about smoke and mirrors. And Amanda nearly got in, but got a lecture about 'maybe next year, if she learns to not depend on ready-mades so much'."

"Like Daydark," Cait guessed. Penny nodded.

Cait continued, "How come the contest was just for Spellwork, anyway? Meg didn't look too happy tonight. She'd have won a Mindcasting contest if they had one."

Penny shrugged. "I don't know why they don't have one. At least there's broomsprints at Beltane, and that's not even a month away. She'll get to show off then."

"Meg can practically fly in her sleep. She'll win for sure." A thrill filled Cait as she picked up Nini, who was about to curl up on Cait's pillow, and hugged the cat. "And I have really big news. Thanks to this amazing cat, I think I've got a way to night-fly. The Belfry folks are going to tell Greengage all about it. I can't wait for our next night-flying class. Wish it were Wednesday already."

But during the next day's before-supper broomsprint practice, Cait had no chance to brag about Nini's talents. Meg was in an evil mood. "I'll be a Hedgie for life with some boring job that pays nada, I just know it." She zoomed in furious circles over Partridge Hall as if she were on her own small racetrack. "And I'll never get out from under Genius Big-Sister's shadow. It's only because of her I can do anything halfway decent in class. And you and Penny will go on to become book-writing bigheads."

Cait hovered in the center of Meg's circle as she took a break from keeping up with her friend's furious rate of speed. "Come on, you can Mindcast circles around Penny and me without half trying. Auclair doesn't give us the grades you get."

Meg snorted. "Only because of my snoopy sibs. When you're at the mercy of a houseful of people all older than you, it's a survival skill."

Cait flew down to the rooftop and sat next to the aviary full of cooing and chirping message birds, while she continued to watch Meg's dizzying circles. Why wouldn't Meg believe her? After all, those midnight study parties were helping Meg's grades. When was this conversation ever going to change?

Conversation ceased as Meg continued her dizzying laps. Then Penny emerged onto the rooftop.

"Hey Penny, Meg's all down on herself again. Thinks she's a below-Hedge Mindcaster."

Penny snorted before answering Cait. "Yeah, right." Looking at the blur above her, Penny called out, "Hey Meg, what's my mood?"

Meg slowed her overhead circuits, closed her eyes briefly, and answered, "Hungry. And wicked happy about that trophy of yours. Still. Don't go snob on us."

Penny gave a smug grin as Meg continued her overhead circuits. "See? I can never do a reading that fast, let alone while flying. Takes even longer when I'm grumpy."

Meg made a face. "Logic. It's suppertime, people are hungry. And you are proud of that prize. And you're also still daydreaming about stealing the Schoodic and taking it to the Caribbean."

"See, I didn't even think about the Caribbean for more than a second." Penny smirked triumphantly. "You almost never study your Mindcasting, and you still do fine in class while Cait and I are stuck in our books."

"All you need is a pack of older sibs," countered Meg. "Cait's turn," and she closed her eyes briefly, opening them wide in incredulous surprise. "Green tulle, billowing yards of it. Did some fashion designer zombify you?"

Cait mimed a punch up in Meg's direction. "Well, we've got to wear something to that Beltane dance. Dance in formal heavy silk robes? I don't think so. And if I wear all green, and put in some gold jewelry, the trumpetvine will look like part of the design." And Cait was again lost in her Beltane reverie.

"Stolen by a dress designer," muttered Meg as she came in for a landing. "Well it's suppertime. Let's go." Meg pulled Cait up from her seat, and they all headed off to the Commons.

Immediately after supper, Cait was back on the Partridge Hall roof with Nini, shakily flying back and forth, learning how to juggle between letting Nini balance the broom while she controlled its speed and direction. And falling off every time she forgot and tried to keep the broom balanced herself. By her second night of practice, she hardly fell off at all, and Nini's anxiously loud purr had settled to a comforting rumble. Cait would have practiced all night, but Meg grabbed her broom at midnight, when she was about to fall off from tiredness. "You can't compete without sleep. You won't impress Greengage at all if you're too tired."

At last, it was time for Broomwork class. Greengage beamed as Cait and Nini walked into the courtyard.

"Congratulations on your furry co-pilot," she began. "I have just received a fascinating letter from a Belfry Outreach office in DC telling me all about a breakthrough with your flying. I only wish I'd thought of it myself. And best of all, the Boston Council of Witches has no restrictions at all against night-flying with familiars. So, shall we begin? Everyone else, in the air, two-team slaloms around the east-court quince and apple trees. Cait, you fly over to that pear tree and back, and show me your new technique."

Cait took up her broom with a mixture of anticipation and nerves as Nini jumped on her shoulders, purred against her cheek, and settled onto her spot on the broomstick between Cait's arms. As she shakily swung back around the pear tree, she could see Greengage looking radiant as she paced back and forth, watching Cait. Then she signaled Cait to hover near her.

"Yes, yes, I think you've got it. How about a lap around the whole courtyard? Show me how many steady laps you can do." Cait nodded, and swallowed her nerves. How far was that? Six times the length of Partridge Hall roof? Eight? Or more? How long could she keep her concentration and remember to let Nini do all the balancing? Time to find out.

The first lap was nice and steady. I really can do this, thought Cait as she began the second lap. Good-bye kitchen jobs. No heavy boats or unaffordable carpets. No being held back while her classmates go ahead. A wobble of the broom and a sharp mind-tap from Nini pulled Cait away from her musings. By the third lap, tiredness began to set in, and Cait swerved too far as she took the last corner. Nini nudged her, but not quickly enough. Both of them landed and bounced on the courtyard groundcover.

"Turf's still nice," said Cait as she reached for her broom, ready to try more laps. She heard something that made her pause. Was somebody clapping? Greengage?

But the teacher wasn't alone. There were Meg and Penny as well, and Andreya, and Minna. All clapping and cheering.

And to one side, Amanda stood scowling. "Sorry, champ," said Cait with a wicked grin. "Guess I'm not gone after all."

Amanda tossed her hair. "We'll see. I'm going to get the best Zoomorphia grade." She stroked the crow on her shoulder, which took off and flew behind the library.

What did that have to do with anything? wondered Cait.

"Good work, excellent work," boomed Greengage. "You've just done 300 broomlengths. In order to cross Salem Harbor at end of term, you'll need to fly 500 broomlengths steadily within five minutes. But if you practice every day over the next four weeks, I think you can catch up with the rest of class. Every day. You can't skip a single one. Congratulations." And she beamed once more. "Full sprints, relay-team division, into the air, everyone," she bellowed at the rest of the class.

Zoomorphia class two weeks later was almost as much fun as being applauded in Broomwork. Right in the middle of one of Graycliff's lectures, a small blur whizzed in through the window and made directly for a mysterious and unexplained shelf tucked in among the ceiling's wide oak beams. Another blur quickly followed it.

"They're back," said the teacher, as she tilted the wide brim of her hat away from her eyes to peer at the shelf, while a Thoughtwrite board borrowed from the Belfry Bats displayed her words. "Early, even. Class, this is our own resident pair of barn swallows. They've been returning to this same nest for six seasons now, and these little birds are exceptionally mellow about allowing a whole pack of humans to watch them go about their nesting business. Exceptional, exceptional."

Graycliff motioned them all to watch the birds as they hopped about, examining the shelf, then zooming out the window to return with muddy twigs and stalks of grass. The class watched in fascination as the swallows began their nest-building.

"Some of you have been observing nests in the wild already, and I applaud your perceptiveness. Remember our ground rules as always; disturb the residents as little as possible, Take nothing from the site unless you know the animal no longer wants it. Lastly, common species can be just as interesting as rare ones. Case in point, our barn-swallow friends here."

To Cait's left, Meg fidgeted in her seat. When Cait signed at her, "Wrong – what?" Meg didn't answer, but burst out of the room the next time all eyes were on the swallows' growing nest, muttering something about "Mindcast from upset bird."

Cait leaned to her right, poked Penny and raised her eyebrows; "No idea," Penny signed back.

As soon as the class ended, Cait and Penny bolted out of the classroom, leaving Graycliff swinging her glasses by the temples in puzzlement. Once in the hallway, they paused. Which way did Meg go?

"She did say something about a bird," said Cait.

"Must be outside then," said Penny. "There's a bunch of bigger trees on the other side of the classroom building. You go right and I'll go left."

Cait saw the ring of light around the tree first, glowing about ten feet up. A faint and agitated whistle could be heard from the tree's branches. Meg stood beneath the ring with her face set in a defiant frown and wand held at the ready.

Amanda stood facing her, shouting furiously, "Well, if a golden creeper decides to put her nest right outside our classrooms when they never even show up in Massachusetts, why shouldn't I get myself an A for bringing in a rare nest? She can always build another one."

Cait approached the tree and looked up. "Golden" was right; the stripes of the bird's gold-on-white plumage glittered in the dappled sunlight which filtered through the newly-budded foliage. The nest itself sparkled; some of the bird's feathers had been woven in among the twigs and grass tucked into the stub of a broken-off branch. A stick sat askew at the edge of the nest, and one blade of grass dangled from the bird's beak.

Amanda's attention shifted as Cait came into view. "No talking with your friend over there! This is between us two. And I don't want to hear her casting any spells, either." Cait put up her hands and backed up to where she had been before, carefully staying within Meg's line of sight, but outside Amanda's. How dense could a girl be? Had Amanda really forgotten that Cait hadn't used spoken spells for more than a semester?

Meg now fired back, "Not until she's done with this nest. How do you know she'll build another one? She might get scared off campus completely. Don't you want her to lay eggs and raise more golden birds? Don't you even care that this bird is screaming, she's so scared and mad at you? Or can't you even Mindcast? Even a Plod can see how upset she is. And there's no way a real Mindcaster can ignore panic like that." Meg extended her wand even further and braced herself.

"Well it's just a bird, not a person, they don't even have minds big enough to Mindcast." replied Amanda. "And this class isn't about Mindcasting, it's about observation, and observation is what I was doing when you got in the way. There aren't even any eggs yet so there."

As the shouting continued, Cait signed at Meg, "The nest – I can hide it. Shall I?"

Meg nodded her free hand in a surreptitious "yes" as she shouted back at Amanda. Cait pulled out her wand and worked an illusion of a leafy new branch in exactly the right spot to make the nest invisible from the ground. As the chartreuse haze descended over the nest, the bird's anxious whistles slowed down and grew quieter.

Amanda appeared to have shouted herself out; she and Meg were locked in a staredown. Cait felt someone tap her elbow; Penny glanced up at the chartreuse branch and signed a thumbs-up to Cait as she also kept out of Amanda's line of sight.

Elsbeth appeared around the corner of the building, gasping for breath as she ran. "There you are, Amanda. Is the nest ready? Isn't it too soon?" Her brow creased as she peered up at the tree.

"This pauper's interfering with my grade," stormed Amanda.

The bird whistled from the branches, and Elsbeth gasped. "You're going to take the nest now? But the bird's still there. You can't do that to a nesting bird, poor thing."

"Hey, whose side are you on?" asked Amanda.

"Yeah, listen to your friend, Amanda." said Meg.

A shadow fell over Cait and Penny as a voice came from behind them. "Do we have a situation here, girls?" Graycliff strolled over to the tree and took in the ring-spell, the dueling girls, and the concealed, whistling bird. Her glasses dangled from her fingers, swinging back and forth for a long moment.

"They say it's a golden creeper," said Cait softly. "That's not in our books." She gently lifted the illusionary branch while Graycliff put on her glasses and peered at the bird and her nest, then nodded at Cait to put the illusion back into place.

"And I'm the one who found it," proclaimed Amanda, chin proudly lifted.

"And you were going to steal her nest," hissed Meg.

At the raising of Graycliff's hands, they all stopped. "Grade raised one level to an 'A' for spotting this rare bird," she announced solemnly. She nodded at Amanda, who smirked. "And dropped two levels to a 'C' for endangering the same. You have clearly not been attending to the parts of my classes which have stressed observation only. Never, never, disturb any animal on its own turf unless it happens to be in imminent danger. Ever." Greycliff's eyes flashed with subdued fury as Amanda stalked off, throwing off Elsbeth's anxious attempts to calm her.

Greycliff now addressed Meg. "Extra credit and an 'A' to Meg Ainslee for protecting – while at the same time not disrupting – this little bird. Nicely-done Ring-Guard spell. I was not aware of it being taught to firstyears, however." The glasses dangled from Graycliff's hand once more as she awaited Meg's reply.

"Big brother always got into my stuff, so I learned to copy how my big sister kept him out of her things," Meg said.

Greycliff nodded. "And the concealment spell?"

Cait raised her hand.

"Well done. A half-level added to bring your grade to a 'B+' for your quick thinking and insight." Greycliff regarded the tree. "I recommend that the concealment spell remain; be sure to renew it every day. Please dissolve the Ring-Guard spell. It has done its work. I believe that Thursday will be an excellent time to lecture the whole class on the observation of rare and fragile species. And that learning to Mindcast small animals, as well as people, is a skill very worth developing. Not everyone can do that, you know." Graycliff nodded in Meg's direction. "Excellent skill to have. Good night."

Graycliff strode off towards the courtyard leaving Cait and Penny jubilant and Meg pensive.

"Meg, do you believe us now? Graycliff says not everyone can do what you just did. And you saved a bunch of little rare birds besides. Champ, champ champ, you are the best Mindcaster!" Cait highfived her as Penny threw an arm around Meg's shoulders.

"We're worrying the bird, let's move," was all Meg said; she looked stunned. "Did Graycliff really mean that? Not everyone can Mindcast animals?"

"Well I can Mindcast Nini sometimes, but only when I really concentrate," said Cait. "Not birds and mice though."

"Don't look at me, I can't even Mindcast my own Nicky," added Penny. "He only shares when he wants to."

"Victory lap around the courtyard!" announced Cait, as she summoned three brooms from the Partridge-Hall roof, pleased with herself for getting a glamour of golden streamers to flutter from Meg's broom.

The next day before breakfast, Meg sent out a Mindcast to Cait and Penny on her way out the dorm, and all three of them walked behind the library to look at the nest once more. The bird now sat there calmly. She no longer threaded feathers and grass among the branches, but only turned her head the tiniest bit to watch them.

May 4, 2008
Witches' Academy
Salem, MA
Dear Aunt May:
Flowers are all over campus, looks so amazing when I fly over the dorms. Wish I could see your orchard; does it look that way too?

Beltane ball was really excellent, and even though it was noisy, I didn't even say "what" once! Penny and Meg have been learning ASL from a Belfry teacher. Such best, best friends! There's the trumpetvine too, and it's all the hearing people who were going "what, what, huh?" We put glamours on our dress robes so they looked like ballgowns, and Corwin said mine's one of the best she's ever seen. Then she put a knot in one of about a thousand cords all hanging from her belt, and that makes the glamour stay put for three hours. I can't wait to learn binding spells like that one, but they won't allow it until we're over Hedge and into our fourth year. Which means that Meg won't learn binding spells at all. I'll miss studying with her Over the Hedge. And I can't stand the thought of broomraces without her, either. For four whole years.

At the ball, Andreya showed up with this ginormous smile, and Meg's signing to me, "Weird girl, what's up with her?" Then she brings her cousin Neil right up to me. The one who guided us to the Eagles practice in Seattle. Best. Dancer. Ever. Especially since the other boys were just sticking to themselves and acting stupid. Belching contest at the punchbowl, can you believe?

Now I have to go study for finals. I can't believe that I'm actually looking forward to seeing Salem Harbor from the

air at midnight, instead of being terrified! Meg and I practice every night; she times me on my 500-broomlength runs. I'm so glad that you and the extension students will be flying over Salem Harbor with all of us firstyears. Yay weird witchy all of us!
Love,
Your onliest niece,
Cait

May 20, 2008
Witches' Academy
Salem MA
Dear Aunt May:
Our golden birds fledged!! Remember the nest we rescued last month? Meg came running in and got us and we all ran out to the tree just in time to see the five baby birds all lined up on a branch instead of being in their nest. Then they all took off and flew just like real grown-up birds, following the mama bird off to where we couldn't see them anymore.
So, Amanda can go ahead and have the nest now, ha.
Ms. Graycliff thinks they waited for us because they know we rescued them. How long do birds remember? Please don't forget to finish teaching me how to train a messenger bird to letter-carry, by the way. You can do that during family reunion, right?
Love,
Your onliest niece
Cait

A brisk wind filled the Schoodic's sails as Cait stood with Meg and Penny, watching the Salem waterfront disappear behind Marblehead. Frustration nagged at her despite all their summer plans for derby, broomracing, and camping. How could Meg still think of stopping at Hedge level after the bird episode? She dangled her hat ribbon for Nini to bat at from her carrier as she sulked.

"I'm going to become a Belfry Bat once I'm a seventh-year graduate," said Cait

Penny nodded. "And I'll be a master weatherworker so I can help you travel. I bet they'll send you all over the place, even overseas. But a proper Speedwind for traveling won't work so well with just you and me." She looked at Meg, who stood with her chin propped in her hands, and a faraway look in her eyes.

"Yeah," answered Cait. "We'll be the best outreach team the Belfry Bats ever had. But we'd be even better with a seventh-year Mindcaster, instead of just a Hedgie."

Cait reached over and elbowed Meg. "Soooo – you are going to do all seven years of Witches' Academy, right?"

"I don't think Ms. Auclair will let you stop at Hedge," added Penny.

Meg blinked. "Hey, I was in the middle of a Brindisi daydream, guys. Don't do that."

An idea struck Cait. "Never mind Brindisi. How about Coach Joe?"

"Coach Joe? He's not cute at all. Now that guy with the nice eyes, Alberto, I'd go for him, but I know you've got first dibs, Cait."

"No, seriously. Both of them are Hedgies, remember? And Coach Joe hates books even more than you. And they're both going to become sevenyears now." Cait bit her lip and watched Penny cross her fingers.

376

Meg leaned on the railing and stared at the waves and swooping seagulls. A cheep drew Meg's attention to Cait's cat carrier. "You know, Nini thinks seagulls are the biggest dopes of the avian kingdom."

Cait's jaw dropped. "She does?"

"I rest my case," said Penny with a smile. "You are the best Mindcaster. Sooo?" she nudged.

Meg paused. "It would be cruel to make Cait race Amanda all alone."

"Yay! Woot, woot," Penny and Cait cheered.

"We need to toast to that. Belowdeck!" announced Penny as she gathered her things. Grabbing Nini's carrier, Cait linked arms with her friends, and all three trooped below.

As the three girls sat together, Cait toyed with a brilliant white seagull feather that Nini had somehow gotten into – and batted out of – her carrier. Waving for Meg and Penny's attention in the noisy room, Cait stuck the feather in her hatband and signed, "Year number one – finished. Six more – three-of-us – together!"

In a burst of spontaneity, their three right fists met and jointly formed the sign, "Together!"

And they raised their bottles of single-fizz once more.

A Guide for the Puzzled Plod Parent:
Magical terms for nonmagical people.

Adel: largest unit of North American magical currency, roughly equivalent to two hundred dollars.

Alchemy: art of knowing the elemental components of any given substance, being able to break it down to said components, and to reassemble, or "transmute", them into another substance. Turning lead into gold is but the most famous – and difficult – example.

Astronologia: the art of using ancient astrological principles in combination with current astronomical knowledge to detect relevant influences on people and one's environment, both short- and long-term.

Blatt: smallest unit of North American magical currency, roughly equivalent to a quarter.

Boh (Hebrew): to come.

Hedge: the division between basic-level magical training which is completed in one's first three years, and upper-level studies which are begun in one's fourth year. Three-year graduates are known as "Hedge witches".

Farsight mirror: a dark, nonreflective glass used to communicate face to face with someone long-distance.

Glamour: an elementary-level illusion-casting spell. It changes the appearance –but not the substance – of an object or person, and its effects are temporary.

Greenwitchery: knowledge of the use of plants for magical and medicinal purposes. For this, wildcrafting and gardening skills are essential.

Lech (Hebrew): to go, to leave.

Loreleien: a solitary cliff-dwelling people originating on the Rhein River, who prefer to live near water. Their language is nicknamed the 'Wizards' Basque' due to its difficulty. Their habit of singing from clifftops is often a dangerous distraction to those navigating rivers below.

Mayim (Hebrew): water.

Mazal (Hebrew): stars.

Mindcasting: the ability to project and to receive mental impressions to and from other people and creatures.

Nixies: these water people appear human at first glance, but have gills rather than lungs, and so are obliged to live underwater.

Orso: second-largest coin in North American magical currency, roughly equivalent to twenty dollars.

Quiller: next-smallest denomination in North American magical currency, roughly equivalent to two dollars.

Sader (Hebrew): to put in order, organize.

Selkies: seal people; they are native to both the British Isles and North America. Born in seal form, they retain the ability to easily transform from seal to human and back throughout their lives. Too often, theft of their seal pelts can leave selkies stranded in human form for years.

Shamayim (Hebrew): heavens, sky.

Shuvah (Hebrew): return, come back.

Spellwork: the use of an already-established vocabulary of words (preferably not in one's native tongue) to cause specific effects in the material world, through use of magical energies.

Spellcraft: the art of creating spells, or of connecting specific words or phrases with the correct energy pattern to reliably attain the desired effect.

Transformation: the ability to change one substance into another, temporarily (Hedge level and below) or permanently (upper-level only).

Zoomorphia: the art of observing and understanding animals well enough to see the world through their eyes, both metaphorically and literally. Few magicworkers are able to transform themselves into more than one kind of creature; full transformation is strictly an above-Hedge skill, usually attained by one's sixth year of study.

Acknowledgements
It may take a village to raise a child, but I am convinced that the same goes for first novels. ILY to all of you, every one. Thank you, thank you!

Ayisha Knight-Shaw, ASL poet, performer, and teacher extraordinaire, and early fan of this book.

Charles Wattles for coaching me on boarding-school dynamics; there'd be no Poe patrol without him.

Fanfiction.net readers, who said kind things about this book's earliest version, and asked for more stories about Cait.

Haley Cheek for sharing her middle-school point of view.

Leslea Newman, for her talent in telling me things I don't want to hear about the manuscript ... in a way that makes me want to do them.

Maida Tilchen and Tom Hubschman of Savvy Press for giving this book a real publisher.

Mikey Krajnak, this book's earliest and most enthusiastic Deaf fan.

Mom, who always knew that I'd find a way to bridge both the Deaf and Hearing worlds, and who's been this book's tireless publicist since its earliest drafts.

Nancy Hutchins, for her enormous patience, good will, and hard work in ushering me into the land of novel-writing.

Nava Ervin, for keeping my Hebrew up to par and for loads of moral support.

Valerie Sutton at www.signwriting.org, who developed the concept of writing in Sign, and all the other folks there who are taking this concept and running with it,

and

Rebecca Gorlin, my endlessly supportive and wonderful wife, who dragged me to my first ASL class in 2004, followed Cait's story from the very first rough handwritten draft, and let me completely hog the family computer. This book would not exist without her.

381

Kimberley A Shaw shares a hundred-year-old house in Boston MA with her fellow-librarian spouse and a pack of feather-stealing chowder-eating cats. Born hard-of-hearing, she didn't fall in love with American Sign Language until after completing mainstreamed public school, Mount Holyoke College (BA), and Simmons College (MLS). She enjoys playing trumpet, travelling, and collecting books in too many languages. A Handful of Spells is her first novel, with a second one, also set in Salem, currently in draft.

Made in the USA
Middletown, DE
03 May 2021

38933142R00231